Haemanism: The Spread

By

Nicoline Evans

Author: Nicoline Evans – www.nicolineevans.com

Editor: Andrew Wetzel – www.stumptowneditorial.com

Cover Design: Martynas Pavilonis – www.whitewhitedog.net

And a big thank you to everyone who has offered me support (in all ways, shapes, and sizes) during this entire process.

Dedicated to those who overcome

Chapter 1

Red streaks covered the set of the sound stage. Prince Mikhail Romanov did his best to behave. He sat patiently as the hosts scurried around, confirming their questions and consulting with their producers. His right-hand man, best friend, and General of the Russian Armed Forces, Kirill Mikvonski, stood in a dark corner, away from the chaos—he wasn't nearly as good at controlling his rage.

The show's stylist crew surrounded Mikhail as he waited on the assigned sofa, dabbing his face with powder and fixing his locks of curly brown hair. They mumbled apologies about the death of his sister, Princess Milena, as they worked, but Mikhail ignored them. He could not engage; he could not waste strained pleasantries on off-camera squabble. Too much rode on giving the perfect on-screen performance and he only had so much energy to put toward this charade. He already toured Europe, successfully solidifying their adoration of him. The media rounds were, admittedly, pure gold. He had hit a groove, he was a natural on set and he needed the same result in North America. This was the big market; they were the key to a future takeover.

News anchors Parker Brown and Mindy Chen returned to the sound stage, took their seats, and reviewed their notes. The show was live so there could be zero slip-ups. It bothered Mikhail that the fake niceties from when he arrived earlier that morning had ceased; he liked it when they sucked up to him, but he bit his tongue. They had to prepare. They needed to deliver an award worthy interview.

News Day New York was the largest morning broadcast in the country, and with him on, ratings were sure to skyrocket. New York City was the epicenter for groundbreaking stories and this was the only show respectable enough to present his with unbiased integrity.

Beyond the perimeter of large cameras was blackness. All he could see was a small monitor on the floor that showed what was airing in live time. A promo commercial for the network's top-grossing reality show was playing. The women on it had surgically altered faces and the screen flashed from clip to clip so fast it felt like whiplash. The colors were bright and though he couldn't hear it he imagined it was excruciatingly loud, just like other commercials he had heard in his hotel room. The Americans had terrible taste in entertainment. It was shallow, hollow, and devoid of any meaning. They were slaves to it, believing every word they heard and adjusting their lives to fit what they saw—it wouldn't be hard for Mikhail to manipulate this population.

"We go live in ten," a voice announced from the darkness.

The show's intro began to play on the small screen. The logo flashed, followed by Parker and Mindy's smiling portraits.

"Are you ready?" Parker asked Mikhail.

"Of course."

Next to the main camera, a hand emerged from the darkness. It counted down from five. As the last finger dropped, the hosts came alive.

"Welcome to *News Day New York*. I'm Parker Brown."

"And I'm Mindy Chen. Today, we have a very special segment for you. Our guest is Prince Mikhail Romanov. He has flown here from St. Petersburg, Russia to share in our grief for the loss of his sister, Princess Milena. I must say," Mindy directed her next comment to Mikhail, "it is quite selfless of you to come here during this time. Our grief does not compare to yours."

"I am devastated," Mikhail confirmed. "She was my best friend. But it has been two months now and I know how much the rest of

2

the world adored her, too. I thought it was important to let everyone know that the Russian royals value the love shown toward us, and the best way to do that was to share this grave moment with the rest of the world. Milena would have wanted it this way. She cherished those who supported her, near and far."

"She was an idol—still is. Ever since your family was rediscovered and ascended back onto the throne, Americans have been watching intently. I'm sure you noticed her stylistic influence while walking the streets of New York."

"I did. She certainly had a way with fashion."

"Yes, and her natural beauty was incomparable. Simply stunning."

"Thank you."

"I beg to differ," Parker spoke up. "Your wife, Arinadya, she compares."

"Oh yes," Mindy corrected herself, "she certainly does. They are quite different, but equally exquisite."

"Yes, I am a lucky man to have such beautiful women in my life. What's even better is that not only are they lovely to look at, but they are also quite smart. Nothing is more attractive than a strong, intelligent woman. I hope Milena is remembered for that as well."

"I can promise you she will be. I'm sure you are not up to date on the trends in American social media, but her translated quotes have gone viral. Everywhere you look, there is her face along with her beautiful words. Much like the posthumous fame of Marilyn Monroe, Milena Romanova will live on forever."

"I am happy to hear that," his unused smile muscles moved with force. Unnatural, but effective, he fooled them all.

"Would it be alright if we took a moment of silence together to remember your sister?"

"Of course."

The lights dimmed and the screen behind them came alive with funeral footage. After extensive editing, Mikhail released this version to the world's media. It lacked all traces of haemanism. No blood, no drugs, no violence, just the opulent parade down the main strip in St. Petersburg. Footage of the blood-stained mourners and the grand proceeding within the Haeman Russian Orthodox Church was not released.

They watched as horse and carriage moved through the crowded streets. There were close ups of strangers within the Russian population sobbing for their lost princess, shots of Mikhail wearing a brave face as he was towed in the carriage, and clips of President Dobrynin consoling the royals as they reached the church steps. The Russian Funeral March echoed through the streets by the traveling brass orchestra. Its eerie melody was hauntingly opulent, the perfect sendoff for someone of Milena's status. The Moscow Ballet danced the Vaganova style as the proceedings journeyed down the long road. Their movements were dramatic, matching the intensity of the music. The short footage ended, leaving the hosts in silence.

"I am left in chills every time I watch it," Mindy said. Her face expressed a mixture of remorse and unease.

"That song really hits a nerve. It fits the mood with unsettling perfection," Parker added. "A bit ghostly, if I'm being honest."

"Yes, Frederic Chopin's *Funeral March* is a tradition in my family. It's the only sonata, I feel, that truly captures the grief."

"I'd have to agree," Parker said.

"I must note," Mindy spoke, "that a certain individual was missing in all of that footage. Many were anxious to catch a glimpse of Arinadya, but she was nowhere to be seen."

"She was there, just out of sight. She and Milena were great friends, so the loss hit her very hard."

"Where is she now? I know the world would have loved to see her with you today."

"Well," Mikhail said, a charming smile forming on his angular face, "amidst the tragedy, we have actually been blessed with some good news."

"Do tell!" Mindy exclaimed.

"We are expecting a child."

Mindy squealed and Parker slapped his knee.

"Congratulations," the male host stated, extending a hand for Mikhail to shake. "I can tell you now, all of America is going to be delighted at this news."

Mikhail shook Parker's hand fast, trying not to squeeze too hard. "It is quite exciting. But due to this new development, it wasn't wise that she be in the middle of that parade, or that she travel around the world with me. She is home, relaxing."

"That is lovely. We are so pleased to know there is some light amongst your recent darkness." Mindy was smiling ear to ear as she spoke directly into the camera. "On that note we are going to take a break. When we return, we will have your local news and weather. Don't worry, we will talk more with Prince Mikhail at the end of our hour here on WMBN."

They were off-air and the small screen on the ground cut to commercials.

"No one told us you had news to share," Parker commented as he shuffled through his notes.

"No one asked me what I planned to talk about," Mikhail responded, unconcerned by the blindside.

"Well, it went fine. I must say, you just caused a media frenzy. My social networks are blowing up with questions and comments." Mindy scrolled through her phone in awe.

5

"When we come back on with you again later, do you plan to announce the rest of your tour of the States?"

"Yes, it will mostly be tourist-like visits. But I suppose your media and paparazzi will be all over it."

"Yes, but you can express your wish for privacy if you like."

"No, it's okay. The purpose of my visit is to connect with the public. I don't want to be hounded, but I don't mind a little publicity."

"That's very generous."

"Can I return to my dressing room? It will be a while before you need me again, right?"

"Yes. One of our PA's will get you when you're needed on set."

"Fantastic." Mikhail gave them a curt nod and departed. Kirill left his shadow and followed the prince into the bright hallway. They entered the green room and Mikhail collapsed into a chair. Without speaking, he motioned to a security camera attached to the ceiling. Kirill grabbed a washcloth and wrapped it around the device, shielding them from its view. Again, without speaking for fear audio might be monitored, Mikhail put out four lines of silve, two for each of them. As the effects steadily seized control of the men, Mikhail turned the TV in the room up to an unbearable volume.

"We need to find Arinadya," he whispered in Russian, low enough that any recording device or eavesdropper could not hear him over the racket of the TV.

"I know," Kirill seethed. "She has made a mess of your plans."

"I cannot dwell on it. It just needs to be fixed. Have our men made any progress?"

"Not yet, but they will. And border patrol is on high alert. She won't get away."

"She can't. As much as I hate to admit it, I need her. She is far too adored to write off now."

"Plus she knows too much."

Mikhail groaned. His head throbbed, his vision was blurred, and his high was formidable.

"No more chatter about it. It's ruining my high."

Fifteen minutes passed before the production assistant knocked on the door.

"Come in," Kirill growled.

The small girl peeked her head into the room. Her thick-rimmed glasses fell down her nose and she pushed them back into place timidly.

"They are ready for you," she informed, her nerves apparent.

"What's your name?" Mikhail asked.

She opened the door a bit wider. "Melanie Cane."

"Come in, Melanie. You don't need to be so skittish. I don't bite." He flashed her a devious smile, one that enchanted the young girl to come closer.

"I have followed your story since the beginning," she explained. "I tried to book a trip to Russia, to see what it's like where you're from, but the paperwork was so complex and I was denied the traveling visa."

"I'm sorry to hear that."

"Yeah, I've been all over the world. Russia is the only place that requires tourists to be pre-approved before making the trip."

"Yes, our security is high, but for good reason. We have many volatile countries around our borders. It's safest for us to be cautious."

"I understand."

"Let me make it up to you. After the show, Kirill will give you a ticket to the ballet. I'm going tonight, you can sit with us."

"I would love that! Thank you so much." She was coy, but could not hide her admiration for the prince.

"You're very welcome, Melanie. I'll be out on set in a moment."

She nodded and left. Mikhail's eyes narrowed. "Tell Abram and Sabine to start with her. She's impressionable *and* has a job with some level of influence."

Mikhail stood and exited the green room. Kirill removed the washcloth from the security camera, turned the TV off, and then followed Mikhail back to the set.

Once the curtains closed, their takeover would begin.

Chapter 2

The frozen dirt hurt as she tossed and turned in her sleep. Bones aching, she opened her eyes. Piled in the corner of the small dwelling were the blankets and pillows Sevrick brought her weeks ago.

She refused to accept his kindness.

Hours lost staring at the ceiling, the tiny beams of light filtering through the air-ventilated holes began to look like stars. They were beautiful, natural, and fell upon her body with warmth. She closed her eyes again and let the light fill her mind. It coursed through her soul, transporting her to a peaceful place where she could be alone. A place she was safe, a place where she couldn't hurt anyone.

"Good morning, Rina."

She squeezed the lids of her eyes tight, not wanting to greet reality—she hated that name. It reminded her of all she lost.

Sevrick stood at her doorway with a tray of food, waiting for her to acknowledge him. She did not budge. She held her breath and wished to disappear.

"I'll leave your breakfast here." He placed it next to the other trays on the ground, all untouched. Despite her lack of appetite, Sevrick returned every day with breakfast and dinner, and after a few days he'd clean up the rotting food she never ate.

He paused in the doorway before leaving, staring at her, hoping she'd talk to him. But as usual, the moment passed in silence and he resigned for the day.

He walked down the long, silent hallway of recovered haemans, through the laboratory, down another small honeycomb of bedrooms, and into the main living space. There, he collapsed onto a refurbished couch and threw his head back to stare at the ceiling.

9

Rina's resistance was maddening. He wasn't sure how much patience he had left.

Nikolai sat on his left and Elena on his right. They were watching the old television Ruslan stole from the city. After bringing Rina into their underground dwelling, a huge raid was made. Along with a massive collection of food, medical supplies, and bedding, they also got a small satellite and TV. The Primos had a few electricians in their group who set up the system, filtering the wires through the tree trunk and into the satellite that sat hidden amongst the tree branches. Pasha had completed most of the hard labor back when he carved those wire tunnels to get electricity into the laboratory. Now, they had solar panels and a satellite concealed amidst the branches of the white elm.

The raid occurred at the perfect time. They scored a large quantity of essential loot right before the haemans began entering the forest in droves. After their princess was officially deemed missing, their search became relentless. It became too dangerous to leave the white elm, and only a few skilled survivors were allowed to exit the fortress on rare occasions when necessary.

The expansion of their subterranean home was complete: all the new living spaces were finished as were the multiple hallways and living coves for the Primos and surviving Scots. Everyone was safely underground. Now, they waited for the haemans to cease their search for Arinadya.

Plans were in the works to cross the Russian border into Finland or Norway in hopes of contacting officials there and letting them know the horrors that engulfed Russia. The Clandes hoped to acquire outside aid in defeating Mikhail and ending the haemanism epidemic. The problem was *getting* across the border. The border patrol was fierce before the princess went missing, and now that she was gone, it was impossible to cross. Scouts were sent to assess the situation a few weeks ago.

They never returned.

The plan to leave and warn the world was put on hold, but they gathered every day to discuss new ideas.

Sevrick's head throbbed. His friends were watching the international news from the United States and he could hear Mikhail's voice resonate from the little TV set.

"I wonder if it'd be easier to get across the border with that douche out of the country," Nikolai speculated.

"No, I bet it would be harder. None of those guards want to screw up while he's away. They'd be murdered. If anything, they are on higher alert," Elena answered.

"It's gross how much they love him."

"Did you watch him with the Brits last week? They're just as pitiful."

"No, but I saw him in Germany. Girls were crying in the streets like he's a rock star or something."

"That's what they were doing in London. I wonder what the British royals think of him."

"He probably schmoozed his way into their hearts as well. Wouldn't be surprised if they're already drug buddies."

"No way, they're too classy."

"So we think. That's how everyone perceives Mikhail and Arinadya, too."

"It's Rina," Sevrick finally spoke up, "and she's not with him anymore."

"Yeah, but they don't know that."

"You won't believe what he's telling them," Elena scoffed.

"What?" Sevrick asked, his interest piqued.

11

"Today, when the Americans asked why she wasn't with him, he said it's because she's pregnant and can't travel."

"Pregnant?"

"Yup. No clue how he's going to weasel his way out of that lie."

"Guess he has half a year to figure it out," Nikolai shrugged. "He'll probably end up telling the world she's dead. Kill her off since he can't hide her running away forever."

"Did she really run away though?" Elena asked, touching on a sensitive subject for Sevrick. "Kinda seems like this was forced upon her. Not by you, Sev, but by circumstance. She wanted to die, not be healed. You just happened to be there."

"She'll be fine. She just needs time."

"It's been two months and she still won't talk to anyone, not even you."

"I'm giving her a chance," Nikolai stated. "I don't know what it's like to be suicidal, but I bet it takes a long time to recover. Those feelings don't just go away. It also says a lot that she'd rather be dead than haeman. That has to count for something."

Elena shook her head. "I'm wary. I just hope she doesn't turn on us."

"I never said that I trusted her," Nikolai clarified.

Sevrick's overwhelming frustration surfaced. "Did it ever cross your minds that maybe she stays hidden and won't talk to anyone because you're all so opinionated? She's already being ruthlessly hard on herself, she doesn't need a bunch of strangers making it worse."

"She doesn't know what we think," said Nikolai.

"She doesn't need to hear it, I'm sure she can feel it. I don't blame her for wanting to disappear. Hearing this garbage makes me want to disappear too." He stormed out of the room.

"I didn't realize it was illegal to have an opinion," Elena huffed.

"He's stressed," Nikolai sighed, feeling bad that he upset his friend. "He saved the girl he loves and she still won't let him back in. I don't even know if she's thanked him yet. He's on edge."

"He's being irrational."

"That's harsh. You'd be a little nutty too if you spent all that time on someone, and when you finally thought you won, you realized the battle was just beginning. I just hope he learns to make peace with the fact that she may never be the same girl he used to love."

"She *can't* ever be that girl again," Elena explained. "Too much has happened, she's been through too much. No one would be the same after all she's done, after all she's suffered." Her voice softened as she considered the recovered version of the princess. "If she ever comes around, he'll need to learn to love the new girl in front of him, not his memory of her. But I'm afraid he'll never stop trying to recover her ghost."

Chapter 3

Sevrick fumed. He wanted to believe Rina was still in there, the girl who loved him back, but he wasn't sure. For the first time, he doubted everything: his conviction, their love, her.

The recovery was supposed to bring her back, but it sent her farther away. He couldn't see the girl he used to know anymore. When she was haeman, he got glimpses of her, but now, she was completely blank. It was as if the transition from haeman to human ripped out her soul. So many years fighting for her, confident that he was right about everything, and now that the time of resolution was upon him, this new uncertainty was crushing. He hadn't expected this outcome. The impending failure was too much to bear.

He walked with purpose to Pasha's room. Oksana sat by her husband's bed while he rested. Though Pasha was recovering, the heart attack and pneumonia was likely the start of his decline into death. Sevrick would never forgive himself for this.

He visited every day.

"How are you feeling today?" Sevrick asked his old friend.

"Chipper. Haven't coughed once yet."

"You'll be back to your old self faster than you thought."

"Sure hope so, this mattress is beginning to take on my shape."

"Next time you're feeling up for a walk, I'll have someone come in and flip it."

"Sevrick, are you hungry?" Oksana asked. "I'm going to fetch some soup for Pasha."

"I already ate, but thank you." Oksana left, leaving the men alone.

"You look tired," Pasha said.

"And you look old."

He laughed. "Well I *am* old. Can't change that. Are you sleeping well?"

"No. Barely at all."

"Why?"

"She still won't talk to me."

"I see. I bet she's afraid."

"Why would she be afraid?"

"Cause she already hurt you, emotionally and physically, as bad as anyone could hurt a person they loved. I saw it with my own eyes. I also saw her cry, in her haeman state." He gave Sevrick a knowing look. "They never cry. Not out of remorse."

"She has to let it go. I have. I'm not holding it against her."

"Bet she's petrified to even go there with you. I could make up a million reasons she might not want to. Putting myself in her shoes, how I'd feel if I was her and you were Oksana. Her justifications for shutting you out could be infinite. You just need to be patient." He paused. "Or you need to move on."

"How can I give up now?"

"I'm not saying give up. Just move on with your life, knowing she's there. Knowing she's safe and healthy. That's what you always wanted."

"Yeah, but I also wanted her to love me again."

"Well, you can't always get everything you want. Move on and maybe, with time and space, she'll surprise you one day. Maybe she'll come around. But don't expect it and don't wait for it. There is no greater misery than waiting for a love that may never return."

"It's all or nothing with me. If I let go, if I move on, I fear I won't ever be able to go back to her. Letting her back in would be too hard. I'd have to relive this pain all over again. While I'm in it, it's easy to hang on, to keep pushing through."

"I think it's time to put yourself first and worry about all the residual effects as they come. You've suffered within her hold for too long. You've done all you can for her, there's nothing left for you to do."

"Trust me, I know. And it's killing me."

"You need to remember what it feels like to be happy. And I hate to be the bearer of bad news, but at the current moment, your happiness isn't likely to come from her."

"I'm afraid it will never come from her."

"That's a possibility and you need to find a way to be okay with that. The fate of your contentment is in your hands, no one else's."

"I know you're right, I just need to get there."

"You will. You're smart."

Oksana returned with a hot bowl of soup for her husband. He sat up slowly and she placed a tray on his lap.

"Thank you, dear." He smiled with love at his wife then ate his food. Sevrick took this as his cue to leave.

"I'll come back later tonight."

"Watch some of the news for me so you can fill me in on what's happening out there."

"Will do."

Sevrick left the room, unsure where to go. He did not want to watch TV with his friends in the main lounge; he was still angry with them. So he walked the long, freshly dug hallways to the new kitchen area instead. Unlike before, they now had a large space just for food storage. Polina was standing in line for soup.

Sevrick approached her, happy to see her out of the recovery hallway.

"Hi, Sevrick." Smile lines creased around her eyes. "I heard they made schav."

"Finally, something other than cabbage."

16

Polina laughed. She was the only recovered haeman in the kitchen. Since Rina arrived, the obtainment of new test subjects slowed. Though there were many more roaming the woods, it was too dangerous to hunt them when they arrived in such large numbers.

"I'm glad to see you out and about amongst the rest of us."

"Yes. It was easy to hide when our hallway was less full, but now, with all the newly recovered haemans, I like to get away. I am starting to feel better, and being around them in their darkest stages takes me back to a place I never want to return."

"I understand. I've been trying to get Rina to open up to me, but she refuses."

"She's scared."

"How do you know?"

"She told me."

"She talks to you?"

"Yeah, we chat often. She has a lot more to be remorseful for than I ever did. It's going to take her some time."

"Do you think she'll come around?"

"It's possible, but I doubt she'll ever live up to the high expectations you have for her."

"What does that mean?"

"Seems to me you want your old love back." Polina shook her head. "That's gone. That girl you knew has morphed into a woman with many dark secrets. You can't pressure her to be anything more than what she has become. She will get through the sorrow and guilt, but she won't reemerge as the person you used to know. She will be wiser and stronger and different. You'll need to accept this if you want to mend things with her."

"If this change is so drastic, will she even be able to love me again?"

17

"Maybe, but it'll have to start from scratch. And it will be hard. Between your expectations for how it *should* be and the reality of what it *is*, you'll most likely feel great frustration."

"As long as she genuinely tries, I'll fight till the end for her."

"I'm sorry it's still a fight. I know you were hoping it would get easier after she was healed."

"Everyone has different advice for me, but I need to do what feels right."

"And what is that?"

Sevrick paused. "I'm still trying to figure that out."

"Well, if it's any consolation, seeing your face every day is helping her. She doesn't say that, but I can tell."

"She doesn't even look at me when I'm there."

"The only time she is calm is during the hours you usually come to bring her food. Most other times, she's engulfed in fits of panic."

"Fits? Why didn't I know this, does she need medical help?"

"No, it's just part of the recovery. Hers are worse than others, but it's good she's getting it all out. I stay with her a lot, hoping my company will give her comfort."

"The fact that she lets you means it probably does." Sevrick sighed. "I'm glad she's letting someone in, even if it isn't me. I don't want her to be alone."

"Don't worry anymore. Let it be. There's nothing more you can do for her right now."

They were at the front of the line. Polina retrieved a bowl for herself, said goodbye, and departed. Sevrick filled a bowl for himself and Rina, then left as well. He took his time heading to her room. It wasn't quite dinnertime, but he had nothing else to do, nowhere else to be. The laboratory was cold and empty. He crossed through it and into her hallway. The last door on the right was hers. As he approached, he heard sobbing.

18

Afraid to upset her, he knocked on the wall next to her doorway before speaking.

"Hi, I've brought your supper a little early. I hope you don't mind."

As he stepped into the archway, the crying ceased. She was alone in the dark with no candles lit. Her eyes remained glued to the ground in embarrassment. He placed the bowl on the floor next to her untouched breakfast, then struck a match and lit the candle mounted to her wall.

"I know I've already told you this, but I'm here for you always. If you ever need me, you only have to ask."

She stayed frozen in place. From the glow of the candle he saw a silent tear roll down her face.

Another futile attempt to spark a conversation.

Sevrick turned to leave.

"Thank you," she whispered.

His heart swelled and his face became tight with emotion. He turned to look at her and found her looking back at him. It was the first time she made eye contact with him since being healed. She wore a raw, unguarded expression. Her words of gratitude ran deep—all the time, heartache, and letdowns he endured for her. The look on her face said it all.

"You're welcome."

She exhaled deeply like she had been holding her breath for months. The words were out, the silence was broken. Her eyes reverted back toward the ground and she retreated back into herself.

As he began to leave, she picked up the spoon and ate a mouthful of soup. Seeing her eat gave him more joy than he'd felt in a long time. It was small, but significant.

Maybe Rina was still in there; maybe there was reason left to fight. Sevrick smiled as he departed, overjoyed that his love might not be lost.

Chapter 4

New York City was alive with energy, partly because it was the holiday season and partly because the locals were gathered in the streets, hoping to catch a glimpse of the Russian royal. Mikhail and Kirill were escorted by security to their limo and then taken to Lincoln Center where the NYC ballet would be performing George Balanchine's *The Nutcracker*. Hearing Tchaikovsky's music played live would ease his homesickness.

They had only been in the United States for twenty-four hours and Mikhail was already itching to leave. The people, the culture, the scenery: it was all grossly foreign. He didn't like it. They were insufferable, and having to play pretend to a population of individuals so beneath him was excruciating. But America's power and influence amongst the rest of the world required that he stay. He had a month-long itinerary of national sights to see. First, the ballet. Tomorrow, they'd visit the 9/11 Memorial and take a tour of the Freedom Tower. Feigning sympathy all day long would drive him mad.

The rest of the schedule was chaotic. They were hitting all the major cities in the country, each of which already had members of his haeman council in place. Two members were assigned to each location immediately after Milena's death. Their job was to infiltrate their assigned city, connect with the youth, and plant the seed of haemanism. Once their area was addicted, it would spread naturally. They were in charge of commandeering the dive bars, popular nightclubs, and underground dealings—the places and events Mikhail could not visit during his trip. Due to his fame and social standings, Mikhail was able to get them all working visas and quality jobs in the U.S. He was hopeful that they were making

21

significant progress and that his visit to each of their cities would only amplify their success.

After his stay in New York, he and his entourage would fly to Chicago. For now he just needed to make his excursion in the Big Apple as successful as possible. Abram and Sabine were by his side now.

"The surrounding boroughs have been easier to infiltrate than Manhattan," Abram explained.

"The Bronx and Queens are booming. Everyone in the underground circle is asking for silve. We suspect it won't be long before it reaches Manhattan. Many who live in Brooklyn commute here every day," Sabine added.

"My visit will help influence those of higher standing. It's not hard to persuade rich people when what you're offering them is power."

"Most of them snort coke anyhow," Sabine said. "Wall Street is riddled with drugs. I can't wait to get my hands on those men."

"Just be careful. They must not boast about it. Haemanism needs to stay relatively secret for now. Until the majority are converted, it can't go mainstream; too many people will be against it."

"We know," Abram reassured his leader. "Most people don't talk about the drugs they use."

"You remember how it was in the early stages in Russia," Sabine reminded him. "Word was spread through friends and people you trusted. That's how it always works. We don't have to worry about bad publicity for a while. Ecstasy has been huge amongst teenagers for decades and it never hit the media until that pop star started singing about it."

"Good point. With the way things work in the U.S., it might be wise to keep silve away from the celebrities until the end," Mikhail advised. "Once it begins spreading more rapidly among the general population, we can get the actors and rock stars on board. Right now, it's more important to get the street rats and Wall Street businessmen. In time, it will trickle into the massive middle."

Both his cohorts nodded in agreement. They reached Lincoln Center and exited their limo. Crowds of people lined the sidewalks but their security team, along with many NYC cops, helped clear a path for them to walk through. The huge fountain was lit up for Christmas and music resonated through the chilly night air. They entered the building to warmth and merriment.

Melanie Cane of the Metropolitan Broadcast Network was standing there alone with her ticket in hand. She smiled with glee at the sight of Mikhail.

"Good to see you again," Mikhail said, smile bright with charm. "Let me introduce you to my friends. This here is Abram Gusev." Melanie had to tilt her head to look up at the enormous man beside the prince. Abram was six foot seven with short brown hair and enchanting brown eyes. "And the lovely lady to my right is Sabine Drugova."

Melanie shifted her focus to the striking supermodel next to the prince. She gulped, instantly intimidated.

"So nice to meet you," Sabine said with a heavy Russian accent. She smiled at the girl and extended her hand. Melanie shook it.

"I have to sit with my guards," Mikhail revealed, "so these two will be your guides tonight. If you need anything, they will help you."

"Thank you. I'm very excited to be here with you and your friends."

"We are pleased to have you. I felt terrible that our strict tourism regulations prevented you from visiting, so I hope this makes up for it," Mikhail lied with precision.

"This is above and beyond kind. I am a nobody in comparison to you. I am just thrilled to be here."

"You must never say those words about yourself again," Mikhail insisted, assuming the pretense of a supportive friend. "If you want to make it, you have to own who you are. Nothing gains respect or admiration like being sure of yourself and all your decisions."

"Especially in this city," Melanie agreed. "Everyone is so cut-throat. Sometimes I feel like I'm being eaten alive."

"Well, tonight you are safe with us," Mikhail's eyes gleamed. "I sense that by the end of the evening, you'll have an entirely new outlook on this matter."

The lights in the entrance hall flashed, indicating it was time to take their seats. Mikhail wished Melanie farewell and made his way toward his private balcony. Kirill and two haeman security guards sat with him. Mikhail wished he could have found an easy American girl to keep him company at the ballet and in his hotel bed, but it was important to behave in public. The masses loved Arinadya. If they saw him with another women, everything would implode.

The ballet was beautiful and the music felt like home. As he flipped through the playbill he noticed many Russian dancers were in the company. He wondered if they were born here or traveled here. If it was the latter, then they left a long time ago. No one had been allowed to leave Russia in years.

After the performance, Kirill followed Mikhail back to their car. Sabine and Abram would take Melanie out on the town, but Mikhail could not join them. They were aiming to strike the bars where recent college graduates hung out, and the prince could not be seen there. Instead, Mikhail made his way to Bemelmans Bar at the Carlyle. It was upscale, fancy, and bound to attract NYC aristocrats.

Mikhail entered the lounge like he owned it. His unwavering confidence silenced the self-righteous lot of guests.

"I'm not one for small talk or modest behavior, so I hope you all like to party," he announced, and the energy in the room lifted. "A round of shots for everyone!"

The drinks flowed and the attendees loosened up knowing they did not need to be on their best behavior around the prince. By midnight, all inhibitions were gone and the haughty guests were acting like they were back in college. Someone began passing the usual drugs around after midnight: cocaine, ecstasy, special K, rush. Mikhail let those circulate for an hour before he brought out the silve. Kirill was in charge of introducing it to the party guests. They could not see Mikhail with the drug; he had to be able to deny it if anything went wrong or anybody snitched.

"A gift from the prince of Russia," the large haeman said as he carefully laid out five lines at a table of wild party guests.

"What is it?" an inebriated man asked.

"It's called silve."

"And what's in it?" a lady slurred, trying to flirt.

"Cocaine and a special chemical, made by me actually, that makes it better than any drug you've ever taken. Trust me, you'll love it. It's the royal drug of choice."

The woman took the dollar bill she'd been using all night and snorted the silve. The drug took immediate effect.

"Oh, it's lovely," she purred.

The men at her table followed suit, ingesting a line each.

"This is quality stuff," one said.

"That's not all," Kirill stated. "Hold out your hands."

The group was confused but they did as he directed. Kirill then took out his pocket knife and opened the blade. He grabbed the woman's hand and gently pricked the top of her finger. With a tight hold on her wrist, he pulled her in closer. His body heat hit her as they touched.

"Now lick it."

She obeyed, licking her blood off the tip of her finger. As her blood recirculated back into her system, Kirill drew blood on each of the men. The men drank their own blood and felt the sensation of haemanism for the first time. Wicked smiles crossed their faces as new strength filtered through their bodies.

"What is it doing to me?" one asked in amazement.

"The recycled blood is augmenting your abilities as a human. You've doubled your strength, both mentally and physically. Drinking your own, enhanced blood makes you more powerful than you ever dreamed possible."

"Silve, right?" another man asked. "Why haven't I heard of this before?"

"It's made solely in Russia."

"But how will I get more once you've gone?" the woman inquired with panic.

Kirill handed them each a silver card with a phone number on it. The numbers were printed in metallic ink, which made the number almost invisible. It could only be seen when the card was tilted in light.

"Call this number. When the person on the other end answers say: Мне нужно силве."

"Mne nuzhno silve," the woman repeated, sounding it out with her American accent. A few of the men took out pens and jotted down the phonetic translation so they could remember how to say it.

"It means *I need silve*. Once you do this, you'll be given a place to meet one of our people. They will assess you and if you pass, you're in."

"Assess?" a man asked skeptically.

"We only share with those we trust."

"Of course."

"Tonight is on me." Kirill laid out five more lines. "But remember, without the blood, the drug is just a drug. With your blood, you receive its full power."

The new recruits consumed their lines as Kirill moved onto his next targets. An evil grin crept on his face: turning the Americans into haemans would be easy.

Chapter 5

After a full day of make believe empathy at the 9/11 Memorial, Mikhail was finally set free from New York's grasp and ready to move on to his next location: Chicago.

Katya Pavlova and Nestor Orlov, his Chi-town haemans, picked him and Kirill up from the airport and brought them to their hotel. They spent the next two days touring the city. The governor of Illinois was so excited to have the Russian royal visiting his home that he personally escorted him everywhere. They spent their afternoons at Navy Pier, mingling with the locals and enjoying the annual Christmas festivities. The governor also took him on a tour of Wrigley Field despite baseball being out of season. Since it was a mid-week visit, these activities were most appropriate.

Katya and Nestor accompanied them everywhere. They weren't as skilled as Abram and Sabine in NYC, but they were learning. These subordinates desperately needed Mikhail's guidance. They were young council members, each in their early twenties. Though they were placed into influential American jobs, they hadn't quite grasped how to combine their fake life with their mission as haemans. On their last night, Mikhail, Kirill, Katya, and Nestor attended an upscale party at the top of Willis Tower. Just like New York, they controlled the party and introduced the silve once the guests were uninhibited. After watching Kirill turn an entire cocktail party onto haemanism, Katya and Nestor understood how it was done. Mikhail suspected they'd do just fine on their own once he departed.

Next up was Detroit. The *News Day* anchors in New York questioned why he'd ever want to go there. It was run down, full of gangs, and prone to violence. Those were the exact reasons why he

28

had to go there, but he told them he loved Motown and wanted to visit its birthplace.

First stop was the Motown Museum, to validate the lie. Osip Razin and Roza Teplova escorted him there. They were two of his best council members. Not only were they long-time haemans, but they also were tough enough to handle the rough streets of Detroit. Osip was thirty-five, built like a Mack truck, and impossible to intimidate. Roza was a sexy twenty-seven year old with the savvy street smarts of a seasoned gang member. Together, they would break Detroit and warp its hardened citizens into haemans.

On their second night they saw an early production of *Faust* at the Detroit Opera House. A bore for Mikhail, but essential. Many of the elite from surrounding states traveled to watch the Michigan Opera perform. After the performance was complete, many of the patrons lingered in the opulent theater as drinks and appetizers were served. The performers joined them after changing out of costume, and the dull event turned into a small party. During this time, Mikhail mingled and determined who fit the role of a potential haeman pioneer. By 9 p.m. he had a list of individuals that would accompany him to Motor City Casino to finish out the night. Kirill, Osip, and Roza quietly invited these chosen individuals to join them in their after party at the casino. No one declined.

The night was complete degeneracy. Barely an hour passed in their private corner of the bar before their new friends were ready to try silve. It was an easy conversion. They embraced haemanism so effortlessly that by the end of the night, the room was covered in residual blood. Mikhail also found himself a one-time lover, a twenty-one year old girl who let him mark her. He used his ring to draw blood from her inner thigh. As they rolled around in bed, her blood smeared all over his groin and she licked it off to keep her high going. It was erotic and the most fun he could recall having in a long time. She was ravenous. They woke up the next morning in a room that looked like murder. A proper mark of violent ecstasy.

She promised to keep their rendezvous a secret and left. Mikhail cleaned up to the best of his ability, left a large tip for the maids, and prepped for his flight to Seattle.

They arrived before the 8 p.m. football game. His good friend Pyotr Tsvetnov was stationed in Seattle with his cousin Zhanna Shepkina, and they arranged for him to watch the Seahawks play.

Pyotr escorted them to the Brotherton Reserve Club, which was the most elite and exclusive suite at CenturyLink Field. The game had already started. The stadium was packed and deafening.

"They are insufferably loud," Mikhail commented.

"It's called the twelfth man," Pyotr explained. "The Seahawks fans are known to be the loudest. It can become so distracting to the opposing teams, it's like they have an extra player on the field."

"It's annoying."

"Just be glad you're in here and not out there. I sat amongst them once and I almost killed a man."

"Can't blow your cover over a barbaric sporting event," Mikhail warned his friend. "You're too important here."

"I know. Anyway, they are playing the Green Bay Packers. Take a seat and enjoy yourself. It will be a good game."

Mikhail took a seat by the window, reluctant to believe this sport would entertain him. The view of the field was impeccable. He did his best to learn the rules of the game with Pyotr and a few other businessmen by his side to answer any questions he had. By halftime, Mikhail was engrossed. The brutal nature of the game was intriguing and he was turning into a fan. American football was physical, ruthless, and often times, bloody. It was the perfect spectator sport. He began plotting ways to begin his own league in Russia. His haemans would excel at a sport like this.

30

The game came to a close with the Seahawks beating the Packers 28 – 24. Mikhail recalled the best hits, imagining more blood and injuries. His version of football would be played by gladiator haemans.

Pyotr and Zhanna took him and Kirill to the player's suite where the enormous football players planned to celebrate their win.

"Do you think it's smart to introduce silve to the athletes?" Mikhail asked, unsure about the dynamic of professional sports and their influence in the U.S.

"No, not during the season. They are tested all the time for drugs; they aren't good haeman recruits," Pyotr advised.

"But offseason," Zhanna interjected, "many let loose for a few months before they go back to training camp. And Americans are obsessed with football. If we snuck it in during that short time frame, perhaps it would spread."

"Alright," Mikhail was deep in thought. "Leave them out of it for now. Instead, we focus on good press. If the players love me, then so will their fans."

"Agreed," Pyotr threw an arm around his buddy and escorted him into the player's suite where the commotion was abundant. "Tomorrow night, we can infiltrate Seattle's elite. I have a private event planned at the top of the Space Needle. You'll hit your target audience there."

They immersed themselves into the mix, socializing and making connections. The entire Seattle Seahawk franchise was there, knowing this particular after party would have the Russian prince in attendance. The schmoozing was intense as all the men wanted a chance to connect with royalty. It was a power trip. By the end of the night, Mikhail had charmed them all.

Monday night at the Space Needle went as successfully as his other stops. The rich Americans loved to spend their money on cocaine, so learning of an exotic form of the narcotic, only available in Russia, was all they needed to give silve a try. They all wanted to be among the first to try the rare substance. Its foreign origin and unattainability gave it added value, making it the most desirable gift Mikhail could offer. As usual, Kirill made the pitch and taught them how to use it, but they knew its derivation came from the prince.

The night ended in a blackout. Mikhail woke up with two strange women in his hotel bed. He didn't remember how they got there, but he did remember some of the dirty things he watched them do to one another. They were beautiful: blonde hair, blue eyes, long eyelashes, and tight athletic bodies. Still high from the night before, they engaged in another intense threesome before getting dressed and parting ways. He gave them both a baggie of silve in exchange for their discretion.

By the time he got to San Francisco on Tuesday afternoon, Mikhail hated Christmas. It was everywhere: lights, ornaments, garland, music. The Americans barfed it up all over their streets, stores, and homes. There was no escaping it. He feared he might punch the next man he saw dressed as Santa Claus. To his dismay, the City by the Bay was a Christmas-themed pit stop. They drove up and down crooked Lombard Street, which was drenched in white lights and ribbons. Even the Golden Gate Bridge was decorated with wreaths, garland, enormous ornaments, and lights.

A heavy fog set in on Wednesday morning, cloaking most of the atrocious decorations. Mikhail was grateful for the temporary reprieve. They spent their second day at Fisherman's Wharf, walking the pier, mingling with the locals, and eating fresh seafood. By noon the fog lifted, revealing the overload of holiday decorations. Carolers were scattered every ten feet, singing rivaling Christmas songs. Santa Clauses rang bells, trying to get people to donate to an assortment of charities. All the restaurants were decked to extremes. Even the boats in the bay were lit up. The entire strip was festive and it was a test of Mikhail's patience not to let his irritation show.

Timofey Emsky and Yana Sizova were his haeman guides in San Fran and he was annoyed they hadn't planned something better for him to do while visiting.

"We thought it best for your image to tour the city," Timofey tried to explain.

"I'm not here to be a tourist, I'm here to infiltrate. I need to make sure the silve gets into the right hands in this community."

"We have the streets covered," Yana cut in. "The high schoolers are all over it. Its popularity amongst the teenagers is spreading like wildfire."

"Make sure they show discretion. Especially on social media. Make them friend you on all accounts so you can monitor their posts. One reference to it and you cut them off."

"I already warned them not to talk about silve, but I'll remind them. So far, its secret is staying relatively contained."

"And tell them to be careful where they draw blood. If their parents see the cuts, they'll step in and cause an uproar. We don't need that crisis on our hands."

"We understand," Timofey bowed his head, aware of the monitoring he had to do with such young recruits.

"I think you'll be impressed by how influential the teens are," Yana told the prince. "Once you see its progress here, you may want to consider striking high schools in all the cities you've breeched. The youth latch on like leeches."

"We shall see. For now, make sure it doesn't backfire on you."

The night was quiet. He spent his time with Kirill, talking strategy and video chatting with his haeman lieutenants back home.

They still hadn't found Arinadya.

Without thinking, he slammed his fist onto the keyboard, breaking it beneath his strength.

The screen went black.

"I will lose my mind if she isn't found by the time I return to Russia."

"We still have half our journey remaining. Calm down and enjoy the ride." Kirill was the only person Mikhail could be around during fits of rage. He was the only person he trusted himself not to kill.

"What's next?"

"Los Angeles and Las Vegas, both of which will take your mind off the disaster back home." Kirill's eyes flickered with mischief. "Hollywood and Sin City—you know it's going to be a good time."

Mikhail thought about it and agreed. A wild romp of depravity was exactly the cure he needed.

Chapter 6

Sevrick returned every day with breakfast and dinner for Rina. She began saying "thanks" on a regular basis, but nothing more. Frustrated, he hoped his consistent presence would help her open up. If Polina was right, just seeing him on a regular basis was helping heal her.

Today was no different. He went to her room with a plate of scrambled eggs. A rooster, three hens, and a goat were kept in an underground pen, so besides a small garden growing root vegetables, eggs and milk were the only fresh produce anyone got.

He placed the plate on the ground and she looked up at him.

"Thank you."

"You're welcome."

"I'm sorry I've been so distant. I can't find the words to explain how I feel."

"It's okay." He stepped in closer, inviting her to keep the conversation going.

"I've thought a lot about what I want to say to you, but every time I have the conversation in my head, it's wrong."

"You're overthinking it."

"I'm not. There is so much pain in the space between us. I don't want to make it worse."

"Ignoring me *is* making it worse. You do realize how much I went through to get you back, right?"

"That's the crux of my dilemma. You want the *old* me back. I can't ever be that girl again. I'm not saying I've changed for the worse—I don't even know that yet myself—but my 18-year-old self is gone. I have persevered through a lot—I have evolved as a person. Most people stay side by side as they change. We didn't have that luxury and I fear we may never meet on the same path again."

"We won't know unless we try."

"But if we try and fail, you're left hurt by me once again. I can't bear that burden. Not again."

"There is no weight for you to carry anymore. I'm fine and you'll be fine in time. The past is behind us and I'm happy to leave it there."

"That doesn't erase it though. It will always be there."

"Yes, but let it shape a better tomorrow for you instead of letting it restrict you from ever being happy again."

"What if me finding happiness doesn't involve you?"

"Then I move on."

"Could you?"

"If I have to." Sevrick sighed. "All I've ever wanted was to see you happy. And if at this stage in life I'm not a part of that equation, then at least I helped you get there. You were never going to find it as a haeman."

She nodded, deep in thought. She inhaled and released, contemplating an idea that visibly scared her.

"What are you thinking about?"

"I'm afraid to tell you."

"Don't be."

She closed her eyes. "Sometimes, I miss my haeman life."

"Why?" His heart contracted as she opened her eyes and examined his expression.

"The fame, the power, the intoxicated elation. I miss the drugs and how they numbed my pain. There are times I wish I had some here with me, just to make the days easier to bear."

"Taking drugs to get through a day is a copout. It's running away. You'll never get better if you hide from the pain."

"Trust me, I am very aware of that. It doesn't stop me from wishing for it though. I am trying to adapt, but I lived like that for a long time."

"I know. It'll take time."

"I still can't imagine ever forgiving myself for the person I was on the drugs. It's such a strange confliction, wanting to return to that life while simultaneously never wanting to be that woman again." Tears filled her eyes. "I guess sometimes I think since I'll never let go of the guilt I might as well give into it."

"Just give it time. In a few weeks, months, or a year, everything will change. I can't predict how, but I promise it will. You're safe here, just wait it out."

"I'll do my best not to go crazy before then," she laughed, but he could tell she was being serious. It wasn't out of the question that she might break before the dust settled. Her mental stability was on the brink and he had to make sure she made it through the storm.

"It will get better."

She wasn't sure if she believed him, so she stayed quiet. He took her silence as the end of her participation for the day and left. After months of silence, she finally opened up and had a real conversation with him. It didn't go exactly how he hoped, but it was a start.

Expressing that she missed haemanism and the fact that he might not be part of her future happiness worried him, but it wasn't enough to make him give up on her yet. She had a lot of internal mending to do and he planned to wait it out until she learned how to heal herself.

Chapter 7

Rina took a bite of her eggs and promptly lost her appetite.

She didn't deserve him.

Polina peeked into her room.

"Are you okay?"

"No."

"I heard the whole thing, it sounded like it went well."

"Yeah, but I'm left here feeling anxious."

"Why?"

"Because he still loves me. I can feel it in the air every time he's near."

"Isn't that a good thing?"

"No," Rina expressed, "because he's wrong and doesn't realize it yet. He doesn't love me, he loves *her*; the girl I used to be. And when he finally understands that, he'll leave." Tears fell down her cheeks. "I just think it would be easier to lose him now than to watch him fall out of love with me."

"You could be wrong, you know." Polina sat on the floor next to her and hugged her. "It's possible his love for you could evolve just like you have. He's not a dense guy, he's got great depth, and I bet he could reach you wherever you land."

"It's too much pressure. One of us will be left broken in the end. And if I'm being honest, I don't think I would survive either outcome. Seeing him give up on me would hurt, but hurting him again would be even worse. I can't bear either weight."

"So it's better to run away without exploring either option?"

"I think so."

"I think you're wrong."

"I'm too stressed."

"Just focus on yourself right now. Don't worry about Sevrick. That'll pan out however it's supposed to. Your health and peace of mind are far more important than rekindling an old love. If it's meant to be, it will be." She kissed the side of Rina's head and pushed her plate of food closer. "Eat up. You're getting too thin."

Rina obeyed, her appetite returned, and Polina left to get her knitting tools from her own room. She came back and kept Rina company the rest of the afternoon.

Sevrick spent the day with Kira and Maks. After arriving at the white elm, Sofiya took them in and treated them like her own. Agnessa liked having siblings and the orphaned Vyborg kids were happy to have a family to join. Nina also took a liking to them, so she was often in Sofiya's dwelling bonding with the children. When Sevrick arrived there today, Nina was showing them her collection of Disney movies. Back when sneaking in and out of the city was much easier, she managed to pack her favorite DVDs into a duffel bag full of her favorite belongings.

"I wish we could watch them," Agnessa sighed, holding the *Cinderella* DVD in her hands.

"I like hearing Nina tell the stories," Kira replied. "Can you tell us the story of Mulan today?"

"I can't right now, but I will come back later," Nina answered.

"I want to hear *Lion King* again," Maks objected.

All three children erupted into an argument of which fairytale they wanted to hear, with pleas for Nina to tell them a story now. Sofiya halted the commotion by reminding them to be respectful.

"No one likes a beggar. Nina said later, so later it will be."

"I'd love to tell you now, but I have to spend the evening with Leonid." She smiled as she left, happy that the children valued her company.

39

Sevrick took her spot on the floor. The kids rummaged through the movies she left, reading the descriptions out loud to each other.

"What's your favorite, Sevrick?" Maks asked.

"I like *Up*."

"What's that about?" Kira asked.

"A love that never dies."

"But that's not possible. Everyone dies eventually."

"Do you still love your parents?" Sevrick asked Kira.

"Very much."

"There you go," he explained. Kira seemed to understand.

"Next raid, I'll do my best to get a DVD player. Can't make any promises, but I'd like to watch movies again, too."

"Then it would *really* feel like Christmas," Agnessa cooed. "You can be our Ded Moroz."

"Nina can be Snegurochka," Kira played along and the children giggled.

Sofiya cut in, "I already told you not to expect Grandfather Frost or his Snow Maiden granddaughter this year. Just because we got a TV doesn't mean the New Year will be any different than the previous ones living beneath the white elm."

"Ruslan let his white beard grow long and wore a red cloak one year," Agnessa protested.

"I know, but I don't want any of you to get your hopes up for presents."

"We didn't get to celebrate with our family in Vyborg, or any of our locations before that either," Kira explained.

"They're just having fun, Sofiya," Sevrick chimed in. "Nothing wrong with a little holiday spirit."

"Yes, yes. I just don't like disappointment. You don't have to deal with the aftermath of their let downs."

"We all know the holidays are different now. They are smart kids, I wouldn't worry too much about them." Sevrick rustled Maks's mop of brown hair.

"If you can deliver a machine to play the movies on, we'd all be grateful. I just don't want any mopey attitudes if it doesn't happen." Sofiya gave Sevrick a stern look.

"She's right," he said, addressing the kids, "I'm not promising anything, I'm just saying I'll try."

"We know." Kira smiled with confidence, her gratitude shining through.

Sofiya grabbed the torch off its wall mount. "It's supper time. Put Nina's movies away and we will head down to the kitchen."

The children obeyed and Sevrick went with them to get his own dinner. He made a plate for Rina too.

"Enjoy your dinner," he said to them as he departed.

"Bye, Sevrick, see you later," Kira said as he left, two plates in hand.

He headed to the recovery wing with both trays of food. He was greeted by darkness upon reaching Rina's room. She sat in the corner, veiled by shadows.

"Dinner is soup and cheesy bread." He placed the tray on the floor.

"Thank you." Her voice was hoarse, as if she'd been crying all day.

"Do you mind if I eat dinner here with you tonight?"

She didn't answer. The long pause was uncomfortable. He wasn't sure if it was an invite to enter or her silent way of telling him to leave.

"I don't have to stay," Sevrick added. Another long moment passed before she spoke again.

"You should leave."

41

Hurt, he tightened his lips and left without saying anything else. He went back to the kitchen and sat at an empty table. It wasn't long before Zakhar and Nikolai joined him.

"You look bummed," Zakhar said, taking a bite of his bread.

"Same old shit," Sevrick answered. His friends knew what that meant and didn't press the issue any further.

"Just came back from a meeting with Ruslan and Alexsei," Nikolai said as he chewed. His eyes blazed with a secret.

"Why wasn't I invited?" Sevrick ignored Nikolai's mischievous look for a moment to address the bigger issue.

"You would've been if we could have found you," Zakhar explained.

"I was with Sofiya and the kids."

"How were we supposed to know that?" Nikolai asked, his words barely understandable through a mouthful of food.

"What did I miss?"

"The border surveillance team came back this morning with good news. There's a small section that, if orchestrated with care, could be breached successfully."

"Where?"

"It's far," Zakhar continued. "There's an unguarded area along the Paatsjoki River in Murmansk Oblast that we could sneak through."

"Murmanskaya?" Sevrick repeated, shocked.

"Yeah, it's the only safe option so far." Nikolai took a break from his food to confirm the location. "Their coverage of the border is no joke. The haeman guards are everywhere."

"It's about 1,200 km from Vyborg," Zakhar informed Sevrick.

"Way past Lake Ladoga," Nikolai added.

"How long of a trip is that?" Sevrick asked.

"A little over ten days if we didn't stop at all, so my guess is somewhere between two to three weeks."

"Which part of the river is it?"

"It's near Pechengsky District in Murmansk Oblast. Right along Route 10. It would bring us into Norway."

"What's nice about this spot is that we could easily cross into Finland from there too," Nikolai said, chewing stale bread.

"So in addition to the three weeks getting there and three weeks getting back, there will be countless time spent trying to contact officials in Norway and Finland."

Zakhar nodded. "There really is no telling how long it will take if we successfully cross the border. We wouldn't leave until the proper authorities were told what was happening in Russia, and there's a good chance we might never get back over the border until Mikhail is stopped. If leaving Russia proves to be difficult, it might be smarter to wait it out on the other side."

"We'd have to play it day by day," Nikolai concluded.

"You both keep saying 'we.' Does that mean the three of us are part of this mission?"

"Of course," Nikolai scoffed. "Why wouldn't we be?"

"That's a long time." Sevrick had Rina on his mind.

"Ruslan, Leonid, Vladimir, and Isaak will be joining us, as well as six other large Primos men."

"Isaak is only 14," Sevrick stated with concern.

"He's ready." Nikolai was confident.

"Alexsei and Oleg aren't coming?"

"No, they will stay behind to keep watch over our community with Elena and Lizaveta."

Sevrick nodded in understanding. "When does this mission begin?"

"Tomorrow afternoon. We can't waste any more time. Mikhail is touring the globe, enchanting the masses with his manipulative charm. If we wait, we will be too late."

"He will turn everyone into haemans and there won't be anyone left to fight on our side," Nikolai added.

"It's crucial we get word out into the international press before whatever seeds he has planted bloom."

"What exactly do you think he's doing on these trips?" Sevrick asked, confused.

"Starting up underground swarms of haemans throughout other nations," Nikolai answered. "Building armies in other countries, using their citizens as his soldiers. Recruiting them. Getting them addicted and loyal to him so when the time to take over arrives, he has already infiltrated his enemies from the inside out."

"If it grows too big before we blow the whistle on him, we won't be able to stop its spread," Zakhar concluded. "For all we know he is slipping his disease into foreign governments, corrupting them with haeman power in order to form allegiances. If that happens, we are screwed. The United Nations cannot be compromised."

Sevrick understood the urgency of this mission and began thinking of ways to make sure everything was in order before he departed. He had to say goodbye to Rina, explain what was happening and why he had to leave. Maybe the time apart would be good for them, but he had to make sure she knew why he was gone. He did not want her to think that he abandoned her.

Sevrick immediately went to Elena's room to consult with her about Rina. He needed those who stayed behind to keep an eye on her. He needed the people he trusted to take care of the one he loved most while he was gone.

Chapter 8

Blood dripped from his arm onto the white carpet.

Mikhail was too high to care.

He and his crew were the guests of honor at the Playboy mansion in Los Angeles and the scene was a haeman's dream. Naked women walked around, alcohol flowed in abundance, and no one questioned the drugs. Those into it participated and those who weren't barely noticed it happening all around them. Seeing the array of specialty narcotics scattered across the party was no big deal and Mikhail loved that places like this existed. It gave him hope that his infiltration of the United States would be complete much sooner than anticipated.

Red streaks lined his vision as his high consumed his senses. The women around him wore panties and high heels, nothing more. It took all his self-restraint not to pounce this easy prey like a feral lion.

Radimir Yashin and Sasha Chernova were his LA correspondents. He was extremely pleased with this stop on the tour and rewarded them both with an extra tin of silve each. Radimir had a large head with intense bone structure and the shadows it created upon his face were intimidating. Sasha was stationed in California as a Playboy Bunny, so she knew the ins and outs of the mansion. She also knew the regulars, so it was easy to find Mikhail the best-suited recruits.

The Playboy mansion was so secluded and known for secrecy that by the end of the night, Mikhail felt less obligated to hide his true self. He felt a sense of security at the party in this establishment and felt no need for Kirill to act as his cover. It was a rush to show the haeman novices how to take the drug and draw blood. It was even more exhilarating to make the incisions for them. He went around the table, fondling and kissing the women, putting them into a state of euphoria as he made the cuts. With his knife he drew droplets of blood in their palms, then transitioned their hand to replace his mouth so they were sucking on their blood rather than him.

"If I don't get one of these women in bed I will explode."

"People are banging everywhere," Kirill pointed out. Mikhail looked past the tunnel vision of his high and noticed for the first time that the shadows of the party were filled with sex.

Invigorated, Mikhail sat in the middle of a group of naked Playboy bunnies. They were still licking up their own blood and taking more hits of silve, but those closest to him began rubbing against him in their blurry high. It wasn't long before the group of girls surrounded him, stripped off his clothes, and took turns pleasing him. It was pure exhilaration and he relinquished control to them. No other party guests even noticed the orgy taking place in the middle of the mansion, they were all too intoxicated to notice anything other than their immediate surroundings.

Mikhail moaned through the heap of bodies that engulfed him, "Kirill, remind me to make more frequent trips here." Then he disappeared again beneath the skin of the ravenous women.

Kirill took note but said nothing. He looked around the room and wondered if he could engage in the fun. He was high on silve, but restrained by his duty to watch over Mikhail.

"My friend," Radimir approached Kirill from the other side of the room. "You look bored. How is this possible?"

"I'm fine, just doing my job."

Radimir waved Sasha over. She approached, arm in arm, with a small, topless blonde.

"This is Lila," Sasha introduced the glossy eyed girl to Kirill. "She asked me who the tall, handsome man accompanying the prince was, so I figured I'd make the introduction."

"I would've done it myself," Lila slurred, "but I wasn't sure if you wanted to be bothered. You seem focused more on work than fun."

"My apologies." Kirill tried not to stare at her breasts as he took her hand and kissed the back of it. "Sometimes I am a bit too serious."

"Go have fun," Radimir told Kirill. "I've got my eye on the prince. You deserve a night off."

Kirill gave Radimir and Sasha an appreciative nod and escorted Lila to a private corner of the room.

Nobody slept. It wasn't until sunrise that the partiers awoke in sluggish fashion. The sun filtered over the perfectly manicured lawn, over the enormous pool, and into the windows of the mansion. As it hit the different groups of people strewn across the property, it reminded them that a new day had arrived. Many subsequently recalled the life they lived outside this haven and the responsibilities they had to leave to take care of. Those who did not have any outside jobs or obligations beyond themselves fell asleep wherever they were: on the couches, on the lawn, on top of pool rafts. By 7 a.m., many of the guests had either departed or fallen asleep. Mikhail and Kirill were escorted out by Radimir and Sasha. They snuck out before any of the partygoers could see them off. It was better this way. Everyone was so intoxicated; he could easily say the women were fame-whores if they tried to reveal their night together.

"No pictures were taken after our arrival here yesterday afternoon, right?" Mikhail asked Kirill.

Radimir jumped in. "Absolutely not. All cameras and phones were confiscated and locked in a safe. We had our eye out for any stragglers all night, but saw none. You're good."

"Fantastic."

They got into their car and Radimir drove them back to their hotel. Sasha sat in the back with Mikhail and Kirill.

"I hate that place."

"Why?" Mikhail didn't understand.

"It leaves me feeling dirty."

"That was the closest thing to a real haeman party I've encountered in America. You should feel at home there."

"But they *aren't* haemans," she tried to explain. "They behave like that without the silve, without the blood. We are wild and violent and sexual, but we aren't classless. Maybe it's just because I see them during the day too. They are superficial and greedy. And while I know we have those tendencies too, there are no smarts behind their weakest traits. No wits or cleverness. They are vapid and it's tough to pretend that I like them."

"Well you better keep pretending," Mikhail warned. "I'm sure it's insufferable at times, but you're doing a good job here and that can't change."

"I know. I just don't like this culture very much."

"I do think you ought to keep a tight leash on the Americans," Radimir chimed in. "They have a tendency to latch on and claim ownership over their interests. You don't want your lifestyle turning into an American thing."

"Yes, you want it to spread from Russia, not here," Sasha agreed. "They will ruin it. They will commercialize it and turn it into a sickening fad. It won't be the same if other countries adopt it because of *them*."

"Interesting viewpoint," Mikhail mused. "I never thought of it like that before. Hopefully the European countries I already visited are growing on their own accord. And if it starts slow and from the underground here, it should unfold how I intend."

"Let's hope," she stated with a sigh.

They arrived at the hotel by noon, but could not stay long. Their flight to Las Vegas was in four hours.

"Good luck in Vegas," Radimir grinned. "Fedor and Roksana are nuts."

"In the best possible way," Sasha added with a smirk.

"I look forward to it," Mikhail replied, even more eager to see what awaited him in Sin City.

Fedor picked them up from the airport in his bright yellow Hummer and drove with reckless abandon to their hotel. Fedor was amped to take the prince out on the town. When he spoke, it mostly came out as shouts. Though his enthusiasm was intrusive, the energy was infectious. Fedor was extreme and their time with him was sure to be unforgettable.

The Palazzo was exquisite. They went up to their room where Roksana waited. She sat in a chair by a glass table, dressed in a skirt short as a handkerchief and a midriff top with tons of cleavage. Mikhail bit his lip with desire as he saw her. They dated once; he even considered making her his bride until he saw Arinadya. Roksana would have been a much more compliant wife, and it would have been more fun with her, but she did not possess the same air as Arinadya, nor was she as breathtakingly beautiful. When it came time to make the decision, the choice was easy. His red headed bride was unattainable, stunning, and a force to be desired. People would flock to her, they'd imitate her, they'd want to become her. Roksana was too much like the rest of them: she blended in, she was one of them. Though her strength and beauty stood out, it wasn't enough to captivate a nation.

"Hello, lover," she purred upon seeing her old flame.

"Hello, Roksy," he knelt down before her and rubbed his hand along her thigh. "I cannot hide my pleasure to see you."

"I am aware." She grinned and removed his hand from beneath her skirt. "We have a long night ahead of us. Patience." She stood up and sauntered to the opposite side of the room.

Mikhail collapsed into the chair, face buried in the cushion where her heat still lingered.

"What's on the agenda?" Kirill asked. Mikhail regained his composure, slowing the blood flow from his heart to his groin with great concentration. Roksana watched, amused.

Fedor's knee shook as he spoke. "Dinner at Botero, then XS Nightclub. We've reserved a VIP booth with bottle service. Champagne and Vodka."

"Sounds good. I'll get changed then we will be on our way."

Mikhail reemerged from the hotel bathroom in an expensive suit. Beneath it was a blue button down he planned to party in after dinner. His brown hair was slicked back, which enhanced his handsome facial features. He was ready to rule the strip.

Botero was pure luxury. Though none of the haemans liked to eat, they each ordered a plate and did their best to consume as much as possible. Mikhail ordered the Australian Grass Fed NY strip. He was surprised how good it felt to have real protein back in his system. The steak revitalized him, giving him energy to take on the night.

XS Nightclub was opulent: golden entranceway, bright lights, clean space. The crowd was excited to have the Russian prince there and the DJ brought him up to the stage twice so everyone could get a good look at him. It was still early in the night, so Mikhail was on his best behavior. Once the booze took over the minds of those around him, he'd have Kirill make the initial strike.

Roksana and Fedor said the lower class locals of Las Vegas were gravitating to the silve. It was widely accepted amongst them; now it was up to Mikhail to infiltrate the upper class. Many would be tourists and they would take their new love for silve home with them; others would keep it going in Nevada. Kirill handed out silver business cards to every new recruit.

Their secluded sofa in the VIP lounge was a safe distance from the heat of the party. Roksana sat beside him as they bided their time.

"How are Radimir and Sasha doing in Los Angeles?" she asked.

"Good. Same story as here. The locals were easy to penetrate. Seems there is a rampant underground drug culture in both cities."

"Did you hit the high levels?"

"I met with socialites who claimed to be humanitarians Thursday afternoon. They are by far the most indecent human beings I have ever met. All I had to tell them was the drug would give them incomparable power and they latched on. Thursday night I had dinner and drinks with Hollywood's elite. It was a small party but it had some very influential people in attendance; top notch producers and directors. People not seen on screen, but who control the masses via entertainment. They make the big decisions, they have the money and the power, they go unseen and are safe from the relentless paparazzi. It was the perfect setup. And they love a good time, so the silve was a welcome treat."

Roksana nodded. "And I suppose Sasha got you into the Playboy mansion?"

"She did. We were there Friday night. Not too many power players there, but the girls are hooked. They meet everyone in LA. It's sure to pass on through them."

"Fabulous." She sounded happy, but there was a twinge of jealousy in her voice. She wasn't stupid, she knew the secrets Mikhail kept. He hadn't changed after marrying Arinadya—he was just as foul as ever. His affection was impossible to capture, and for that, Roksana equally loved and hated him.

She caught him staring at her chest. All he saw was skin beneath the red fog of his high and he wished to rip the clothes off her body and bury himself inside her. She grabbed his face and redirected his gaze.

"Patience, love. We have work to do."

Again, he had to collect himself from the primal cravings that overcame him every time he looked at his former lover. He remembered how she felt, how she tasted—he had to have her again.

Fedor approached the table with a small group of well-dressed people.

"Prince Mikhail, I'd like you to meet my new friends."

"A friend of Fedor is a friend of mine. Please sit down," Mikhail said with artificial kindness. As they settled in, Roksana introduced herself and got the conversation going.

Fedor stood close to Mikhail's side and whispered into his ear.

"The two men own hotels in Las Vegas. The bald one owns the Venetian and the one with the buzz cut owns the Bellagio. The girl in green runs all entertainment at Caesars Palace. The girl in red manages Aria. And most important is the red head in black."

"Who is she?" Mikhail asked, scanning the attractive woman in her thirties.

"Mayor of Sin City. They saw me with you earlier and approached me at the bar to see if I could get them into your circle. Your presence has brought a lot of influential people into the club."

"What do you know about the mayor?"

52

"Only that she's mayor of a city like this for a reason. She keeps her personal life hushed, but I've heard rumors, and they are dirty."

"Sounds like my kind of woman."

"Indeed."

Mikhail took his seat amongst Las Vegas's elite and began charming them. They had a waitress on task to make sure the drinks never ran dry. To Mikhail's delight, redheaded Mayor Genevieve Scott brought out the cocaine before he had to feel out what their vices were. Within the hour, the cocaine was replaced with silve. The rush of dominance the Russian drug gave these powerful people was enough to convince them they needed more. They took Roksana and Fedor's contact info so they'd have access to the Russian delicacy whenever they pleased.

"This will be a huge hit in my clubs," Christoph Glade, owner of the Bellagio, expressed between hits.

"Same with mine," Burt Fernstein said as he carefully pricked the tip of his fat index finger. He sucked on the blood for a moment before speaking again. "What's the street cost?"

"Don't worry about that yet," Roksana nuzzled up next to him. "We will work out details tomorrow. Tonight is for fun."

Burt did not press the issue as he was too busy enjoying Roksana's body pressed against his. He was a rich man, unattractive but entitled. Attention from beautiful women was nothing new, but Roksana was a step up, even for him. Mikhail watched as she silenced him with her sexuality. The man was at her command. Watching her manipulate him was a turn on and Mikhail was counting the minutes until he had her alone in his room.

The night was as crazy as the Playboy mansion, but mostly because Mikhail had one goal in mind: Roksana. After planting the seed amongst their new powerful friends, Mikhail felt no need to push it further. Fedor was now in with that crowd and he would surely make more useful connections in the weeks to come.

At midnight, while everyone was dancing, Mikhail grabbed Roksana by the hips and slammed her pelvis against his. He leaned in and whispered into her ear.

"I'm going up to my room. Leave the club in ten minutes and meet me there." His heat encased her, leaving her breathless. She licked his ear before he pulled away, indicating her obedience.

On cue, she knocked on the hotel door. When he opened it, she pounced, taking charge and giving him no time to object. He let her take the lead as they fell into bed. Like he expected, the sex was the best he'd ever had. It was wild and dirty, it was passionate and aggressive; it was haeman.

When morning came, they remained naked in bed. Tired from their lack of sleep.

"You could have had me forever," she said as she traced the scars on his chest with her finger.

"I'm sorry if my choice upset you." He wasn't sorry, but he did hope to keep Roksana forever, just on the side.

"She seems miserable."

"She is, but she plays the role well. She is everything I need her to be."

"Everything?"

Mikhail's eyes narrowed mischievously. "No, but that's why I have you." He caressed her torso, but Roksana did not take this as a compliment.

"And every other girl you come across."

"What do you care? I have no doubt you have your pick of men here."

"I do."

"So why are you acting jealous."

"Am I the best?"

"Without a doubt." He meant it.

"Then don't I deserve a title? Don't I deserve the power you gave to the no-named girl you married? She doesn't give you what I give you. Why her?"

"Because no one knew her before I made her what she is today. You were too popular. You were one of them, part of them. I needed someone they couldn't reach. Someone they weren't already friends with." He wasn't convincing her. He tried again. "Someone I could control."

She finally began to understand. "If what you were looking for was a pawn, then I guess it's a sign of respect that you chose her over me. I am nobody's play toy."

She was wrong, but Mikhail let her believe whatever put her in a better mood. It wasn't respect; it was where he placed their value. Roksana was of no use to him in the greater picture, Arinadya was.

"Are you still mad at me?"

"No." She smiled and kissed him, trying to seize control over their next romp. But Mikhail flipped her over and pinned her to the bed, dominating her completely. As he leaned in to bite her lip, a knock came from the door. Mikhail sat up.

"Who is it?"

"Kirill. Our plane to New Orleans leaves in an hour."

Mikhail looked at the clock on the bed stand and cursed.

"I hate to do this, but we need to part ways. I'll make sure you make it back to Russia soon." He kissed her cheek, jumped out of bed, and pulled on his pants. She lay there, shocked and vulnerable. Dejected and displeased.

With a huff, she put her clothes back on and stormed out of the room. Kirill entered behind her.

"You shouldn't be upsetting our roots in these cities."

"She's not mad, just frustrated. We were about to go again when you knocked. She'll calm down." Mikhail was tossing his belongings into his suitcase.

"Fedor is taking us to the airport in fifteen minutes."

"I'll be ready. Any word on Arinadya?"

"No, not yet. Just keep your mind off it. They will find her."

"Give me my tin," Mikhail demanded with an outstretched hand. Kirill took a small container out of his pocket and handed it over. Mikhail unsnapped the clasp and opened the lid. Inside was a large amount of silve. "Do you want a line?"

"Not before we fly. I get anxious in the small plane. I don't want to hurt anyone."

Mikhail arranged three lines of the silver drug for himself and snorted them consecutively without pausing. "Let's go."

Chapter 9

The men were ready to leave, but Sevrick still needed to say goodbye to Rina. Between packing and planning, he had zero downtime to give her a proper farewell. He wanted to explain why he was leaving and where he was going. He did not want to disappear on her.

Packs of food and supplies were piled by the main door leading up to the field around the white elm.

"Everyone carries two bags," Ruslan instructed. "This should last us until we cross the border. From there, we hope to be welcomed and accommodated by the Norwegians."

"We aren't leaving yet, right?" Sevrick asked.

"Well, I'd like to."

"You've kept me in that damn meeting room since I woke up," Vladimir objected. "I need time to say goodbye to my wife and children."

"Fine," Ruslan conceded. "Everyone meet back here in a half hour."

Relieved, Sevrick raced to Rina's room. He already spoke with Elena and Lizaveta. They agreed to bring her food and offer her company on his behalf. Though they seemed hesitant, he had enough faith in their friendship that they would not let him down. Polina also promised she'd remain by Rina's side. Between the three of them, Sevrick felt better about leaving her for so long.

He arrived at her doorway and saw the breakfast on the floor untouched. Rina sat in the dark corner, facing the wall. He lit a candle.

With a slight turn, she glanced at him, then returned to face the dirt wall.

"You didn't come this morning," she stated.

"I know, I'm sorry. They had me locked away in meetings. I made sure Elena brought you something to eat."

"I can get food on my own."

"But would you?"

She didn't answer.

"Okay, well please eat. You should be gaining weight, not losing it."

"I'm doing just fine," she said to the wall.

Frustrated, Sevrick entered further into the room.

"Why won't you look at me?"

His voice was closer and Rina turned in surprise at his sudden proximity. His absence this morning hurt more than she ever dreamed it would.

"I didn't get much sleep last night and then you didn't come this morning. I'm sorry." She tried to justify her bad mood without revealing too much.

"Well, I'm here now."

Rina nodded. She was happy to see him, but afraid to tell him.

"Can I sit?" he asked, hoping she'd engage before he left.

"If you want to."

Sevrick sat across from her on the ground. They sat in silence for a painful minute.

"How are you feeling?" he asked.

As she repeated his question in her head, she grew tired. She felt distraught, conflicted, torn apart. Everything hurt, inside and outside. Her mind, her heart, her body: all of it ached. The indecision she struggled with tormented her, the days felt never-ending, and she could not predict how she'd feel from one moment to the next. Her thoughts and opinions shifted like wildfire, her moods were fleeting and impossible to maintain. She caved beneath the bad times and grew too hopeful during the good. It was frightening. Her unpredictability made it impossible for her to depend on herself. She didn't have any clue who she was anymore.

"I'm fine," she answered.

"You can talk to me," he said.

"I don't know who I am."

"This is a fresh start—you can be whoever you want to be."

"No, I can't."

"Why not?"

"Because you're here. I don't want to let you down and I'm afraid I will. The pressure makes it hard to breathe."

"Stop worrying about me. I get it, trust me. Between your warnings and everyone else's I know things between us might never be the same. I just want to be here for you, regardless of what that means for us in the end."

"Sometimes, I want to run into your arms and hide there forever. I want to heal and grow into something we can be together." Tears filled her pretty blue eyes. "Then other times, the thought of you sends me into a cold sweat. The expectations, the pressure, the pain, the fact that I destroyed what we had and I am capable of doing it again."

"If you let that go, we could build something new. It doesn't need to be exactly the same as it used to be."

"Maybe. But I also worry that one day you'll finally feel the extent of what I put you through. It might hit you like a brick wall one day, down the line, and you'll resent me for it."

"I don't think that'll happen. I'm already dealing with all we've been through and I don't hate you for it. I just want to see you rise above it."

"And if I don't, *then* you'll resent me for it."

"Rina, stop. You're already rising above it, just by being here. You *will* get better and you *will* be happy again. You're so much more than that damn addiction."

"And other days," the tears fell faster now, "I miss the high. I miss the numbness. I want to go back. Not to Mikhail, I hate him, but to the *lifestyle*. The power, the fame, the adoration. Mostly though, I miss that high."

Sevrick sighed. He had no good answer for this.

"I've never experienced that feeling so I wouldn't know, but I assume once you find some kind of happiness outside that lifestyle, you won't have any desire to return to it, for any reason."

"Maybe."

They sat in silence again, unsure where to take the conversation. Rina's face was tight in thought. Eventually she looked up at him.

"I do love you," she confessed. "This wouldn't be so hard if I didn't."

Hearing her say those words was all he ever wanted, all he'd been waiting for. He grabbed her and kissed her. His relief, excitement, and love radiated into her.

Shocked, she resisted, keeping her lips locked tight and refusing to kiss him back. But as his energy poured into her, she slipped into the moment, letting it consume her. She kissed him back and the feeling of love was returned to him.

The kiss was passionate, but reserved, full of love rather than lust. The chemistry between them returned without force and they both felt it. It flooded the space between them.

Suddenly, Rina pulled back. Out of breath and petrified, she began to panic. The tears were silent and she wiped them away with fury as they fell.

Sevrick was confused. "What's wrong?"

"Why did you do that?"

"I'm sorry," he stammered, unsure what went wrong. "It just felt like the right thing to do. I didn't mean to upset you."

Her panic turned into a fit. She couldn't catch her breath and her walls of fear began closing in on her. Sevrick did not see the signs of her rapid decline.

"Didn't you feel it too?"

Rina frantically looked around the room for an escape, but Sevrick sat in the path leading to the door. She was trapped and the claustrophobia was suffocating.

"No," Rina said to herself, mumbling the word repeatedly as she stood up and backed toward the wall.

"You didn't?" he asked, the hurt rang clear in his voice.

"No, I did." Her body was pressed against the wall. The pressure of her limbs against the frozen dirt was fierce, as if she was hoping to create a new exit to escape through. "I didn't want that. I wasn't ready for it," she sobbed. "It can't happen like this."

"What can't?"

"My recovery. It can't be dependent upon you or drugs or anything other than myself." She sunk to the floor, knees covering her face. "I have to do it on my own, otherwise it won't be real and it won't last."

"There's nothing wrong with getting a little help from those who care about you."

"Stop!" she bellowed. "I can't accept your help. I don't want it. It won't be good for either of us in the long run."

Sevrick stood up, angry and rejected. The long suppressed embarrassment he kept contained began to surface.

"You're making me look like a fool."

"That's not my intent," she pleaded. "Can't you understand my reasoning?"

"Yeah, I get it, but it's ridiculous." His face tightened with anger. "The last time you dealt with everything by yourself you tried to commit suicide."

The tension between them was electric. Rina did not wish to remember that day on the cliff, but he could not forget it.

"Just let me do this alone," she begged. "Please."

Sevrick nodded absently as he backed away and left.

"I'm sorry," she called out as he stormed off.

Her voice echoed through the hall and reached him as he entered the laboratory. Before he closed the curtain separating the hall from the medical room, a faint set of sobs reached him. The sound of her crying stung, but he did not return to comfort her.

He made his way back to the main living space where his travel companions waited for him.

Nikolai tapped his watch-less wrist.

"Sorry," Sevrick muttered. "Let's go."

The thirteen men left the white elm in hopes of finding rescue beyond the borders of Russia. Sevrick left the white elm in hopes his love would find solace in his absence.

Chapter 10

Ruslan led the way up the intricate maze of levels beneath the tree. When he reached the top, he peeked into the field from beneath the roots.

There were haemans in the distance.

"We can't go this way," he said as he dipped back down. "They are scattered along the edge of the east forest."

"Then we exit to the west, through the tunnels leading out beneath the Scots Pines," Vladimir suggested.

No one had used those exits since the burial of the Scots. After the massacre, they buried the bodies, but no one dared go near the site. The memory of that loss hurt too much to revisit.

"It might be our only choice," Zakhar agreed, understanding the Clandes hesitation to take that route.

Ruslan conceded. "We need to move on from that at some point. No sense having exits we refuse to use."

The men maneuvered back through the tight spaces beneath the tree, into the hall leading to their large wooden door, and back into their living space.

"Trouble already?" Alexsei asked, scanning the group but focusing on his adolescent son, Isaak.

"It's alright, father. We are just using an alternate exit."

"There are haemans surrounding the border of the forest leading to St. Petersburg," Ruslan explained. "It's safer to exit through the Scots Pines."

"Be safe," Alexsei requested as the men walked past him. Isaak gave his father another farewell hug before following the group to the other side of the underground fortress.

Vladimir led the pack this time with his six Primos right behind him. The Clandes covered the rear.

"It worries me that they are constantly in the forests now," Benedikt Zharkov of the Primos expressed, giving voice to the obvious.

"It's because of that girl," his comrade Konstantin Vazov replied. "The red-headed bitch we are foolishly housing."

Sevrick pushed past Leonid and Nikolai, ready to strike Konstantin in the face, but Zakhar stopped him.

"Not worth it," he said softly. "Keep your cool. They don't know your past with her. I'll tell them to lay off in private."

"I say we give her to them," Jurg Mashir, another Primo added. His square head was inches from the seven-foot ceiling as they walked. Sevrick hoped it slammed against an archway.

Ruslan tried to stop the conversation. "She is no longer haeman, she is one of us. And we do not turn in our own."

"But you can't deny that the haemans would leave our forests if they got her back," Vladimir said in agreement with his men.

"Whether they would or wouldn't, it doesn't matter. She's with us now," Nikolai said in defense of Rina.

"You're all too soft," Konstantin continued. "I'd have let her fall off that cliff."

Sevrick pushed past Zakhar and lunged at Konstantin. Despite the significant height difference, Sevrick managed to knock him to the ground.

He cursed as he struggled to keep Sevrick's hands from clasping his neck. The bustle only lasted a moment before the other men pulled them apart.

"What's wrong with him?" Vladimir demanded of Ruslan.

"Nothing at all," he explained. "He and Rina have history."

"It was *you*?" Jurg's mouth was agape.

Benedikt grunted in disgust.

"I still say you should've let her fall." Konstantin straightened his shirt and stood up straight.

"Shut up." Vladimir reached up and smacked the back of his head.

"If there are any other sensitive subjects I ought to know about, please divulge," Konstantin said sarcastically. "And I'll tread lightly in conversation around the girly men."

Vladimir smacked his head again.

"Everyone, swallow your pride," Ruslan demanded. "This trip has no room for sensitivity *or* cruelty. We are grown men, act like it."

The argument was over and they walked again in silence. When they reached the door, Ruslan went up first.

"Coast is clear."

The men filtered up the dirt-carved stairs. The door was made of branches and covered in leaves and moss for camouflage. Leonid exited last and when they put the door back in place, it disappeared into the scenery.

Quietly, they walked through the dense wall of trees. Ruslan led the group with a map and compass while Zakhar trailed behind with a broom to cover their footprints. There was a light covering of snow and it was imperative they did not leave an easy path for the haemans to follow.

The journey was going to be long and Sevrick hoped the days passed faster than that afternoon had. They walked in silence for hours, only talking when it concerned directions. They had to hide from haemans twice in their first hour of travel. By the time they set up camp to rest, Isaak was a nervous wreck.

"I told you he was too young," Sevrick mumbled to Nikolai.

"He'll be fine. In a few days, he'll adjust."

Isaak stayed close to Ruslan the following day. Everyone was in poor spirits after their damp and restless sleep. No one talked as they followed Ruslan through the snowfall.

It was late when they reached Lake Ladoga, but Lyov, leader of the Lads, was up. He welcomed them into his home without hesitation.

"Nice to see you again, Lyov," Primo Marat Usov said as he shook the snow off his mop of long brown hair and entered the cave.

"You too, Marat."

When the Primos first arrived at the white elm, many of them bunked with the Lads until the expansion of the underground fortress was completed.

Marat, Jurg, and Konstantin got comfy by the fire pit at the edge of Lyov's lakeside cave.

Ivan Dudin and Artem Kozlovsky left to visit the family they stayed with a few months ago. They wanted to spend time and show appreciation to those who housed them when they had no home.

Benedikt sat on the floor with Isaak, telling him stories from his travels and about the younger brother he lost to haemanism. Sevrick listened to make sure he wasn't frightening the boy, but after a few minutes realized the advice was solid and helpful. His stories were intended to invoke confidence within the teenager, not fear.

"Thank you for taking us in," Ruslan said as he shook Lyov's hand. "Your kindness is greatly appreciated."

"Anytime. Where are you headed with so many men?"

"We found an unguarded section along the border. We plan to sneak through and inform officials in Norway about the haemans."

"Norway?" Lyov asked incredulously. "You're walking all the way to *Norway*?"

"It's crazy, I know, but it's our only option. We can't sit back and wait it out any longer."

"They'll die off," Lyov objected. "If we hide and wait it out, they will die by the next generation. They are sick. They don't reproduce. They can't survive."

"We stole a satellite TV and have been getting the news. Mikhail is traveling the globe, winning the hearts of millions. He's visiting on the premise that he wants to mourn the death of his sister with those who loved her from afar, but we are positive he is infecting these countries with haemanism during his visits. If we don't stop him now, the epidemic may spread. He may weasel his way into power in other countries. People need to be warned before they fall victim to his charm."

Lyov was speechless. They had no television or Internet; they had no insight into the happenings of the world around them. This was terrible news.

"Can we help?"

"It's probably wise that we don't expand our group to be any larger than it already is. It's tough staying out of sight when you have so many large men accompanying you. I'm actually contemplating leaving some of them behind," Ruslan revealed.

"Why's that?"

"We've been traveling for two days and it feels like we are hiding from haemans once every hour, at the minimum, probably more. They are everywhere."

"There's a rumor that Princess Arinadya is missing. They are probably out looking for her."

Ruslan did not want to divulge that they had the former princess in recovery at their home. If the haemans ever raided Lake Ladoga, it was better that none of Lyov's people had this information. "Possibly. In any case, it's making the journey more difficult."

"Anyone who wants to stay behind can remain with us, or return home," Lyov offered. "But good luck getting any of those Primos to turn around now. I lived with them for a few weeks and they are stubborn as hell."

"Yeah, try living underground with them," Ruslan joked.

The men were scattered among the small living quarters of the cave. It was warm, they were shielded from the snow, and they were grateful.

By morning, the snow ceased and the men began gathering their belongings to head out again. Their spirits were lifted after a decent rest and they thanked Lyov as they departed.

No one stayed behind.

"If you think of any way we can help, please let me know," Lyov insisted of Ruslan as he left.

"Of course. And once we have more news, I will make sure it is relayed to you and your people."

"Thank you."

They made their way north, keeping a safe distance from the actual border, but following its trajectory from afar. They could occasionally see the fence and the haemans that surrounded it. Every few feet, a guard was stationed to keep tourists out and Russians in. Seeing the fence helped Ruslan navigate.

Zakhar's duty on the broom was much tougher now that the snow was so much thicker. He passed the job onto Nikolai, who begrudgingly accepted.

"Walk in a single file line," Nikolai whisper-shouted from the back of the group. Everyone obeyed, but it only lasted a few minutes before they forgot and began walking in clusters again.

"C'mon, guys," he complained as he lagged behind, brushing away various shoe marks. "This is the worst."

Isaak hung back to try and help, but they only had one broom.

"Do me a favor and go tell them they all suck," Nikolai requested.

"Really?"

"No," Nikolai huffed. "But this job does."

Isaak felt bad he couldn't do more to help. He walked a few paces in front of him, trying to step in the footprints already left by the men ahead. He scanned the scenery while Nikolai mumbled in frustration to himself.

"Wait," Isaak said out of the blue. "I have an idea."

Nikolai stopped what he was doing and watched Isaak race to a nearby pine tree. He examined the branches before picking one and breaking it off the trunk.

"A second broom," he said with a proud smirk.

"Ah! You're my new best friend," Nikolai exclaimed.

Isaak covered the trail he made to the tree then began helping Nikolai cover the trail of footprints.

"I hope this snow melts soon, or that it snows again, because even though we are covering the footprints, it'll never be as smooth as the untouched snow," Nikolai thought out loud.

"It's December," Isaak said bluntly. "It will snow again."

Nikolai laughed and they continued sweeping.

The group continued onward, tackling each obstacle as it came. Snow, haemans, sleeping arrangements, food: all of it was manageable if handled in small doses.

Leonid rationed the meals and Benedikt carried the two tents, though they made shelter out of nature whenever possible since the tents were a hassle to set up and take down. One rifle and pistol per man, so they were well armed if ambushed by haemans. A storm rolled through later that night, settling everyone's nerves about their poorly covered tracks.

Sevrick was beginning to find relief in his distance from life beneath the white elm. Fresh air and space was proving to be therapeutic. Being with his closest friends on a mission to save their beloved country was a perfect distraction from the heartache he left behind.

Chapter 11

The trip to New Orleans was long. Between the four hour flight and the switch of time zones, it was night when they landed. Mikhail was still exhausted from his weekend of heavy partying and was eager to get to his hotel and sleep.

Valeriya Gorelova and Demyan Vazov were his contacts in Louisiana. They picked him and Kirill up and drove them to the French Quarter where they'd be staying the next few days.

"Why was I advised not to cover the big cities in between? Phoenix, Dallas, Kansas City? Feels like we are missing a huge chunk of the country."

"They are too conservative," Valeriya answered Mikhail as Demyan drove the large SUV. "It's better the haemanism trickles into those states naturally through their borders. Same with the states in the Midwest. Not worth the risk this early in the game."

Mikhail massaged his forehead. "Make sure it spreads. Otherwise, we lost a large piece of their population. I need the majority on board before the takeover."

"We know," Demyan assured him. "New Orleans latched on fast, low class and high class alike. We got into places we never imagined we'd reach without you. You're going to be very pleased when you arrive. It's like the early days of your rule in Russia. Everyone is alive with change."

"I look forward to seeing it. The agenda says I'm here until Wednesday night, what do you have planned for me?"

"New Orleans is famous for its Mardi Gras celebration. Normally it happens in February, but the town is so excited for your visit, they have organized a similar festival in your honor. They aren't announcing it to the masses, but everyone in the area is throwing an additional series of Mardi Gras parades for you."

"Wait until you see the scars," Valeriya said with excitement.

"Already?"

Both his New Orleans correspondents nodded.

"I'm intrigued." Mikhail smirked. "Sounds like New Orleans has progressed the furthest into haemanism thus far."

"Yeah, between those who are hooked and loyal to you, and those who just admire you from afar, your visit here is certainly welcome."

"Make sure I am always aware when I am safe to express my own haemanism and when I must keep it concealed. If it's as far along as you claim, I think my new followers would like to witness me in all my haeman glory."

"Absolutely," Demyan agreed. "We can find some safe spots for you to show them your true self."

"There just can't be any cameras," Kirill reminded them. "New Orleans might be ready, but the rest of the country isn't."

"Of course," Valeriya agreed. "We don't want to spoil the progress we've made here either."

The SUV pulled up to The Roosevelt New Orleans and Mikhail made it into the hotel without much fuss. It was late and the population didn't expect to see him until tomorrow. He was grateful for the momentary break in social interaction. After Los Angeles and Las Vegas, he needed one night to himself.

The hotel was designed with Parisian luxury. The French inspired architecture was clean, the colors were neutral shades with pops of rich blue, red, and green, and the layout was open. Walking through it felt like walking through a palace in Russia. The atmosphere was extravagant and he felt at home.

He made his way through the lavishly decorated foyer and onto the elevator. His suite was on the top floor with two separate bedrooms in it: one for him and one for Kirill. Demyan and Valeriya were staying a floor below them during his visit.

They entered their suite and Kirill dropped their bags.

"I need silve," Kirill expressed.

"I'll never fall asleep if I take a line with you at this hour. I told you to take some before the flight."

"I don't trust myself," Kirill reminded him. "I hate flying and I'm afraid a full high in a flying can will result in murder."

"We fly private. I don't see what the issue is. There are no strangers besides the wait staff and pilots."

"I get claustrophobic. And that feeling doesn't combine well with my rage."

Mikhail rolled his eyes. "Take a line if you want. I'm taking a small hit of blood then going to bed."

He walked into his bedroom and shut the door behind him, leaving Kirill to his own choices. The room was white, but Mikhail had a feeling it would be streaked with red by the end of his stay.

He sat on the bed and unscrewed the flask from his belt. It was filled with a day's worth of blood. He took a sip, letting the light dose of chemicals enrobe him. The room spun as he removed his clothes, carefully unlatched the belt's needles from his skin, and cleaned himself off. Once all the residual blood was off his waist, he got into bed naked. The mattress was soft and his high was a warm blanket around his thoughts. It soothed him into a deep slumber, one that would revitalize his energy for the days to come.

New Orleans proved to be as evolved as his cohorts claimed. Exiting his hotel the next morning to a horde of newly crafted haemans brought joy to Mikhail's dark heart. They were informed, they were in the loop—he could see the knowledge in their stares. Due to its geographical location, this city was warm in December and the crowd wore their scars like trophies, putting them on display rather than hiding them beneath clothing. He wanted to express his pleasure and shout how proud he was to claim them as haemans, but maintained his reservations. It was daytime, there were cameras and videographers, so he could not act foolishly.

The December-themed Mardi Gras celebration lasted the entire three days he was there. Every afternoon and evening, floats and costumed partiers paraded through the French Quarter. It was always on a different street with different routes, which gave Mikhail an opportunity to see the whole area, but the theme stuck to true traditional Mardi Gras. No unwanted sights of Christmas-related commercialism.

Like all his other stops in the United States, he had Kirill and his local correspondents, Valeriya and Demyan, checking the Internet for press regarding his visit. After each day of public pleasantries and each night of rowdy partying, they scanned the news and social media sites to see what people were saying. As Mikhail had carefully manipulated, the only pictures people were taking were the socially acceptable ones, images that wouldn't alarm the more conservative members of this enormous population. He was controlling them by physically removing phones and cameras from his late night binges. He was governing their ability to share by stripping them of their belongings, but they all went along with it, never questioning his motives because partying with Russian royalty was far more important than objecting to his rules and being denied a night in his presence. Through stringent screening, his people managed to allow only genuine admirers into their circle, and so far, their radars had been on point. The only posts and "evidence" of his trip to America were of the nature he crafted. He was getting respectful attention and strengthening his image amongst the masses. Everything was going as planned.

74

His last night in New Orleans kicked off with a parade that made a square along Bourbon Street and Chartres Street. It was the most visually stimulating masquerade thus far. The people were dressed in costumes of green, purple, and gold. They wore masked headpieces decorated with feathers, ribbons, and gems, and the people on the balconies surrounding the parade's progression threw beaded necklaces down for the partiers to wear. By the end of the parade, many of those marching alongside the floats were neck-deep in beads of all shapes and sizes. The women who flashed the spectators were given the most beads. The music was a blend of the classic jazz New Orleans was best known for: Ragtime, Creole, Cajun, Zydeco, and the Swamp Blues. This mix of styles helped shape the local music through the years. The musicians switched between them, keeping the energy up. All songs were lively and roared for miles in all directions.

As the parade ended, the party continued and the music shifted from jazz to contemporary hits. This was Mikhail's cue to leave the crowd.

The Carousel Bar reserved their entire venue for Mikhail and his pre-approved guests. Demyan organized the guest list and the bar was packed when Mikhail arrived. There was a basket filled with phones and cameras next to the bouncer at the front.

Everyone in attendance was haeman—their gaunt appearances, the small stains of residue blood on their clothes, and the scars revealed their true nature.

"You can act freely here," Valeriya whispered into Mikhail's ear as he scanned the room in awe. His chin dipped and his eyes remained locked on the scene in front of him.

"I've been waiting for this," he said, hunger in his voice. He tore off the light overcoat he wore to hide his scars and cracked his neck. Finally, he could appear as he truly was: powerful, invincible, *haeman.* As the scars on his forearms were revealed, the crowd stared in admiration. As willing participants to this new lifestyle, Mikhail was who they strived to emulate. He was the goal, he was the level of haemanism they wished to reach. And though they never would, the drive to do so would keep them on his side until their deaths. The drug's addictive quality was eternal and the only person to escape it, out of thousands, was Leonid. Mikhail still wasn't sure how, but the odds favored the drug. Proof of that lived in Russia—through all these years, he had only lost one.

The night carried on with open drug use. Everyone in attendance was on silve, so they didn't need to be discreet. He behaved himself for the sake of his overall image—the newly married prince who was grieving his sister—but all other pretenses were dropped. He could use the drug without secrecy, he could show his scars proudly, he could engage in slightly heightened behavior without fear of being questioned. *Why are you so fast? Why are you so strong? Why are you so violent?* Everyone here already knew those answers because they developed similar qualities. It was liberating to spend a few nights without such restrictions.

The silve flowed like water and the crowd consumed it with great thirst. The blood quenched them, the silve empowered them; it was three days of intense intoxication.

As suspected, Mikhail's white bedroom was mostly red by the time they departed Thursday morning. Valeriya and Demyan would see to cleaning it before the regular maid service arrived to tidy up for the next guest.

He and Kirill were off to Miami to finish their third week in the United States. His plans were shaping up nicely and it wouldn't be long before phase two of the takeover could begin.

Chapter 12

A week passed with no sign of Sevrick. Rina recoiled into the darkest shadows of her room, hoping to hide from the feeling of abandonment. Each day she went without seeing his face her heart ached more. Did she finally succeed in pushing him away? Was he finally fed up with her?

She feared her nightmares were finally coming into fruition: Sevrick saw her for the monster she was and resented her for the years he wasted trying to save her. Every day that Sevrick did not come to see her, the reality of her fears were further confirmed.

Polina stayed by her side whenever Rina let her come close enough, and two women from Sevrick's group took his place in delivering breakfast and dinner. Rina hated their visits. Seeing them validated her suspicions. She should have accepted Sevrick's kiss instead of fighting away the feelings it brought back to life. His disappearance was her fault.

Elena brought her breakfast, which meant Lizaveta would bring her dinner. They alternated; neither came twice in one day. Rina never talked to them, and after the first few failed attempts at conversation, they stopped trying. It was better this way. Rina could sense their long-held dislike for her and didn't imagine they truly wanted to befriend her anyway.

As the days passed and Rina grew more insecure about Sevrick's sudden lack of interest in her, she contemplated asking one of the women where he was. They would know his whereabouts and why he no longer came, but Rina wasn't sure if she was ready for the truth.

Polina spent most of the day in the small common room the rehabilitated haemans often gathered in, which meant Rina spent the day alone. Rina never went with them because she still didn't feel right amongst the survivors: the Clandes, the Primos, the rehabilitated. The other recovered haemans had been regular citizens; she was the princess. She was responsible for a lot of terrible things and was the reason many dove further into the dangerous addiction. Worst of all, her presence alongside the prince kept the masses on his side. They liked her, so they put up with him. Though she was gone now and hoped the population realized that soon, it didn't change the fact that she enabled and encouraged them from afar to continue their destructive ways.

She sighed with guilt. It was hard not to feel defeated without the drugs.

The hours passed slowly and Rina had no concept of time until Lizaveta arrived with a bowl of soup.

She placed it on the floor and stood in the doorway staring at her. Rina could feel Lizaveta's eyes boring into her back.

"Thank you," Rina said without turning to face her. She hoped it would make her leave, but Lizaveta remained. She didn't say anything, she just stared. Another minute passed and Rina shifted her head to look over her shoulder. Lizaveta stood there, her expression a mixture of bitterness and pity. Rina widened her eyes in question but instead of explaining why she wouldn't leave, she stepped into the room.

Silence.

Rina decided this was her chance to ask about Sevrick. Maybe she'd be wrong, maybe it would set her fears to rest.

"Does he still love me?"

Lizaveta's nostrils flared in annoyance. "Probably."

Rina nodded, sensing Lizaveta's resistance and aware that she might not get the answers she needed.

"He shouldn't though."

"His love for you is destructive," Lizaveta agreed. "For him and everyone around him."

"I'm sorry. I told him to let me go."

"Yeah, well, we all have. Seems there's nothing that can change his mind."

"I just want him to be happy. And safe."

"He never will be with you around," Lizaveta said with venom. "You don't belong here. You're no good."

Rina ignored the hurtful insult, partly because it wasn't worth the fight and partly because she agreed.

"Why has he stopped coming to see me?"

Lizaveta paused, taken aback.

"Do *you* still love *him*?"

Rina did not respond but Lizaveta read the answer all over her face.

Lizaveta's wrath was potent. "You act like you want what's best for him, but then you keep him on an invisible chain. You must realize what you're doing. You can tell him to let go a million times, but if you're giving him slivers of hope, he'll never move on."

Rina's anger grew. "That's not what I've done. If I have, it was not intentional." Her heart rate quickened. "You're rather opinionated about the matter, more so than a casual friend would be."

Lizaveta scoffed. "Everyone has an opinion on this drama fest he's created, you just haven't heard the rest."

"Lovely. Thanks for my dinner, you can leave now." Rina gave her a wicked glare, one she wore often as a haeman, and turned to face the wall again.

"You are rotten. You're a goddamn disease." Lizaveta's voice quivered "One day, in one way or another, you'll end up killing him."

She stormed out of the room. Rina could hear her footsteps and sniffles as she hurried away.

The shock of the conversation hit her all at once. Her eyes welled as the adrenalin left. *Lizaveta was right, she would be the death of him.*

The panic set in and her lungs began to close. If she wanted Sevrick to be happy, to be safe and healthy, she could not be around. Right now, they were no good for each other. She had to leave; it was the only way.

Chapter 13

Rina tucked her long curls of red hair behind her ears. She had to leave immediately. She threw on her hooded pea coat and boots, which were in a heap in the corner—she hadn't touched them since she woke up from her rehabilitation. The bedrooms attached to her hallway were empty, so she made it to the laboratory with no encounters. She pushed through the curtain door and saw the vacant medical beds.

In the corner was a small desk with notepads and pens scattered across it. She ripped out a piece of paper and began writing.

Sevrick,

I'm sorry I left without saying goodbye. I love you too much to stay. My being here is holding us both back, so I must go. I will head away from the city and cross the border. I will heal and learn to love myself again outside of Russia and away from haemanism. I hope you can understand my choice. I will be okay, and so will you. I am grateful for all you have done for me, but it is time that I go. It's what's best for us both.

I'll love you always, in this life and the next.

Rina

Her tears made the fresh ink run. The letter wasn't as articulate as she wished, but it captured her point. It let him know that she had not run back to her life as a haeman. She made it clear she loved him, but that it was time they both let go. It would be happy closure for him, she hoped.

She folded the note, wrote his name on the outside, and left it on the desk for Leonid to find. She trusted that he would deliver it directly to Sevrick.

She grabbed one of the less expensive looking compasses from the top drawer of the desk and a map of western Russia. As she turned to leave, she caught sight of herself in a mirror. It was the first time she saw her reflection since being healed. She still looked like a haeman: her skin was pale, her face was gaunt, and the scars on her neck were still prominent. Her long red hair was flat but recognizable. She looked too much like the person she no longer wished to be.

A pair of scissors gleamed under the harsh fluorescent lights. She grabbed them, pulled her hair into a ponytail, and chopped off the long curls. Five inches of curls hung in her grip and her hair now ended at the top of her shoulders.

The color was still a problem.

She looked around the room and saw a set of winter clothes hanging on a coat rack. A black knit hat was tucked into one of the jacket pockets. She put it on and examined her reflection again. Her red hair peeked out at the bottom, but it was better than all of it showing.

She took a pair of possum fur gloves that had fallen on the floor and left the laboratory. She followed the hallway into one of the living spaces. No one paid any attention to her, but she kept her gaze down just in case. She had no idea the layout of this underground fortress or how to get out. There were multiple causeways leading off this room and she could only imagine the maze of paths leading off those. She needed guidance.

A young girl sat in the corner of the room reading. The moment Rina looked at her, the girl felt her stare and looked up from over the edge of her book. Rina gave her a small smile and the girl closed her book and walked over to her.

"You have beautiful hair," Rina said as she scooped and dropped a handful of the girl's red locks. It landed gracefully on the girl's shoulder.

"Thanks," she said with a smile, looking up at the tall woman and noticing the red hair beneath her hat. "I've never seen you before. My name is Kira."

"Hi, Kira," she said. She stumbled for a moment, not wanting to reveal her true identity—the girl might tell someone before she got far enough away. "I am Nadya."

Declaring this new identity was liberating. The relief it brought surprised Rina.

"You were a haeman?" Kira asked as she examined her appearance.

"I was, but I am healed. I have a favor to ask you."

"What is it?"

"I was tasked with retrieving firewood from the forest. Problem is, I'm still kind of new here and I don't know how to get above ground. Could you point me in the right direction?"

"Was it an assignment from Alexsei?"

"Yes," she lied.

"Okay, follow me."

Kira led her through a web of pathways. The route was organically built and hopelessly convoluted; there was no way she'd have ever found the exit on her own. Five minutes later they reached a dead end. Kira stopped and pointed up. There was a wooden plank set into the tunnel ceiling.

"This is it. Just push up," the girl instructed.

"Thanks," Rina said and smiled at the girl.

"Nadya, do you want me to wait for you? I can lead you back and help carry the wood."

"Oh, that's so kind of you, but I think I can remember the way. I don't want your family to get worried and wonder where you went."

Kira thought of Maks and how he suffered terrible separation anxiety whenever she was away from him too long.

"Alright," Kira conceded. "Maybe you can have dinner with me and my family when you're back. Nina usually joins us. It's a lot of fun."

Rina knelt down to speak more directly to the young girl. She reminded her so much of herself at a young age, in appearance and personality.

"I would love that."

"Great! See you later." Kira smiled and walked away. Rina wondered if maybe there was a life for her in the white elm after all; a small sliver of joy she might have found if she ever left her room. But it was too late, she couldn't turn back now. Her mind was made up and maybe one day she could return. Maybe, with space and time, everything would resolve itself naturally.

She pushed the door open. There were crevices carved into the wall, creating an inverse ladder, so she climbed and pulled herself onto the forest floor. She placed the door back into its nook, making sure all the carefully glued camouflage stayed in place and blended with the earth around it.

Turning to face the dense forestry before her, she took a deep breath and began to walk.

Map out and folded to the section that mattered, she followed her compass northwest. There wasn't much visual guidance to follow as the map of Karelian Isthmus was mostly woods, but heading in the direction of Finland's border was her best bet. Eventually she would hit highway E18, which had a few routes to different parts of the border. E18, A127, and A124 would all get her out of Russia, but she knew the haemans were on guard and she had to be careful. They could not see her. As she neared her destination, she hoped the safest route to take would present itself.

The snow began to fall a few hours into her trek. She lifted her oversized hood to shield herself from the cold. The rest of her outfit was rather inappropriate for a journey like this—all she had were the leggings and thin sweater she wore to the cliff. Sevrick had offered to get her a new outfit, but she always refused. Now she wondered if living in her suicide-outfit all this time had made healing harder. Sevrick's old bloodstains were still on the collar of her shirt; blood from the wound *she* gave him. The blood held memories; and though it was old and dried it held fresh reminders of all the pain she caused.

Her boots were warm, thankfully. They were waterproof rubber on the outside, Arctic Fox fur on the inside.

She kept moving forward, hoping to make this trip a quick one since she had no food or shelter. Walking to the border without stopping could take less than two days if she hit the closest town, Nuijamaa, Finland. But there was no predicting her path until she saw where the haemans guarded the border.

As the aching of her weak body intensified, she found herself wishing she had silve to numb the pain.

She shook her head.

It was time to heal, still, the appeal of a quick and easy fix taunted her.

Haemanism *wasn't* natural, like they claimed for so many years. It *wasn't* a gift from God, coursing through human veins, waiting to be discovered. She could drink her blood in the forest, but that would do nothing for her. She wondered how many haemans in the city still believed this lie. At this point, it couldn't be many. Most were aware that haemanism wasn't natural, and though they didn't know what caused their blood's power, they chose to remain ignorant. The addiction was more important than the values they held before turning into monsters. They'd rather be lied to than lose their haemanism.

Days passed and Rina found herself needing to stop often to rest. She ate snow to prevent dehydration, but the more she consumed, the worse she felt. She never went camping, never learned how to survive in the wild, but she knew something wasn't right. The snow seemed to be making her thirst worse. By the third day, her lips began to blister and she couldn't shake her shivers. She was drowsy and disoriented, tripping over her own feet as she walked. Her mind became foggy and the lines on the map began to blur. Unsure what was wrong, she found a snowless spot beneath a tall pine tree and sat down. The branches overhead kept her shielded from the harsh weather.

"What am I doing wrong?" she asked aloud. Three days without food was no issue, that couldn't be the problem. She went weeks without food as a haeman, and multiple days without it beneath the white elm.

The snow continued to fall and she watched it from her dry space beneath the tree branches. It was peaceful and beautiful and Rina's fuzzy vision only enhanced its enchantment. She imagined the snowy landscape paintings in the Winter Palace coming to life. Majestic and graceful, she was entranced. It wasn't until the sun set and night befell her that the snow's hypnotic hold let her go. The dark of night erased the snowfall from her sight, forcing her to reacquaint herself with her current predicament.

She cursed beneath her breath, aware she lost another day.

The bottom branches of this tree were huge and thick, protecting her from the onslaught of the blistery storm. It was dry and a few degrees warmer than it was in the open air. The lost day granted her a proper shelter, and for that, she was grateful. She'd get a decent night's rest and tackle a new day tomorrow.

The morning sun came with a migraine. She sat up, clutched her temples, and cursed beneath her breath.

There was no time to waste. She had to keep moving.

The storm had ceased, leaving a thick layer of snow on the ground. After a few steps, she looked backward. Any tracks she left previously were gone, but the new ones she was making in the snow were troubling. She sighed, resigned to the fact that there was nothing she could do to prevent it except hope, begrudgingly, that it snowed again.

A few hours into the day she reached the meeting point between highway E18 and A127. If she followed A127, she'd get to Nuijamaa by nightfall. If she followed E18, she'd be heading southwest and would need to veer off into the woods in search of a spot along the border she could pass through undetected. Follow the highway to the border or venture into the pathless woods—equally dangerous options.

Rina coughed, spitting up small traces of blood. She was already sick; if she didn't find help in Finland soon, she would surely die in the forest.

At the fork in the road she went right, following A127 toward Nuijamaa. From here on, she'd need to be even more watchful for haemans: they'd recognize her, they'd capture her, and she'd be brought back to Mikhail.

Rina shuddered at the thought.

By midafternoon, a sudden drop in temperature left Rina in a fit of shivers. She pulled her hood further over her face and kept her head ducked. The wind was relentless.

The road wasn't plowed. Still, she followed it, knowing the map wouldn't lead her astray. A127 led straight to her destination. If she followed its course, she'd soon land in a friendlier place.

Head down and hood up, she carried on. It was impossible to hear anything above the roar of the wind, so as the armored Kamaz truck approached, she did not notice. It wasn't until its headlights reached beneath her hood that she became aware of its presence. The sudden shock and fear left Rina momentarily paralyzed. As the haeman men climbed out of the high-tech ice vehicle, she regained her wits and ran. She left the road and headed toward the forest where she could find a place to hide.

The men shouted after her as they grabbed their rifles and gave chase.

She ran as fast as her strained lungs allowed. But these men were haemans on silve; she knew they would catch up. Still, she ran, hoping to find a hideaway before they gained too much ground.

But there was nothing, no safe place to hide. Tears fell and froze on her gaunt cheeks.

"Stop or we will shoot," one shouted, but Rina did not stop. She would rather die than be captured. She wished for the bullet as she kept running, waiting for it to pierce her and end this hunt. But it never came. Instead, she was tackled to the ground, flipped over, and slapped hard across the face. Her skin was so numb from the cold she barely felt the sting.

"Foolish girl," the guard spat. She still looked haeman to him. "Why are you out here?"

"Fresh air."

"Lies."

He yanked Rina up by her skinny bicep. This time, she felt his strength. Her bone felt brittle beneath his relentless grip. He dragged her to his truck, still unaware of the identity of his captive.

Rina's mind raced. She had to get away before he got a good look at her face.

He dragged her next to his enormous Kamaz truck and banged on the side for the driver to unlock the doors. It wasn't a typical Russian ice truck. The tires were as tall as her and roll bars were added like a cage around the vehicle. Though she was tall, he managed to toss her into the back seat over the middle console.

"Not sure why you're so resistant," he said annoyed. "You can't leave anyway. Next trip back, we will return you to the city."

"Why would you want to leave anyway?" the driver asked her. "You can't be haeman anywhere but Russia, at least not yet."

Rina didn't answer. The other guard who hadn't caught her finally reentered the truck. He jumped into the back seat next to her.

"Sorry," he said, "I was radioed by Filipp. He wanted to remind us that the prince is nearing the last week of his trip."

"What an asshole," the driver complained. "Like I can't keep track of the date myself. I don't know how he got promoted with us."

"If he's so concerned, maybe he ought to come out here and help us look. It's like trying to find a specific grain of sand at the beach," her captor added.

"He's in charge of maintaining order at the palace, he can't leave," the haeman next to Rina said. Then he looked at her. "What's her deal?"

"No clue, she won't talk."

The backseat haeman grabbed her face, pressing hard into her cheeks, and pulled her closer. He examined her beat up appearance.

"Did she say her name?"

"I told you, she won't talk."

"Look at her face." He shoved her head between the two front seats. The other haemans turned to observe. They both squinted

89

their eyes in scrutiny as their brains looked past her sick appearance, bruised cheek, and scabbed lips. "Am I wrong?"

Her captor ripped the knit hat off her head, revealing the blaze of hair hidden beneath. The men gasped in unison.

"Call Filipp back," the driver said as he shifted the truck into first gear. "We've found the princess."

Chapter 14

Two weeks into their journey and they were still stuck in Russia. Sevrick worried that the constant sight of haemans would continue until they crossed the Norwegian border.

Over time, Benedikt, Artem, Marat, Jurg, and Ivan began fitting in nicely with the Clandes. Artem had a similar story to Sevrick, which he shared in private one night, and it brought the men closer as friends. He often told Konstantin to shut up on behalf of the whole group whenever he poked fun at Sevrick for still loving a haeman.

Ruslan and Vladimir led with authority. They predicted they'd reach Kirkenes, Norway in a week. Nikolai was enjoying his role as Isaak's mentor. He was the youngest amongst the men at twenty-four years old, so it was natural for him to adopt Isaak as a younger brother.

Benedikt often hung by them, using Nikolai and Isaak as fillers for the bond he sorely missed with his own brother.

"I wish I had a brother," Isaak said after Benedikt recalled a fond moment he had with his own.

"We're your brothers now," Nikolai professed, grabbing Isaak's shoulder and pulling him in close.

"I miss Filipp," Benedikt confessed, still lost in old memories of his brother. "But he became a different person after the drugs took over."

"I'm sure he misses you too," Isaak said.

"Deep down, maybe." Benedikt shook his head. "We went through a lot together. Our parents died when we were very young and we were passed through countless abusive foster homes. For years, we went from one awful family to the next. I was Filipp's unofficial guardian through it all, keeping him safe and protecting him the best I could as we grew up under abysmal government care. At the end of the day, we only had each other."

Benedikt paused, choking on memories of the past.

Nikolai cut in. "Let me guess, then the Romanovs came back?"

Benedikt nodded. "Filipp bought the lies the royals sold, and I blamed myself for not preventing his downfall into haemanism. I left, escaped into the woods and found the Primos. When we went back to save him, Filipp declared he no longer had a brother." Benedikt took a moment. "I was dead to him."

"It was the drugs that made him that way," Nikolai insisted.

"I don't even know if he's still alive."

Sevrick wasn't part of the conversation, but he listened in and suddenly understood why Benedikt wore such a hard shell; he was still mourning.

Isaak was a positive addition to the group; his youthful energy kept them all in good spirits. Whenever there were clear signs of no haemans around, Isaak, Nikolai, and Benedikt challenged each other to speed battles. Nikolai won every time.

Isaak was quickly adjusting to life outside the safety of the white elm. Sevrick was impressed. He never complained, often came up with helpful ideas, and never behaved in a manner that risked their mission. Alexsei was going to be very proud when he heard how well his son did.

Zakhar and Leonid spent most of their time talking strategy. They kept their ideas hushed until they were solid enough to share with the group. Zakhar always presented them, as the Primos were hesitant to show respect to Leonid, who still looked like a haeman. Despite spending so much time with him, they still weren't able to separate his appearance from his reality. They saw him and thought *monster*, even though he was the kindest amongst them.

Artem walked next to Sevrick as the group continued north. They were the same height but their looks were polar opposite. Sevrick had dark brown hair, long on top and buzzed along the sides, piercing blue eyes, and a medium complexion. Artem had sandy blonde hair that fell to his shoulders that he often wore in a small, low bun. His eyes were bright green and his complexion was fair. He was originally from southwest Russia, near Ukraine where people were Slavic. He spoke of his heritage often, and proudly.

"I'm surprised we haven't seen any haemans yet," Artem commented.

Sevrick hadn't noticed until his new friend pointed it out, but he was right. It was almost dusk and they hadn't seen any.

"I wonder where they are. Mikhail should still be in America. I doubt they'd lessen the guard until he came back."

Artem shrugged. "Maybe we are further north than we realize. Perhaps they didn't think this area needed as much protection."

Sevrick shook his head. "Our lookouts said the entire forest was loaded with haemans and the only safe spot was the one near Kirkenes. We are a week away, we should still be dodging them."

Artem creased his brow. "We have no access to the news. I don't know what would pull them away."

Sevrick was deep in thought. The guards along the fence were border patrol; those further into the woods were tasked to prevent anyone from getting near the border in the first place. That was what the men determined. Then Sevrick stopped, consumed with new thoughts.

"Why have you stopped?" Artem asked from a few paces ahead.

"What if we are wrong?"

"About what?"

"The reason haemans are littered through the forest, in addition to those stationed at the border."

"It seemed like a solid thought to me: they don't want anyone getting near the border. If they can stop them before they reach it, they can prevent any mistakes."

"It makes sense, but what if there is more to it? What if there is more to their job than stopping *anyone* from leaving?"

"What do you mean?"

"Like stopping a *specific* individual from leaving. And maybe, they are also tasked with *finding* that person."

Artem went quiet.

"You mean the princess?" Artem finally asked, his tone hesitant. "Sorry, I mean Rina."

"Yeah."

"I always assumed part of their job out here was to find her, too."

"Same, but now they've stopped looking. Why? What does that mean?"

"Maybe they realized they're never going to find her, that they are wasting their time. I bet the next time we have access to the news, we will learn they've announced her death. Killed her off in some way."

Sevrick released a heavy breath. "That makes sense."

"She's safe at the white elm," Artem reassured him with confidence. "They must be giving up. If Mikhail is trying to take over countries beyond Russia, he can't waste his resources on finding someone that cannot be found. It's been months, they'll have to call it quits at some point."

"You're right. I don't know why I got so nervous."

"I get it. I lost my wife to that world too." Artem patted Sevrick on the back. "I still get anxious when I think of her, or things involving her. Don't worry."

"Thanks." Sevrick appreciated Artem's empathy.

"Why can't you girls keep up?" Konstantin shouted back to them from the front of the group. They ignored the insult and hustled to catch up.

"Ruslan told me you were carrying the food bag today," Benedikt said to Sevrick.

"Sure am."

"Can I grab a snack?"

Sevrick turned sideways so Benedikt could unzip his extra pack and take what he wanted. He took a pack of crackers and closed the bag.

"Thanks," he said as he ripped the package open. "And just ignore Konstantin. I'm not sure why he won't drop his issue with you."

"It's annoying."

"I know. Sorry again that I fed into it when we first left the white elm. I didn't realize how personal it was until I talked to Leonid. We often forget it's not just bad choices spreading through Russia, but a disease. After the bad choice is made, you're pretty much a slave to it."

"Yeah, but I got her out. It's possible to beat."

"Seeing Leonid, hearing about your fiancée, and being reminded about all the other haemans you guys saved, I had to reevaluate my sense of humor. None of this is funny, it's quite grim. I guess I thought joking about it might make the situation feel less dire." Benedikt shook his head. "It didn't."

"I appreciate you saying this to me."

"My younger brother stayed in Moscow."

"I'm sorry."

"Yeah, I just need to stop masking my sadness with anger. I take my disappointment in Filipp out on everyone else. Seeing you own

95

your grief is helpful. Most men wouldn't let it show, but you do. I'm working on doing the same."

"I'm glad to hear that." Sevrick felt honored that Benedikt opened up to him voluntarily.

Benedikt nodded, gripped Sevrick's shoulder in camaraderie, and caught up to Ivan.

"See," Artem smiled and gave Sevrick a shove, "we aren't so bad."

Sevrick rolled his eyes and laughed. The Primos operated differently than the Clandes; they were brash, blunt, and ruthless, but they meant well. As time passed, they began to grow on him. Once the outer layer was breached, they weren't so terrible. They just hid their struggle behind tough exteriors, an act of self-preservation that Sevrick understood well.

Chapter 15

Miami passed in a blur. New Orleans had been so successful, Mikhail didn't care what happened at his next stop. Darya Vashneva and Vadik Nuriyev escorted him through the Latin-influenced city. Once again, he couldn't escape Christmas. The holiday was a week away and the timing of this trip couldn't have been worse. It didn't matter though; the next time he came to the United States, the country would belong to him. His haemans will have taken over and Christmas would be a thing of the past.

Though he had a fun weekend in Miami, he was ready to go home. Russia was where he belonged.

D.C. was next. They left Miami Sunday afternoon, dizzying hangovers intact, and made it to the country's capital by nightfall. Larisa Aristova and Nazar Yedemsky greeted them at the airport. Both haemans were placed in government roles and tasked to work their way up the ladder.

They wore business suits and looked as stiff as seasoned politicians. Mikhail smiled at the sight of them.

"You both look ridiculous."

"Just playing the role you gave us," Nazar said, shifting uncomfortably in his suit.

"Any progress?"

"It'll take time," Larisa explained. "We need to earn their trust and respect, prove we have something worthwhile to offer before getting higher up in the political food chain."

"I have no doubt you will both succeed. And after you're seen by my side the next few days, the politicians will be clawing at each other to get their hands on you. Snatching people with powerful connections is just as good as having those connections themselves.

They'll want you on their side if it means the Prince of Russia is only a phone call away."

Nazar smirked, excited for the chance to use his manipulative wits against the best in America.

Larisa filled them in on the itinerary for their time in the capitol. It included multiple meetings with local representatives, a tour of the historic monuments, and a night with President Nathaniel Ward watching a classical Russian performance by the National Symphony Orchestra. Mikhail scanned the itinerary.

"Kenneth Arnold?"

"He demanded to meet with you. We told him 'no' multiple times, but we were overruled. President Ward put together the final schedule and included that meeting."

"Well, that'll be awkward."

"I'm surprised you weren't summoned to meet with the Secretary-General. The United Nations is still mad that you made Kenneth move back to the States," Larisa commented.

"I'm not sure how you've gotten away with it this long," Nazar added. "Every country has a U.S. ambassador living in their territory. They aren't happy about your lack of cooperation."

Mikhail tightened his scowl. "That's a damn shame because it's not changing. I kicked all the ambassadors out. The U.S. shouldn't take it so personally."

"Well," Larisa said, "they are all offended. If I'm being frank, there's a good chance they will lose their patience soon. I've heard chatter that you need to let the ambassadors return or they are going to alter the conditions of your membership with the U.N."

"Threats?" Mikhail laughed. "Hilarious. In a few months' time I'll have seized control of all their governments."

"They are biding their time due to your recent loss," Nazar explained. "I hope you have your next move planned because the allotted time for grieving isn't long in the States."

"Don't worry about my plans. After seeing the progress across the nation, it won't be long."

"It better be smooth, or they will fight back," Larisa warned.

"No," Nazar corrected, "they will fight back regardless. It's just a matter of how many of their own have turned on them. If you get the majority, it will weaken America's strength."

"Any chance we can infiltrate the military? Get their soldiers on board?" Mikhail asked.

"Not a chance," Larisa answered. "But if you get the general population they will rebel from within, keeping the armed forces distracted with the fight at home while you take your army elsewhere."

"And don't forget," Nazar added, "haemans have the advantage. We are stronger and faster, the foreigners you recruit to your side will be huge assets in fighting their own armies for you."

Mikhail relaxed into the leather car seat. "This will be like stealing from a child."

"Let's hope."

They made their way to the Ritz-Carlton through D.C. traffic. Kirill barely spoke. His best friend and deputy was fading. They were on their fourth and final week in the U.S. and Kirill's pleasant façade was dissipating. He was never good at pretending to be anything other than his severe and volatile self, but Mikhail needed him to keep up the front a few days longer. Washington was their most important trip, and they both had to be on their best behavior.

Monday was torturous. Members of the Senate and the House of Representatives wanted to meet him while he was in town. Mikhail wasn't sure why Larisa or Nazar let these meetings make the itinerary, but he had a feeling they didn't have much say in the final schedule. He made the best of it, put on his most charming smile, and wooed his counterparts. Learning that the U.N. was angrier about his lack of ambassadors than he realized meant he had to keep enrapturing every person he met. They were only being lenient with him because they saw him as an international ally. Mikhail did his best to keep the grin off his face as the multiple politicians he met melted in his grip.

Tuesday was filled with a tour of the National Mall. Between the Washington Monument, the Lincoln Memorial, and all the museum stops along their walk, Mikhail's chemically laced blood raged. The tour was boring and uninteresting; he did not care for American history or the way his tour guides acted like their country's past was more important than any other nation's. As if the current fate of the world was written by Americans, and Americans only. At the WWII Memorial, the tension came to a head.

"Where's Russia in this memorial?" Kirill asked.

The chipper, overly confident tour guide pointed to the right-side wall. "That wall is the Atlantic arch of the memorial and it depicts scenes from the European theater. The last image shows American and Russian soldiers shaking hands. It symbolizes the combined efforts both of our countries made to stop the Nazis."

"It's awfully small."

"Well, we are in America, are we not?" the tour guide jested, indicating the memorial would naturally be made with an America point of view, but Kirill did not find any comedy in the comment. His harsh glare caused the tour guide to gulp.

"So because we are on U.S. soil, that diminishes the role the Soviet Union played during WWII?"

"Well, of course not—" the tour guide stammered.

"You do realize how much area we covered? We pushed Hitler all the way back to Berlin."

"Only after the non-aggression pact Stalin made with Hitler was broken. Russia was not helping the Allied forces until Hitler went back on his word and began invading Russia. That was 1941. You were fighting Hitler off your *own* land until mid-1943. We received no help from the Red Army until the end of 1943, maybe the beginning of 1944. And this was all after you tried taking other benign, neighboring countries for your own political reasons. You only decided to flip sides against Hitler, your former partner in crime, *after* his alliance no longer served you. With all due respect, Russia's participation in WWII was self-serving."

Kirill lunged at the skinny tour guide, a teenage boy half his size. Nazar grabbed Kirill's arm before he got very far and pushed him out of the small crowd of tourists.

"You ought to show a little more respect," Mikhail sneered at the boy, who now cowered in the presence of royalty. Kirill was just a man, but Mikhail was a ruler.

"I apologize, obviously much has changed since then. You're no longer the Soviet Union, Stalin is long gone; the depiction is really no reflection upon you personally."

"But that is *my* history, and despite your assumptions about my ancestors' motives, we helped the Allies win that war. Without us, there's a good chance you would all be speaking German right now."

"Point taken. I am sorry for offending you."

Mikhail wanted to rip the boy's throat out so he could never speak poorly of Russia again, but he behaved.

"Let's carry on," Mikhail insisted.

The young, humbled tour guide took a deep breath and led the group onward, taking greater care in the things he said around this crowd. Mikhail fell back and found Nazar holding Kirill against the backside of a pillar on the Atlantic Pavilion.

"Calm down," Mikhail said to Kirill, who was fuming. "He is an ignorant American child."

"They all think that way, that they own the whole damn world. They think they are the epicenter in which every other human being on this planet revolves. They are not the fucking sun! I can't withstand another moment in this country, surrounded by narcissistic and oblivious fools."

Mikhail took Nazar's place and held Kirill by the shoulders. "Soon we will be in control. *We* will be the epicenter they have no choice but to revolve around. We will be the powerhouse the rest of the world views as bullies. The U.S. will lose their upper hand and we will take their place at the top. Just be patient."

"I'm trying," Kirill said through clenched teeth.

"One more week, that's all."

Kirill nodded silently and Mikhail stepped back.

Mikhail understood his friend's rage—the Americans were vapid narcissists. They were empty, lacking depth, and Mikhail was happy to fill their void with haemanism.

On Wednesday, Mikhail was scheduled to spend the entire day with Kenneth Arnold, the U.S. Ambassador to Russia. Even though he was forced by Mikhail to move back to the States, his role remained. He called Mikhail on a weekly basis, often times receiving no correspondence or being redirected to one of his high-level council members. Kenneth was no fool, though; he took his job seriously and refused to back down.

Mikhail was escorted into a large office, his small group of companions close behind.

"No," Kenneth said as he saw Kirill, Nazar, and Larisa, "it will just be me and the prince for now."

Mikhail took a seat across from Kenneth's large desk and nodded at his friends to go. They shut the door behind them, leaving the men alone.

"How have you been, old friend?" Mikhail asked.

"If you answered any of my phone calls, you'd know."

"I apologize, I am a very busy man. I make sure you are connected with the most well-informed members of my team."

"You realize you don't call the shots. President Dobrynin does."

"You're right, so why are you always trying to contact me?"

"Because I'm onto you." Kenneth was a big man and his anticipation for this conversation was revealed through his heavy breathing and sweaty brow. "You're in his ear. In fact, I think you call *all* the shots."

"I have influence, of course, but when it comes to politics, I have no interest."

"I don't believe you."

"That's fine, you don't have to. But your issue isn't with me, it's with Timur Dobrynin."

"He may have announced the ejection of all international ambassadors from Russia, but *you* made the call. He spoke on your behalf. He has been *your* fall guy ever since you were found in the slums and placed into a seat of power."

"You're mistaken."

"What did you do to Tim? I knew him long before you came around. He was a decent man and we worked well together. It only took a year or so before he flipped and I no longer recognized him. Only took two years before you had him wrapped around your finger and dispensing orders on your behalf. I may have only been in Russia with you as royalty for two years, but I saw things. I heard rumors. I was well-connected and able to piece together the fact that you can't be trusted."

103

"If that is so, why haven't you done anything about it?"

"So far, you haven't done anything suspicious enough to investigate and ruin the relationship between Russia and the United Nations. They are furious about the lack of ambassadors in your country though. You won't get away with it much longer, and they do not like the restrictions you've placed around your borders, preventing virtually any outsiders from getting in. I told them you're hiding something, but they think I'm still bitter about the expulsion."

"You sound bitter to me too. That happened, what, eight years ago? Maybe more? Time to move on, Kenny."

Kenneth shook his head. "I'm on to you. I don't know what you're doing over there, or what you're planning, but I don't like you being on my home turf. If you try contaminating my country with your infectious influence, I promise you will fail. We are proud, we are strong, and we are brave. We will not bow to you as easily as the Russians did. If you try anything devious here, you are in for a fight."

"Your pride is a lovely thing. Hold tight to that."

"Do not mock me."

"I'm not, just admiring your conviction." Mikhail stood up, placed his hands on the desk, and leaned in close. "Stop being paranoid. It's a bad look." He stood upright and walked along the wall of bookshelves, scanning the pictures and reading the book spines. "Can we let my friends join us again? Or would you like to continue our intimate date?"

Kenneth stood up, his face red with frustration. "This isn't over. I will figure out what you're scheming and put a stop to it."

"Fine, fine." Mikhail had his back to him as he continued to observe the many trinkets scattered around the room. "If it makes you feel important, by all means, do your worst."

Kenneth stormed out of the room, leaving the door open for Mikhail's friends to enter. A U.S. guard stood watch at the doorway, making sure the Russian visitors did not snoop through any of Kenneth's personal items.

"You weren't supposed to upset him," Larisa moaned.

"It's hard not to—he's so moody."

"The U.N. will pounce if Kenneth has any influence," Nazar added in a whisper, making sure the guard could not overhear them.

"If I read the situation correctly, he has zero say in the matter. I got the impression that no one takes him too seriously." Not wanting to talk there any longer, he changed the subject. "Full day with Kenneth cut drastically short. What do we do now?"

"Well, we will be on call in case Kenneth still wants to do lunch or dinner or meet again. Otherwise, anything we want."

"Let's grab a drink at the Russia House Lounge. You'll get a kick out of the stereotypical ambiance," Nazar suggested.

"I think they do a decent job on the food and atmosphere," Larisa interjected.

"I'll be the judge of that," Mikhail said as he led them out.

The Russia House Lounge wasn't as bad as Nazar implied it would be. The food was close to authentic and the overall vibe wasn't too different from the lounges in Russia. Mikhail was content to waste the afternoon there. They ordered a bottle of vodka and a few plates of appetizers to pick at. Larisa and Nazar ate more than Mikhail and Kirill; their appetites had returned since leaving Russia. In order to keep up their political game in D.C., eating out was an essential part of networking.

An hour into their leisure time, Kirill's phone rang. Mikhail snatched it off the table and saw a Russian number displayed on the screen.

"Hello?" Mikhail answered.

"Hello, General Mikvonski. I have news."

"This is Prince Mikhail Romanov, your Haeman commander and Marshal of the Russian Federation. Who am I speaking to?"

"Lieutenant Roman Vershinin. I'm stationed at the border, a few kilometers inland from Nuijamaa, Finland with Lieutenant Sergei Greshnev and Lieutenant Edik Ozerov."

"What is your news?"

"We found her." A shrill, female scream accompanied the rumble of the truck engine. "We are delivering her back to the Winter Palace now."

"Say her name." Mikhail's eyes were closed, afraid to assume who his soldier meant.

"Arinadya."

The piercing scream came through the phone again and Mikhail could hear the physical struggle taking place inside their vehicle. He listened and enjoyed hearing the sound of her dismay.

"Keep her sedated until my return."

Mikhail passed the phone over to Kirill, who mouthed Arinadya's name in question. Mikhail nodded.

"General Mikvonski on the line," Kirill stated. "Who am I speaking to?"

"Good evening, General, it's Roman. We found her."

"Great work. Get her back to the palace safely and don't let anyone but the nurses see her. This mission is still covert, only specially tasked sects of the military were assigned to this search and seize. No one can know she wasn't at home on bed rest."

"I know, don't worry."

106

"I'll be in touch with follow up orders." Kirill disconnected the call, giving Mikhail a grin. "Told you they'd find her."

"I cannot wait to get my hands on her." Mikhail felt relief and terrible anger simultaneously.

"She's pregnant, remember?" Larisa chimed in, sarcastically.

"I meant that in a loving way." Mikhail faked a smile, ending the conversation. "Do I have any pre-arranged press time here in D.C.?"

"No, but I can set that up if you like."

"Do it."

"Tomorrow is your day with President Ward. Can it be during that, or separate?"

"Just something that guarantees I am on televisions everywhere."

"Shouldn't be a problem."

Mikhail sipped on his Moscow Mule, thinking of his pretty bride's face. She was a rebel, a dirty traitor, but she was *his* disobedient wife, *his* property to punish as he wished. As mad as he was, now that she was found he was even more compelled to her. He was eager to place his crippling love all over her again. He shut his eyes and his hands recalled the feel of her.

One more week.

Chapter 16

Arinadya was not cooperating.

Mikhail wanted a picture of her with a pregnant belly to show the world during his public appearances with the American President.

The palace staff tried cleaning her up, dressing her in a gown, and putting make up on her, but she fought the nurses, stylists, and guards in everything they did. When they finally got her dressed and styled, Gavriil hissed through his daggered teeth.

"It's useless," the hair stylist groaned. "Her hair is chopped short, her face is bruised and scabbed, and her body is too skinny to look pregnant. It will take time and healing for her to look like Mikhail's flawless haeman bride again."

After a few more hours of failed attempts at a photo shoot, the nurses sedated Arinadya and the stylists dressed her in a delicate, silk nightgown. While unconscious, the make-up artists tackled her beat up face, covering the bruises with foundation and masking the hypothermia and dehydration scabs beneath lipstick. They strapped a small, fake pregnancy belly onto her, and then maneuvered her into an elegant sleeping position. With the right lighting and staging, they were able to get a presentable shot. It looked like a beautiful maternity picture one might see in a professional magazine. Arinadya appeared to be slumbering in peace with a loving hand placed over her belly, protecting and staying connected with her unborn child.

They emailed the picture to Kirill and it was printed for Mikhail to bring with him to his evening with President Ward.

He met the president in the Oval Office of the White House. There, photographers and reporters for the most prestigious news channels were in attendance. Mikhail and President Ward sat in large, singular sofa chairs placed side by side and smiled for the cameras. WMBN was there, and so was production assistant, Melanie Cane. Her sleeves were rolled up and Mikhail could see the pink, healing scars on her forearms. She was on his side.

When it was time for the Q&A, the field reporter Melanie was assisting spoke first.

"Prince Mikhail, how have you enjoyed your visit to the States?"

"It's been wonderful. I was fortunate to visit many of your cities and all were equally beautiful in their own distinct ways. I am sad to be nearing the end of my trip."

"We've enjoyed watching your visits to cultural establishments and historical landmarks from afar," another reporter said. "What was your favorite visit?"

"It's hard to say. I felt quite welcome at all locations. I cannot choose, but what I can say is that I value the place American citizens have allotted me in their lives. The overwhelming interest and care the people have shown toward me, Milena, and Arinadya is greatly appreciated. At times, I felt like I was home."

Kirill stood in a dark corner, cringing, as the lies poured from Mikhail's mouth. They were thick, elaborate, and the media ate them up. Nazar and Larisa were with Kirill and did their best not to chuckle at their prince's gushing falsities.

"You had something to share, right?" President Ward asked, steering the conversation to Mikhail's picture.

"I do." He picked the picture off the table next to him and held it up for the cameras to capture its image. The room oohed and aahed at the sight of their favorite Russian royal sleeping with a swollen belly. She looked fragile in the picture, delicate and lovely as ever. The international public had gone too long without a glimpse of her and this small sighting was exactly the fuel they needed to reenergize their love for her.

"She looks beautiful," a female reporter said. "Will this picture be sent to our stations so we can post a clear image on our broadcasts?"

"I can have that arranged." Mikhail smiled at the woman.

After a few more minutes of pictures showing the two leaders bonding, the media was escorted out of the room. President Ward picked up the picture and took a good look at it.

"She is stunning," he commented.

"Thank you, President Ward."

"Oh, please, call me Nate. No need to be formal with one another."

"Agreed. Mikhail, without the prince prefix, works for me."

"Fantastic," Nate grinned. He was an older gentleman, skinny in stature with a tuft of white hair topping his tall frame. His wrinkles intensified as he smiled with warmth at Mikhail. "You are going to love the National Symphony Orchestra. They are playing the works of Shostakovich and Dvorak for us tonight."

"Waltz No. 2 by Shostakovich is a favorite of mine. I look forward to hearing it."

"Great. It's almost 6 p.m., we ought to head out. Show starts at 7 p.m. and D.C. traffic is terrible."

The men were escorted to the president's limousine and driven to the Kennedy Center where they'd hear the orchestra perform. Dvorak was Czech, so his music was not of Russian influence, but the power behind the strings and flutes was still beautiful. Shostakovich *was* Russian and the music reflected the heritage. Mikhail closed his eyes and listened. It brought him back to his roots and his bones relaxed as the songs took him home. The night was divine, partly because he got to hear classical Russian music played live by a very talented orchestra, but also because Arinadya was back in his possession. He did not have to worry anymore, he did not have to stress on the flight back to St. Petersburg that he still had a huge obstacle left to tackle. It was taken care of.

The evening ended with a cocktail and conversation in one of the Kennedy Center lounges. Nate and his security stayed with him until 11 p.m., then he and Kirill were taken back to their hotel. They had an early flight and only three days left before they returned home.

The next morning they flew to Philadelphia, Pennsylvania and spent the entire day touring the historic section of the city. Isidor Kozlova and Kazimir Leshev were his haeman spies in Philly. They organized the horse carriage tour and set up a night in an underground bar for Mikhail to get a taste of the scene. It was raw, dirty, and unpredictable. The locals were crass and self-assured, so confident they appeared unapproachable.

They set up in G Lounge and Mikhail had a fun time putting those who did not cater to him in their place. By the end of the night, the entire club was tailoring their evening to revolve around his presence. It was a power trip to sway such smug individuals to his beckoning. Around midnight they moved their personal party into the Mogul Room, which had a steel door and walls that were three meters thick. The silve began to flow and the high was ripe. The entire room was violently intoxicated and Kirill had to guard the door to make sure none of the newbies left and took their newfound strength out on the partiers beyond their room. Philadelphia was a boastful place full of brazen and presumptuous people. Once Mikhail had the majority converted, they might turn out to be his best haeman warriors. The fight was already in them, all they needed was a cause.

Last stop was Atlantic City, New Jersey. Many of the Philly partiers followed him there Saturday night, including Isidor and Kazimir, his haeman moles. Galina Mishin and Sevastian Babikov were stationed in Atlantic City and did not appreciate the Philly haemans impeding upon their territory. Again, the population here was loud and aggressive, perfect pawns to turn into haemans. By the end of the night, Galina and Sevastian got over their territorial issues and enjoyed a good party with the rest of them. The casinos were wild, the people were wasted, and the environment was Mikhail's for the taking.

As with most of his partying in the States, the night passed in a blur. He woke up on Sunday in a strange girl's hotel bed, unsure how he got there or what they did together. The girl slept soundly despite his abrupt awakening. He looked her over and she had fresh wounds on her inner thighs—Mikhail's signature mark. He could determine the rest of the night's happenings from that alone. Her phone sat on the bedside stand. Unsure what might be on it, he smashed it into pieces before getting dressed and leaving her room without saying goodbye.

Kirill had both their bags packed and Sevastian drove them to the airport. Galina filled them in on their progress in New Jersey during the long car ride. She had mostly good news, which helped lighten the pressure of Mikhail's migraine. They were hitting the NJ suburbs, infiltrating the teenagers like Timofey and Yana were doing in San Francisco. Mikhail gave them the same warnings he issued to his haemans in Northern California and Galina swore they were monitoring their youthful recruits carefully.

"Social media cannot be my downfall. I will tear apart every city on this planet if those damn websites thwart my progress."

"We understand. We are keeping a close eye on it," Sevastian said, calming Mikhail down.

"You better."

At the airport, their bags were placed in the undercarriage of their private jet and they boarded the small, luxurious aircraft. The flight back to Russia was long, but much anticipated. Mikhail finally felt like he could breathe again. No more pretending, no more faking the perfect persona; he could finally return to his home and relax back into his normal self. The tour was over: he checked on his foreign cities, watered the seeds planted by his haeman moles, and watched them blossom further. Now he had some time to kill while they grew into the army he desired.

Chapter 17

"Is that it?" Zakhar asked, pointing at a section of the Paatsjoki River where the rapids were rough and white. All the men paused to look in the direction he indicated.

"It *is* what the scouts told us to look for," Ivan shrugged.

They were a few kilometers away from the border, which maintained its fences this far north. But the further north they went, the further the haeman border guards were spaced out. The last guard they saw was an hour south from where they were now and they couldn't see any guards in the distance moving forward.

"Even if this isn't it, it seems like a pretty safe crossing point," Konstantin noted. "I say we go for it."

"I agree," Ruslan chimed in. "There isn't a haeman guard in sight, and hasn't been for a while."

Vladimir stepped to the front of the group. "Let's go. Marat, you first. You're our best climber."

Marat approached the fence, which was made of tall chain link and crowned in barbed wire. He picked up a branch and threw it at the fence to see if it was electrocuted. When it hit, nothing happened.

"Looks like it's just there to prevent people from climbing over. We will need to cut it if we plan to get over this without slicing up our hands." Marat took off his gloves and stepped closer to the fence. In contemplation, he touched a piece of the spiked wire that weaved in and out between the chain links. The moment he touched it, he hollered in pain and was tossed backwards by the shock it sent through him. The fence was electrocuted; the branch test hadn't triggered it.

The men rushed to Marat's side to see if he was okay. The tips of his fingers were black where he touched the fence and his breathing was slow. He was conscious—the current hadn't coursed through his heart.

"Okay, new plan," Nikolai spat out as Marat sat up.

"We have time," Leonid said. "Let's think it through."

"What is there to think about?" Konstantin argued. "We can't climb it."

"Maybe if we walk a little farther we can find a section of fence that has trees near it. Then we can climb those and jump over," Ivan suggested.

"This fence is at least 6 meters tall," Nikolai objected. "We will break our ankles trying to do that."

"We also might not find another spot along the fence as devoid of haemans as this one."

"Is there any way to short circuit the electricity?" Artem asked. "The buzz it makes is barely audible, it would take a while for the haemans to realize what happened."

Jurg looked at the fence in contemplation. He had been a contractor before escaping the city. "It's obviously waterproofed for snow, so we can't cut the wires without getting electrocuted ourselves, and we don't know where the main power box is. If we did, we could break it by shooting it. Unless someone knows another way, I don't think it's possible."

The group broke into disarrayed chatter.

"We could always dig under it," Isaak said amidst the murmuring. His voice was not loud, but enough of his older counterparts heard him to stop their own thoughts and focus on his.

"Dig under?" Benedikt asked, confirming what he heard.

"I mean, it's what we're best at. I can't remember a time in my life where I *wasn't* digging. If we get deep enough, we can crawl under the electricity."

The men went quiet.

"I don't see why that wouldn't work," Jurg said.

"You're brilliant." Nikolai grabbed Isaak's shoulder with pride, then knelt by the edge of the fence. "Hardest part will be breaking ground. The earth is frozen."

"We've done it before," Ruslan said, "we can do it again."

"Luckily, we have time," Vladimir said as he scanned their surrounding area. "Unless they walk the fence perimeter, it seems this area has been foolishly neglected."

"Good point," Ruslan said, picking up on the idea no one thought of. "It may seem like we have time but we cannot be sluggish. They may, in fact, pace the fence this far north. Maybe there's so little action here they are tasked to larger sections. If that is the case, we could have a haeman upon us at any time. We must start now."

The men got to work. It was a dry night and they had no trouble building a small fire over the spot they planned to dig. Once the frozen soil was thawed, they used their knives to carve into the earth. Once one layer was chopped up, they used their hands to remove the dirt. Upon hitting frozen ground again, the fire and knives came back out and they repeated the process.

It was exhausting. Sevrick was covered in sweat beneath his many layers.

It took three hours to dig a ditch deep enough for their biggest men to fit through; Vladimir in width and Konstantin in height. Once the hole was a decent size, Isaak went back and forth beneath the fence to help widen the hole from the Norwegian side. He was the smallest and was able to easily maneuver through the ditch without risk of electrocution.

It was dusk by the time they were finished. They progressed in size order: Isaak first, followed by Leonid, Marat, and Ivan. Middle-sized guys were Nikolai, Zakhar, Sevrick, and Artem. The last group to make the crawl were the biggest men. Vladimir went first in this set since he was the widest. It was helpful to have assistance on both sides of the fence, directing him which way to move in order to prevent electrocution. Ruslan went after him, also on the hefty size but more athletically built. They both made it through with guidance. Last up were the tallest men. Benedikt slithered beneath the fence with no trouble. Konstantin struggled due to his long limbs and broad shoulders.

Jurg went last. As his feet crossed the invisible border, shots fired into the night sky. Sevrick and Zakhar pulled Jurg through and the rest of group tensed. More shots, followed by angry shouting. It was coming from the south and approaching fast.

"Haemans," Sevrick hissed. "We need to run."

"But the hole," Isaak protested. "We need to fill it back up or else they'll use it to follow us."

"There is no time," Nikolai said as he grabbed his arm.

Like a protective older brother, he yanked Isaak along and followed the pack of men away from the fence and toward Paatsjoki River. Isaak fell behind to check on his uncle, who was at the back of the pack with Leonid and Vladimir.

"Can they leave the border?" Artem asked, panting but not breaking speed. He, Sevrick, Zakhar, and Nikolai led the pack.

"No clue," Nikolai said between heavy breaths.

"Not far," Zakhar added, "is my guess. They have a secret to withhold."

"The Norwegians can't see them," Sevrick confirmed without slowing down.

"Guess it'll depend what's more important," Nikolai panted. "Keeping their secret or stopping us."

The men ran in silence for a moment before Artem spoke again.

117

"They won't stop until we're stopped," he heaved. "We *are* the secret, just as much as they are."

Realizing he was right, the men collectively ran faster. As they increased their pace, so did their comrades behind them.

"They are at the fence," Leonid shouted to the rest of the group.

"How many?" Sevrick turned and ran backwards for a moment to assess the situation. He could barely see the fence anymore, let alone who stood on the other side of it.

"Two, I think," Leonid answered.

Shots fired in their direction. Sevrick ran along the outside edge of the group and felt a bullet whiz past his ear. He picked up his pace, motivating the others to do so as well.

They ran another kilometer before reaching the edge of the river. The fence was just a contraption put in place by Prince Mikhail to ensure his territory was secure. The Paatsjoki River was the true border between Russia and Norway.

"The river is too wide and too rough," Zakhar huffed as he caught his breath.

"Let's run south along its bank," Sevrick suggested. "I was keeping an eye out as we walked and I remember it being much thinner during yesterday's walk."

Vladimir, Ruslan, and Leonid caught up with the group.

"You guys okay to keep running?" Nikolai asked with skepticism. The three men looked drained.

"We have no other choice, so yes," Vladimir answered with more conviction than he felt. The men took a moment to catch their breath and Benedikt approached his leader quietly.

"Did you see their faces?" he whispered to Vladimir as the other men were distracted. Vladimir knew Filipp before he fell into haemanism.

"No," Vladimir answered apologetically, aware that Benedikt had been hoping for a sighting of his younger brother for years. "It was too dark."

Benedikt nodded solemnly and dropped the subject.

"Did they follow us beneath the fence?" Zakhar asked, getting the entire group's attention again.

"Last I could see, they were at the fence, screaming, cursing, and firing at us." Vladimir turned and showed the group where a bullet clipped him along his bicep. His thick winter jacket took most of the hit, but blood still trickled from where it grazed his skin. "I think they only saw the three of us at the back, not the whole group."

"They were on their two-way radios getting directions on what to do," Ruslan added. "I never saw them crawl through our ditch to follow us, but we lost sight of them a few kilometers back."

"Then we better get moving."

They ran without stopping for half an hour.

"If the haemans followed us, we'd be caught by now," Nikolai said with exhaustion.

The men agreed, happy to turn their run into a brisk walk. They remained cautious about the haemans guarding the Russian side, making sure they weren't spotted as they snuck along the river.

When they reached a section that was crossable, it was about four hours south of where they breached the electric fence. The men reluctantly stripped down to their skivvies, placed their boots, socks, and pants into their packs, and entered the freezing water. It was a mellow current and the water never got deeper than their thighs.

Once across the river and officially in Norway, the men redressed and created a small fire pit to warm up. There was no sign that the haemans followed them, so they felt comfortable relaxing for a while.

"I wonder why they didn't chase us down," Sevrick thought aloud.

Konstantin laughed and placed a hand on Vladimir's shoulder.

"They probably only saw this fatty holding up the rear and assumed he'd get eaten by a bear before he ever made it to civilization."

"Not funny," Vladimir grunted, but the rest of the men got a kick out of it.

"I really don't think they saw the whole group. If they knew we had such large numbers they'd have followed," Leonid added more seriously. "One or two people isn't worth the chase."

"Or maybe we just lost them," Nikolai contributed. "We ran south. I bet once they realized we didn't go straight through the water, they assumed we ran north. It's more natural to move forward, not backwards."

The men shrugged. There was no way to determine what happened or why. They were just grateful to no longer feel like prey.

Chapter 18

The electric fence burned his back as the bottom bar ripped his shirt and scraped his skin. The shocks were intense but his high numbed the pain.

"Push me through," Sergei shouted. "We have to stop them."

"Your back is raw. I told you this was a bad idea," Edik said as he watched Sergei struggle to get under the fence. It wasn't that he was too big, he was just moving too fast. "Come out of that ditch and put your coat back on. I told you to wait until they flipped the main switch and turned the power off."

"They ran! We have no time to wait," Sergei fought through the electric currents shooting through his body.

"You're going to regret this as soon as your high wears off."

Sergei roared with frustration and managed to get his pants snagged on a piece of jagged metal. Just then, a call came in over Edik's radio.

"We conferred with Kirill," the voice spoke. "He says to let it go. Putting power out along the whole border, sending half the guards on a manhunt, and giving others a chance to escape is more risky than letting a few get away. You say you saw three, maybe four. Those numbers are small, their voice is weak. Norway is a minor player in the bigger picture; we have little to worry about from them."

"They need to die!" Sergei shouted with rage.

"If you put it down for a few minutes, just Sergei and I will give chase. See if we can catch them. The river here is wide, I doubt they got far," Edik said more reasonably.

"No, the order is made. The damage they could cause is less than what may occur if we slackened our border control now."

"Alright, understood."

The crackle from his radio disappeared.

"You heard him. Quit it."

Sergei's body went slack in the ditch, giving up and giving in to the relentless wounds he inflicted upon himself.

"I need silve," he whispered. Edik ran to their truck and retrieved a vial for his friend. He returned to the fence, pulled him out of the ditch by his rubber boots, and helped him put his jacket back on. Sergei was shivering, not only from the cold, but also from the traumatic injuries all over his body.

"You're a dumbass," Edik spat as he helped him into the truck. "I need to get you back to the city. You need medical attention."

"No, I don't."

Edik picked up his radio. "Lieutenant Ozerov here. I need men at the Kirkenes border immediately. I am heading back into St. Petersburg and I need this section of the fence covered."

After a moment a voice answered.

"Two of my men are headed north toward your location. They'll be there within the hour."

"I won't be here. Tell them over radio to stand guard until I return."

"Got it."

Edik put his radio down and directed the truck back toward the city. The drive was long and filled with Sergei's agonized moaning. The drugs weren't enough to numb the pain completely. By the time they reached St. Petersburg, Edik was anxious to get away from his injured companion. The non-stop whimpering was unbearable. He parked at the Winter Palace where the other lieutenants were stationed, helped Sergei into the mansion, and let the nurses take him from there.

Edik headed to the east wing where the lieutenants, senior officers, and generals were stationed. Since Mikhail left the country his officers remained in the Winter Palace, using it as their strategic headquarters.

Filipp and Roman stood at a massive rosewood table with their commanding officers. Maps were scattered all over the table's surface and the men talked invasion tactics. Lines diagrammed the planned route the haeman army would infiltrate once word was given that the majority of their European neighbors were successfully morphed into haemans. It wouldn't be long; it only took a year or two to spread through half of Russia's population. The subsequent years following turned the stragglers and pushed those resistant to the change out, but the bulk of the transformation happened very early on.

The European invasion would be slick. They hoped not to draw too much attention to themselves as they swept their bordering countries under Mikhail's reign. Takeover of the United States would follow and they needed the recruited European soldiers to help fight the Americans. The Russian Haeman Federation Air Force was in the room this afternoon and its supreme officer was explaining their plans to attack the States by air.

"If we can keep our European gains relatively quiet, we can take the war to them," said Air Force Supreme Officer Dominika Mikvonskaia, cousin to Kirill. "It would be to our advantage. They haven't won a war on their home turf in centuries. They won't know what to do."

"The masses will go into a panic, making it harder for their military to do their job," Filipp added.

"And our haemans will be there to fight them from the inside. They'll be so busy trying to subdue them that they'll likely miss our attack from the air until it's upon them." Dominika grinned; her wicked smile and dark, cavernous eyes were the same as Kirill's.

"Perhaps we should instruct the U.S. haemans in hiding to start causing chaos as we move through Europe. It will take the attention off of us and what we're doing," Edik added as he joined the table.

"Great idea." Dominika scribbled it into her notepad. "Kirill has already told me that the American media controls the minds and opinions of the masses. If they are wrapped up in that, the battle on drugs, the fight against a subculture uprising, or whatever spin they put on it, then it's likely very few will have their eyes on us."

"Just make sure our haemans in the States do not reveal silve as a Russian-made creation. If they do, and they are struggling to eradicate it from their country, then *all* eyes will be on us. They need to think it came from somewhere else," Army Supreme Officer Aliona Rusanova warned. Everyone nodded in agreement. She was beautiful and dainty looking, but her strength was greater than most. Her gentle demeanor was the perfect disguise for her volatile temper.

"They'll blame Mexico," Filipp scoffed. "They always do."

"When does Prince Mikhail and the general return?" Edik asked.

"Tonight," Aliona answered.

"Good thing we found Arinadya when we did," Roman said with relief. "Might not have been alive come tomorrow if we hadn't."

The supreme officers looked at the lieutenants in the room condescendingly, then returned to converse with others in their rank around the table. Filipp, Roman, and Edik took this as their cue to leave.

"Where is Sergei?" Roman asked, realizing his buddy should be there with Edik.

"With the nurses," Edik answered. "He lost his cool. A few people crossed the border into Norway. They dug a hole under the fence and crawled through. Sergei was so furious that he stripped off his bulky coat and ran at the high-voltage fence like a raging bull."

"He got electrocuted?"

"A couple times. Didn't seem to feel it because of the high. But by the time we got the order not to follow the escapees and I dragged him out from the ditch, he was shaking in pain. Gave him some silve to numb it until we got back here, but he's in bad shape."

"Will he be okay?" Filipp asked, cringing.

"Yeah. He just needed medical attention, otherwise the electrical burns would have gotten infected. I'm just glad the voltage didn't hit his chest. We are already amped up, last thing we need is an extra kick to the heart."

Roman and Filipp shook their heads, realizing it could have been any of them acting so foolishly. They were haemans, they were irrational; this type of unpredictability was one of the few cons to living this lifestyle.

"Do we know who escaped and how many?" Filipp asked. His fellow haeman soldiers did not know about his condemned brother, but he couldn't help but wonder if Benedikt was one of the escapees.

"No. Kirill said to leave it alone, so we didn't investigate. Can't imagine it'll make any dent in what we have going on. A couple nameless Russians won't have any pull with leaders in other nations."

The men nodded in agreement and walked down the hall toward the room where Sergei was resting. Edik didn't want to see the injuries again, but the others did. It was on the opposite side of the palace. As they crossed through the main hall, they could hear the sound of screeching tires. The men stopped in their tracks on the second floor balcony with the front door in sight.

Mikhail barged through, snow in his hair and fire in his hazel eyes.

"I'm home!" he shouted, his voice echoing through the massive building. All distant noise ceased and the palace froze beneath the prince's authoritative return.

Chapter 19

"Where is she?" Mikhail demanded as he ascended the staircase and made his way toward the lieutenants. His approach was menacing and the normally confident men shrank beneath his presence. They recoiled internally while remaining stoic on the outside. It was an attempt at respect: to Mikhail, who did not like cowards, and to themselves, to preserve their manhood.

"In the west wing, sedated," Filipp answered.

Mikhail stormed off without another word. The men released a collective breath, and continued their trek to see Sergei.

Mikhail tore off the many layers of clothes he wore and tossed them to the floor as he made his way to Arinadya's second bedroom, which was the room she stayed in when she wasn't summoned to sleep with him. The trail of clothes he left was long, but the maids were quick to tidy his mess.

He charged through the bedroom door to find Arinadya on the bed, unconscious, and three nurses huddled in the corner snorting lines of silve. Two of them hurriedly stopped when he entered, the third was too high to process the new situation. Mikhail ignored her and spoke to the attentive nurses.

"What happened to her hair?" Mikhail asked, enraged over this small detail he hadn't noticed in the carefully orchestrated picture.

"She arrived like that."

"Is she healed of haemanism?"

"It appears so. She is weak, slow, and mentally fragile. Her time in the woods cleansed her system of silve."

"Or, she found Leonid and he cured her," Mikhail scowled. "The withdrawals are too intense to survive without some kind of antidote. No one can white knuckle it."

"Perhaps. I don't know how it came to be, but she is silve-free. She hasn't been awake long enough to determine if she is still in a suitable place to easily relapse. Maybe she misses it. Maybe her haemanism was stripped from her against her will. We won't know until we talk to her."

"When will she wake?"

"The last sedative we gave her should wear off soon."

"Don't give her another until I've spoken with her. As soon as she wakes, call me."

"Certainly." The nurses began tying Arinadya's wrists and ankles to the bedposts so she could not fight them or run once she was conscious. Mikhail exited and made his way to the military headquarters temporarily stationed in his home. Dominika greeted him and Aliona pulled up a chair for him to sit in while they told him their plans. Kirill was already at the map-covered table.

Mikhail listened to the supreme officers speak, pleased with the strategy. As usual, he felt his plan was panning out exceedingly well. It would be a few months before the next phase could roll out, so he prepared to hunker down.

This time would be spent getting Arinadya back into presentable shape. She had to be perfect by the start of the invasion. First order of business, after determining her mental state, was to get her pregnant. If it worked, she'd stay off silve and deliver a royal child to Mikhail. Having a baby for all of the haemans to obsess over would not only strengthen their loyalty to him, but also give them hope for their own futures. Many believed they could never reproduce, and seeing it happen would give them hope that haemanism could live on through generations. It would allow them to believe that they too could create their own legacy within this new world, something to attach their name to with pride, something that would live on long after they died.

Mikhail was not sure if it would work; his sperm was likely altered and Arinadya's insides were probably a mess, but with her being "cured" for a decent stretch of time, maybe it was possible. Maybe they could extend their family's reign through the birth of children. If it worked, Mikhail had all the more reason to find Leonid and demand a cure. It was the only way to ensure his new empire wasn't birthed and deceased within a single generation.

A knock came from the war-room door. It was one of the nurses. She looked frazzled.

"The princess is awake."

"Does she know I'm back?"

"No. She's been too busy fighting her restraints, screaming, and sobbing." The nurse tucked a flyaway strand of hair behind her ear. "I suggest you come at your earliest convenience. At the rate she's going, she'll knock herself out."

"I see. I'll be there shortly. You may leave."

The nurse departed and Mikhail took his time wrapping up the meeting. Arinadya could wait; she could fight until her skin was raw for all he cared. Her current state of disgrace was her own fault and he'd let it carry on as punishment for her treachery.

When the meeting ended, he sauntered down the hall toward her room, casual and deliberate in his slow pace. He could hear her sobbing in the distance. The cries came between bouts of screaming. She was trying to escape, but all her haeman strength was gone. She could not break free.

Mikhail stopped at the door, reveled in her agony a moment longer, then pushed it open. The door swung and he remained in the doorway. At the sound of the faint creak, Arinadya froze. She was facing the wrong way and could not see him, but she felt his presence. Saliva gathered in the back of her throat as she waited for any indication of what lurked behind her. Her fear was tangible—Mikhail felt it flitting through the air.

He took a step closer; Arinadya shivered. The tension between them was frigid.

"What do you want from me?" she asked, still hazy from the sedatives but very aware of her new, dangerous situation.

"I want my beautiful haeman bride back."

"She's gone. I killed her in the woods."

"No," he smirked and walked to the other side of the room so she could see him. He sat next to her on the bed and caressed her bruised cheek. "She's right before me. With a little work, you'll be back to normal in no time."

The tears fell despite her determination to hold them back.

"Please don't. I can't go back to who I was. It will kill me."

Mikhail shushed her and addressed the nurse.

"I'm hoping to have her knocked up soon, so she needs to stay off the silve." He looked back at Arinadya who wore a horrified expression. "No crack babies allowed in the royal family." He kissed her forehead and stood up. "I'll be back to interrogate you further and get the answers I need, but for now, rest. You're of no use to me in this hostile state."

"I'll remain in this state until you let me go."

"Ah, like old times." Mikhail grinned, but his glare was evil. "I don't know why you choose to make everything so much harder on yourself. If you complied, if you gave into me, you'd be much happier. I promise."

Arinadya broke eye contact with him.

"Typical," he scoffed. "Your defiance will be your undoing."

He left the room, leaving her alone with the nurses. Her fire was extinguished; the sight of her old captor smothered the flame. Now she lay motionless, numb to the battle lost. Her wrists and ankles bled but she did not feel their sting. Eyes glazed over, all she could see, hear, or feel was Mikhail.

Chapter 20

Due to where they crossed the border, the trip through the outskirts of Kirkenes, Norway was treacherous and devoid of civilization. They hadn't anticipated the density of the forest or the lack of community along the way. Though the terrain was tough, it would have been miserable in Russia, too, and all agreed it was safer to be on this side of the border.

The weather remained frigid as they moved farther north. Each night they found thick pine trees to sleep beneath and watched the Northern Lights dance across the dark sky. Sevrick had only ever glimpsed Aurora Borealis in pictures. The sight was entrancing and never failed to soothe the group into a peaceful slumber.

As they approached their third day in Norway, the finish line was close. Their pace was slow now that they were no longer in a place where haemans hunted them, but they were almost there. Kirkenes was one of Norway's smaller cities, but they were certain they'd find someone there who could spread the word. Or help them travel more comfortably to a place where they'd be heard.

"I think we are half a day's walk from the city," Ruslan said, looking at his map. It was covered in scribbles and a long line indicating where they had traveled thus far. It was a guesstimate, but he was a skilled cartographer so his markings were close to accurate.

They settled in for the night beneath a broad Scots pine tree. Its trunk was so wide in diameter that all thirteen men were able to find a spot to sit and lean against. The thick, low-hanging branches overhead kept them shielded from the harsh winds.

Sevrick looked up from his resting spot through a gap in the branches that revealed the sky. He watched the green swirling lights of Aurora Borealis slowly waltz across the night's black canvas. The colors moved so slowly, so deliberately, he found himself slipping into a sleepy, hypnotic state. A canvas of nature was sealed to the back of his eyelids as they closed.

The morning came accompanied by the songs of chipper Bohemian waxwings. The birds greeted sunrise with a harmony of melodies, making sure the rest of the world came back to life at the sun's reemergence. Sevrick wished to sleep longer, but the birds' relentless songs prevented that. Half the men remained asleep despite the noise so he didn't rush to get up. Artem was to his left, slumbering through nature's alarm clock, and Isaak was to his right, awake and staring into the boughs above.

"I need ear plugs," Sevrick said to Isaak, but the boy put a finger up, hushing him. Without breaking his gaze, he pointed, showing Sevrick what he was observing.

Sevrick leaned in closer to get the same vantage point. A few branches above them sat a great grey owl. It stared down at them, watching their behavior intently.

"Do you think we are beneath its nest?" Isaak asked in a whisper.

"Would it be bad if we were?"

Isaak nodded without speaking. The owl tilted its head, barely blinking as it watched the humans below.

"I don't see a nest," Sevrick continued, looking for any sign of the owl's home.

The owl let out a low-pitched hoot, which lasted seven seconds. As it finished its call, its small eyes bore into the men, waiting to see what they'd do next. They stayed perfectly still and the owl repeated the call thirty seconds later. Again it waited for the men to react.

"It wants us to leave," Isaak revealed. "That's a territorial hoot."

Sevrick broke his gaze from the owl to look at Isaak in bewilderment. "How do you know?"

"I like to read." Isaak rolled up his sleeping bag and began getting his pack together while maintaining eye contact with the owl. "They are very protective over their nests and get aggressive when threatened."

"It's just a bird."

"Take a closer look at its talons. They are razor sharp. One quick scoop and it could gouge our eyes out."

Aware that it was better to leave than linger, Sevrick used his elbow to nudge Artem awake.

"Time to go."

"Why?" he asked through a yawn.

"We pissed off a bird."

"Huh?"

There was no time for explanations. Sevrick slithered out from beneath the tree branches to wake the rest of the group. He circled the tree, shaking the boots of the men as he walked around. Those who weren't awake slowly got up and Isaak passed the message to depart quietly around the tree. The men obeyed, unsure what danger they were in, and they met a few feet away from the tree. Konstantin remained beneath the tree, unwilling to obey Sevrick's order to wake up.

"Konstantin, get up!" Vladimir demanded, but his subordinate barely acknowledged him.

The owl repeated its hoot, this time the low-pitched call sounded more like a growl. The bird hopped from branch to branch until it was perched above the spot where Konstantin slept. After a moment, the growl returned. The owl flared its face feathers and dove at the human ignoring its warnings. Konstantin screamed as the owl's talons sliced the back of his neck. He grabbed his pack and frantically crawled out from beneath the tree. Blood poured from his neck, staining the snow as he stumbled to stand up. Once out from under the tree, the owl ceased its attack and returned to a peaceful state upon its nest.

"What the hell?" Konstantin grunted, pressing the wound on his neck.

"It's a great grey owl. We were beneath its nest," Isaak explained. "You're lucky it only got a small piece of you."

"A *bird* did this?" Konstantin asked with outrage. He removed his hand from the gash and the blood flowed out faster.

"You should've listened," Benedikt, his closest friend, told him bluntly.

"Give me your gun," Konstantin demanded. His own was still under the tree. As he yanked it off Benedikt's shoulder, Vladimir jumped in.

"Stop." He snatched the gun from Konstantin's grip. "It's over now. Pour some rubbing alcohol on it and wrap it in gauze so it stops bleeding. We ought to be on the road now. You're wasting our time."

"I'm bleeding!"

"Man up. It was a goddamn bird, you wuss." Vladimir threw his pack over his shoulder and began walking. "You'll be fine."

Benedikt stayed behind to help his friend dress his wound before they followed the others.

By dawn, they were upon the town. The pathless forest gradually gained trails, which eventually turned into dirt and paved roads. Houses began to pop up intermittently, showing signs of human life. It was only an hour after sunrise and the streets were barren. They were in the town for a while before they came across commercial buildings.

135

"Do you hear that?" Leonid asked and the men stopped to listen. Organ chimes echoed through the morning air, calling for the townspeople to greet the day. It was peaceful, much calmer than the erratic waxwing chirps they woke up to. The men followed the sound down the street and came across the source. Kirkenes church stood tall before them.

"Can't hurt to try a church first," Ivan shrugged. "If we get the priest to hear us, the rest of the town will likely listen too."

Ivan and Marat were the only men in the group who could speak Norwegian. Ivan's grandparents were both Norwegian and Marat chose to learn it while studying to be a linguist at Moscow State University.

"It's worth a shot," Marat added. "If nothing else they can point us in the right direction."

They entered the church. The three altar boys in the distance halted their morning chores to observe the weathered men now standing in their house of worship. The town of Kirkenes was small, so it was not common to see unfamiliar faces. They did not know what these strangers wanted so they waited at a distance for an explanation. Ivan spoke to them.

"Hello, neighbors," he said in Norwegian. At the sound of his Russian accent, the boys took a step back. "We crossed the Russian border in hopes of speaking to someone with authority here."

"No one has crossed that border in years," the oldest of the altar boys said. "We've seen the border patrol set up there. We don't want any trouble."

"We haven't come to cause trouble. We need help."

"From us?" the youngest altar boy asked.

"Yes. And from your priest. And hopefully the local authorities here too."

"Father Norgaard is sleeping."

"We don't mind waiting."

The boys looked at each other, unsure how to proceed. The oldest spoke up.

"All who come in peace are welcome here. Please make yourselves comfortable and let us know if there is anything we can do for you while you wait."

"Thank you," Ivan said, leading the group to a long pew to sit. The boys got back to work preparing the church for morning mass.

Despite the hard wood surface and rigid shape, sitting down in a proper seat felt wonderful. Sevrick's knees ached. He hadn't noticed their tender throb until this moment.

An hour passed before the priest descended a hidden staircase and entered into the crossing through a small door. He saw the strangers sitting patiently in the front of the nave and spoke loudly from the altar.

"Have you come to us from Russia in peace?"

Ivan stood up. "Absolutely."

Marat also stood, ready to act as their translator.

"Your Norwegian is quite good, even with the accent," the priest noted.

"Thank you, Father. My maternal grandparents were Norwegian. They moved to Russia when my mother married my Russian father in order to be closer to them and their grandchildren."

"I'm glad they kept their heritage alive through you."

"As am I."

"So tell me, why have you and your friends come here? If I am to make assumptions based off the overall appearance of your group, it looks as though you walked."

"We did."

"That's a lengthy journey. To make that trip, in the dire manner in which you did, I must presume your reasons are of great importance to you."

"We came because we need help. I'm not sure if Prince Mikhail visited Norway, or if you saw any of his international tour on TV, but he is a menace to humans everywhere."

"How so?"

"His malignant influence. He's turned the majority of the Russian population into drug-fueled monsters and we think he aims to do the same in other countries."

"How is that possible? His royal title is an honorary one," Father Norgaard interrupted. "It holds no governmental power. He has no reign over your country."

"That's how it started but everything changed. Not even a year into his new role he had President Dobrynin under his control."

"How?"

"The drugs. Mikhail came from the underworld of Russia; a place that is foul, violent, and misguided. He and his friends created a drug called silve. They were avid users when he, his sister, and their few extended relatives were discovered to be descendants of the massacred Romanov family. When Mikhail took the throne, he brought the drug with him. Eventually he dispersed the silve to the population. It was a quiet invasion; one most didn't realize was happening until it was too late. It had a very successful trickle effect. Suddenly our families, friends, coworkers, and neighbors were latching on and succumbing to Mikhail's forced lifestyle."

"How was it forced?"

"They put the drug into the water system."

"I'm confused. Why? What does this accomplish for the prince?"

"It's more than just a narcotic. After taking the drug, the user cuts and then drinks their own polluted blood. The recirculation of the chemically enhanced blood makes the user powerful. Their strength and speed are intensified, their emotional capacity is hardened. They are unbeatable in this state."

"They are sickly super humans," Ivan added, "with unnatural aptitudes and warped mindsets."

"I see," Father Norgaard said, processing this information with care. "I assume that explains the dystopian-like scene that has emerged at our border over the years."

"Yes," Marat confirmed. "What you see at your border is a small example of what has taken over our entire country."

"I don't understand how so many people fell for this atrocious manipulation."

"Well, he was smart about it. The whole takeover was gradual. Like I said, by the time we realized what he was up to, the majority were already victims, addicted and irretrievable."

"He tricked them all," Ivan added. "The masses adored him and the princess—they wanted to be just like them. After a safe amount of time, he showed them what drinking their own blood would do. No one knew he put a drug into the public water system; he said the strength it gave them was a gift from God. He said it was natural, because the power came from within us. He said to deny this newly discovered gift was a sin. People ate up his lies and jumped on his bandwagon."

"They created an entire religion around it," Marat added.

The priest frowned. "So they all thought drinking their blood was giving them greater abilities, when in fact it was the drug?"

"It's a combination. The drug on its own only numbs the brain, making them morally corrupt. Drinking the drug-laced blood gives them the physical powers."

"And blood without any chemicals in it obviously has no effect at all," Ivan concluded.

The priest sighed. "And they believed it because they did not realize they had the drugs in their system."

"Exactly," Marat confirmed. "We assume most know the truth by now, but they don't care because they'd rather ignore the hard facts than give up their lifestyle. They are addicts; they live for the powerful high. Some still spout that it's a gift from God. It makes them feel better."

"There are still some who have no clue," Ivan sighed. "And they never need to know since the drug is now in everything they use: water, toothpaste, nutrient pills."

Father Norgaard left his podium and one of the altar boys placed a wooden chair in front of their Russian visitors. He sat closer to them now, facing them in conversation and taking in every word they said with great concern.

"The addiction is called haemanism and the addicts are called haemans," Ivan explained. "They are lethal. We barely made it across the border alive."

"We would have tried to spread this information past our borders sooner, but it was always too dangerous," Marat went on. "When we heard he was scouring the globe, planting his seed in other innocent cultures, we knew we couldn't wait any longer."

"He did not visit Norway," Father Norgaard said.

"Sweden?" Marat asked.

"Yes."

"It will spread. I doubt it will take more than a month before you start to see a change."

"What are the warning signs?"

"There will be more violence. Fights and murders over trivial issues. Things people never cared to fight over before. Physically, users become very pale, skinny, and scar-ridden. Eventually they will learn to hide the blood use, but at first they are always sloppy.

It will be stained all over their clothes, typically the ends of their sleeves." Marat pointed to Leonid. "He used to be a haeman. He's recovered now, but he still has the appearance of one."

"So there is a cure?"

"Yes. It took our friends here," Ivan said, motioning at the men sitting along the pew, none of whom could understand a word of their conversation, "a long time to figure it out, but they did. Problem is, it's not a wave of a wand and—*poof*—everyone is back to normal. It's an extensive medical procedure that takes time. We've been capturing haemans and forcing the rehabilitation on them. They are usually grateful in the end, but sometimes they're not. Sometimes they fight it and die during the process."

"If we want a larger turnover of healed haemans, we'd need more scouts, more soldiers capturing them, and a lot more hospital beds dedicated to the cause," Marat added.

"Is that what you want from us?"

"No. Not yet, anyway. What we really need is a way to warn the rest of the world about Prince Mikhail, what he's done to Russia and what we suspect he's planning for the rest of the world."

"Which is?"

"Global domination."

Chapter 21

"A world takeover?" Father Norgaard asked, appalled. "Do you think he is capable of that?"

"Absolutely," Ivan answered. "If he approaches it like he did in Russia, it's only a matter of time before he has armies devoted to him."

"I know your town is isolated, but you must know the global adoration other nations have for him. They admire him, idolize him, put him on a pedestal without any clue who he really is. He is a master manipulator. Just like the Russians, other nations won't know what happened until they are prisoners to the lifestyle."

"This is a very big accusation," Father Norgaard said while looking down at his folded hands. "And if it's true, I imagine Prince Mikhail's retaliation against those who try to get in his way will be harsh. Deadly, if I am processing all you've told me correctly."

"But if we don't speak up and warn the rest of the world, we are doomed. He will turn the masses into haemans and kill whoever chooses not to join."

"You're referring to many people with many different mindsets. How on earth could he possibly sway millions?"

"If we don't say anything and let him continue his work without any resistance, it will be easy. He will conquer the world without breaking a sweat."

"We already think he's building small armies across the globe," Ivan added. "If he gets the silve to the masses and teaches them how to use it, it won't be long before it spreads naturally. He will barely have to do any work. They already love him and he's giving them the tools to be part of his world. Once they're addicted and on his team, all he will have to do is give the order and there will be international mutiny. Having Mikhail as their new leader, be it president or prince, means easier access to the haeman lifestyle. Once addicted, they will fight to the death to keep access to their high."

"All previous loyalties will be terminated at the start of their haeman lives," Marat confirmed. "All that will matter is the drug, their new lifestyle, and their provider: Mikhail."

"How do I help?"

"We need to get the word out. Can you get us in contact with any Norwegian government officials?"

"Absolutely. I am in high standing amongst our community. I can connect you with those best suited to help."

"Thank you."

"I must warn you, though. This is an enormous accusation. I am willing to believe your word, but it may take a bit more convincing with them."

"That's fine. We will do whatever is needed to stop him."

Father Norgaard stood and waved for the men to follow him. He led them into the backyard and they crossed through the snow-covered grass. Behind the church stood the police station. He escorted them in and security let them pass, no questions asked. They entered a room full of cops at desks, all of whom stopped their work to stare in question at the dirty, armed, and unannounced visitors.

"What's going on, Father?" a large, big-bellied cop asked.

"Sorry, Boone, I normally would have called but these men walked here from Russia to ask for our help. I didn't think it kind to make them wait any longer."

"They *walked*?"

"Yes."

"Have they told you why?"

"Yes, and it is worth a listen."

"Okay, let me get Chief Dahlby. We can use a conference room."
He left and the rest of the cops got back to work, though they all
kept a trained side eye on their strange visitors.

He returned with a tall, thin, blonde man who was in his mid-
fifties.

"Welcome to Kirkenes," he said to the men. "I am Chief Johan
Dahlby. You already met Officer Eike. Follow me and we can sit
down for a chat."

He led them to a large conference room with no windows and a
solid, steel door.

Together, Ivan and Marat explained the situation to Chief
Dahlby and Officer Eike, both of whom listened with shock and
confusion. It took an hour to explain all the details and answer their
questions. Once they were out of inquiries and understood, they
took a moment to reflect.

"I'm not saying I don't believe you, but those are some wild
accusations," Chief Dahlby expressed.

"We know it sounds crazy, but it's the truth," Ivan said. "He's in
the United States now, so we should warn President Ward before he
leaves. Maybe they can confront him directly."

"It's too late for that," Eike said. "He returned to Russia a few
days ago."

"I don't have that kind of access anyway," Dahlby added. "I'd
need to get word to our own government officials and they'd
contact the leaders in other nations."

"Okay, let's do that then," Marat said eagerly.

"It won't be easy. I may be Chief of Police in Kirkenes, but I am
pretty low in the chain of command when it comes to Norway's
leading officials. There are many channels I'll need to go through to
get this piece of information to someone who will make it matter on
a bigger scale."

"They are going to want proof," Officer Eike added, looking at his boss.

"You're right." The chief looked back at Ivan and Marat. "How are we going to prove this is happening? We have nothing but your word."

"If it gets to individuals with authority, they can demand Mikhail let them into Russia to see for themselves. They can demand answers. Let him scramble, I promise he will reveal a crack somewhere."

"They won't accuse him without proof. Those allegations would ruin international relations. Russia is a powerful force, even without your claims of their new superhuman abilities. It would be too risky to wrongfully insult them and turn them into an enemy. There has to be proof upfront."

"Leonid is proof," Marat offered. "He used to *be* a haeman." He placed a hand on his shoulder and though Leonid couldn't understand the conversation, he got the gist of what was being discussed.

"Not only was I a haeman," Leonid said to Marat in Russian, "but I was one of Mikhail's best friends during the creation of silve and haemanism, and also during his first few years as prince." Ivan translated to the Norwegian policemen.

"I mean, that's something, but again, it'll be his word against all of Russia. They won't piss off Mikhail just because some random guy with no notoriety claims to be his ex-friend with incriminating secrets."

"Then what kind of proof do you need?"

"Video or audio of Mikhail confessing to any of this. Documentation with Mikhail or Timur Dobrynin's signature. Official government letters with the Russian seal, revealing truth to haemanism. Something solid to work with."

145

Ivan buried his head into the palms of his hands and translated this to his Russian friends.

"That's impossible," Ruslan said with panic in his voice. "Not only would we need to go back to retrieve that kind of proof, but we'd also likely die trying."

Ivan translated and added, "We don't have that much time to waste. He will be ruling the planet before we can fetch that kind of evidence."

Chief Dahlby sighed. "You'll need to go to Oslo. It's where our Prime Minister resides, as well as other influential people. I will accompany you there and try to get you in touch with the contacts you need."

"That would be great," Marat said, accepting the offer. "You and Father Norgaard believed us, maybe the others will too."

"We will leave tomorrow. Tonight you will stay in a hotel in Kirkenes. Boone," he said addressing his officer, "take a few pictures of them in this state before they wash up. If the others see what we saw upon their arrival, it might help their cause."

"Sure thing, boss."

They took the pictures, cleaned up, and had their first good sleep in weeks. Finally having a chance to relax in a secure environment, Sevrick's mind wandered back to Rina. Knowing she was safe at the white elm was the only reason he agreed to leave. Polina had become a good friend to her, and his own friends would never let anything happen to her. They'd take care of her like family, on his behalf. But still, he wondered how she was doing, if the space and time without him was helping her heal. He hoped it was, he wanted her to solve the issues she needed to tackle on her own so they could finally solve the one remaining between them. It made no sense to give up without a fight; they'd been through too much to throw it away. He'd let her work out the internal struggle alone, he understood why she felt she needed to, but he'd be there when she came out on the other side, waiting to see if their love survived.

Chapter 22

Pictures of a sleeping, pregnant Princess Arinadya flashed across the community TV screen.

"He'll never forgive us," Elena said in defeat, face buried in her hands. It was almost two weeks since Rina disappeared from the white elm. Though the note she left said she planned to leave Russia, only a few days passed before a picture of her surfaced indicating she was back in Prince Mikhail's grip.

"We didn't force her to leave, she made that choice on her own," Lizaveta said defensively.

"It *is* our fault." Elena was angry with her best friend and couldn't hide it anymore. "Polina heard your conversation. You encouraged it!"

Lizaveta was taken aback; she hadn't told anyone about the fight with Rina and she didn't realize anyone was listening.

"I do feel bad about that, but I never told her to leave. I never implied she wasn't welcome here."

Elena shot her a nasty glare and returned her attention to the screen. The photo of Rina flashed across the news continually. In the two weeks since she ran away, this was the only photo they shared with the public.

"It's a bit odd," Elena speculated. "You'd think they'd be showing her off non-stop now that they have her back."

"Maybe it's the only decent picture they could get of her," Lizaveta responded, not realizing how bitter her comment sounded.

"Or maybe she got beat up when they captured her and she's still fighting them," Elena wondered out loud. "I don't believe she intended to land back in that situation."

"Yeah, but it's only a matter of time before they have her hooked again. I'm not trying to sound mean, but she was barely recovered. She'll fall back into that life with ease."

"I hope you're wrong."

Lizaveta thought of Sevrick. "I do, too."

Nina walked into the room and sat beside them on the couch. Kira, her small admirer, came in behind her and sat on the floor. Nina braided her long red hair as she spoke.

"Do you think the guys have access to the news?"

"If they crossed the border, maybe," said Elena.

The women sat in silence, quietly hoping their friends and loved ones survived the journey. The time they predicted it would take to get there came and went, and all anyone at the white elm could do was wonder. There was no way to send word back that they made it. The scouts were out scouring the forests for any signs but there were none. No dead bodies, which was good, but also no sign of their success. Worst case scenario, the haemans captured them and their bodies were nowhere to be found. Though it was a possibility, no one talked about it.

Alexsei had a second team ready to send out if no word or sign of their success came within the next two months. Warning other countries of their dire situation was their only chance at survival.

"Sevrick is going to freak out when he sees what happened. I hope they don't find out anytime soon," Elena said, refusing to speak of their friends as anything but alive.

"I still feel bad about leading her to the exit," Kira said, her small voice lined with guilt. "I didn't know who she was."

"Don't feel bad about it, no one blames you. Not even a little bit," Nina responded.

"You were just trying to be helpful," Elena smiled at Kira. "She would have found a way out with or without your help."

149

"Will Sevrick be mad at me?"

"Not a chance." Elena answered with such certainty that Kira had no choice but to believe her.

"Do you think he will go back for her again?" Nina asked, tying off the braid in Kira's hair.

"Another reason why I hope he doesn't find out for a while," Elena groaned.

"He better not go after her," Lizaveta said.

"Didn't think of that when you convinced her to leave, huh?" Elena snapped.

"I didn't tell her to run off." Lizaveta bolted up in anger. "This isn't my fault. I can't believe you're pinning that psycho's actions on me."

"No one is blaming you," Nina said, trying to calm her down.

"But you certainly didn't help the situation," Elena said, fanning the fire.

"Screw you, Elena. I'm allowed to have an opinion; I'm allowed to have feelings. It's not my fault she couldn't handle hearing them."

"Your intentions when sharing them were bad. You wanted to hurt her, wanted to cause her pain. You should've kept them to yourself."

"I'm tired of being dealt the crappy hand. I'm tired of keeping my mouth shut when it comes to that situation. I've done it for years. I thought you, out of everyone, would understand."

"I do, but it doesn't make it right."

"Fine, I'm the bad guy. Sevrick can hate me when he finds out I'm the reason she left the white elm. Happy? I'll take the blame so no one else has to."

Elena groaned. "All I'm saying is you didn't help. Rina is a grown woman, that choice was hers, no one else's."

"Pretty sure you just said otherwise."

"I'm mad, okay? Not only am I suddenly concerned for one of my best friend's mental health, yet again, but also the state of Mikhail's control. The fact that he got Rina back is bad. You've heard all the recovered haemans views about her: they loved her more than they idolized him. She was the reason their loyalty to the prince grew. Having her back means he's more powerful than ever."

Lizaveta's strong stance crumbled and she collapsed back onto the sofa. "How do we fix this?"

"We don't. She's gone. We just hope it resolves on its own."

"Before Sevrick gets back and goes on a suicidal crusade to rescue her," Nina added.

Elena grabbed the remote and changed the channel, hoping to find any sign of their friends on the international news.

Chapter 23

Mikhail grew tired of Arinadya's resistance fast: she fought the nurses, she fought the guards, she fought him. The sedatives knocked her out, making her useless, but it was the only way to stop her incessant hostility. Mikhail needed her compliance, he needed her pleasant obedience, and he was not getting it.

After a week of suffering her nonsense, he had enough. He summoned two of his haemans back from the United States: Roksana Zheglova from Las Vegas and Isidor Kozlova from Philadelphia. Both cities were fine with one haeman correspondent, so they got on flights and returned to St. Petersburg. Their new task was to wrangle Arinadya into suitable shape for public viewing. They'd been back for three days and Isidor was doing a better job at gaining Arinadya's trust and friendship than Roksana. This didn't surprise Mikhail; Roksana was envious and wanted Arinadya's role as Mikhail's wife. He liked the jealously but monitored it closely. His bride could not be murdered over pettiness.

Whenever Roksana's covetous desire for Mikhail threatened to boil over, he took her to bed and silenced her homicidal urges. It benefitted them both: she was still the best he'd ever had.

Another day of extreme patience awaited him; he was shocked he'd made it this long with no casualties. Between Arinadya's insufferable transition back into the woman he married and waiting for news from his haemans stationed all over the world, his temper was on the fritz and nothing, except sex, soothed it.

"I could be sleeping right now," Mikhail announced as he entered the war room.

This meeting with Kirill and his supreme officers, Dominika and Aliona, would be as pointless as all the others of late. They had their plans of attack mapped out and ready to go; nothing new would come until they had word that enough people had converted to haemanism and it was time to strike.

"It's early, but regular meetings are crucial," Army Supreme Officer Aliona Rusanova explained.

"Our senior officers put together an interactive map of the spread," Air Force Supreme Officer Dominika Mikvonskaia said. Kirill turned off the lights and she switched on the projector. "It starts showing a regular world map with red dots located in the places our haeman correspondents started their recruitment. Based on the reports we've been receiving, my senior officers have been updating the map diagramming the spread of haemanism. It progresses day by day. Watch."

She pressed "play" and the map came to life. The dates flashed rapidly at the top corner of the screen and as the days passed, the red dots expanded, smearing across the map like an infection. It was slow, but steady, and in the short amount of time his haemans had been deployed, the haemanism spread at an impressive rate.

"Europe is moving a bit faster," Dominika said. "We think it's because the first leg of your tour was there. Your presence sped up the growth in all locations. The U.S. is quickly catching up."

"You can see that the surrounding areas around all starting points are now drenched in red. While that doesn't mean 100% of the population is now haeman," Aliona explained, "it does indicate the majority are and those locations are ready for invasion."

"I suggest we wait a few more weeks before we make our first strike," Kirill said. "We need more progress in the U.S. before we attack Europe. They need to be distracted with their own infestation so they aren't worried about outbreaks in other countries."

"I agree." Mikhail was pleased with this comprehensive view of his takeover. "If it still needs time to blossom, we give it another month. Two months, tops. I can't wait much longer than that."

"I think that will be plenty of time," Aliona agreed.

"Fantastic. Leave me with Kirill."

The women exited the room and Mikhail slumped into his chair.

"I can't get Arinadya to relax. The people can't know she disobeys me. They follow her lead."

"The silve isn't helping?" Kirill asked.

"I decided not to give her any."

"Why? That's the fastest way to get her back to her old self."

"I want to get her pregnant. And if I succeed, she can't be on silve. The baby can't be deformed."

"I see," Kirill said in thought. "Perhaps I can return to my old chemistry lab and whip up an obedience pill for her."

Mikhail sat up straight. "Could you do that?"

"It'll require a few test runs, but it's possible."

"Tell me when you need test subjects and I'll have them delivered."

"I'll get to work on it today."

"Thank you. You're a loyal friend."

Mikhail left to find Roksana and Kirill went into the basement of the palace where the silve was created and stored. It was an enormous factory with many haeman workers slaving day and night over the production of the drug. Most of the process was now automated, but the workers acted as button pressers and watchful eyes, making sure nothing went askew. Kirill was still the only person on the planet who truly understood how it was made. He walked through the factory, past the large machinery and tired workers, and into the small laboratory where his chemistry set was located.

154

He planned to start with scopolamine, a mind-control drug known as "Devil's Breath" in Colombia. It came from the seeds of the blossoms on the Borrachero tree. The seeds were chemically altered into the powerful narcotic. Due to its felonious popularity, Kirill secured three kilograms of the drug years ago.

Scopolamine eliminated all free will while keeping its user awake, articulate, and functioning. It was often used by criminals to make someone lie, steal, or kill for them. Victims under the effect of scopolamine would do anything they were told and have no memory of it when the effects wear off. Too small a dose would have no effect, too much would be lethal. He knew one gram was deadly, so he started the trials with less. His goal was to find the dose that kept Arinadya under its spell for 24 hours at a time.

He got to work liquefying the drug. By evening, he had a suitable first trial.

A female haeman comparably sized to Arinadya was delivered to Kirill in the palace basement. She was handcuffed and fighting the guards who escorted her. Kirill gave her the injection and within minutes, she succumbed to the narcotic. Her struggle ceased and her face relaxed. She seemed completely normal. If Kirill hadn't seen her discord upon arrival he'd have never known she was under the drug's hypnotic spell.

As he began to dole out orders to see how she'd react, she began convulsing. She clenched her chest, gasped, and fell to the floor.

Dead.

Kirill sat against the side of his desk, puzzled. Was the dose too high? Then he realized he hadn't calculated the silve cocaine already running through her system—this would be harder than he anticipated. Arinadya had no silve in her. Finding an accurate test subject would be impossible—there were no test subjects in Russia without silve in their system, so the only alternative was to test it on

Arinadya. Starting with the lowest dose possible and working up until it had the desired effect.

He prepared a liquefied solution of scopolamine in the smallest dose and brought it up to Arinadya's bedroom. He placed the syringe on the dresser and waited for the nurse to fetch Mikhail.

"What is it?" Mikhail demanded as he stormed into the room, shirtless with his belt undone.

"Slight snag in the trials. Every test subject will have silve in their system. That combined with any dose of scopolamine is lethal. They'll all die of heart attacks, regardless of the dose. It also is a terrible indicator on how it will affect Arinadya as she doesn't have silve coursing through her anymore."

"So what's your solution?"

Kirill picked up the needle.

"We test it on her."

"She cannot die, you do realize that?"

"Of course. I will reverse the trials. Instead of starting at high doses and working down, like I did with the first test subject, I will start at the lowest dose and work up. The trials on Arinadya stop the moment we find the proper dosage."

Mikhail paused before answering.

"Fine. But if she dies on your watch, you die too."

The threat was real. Kirill didn't doubt Mikhail would have him executed if he failed. Arinadya was crucial to the takeover's success, especially amongst the Russian haemans, so they could not lose her now.

The trials started the moment Arinadya woke up from her latest sedative. To ensure the sedative was out of her system, they waited until she began to fight her restraints then injected her with the first test dose.

She continued screaming at a volume that made everyone in the room uncomfortable. Slowly, the screams dwindled into a sob. The scopolamine didn't work.

"I had a feeling it would be too low. We'll try again tomorrow," Kirill said.

"Why not tonight?" Mikhail asked.

"It needs to be out of her system before I administer another injection. It's the only way to guarantee clean results. If we don't wait, there's no way for me to know what the *real* dosage coursing through her system is. Plus, there's a better chance I'll accidentally kill her that way."

"Whatever," Mikhail said, frustrated.

Arinadya spent the night and following day sobbing and thrashing beneath her bindings.

Twenty-four hours passed before Kirill returned with a stronger dose. At the sight of Mikhail, Arinadya's fit intensified, so he stood in the corner to watch.

The needle slipped beneath her skin and into her vein. Kirill plunged the drug into her system, took a step back, and waited. Her frenzied nature calmed and she laid still for the first time without any sedatives.

"If I take off your restraints, will you behave?" Kirill asked.

Arinadya blinked blankly a few times before speaking.

"I hate you."

The words fired from her mouth like acid.

"It's not enough," Kirill said, surrendering a second time. "It calmed her down, but it wasn't strong enough to alter her mind."

"Damnit," Mikhail grumbled. "How will we know when it's enough? What if we think it's the right dose and she's being compliant and it wears off at the wrong moment? For example, during a public appearance. Or during a moment when no one is watching her. She could escape again."

"This will be a long series of trials and error. Once we find a dose that works, she will never go unsupervised. Not until you get her back on the silve and control her that way."

"She's only going back on the silve if I can't get her pregnant."

"Fine, then for now, you have to do this my way."

"Let's hope tomorrow brings more success."

By 3 a.m. the small effects of the scopolamine wore off and Arinadya woke up half the palace with her ear-piercing shrieks. By dawn, she had tired herself out and her screams were reduced to whimpers. Both Kirill and Mikhail were eager for the third round of the trial.

The next evening, Kirill and Mikhail entered her bedroom to find her drenched in sweat and tears. She wasn't eating, she wasn't sleeping, and it was showing. Her face was gaunt and her eyes looked bruised with exhaustion. Though she was always skinny, she was losing weight in an undesirable way. The few curves she maintained were shrinking, making her look like a corpse.

Kirill approached, syringe in hand, and administered the third dose. She didn't fight it—she couldn't. She was so defeated, all she could do was snivel pathetically in protest.

The drug coursed through her and she was quiet again. Her eyes opened and closed a few times to readjust before she looked up at Kirill. She said nothing and wore no expression to reveal her current emotion. Kirill took a moment to stare back and observe before speaking.

"How do you feel?"

"Fine." Her voice was level, her eyes alert.

"Grab me a plate of food," Kirill demanded to one of the nurses. She left and returned with a bowl of strawberries.

"Eat." He placed a strawberry in front of Arinadya's mouth and she bit into it. After chewing and swallowing, she took another bite. Kirill smiled.

"I am going to take off your restraints. Do not run."

He and the nurses worked together to unleash her. Once she was free, she sat up and touched the wounds on her wrists.

"We will tend to those and have them healed. Might make nice scars."

Arinadya noticed Mikhail standing in the shadows. She did not freak out or get angry at the sight of him, she just stared apathetically.

"Hello, my love," Mikhail said, stepping into the dim light. "I am very happy to see you again."

"It's been a while." Her mind was swarmed with fluff and fog—the drug had complete control of her.

"You will respect me, obey me, and submit to me. You will conform to your role as my wife. You will enjoy being the adored haeman princess again."

"Okay."

"Leave us," Mikhail demanded and everyone left the room. He locked it after they departed. Then he stripped down and crawled into bed next to her. She wore no expression but he could sense her heart rate quicken. "Relax."

At his command, she steadied her breathing and calmed down. He touched the side of her face and let his fingers drag along her skin as he steered them downward. His hand reached her panties and dipped beneath the fabric. She didn't flinch.

Mikhail slithered into her.

Chapter 24

Sevrick and crew spent three months in Norway before getting a meeting with Prime Minister Greta Calland, who turned them away after realizing they had no solid proof of Mikhail Romanov's wretched reign. She believed there was truth to their claims, but no one wanted to go against the Russians without sturdy footing. They contemplated going back to retrieve evidence many times, but it never seemed wise. They had to find a way to convince them without running back into harm's way.

After a few months of relentless badgering from their Russian visitors, the Norwegians finally agreed to an informal meeting where they'd call in the leaders of Sweden, Finland, and Denmark. Prime Minister Calland called the meeting in hopes that fresh opinions from outside leaders might help them all determine how to deal with the news.

Ruslan and Vladimir spent the week preparing the men on how best to present their case. The Norwegians believed them, but now they needed the Swedish, Danish, and Finnish on their side too. The more people of power that were made aware of Mikhail's devious deeds, the better.

Sevrick was tired and missing Rina terribly. Four months felt like four years and he hoped she was okay. He was certain she was—he left her in good hands—but he wanted to be back with her. He wanted to see if this time apart helped their situation. Maybe when he returned he'd find she missed him too.

The other leaders met them in Oslo for the meeting. The Russian men made their way through Prime Minister Calland's home and into the official boardroom where she held private meetings. The four leaders and their deputies were already sitting around the table. A TV was perched in the corner and played the news in

Russia. No one spoke, they just took their seats and watched. Norway didn't broadcast foreign news at their hotel, so this was their first look back into Russia since they crossed the border.

The Russian news reporters, both haemans, kept their stories light. They talked about traffic, pollution, and the weather. They even told a heartwarming story about a man who had a heart attack and his dog got him medical attention in time by alerting neighbors. Watching the haemans hide the *real* news in Russia infuriated the men.

"It all looks normal to me," Prime Minister Calland said in Russian. Everyone there now spoke the same language. Their neighboring leaders learned it years ago. They had to, being so close to Russia's border.

"They're masking the truth," Artem said. "Those reporters are haemans."

Everyone was filled in on the situation previous to the meeting.

"They do look a bit pale," Prime Minister Emelie Braff of Sweden commented. "Nothing I'd deem suspicious though."

"Do you see the scars on the female's neck?" Benedikt pointed out. "Or the similar scars on the man's wrists?"

They all looked closer.

"I see them," President Absalon Hummel of Denmark said, "but I cannot claim to know their origin."

"To believe your story is asking for a lot of trust from us. The safeties of our countries are on the line," Prime Minister Fredriik Kurtti of Finland added. "We could ruin relations with an accusation like yours. You are common citizens with no political or military stronghold. I'm amazed you've gotten this far."

"We've gotten this far because what we say is true and deep down you all believe it. You know something rotten is taking place across the border and you're listening to us because we are the first to make it across to shed light on the situation." Ruslan was exasperated. He needed them to take action.

"We can't wait much longer to act upon this," Vladimir went on. "Too much time has passed. I will not be shocked if we begin hearing news of haemans popping up all over the globe soon. It's only a matter of time."

"If that happens, we will certainly feel more inclined to call Prince Mikhail and President Dobrynin out on the issue," Norwegian Prime Minister Calland said.

"If you wait that long, you'll be too late," Sevrick jumped in. "If we see one addict make it to the news we'll know there are thousands more living in secret. This addiction runs rampant and once it takes hold it doesn't let go."

"It spreads like a virus," Artem went on. "And we think Mikhail intentionally planted the disease in countries all over."

"To what end?" Finnish Prime Minister Kurtti asked.

"His domination over the world," Leonid answered. "The haemans are his army. He'll use them to take down nations, one by one."

"And you used to be a haeman?" Swedish Prime Minister Braff asked.

"Yes, I was Mikhail's best friend. Regrettably, I helped invent haemanism. I have no way to prove it, but I promise it's true."

"Again, believing this requires an enormous amount of faith," Danish Prime Minister Hummel said.

The TV flickered to a new story and Prince Mikhail's smiling face filled the screen. The meeting paused to watch the segment. Mikhail stood on the outdoor balcony of his palace and looked out upon an enormous crowd. The camera briefly panned the back of the crowd once and never returned its attention to them. Too many reckless haemans were there that could not be shown on air. The focus stayed on Mikhail.

He waved and smiled. The reporters' voices spoke of a big reveal as the footage remained on the live event. After a minute of anticipation, Mikhail moved the curtain and grabbed a tiny wrist from the shadows of the adjacent room. He pulled the body forward to reveal Arinadya in a skintight dress that showcased her small baby bump.

The leaders of their neighboring countries kept their eyes glued to the screen, but all the Russian men immediately shifted their gazes toward Sevrick, whose heart barely beat. He watched the screen in horror. The world around him disappeared, he could not feel the many concerned eyes on him. All he saw was Rina back with Mikhail. She was pregnant. Even worse, she was smiling.

"Is this real?" Sevrick shouted, unaware of his volume. "Is this old footage?" he asked desperately.

"I don't think so." Artem stood up, ready to grab him before he ran. "She has a baby bump."

"Is *that* real?" Sevrick's voice cracked with hysteria. "Why is she smiling?"

The leaders attention was now back on their visitors.

"Why is your friend acting this way?" Prime Minister Calland asked Ruslan. "It's just the princess. It's old news that she's having his baby."

"Rina, Arinadya, was Sevrick's fiancée before the haemanism took over. He spent years trying to rescue her from the prince and only recently succeeded. She was living with us in our underground fortress when we left to come here." Ruslan shifted his gaze back to the screen and observed the happy royal couple in bewilderment. "I don't understand how this happened."

163

"Well, this is a whole new twist I don't think I can possibly buy into," Prime Minister Hummel proclaimed. "It's all starting to sound like a television drama."

No one listened to him; they were too concerned with Sevrick's mental stability. He was shaking and pacing, blind to the room and the people in it. His head spun around this new development. It wasn't possible. Rina was safe at the white elm. He looked back up at the screen. Her hair was cut and her belly was swollen; all new looks. He cringed.

"Artem and Zakhar," Ruslan spoke softly, "can you escort Sevrick outside? Help him decompress while we wrap up this meeting."

The men grabbed Sevrick by the elbows and guided him out the door. Sevrick was unaware of the shift in his direction, he was too wrapped up inside his own head. Initially, his heart seemed to stop. The sight of her with *him* was enough to strike him dead. As the image of them together sunk in, staining the backs of his eyelids, his heart kicked up a notch, working overtime to make up for the momentary pause. It beat so hard it hurt.

When they exited the room, he collapsed into a chair and clenched his chest. His friends watched on with sympathy.

"Let it out," Artem suggested supportively. "It's just us now. Let it out so we can move on."

Sevrick looked up at his friends with desperation in his eyes. "There's nothing to let out. I am enraged, I am confused, I am heartbroken. How did this happen? She was safe with us."

"I don't know," Zakhar said. "We left her in good hands. She must have run off."

"She wouldn't."

"There really isn't any other explanation."

"I talked to her. She was struggling, but happy to be out of the haeman world. She'd never go back to it."

His friends shook their heads, unable to offer anything to ease Sevrick's distress.

"Making up scenarios in your mind isn't going to help you or her. Or us," Artem finally said. "We will deal with it when we get back into Russia."

"She needs our help *now*. Maybe she was kidnapped. Maybe she is a prisoner."

"She looked pretty happy to me," Zakhar said cautiously.

Sevrick buried his head into his hands and shut his eyes. All he could see now was Rina holding Mikhail's hand while wearing the beautiful smile he spent weeks trying to coax out of her during her recovery at the white elm.

And the tears finally fell.

Chapter 25

"Breaking News. Reports have come in regarding the school shooters at San Francisco High School. As we all know, they massacred 98 of their classmates along with 5 teachers. It is the largest school shooting in American history. After their incredible getaway and a seven-day manhunt, police located them at Muir Woods National Monument. The redwood forest is currently under lock down. We have helicopters there now, overlooking the scene."

"Turn it up," a voice pleaded from the back of the crowd. Elena raised the volume and the inhabitants of the white elm did their best to squeeze into the large living space. Many sat along the walls of the attached corridors listening because the room was too packed and couldn't hold everyone.

The content on the TV screen was split in two: the news anchors in NY on one side and the helicopter cam on the other. They were seeing everything live.

"The culprits are two male seniors and a female junior. Reports from survivors say the students were popular. They were trendsetters and athletes. The sight of them opening fire on their classmates was a shock to all," Mindy Chen of WMBN's *News Day New York* reported from the safety of her East Coast desk. *"Some claim they were eliminating the 'weak links' but refused to explain what that meant when questioned further. It's too soon to make assumptions and police are doing their best to capture the assailants alive."*

Shots fired. Everyone in the room tensed.

"Man down," Parker Brown shouted as he watched the small screen showing the live helicopter footage. Viewers saw the same footage on the left side of the split screen. A cop fell to the ground as one of the teenagers propelled out from their hiding spot and opened fire on the line of police guarding the area. Like an action

166

movie, the young boy leaped out of his hiding spot, ran unguarded toward his enemy, and screamed as he fired. He was wielding a semi-automatic rifle. The cops were lucky this daring maneuver only got one of them.

"These kids move like professional stunt men," Mindy commented. *"It's unnatural how evasive they are."*

"They almost seem to blur as they run, no?" Parker replied in question.

"I noticed that too. Clearly, it's a result of the camera quality, but there's no denying their athleticism. It's a shame they didn't use their talents toward something more productive."

Gunfire sounded again and the female student fell to the ground. Her left shoulder bled through her light overcoat as she stumbled. She carried on, hobbling back toward one of the boy's hiding spots.

"Stop or we'll fire again," one of the policemen shouted. The girl ignored them and hurried to her friend's side. As she did, she wiped up some of her blood with her right hand and licked it.

Both news reporters' mouths dropped.

"Did she just do what I think she did?" Parker asked.

Mindy hesitated before confirming. *"She just licked the blood off her hand."*

The cops moved in on the students, keeping their riot shields in place as they inched forward. The girl made it to her friend but blew the secrecy of the spot as she did so. They had two of the students in range for seizure. The cops switched to their tranquilizer guns and charged. The students fired, clipping a few officers in non-lethal locations, essentially giving the cops the time to succeed in their capture. The third student emerged from his hiding spot during the ambush but could not stop it. He fired at the backs of the policemen, injuring two, then sprinted away from the scene. His friends were captured and there was nothing he could do to help them now. He

167

ran toward the cop cars at inhuman speed, visibly blurring as he did so. The reporters could claim it was a trick of the light but all the survivors in the white elm knew better. The boy aimed to run between two of the cars but a cop in hiding jumped out at the last second and shot the kid in the leg. He howled in pain and fell to the ground. In front of the cop car he writhed, crawling in an attempt to get away. The officer apprehended and handcuffed the young criminal, then threw his body against the hood of the car. The boy shouted obscenities but the helicopter camera could not pick up the audio.

"*What do you think he is saying?*" Parker wondered.

"*Not sure, but we'll find out in due time. Besides armor, cops are equipped with body cameras. Every moment will be captured and all relevant and appropriate footage will be released for public viewing.*"

"*If you're just tuning in, the school killers have been caught. The manhunt is over and the families of the victims can find closure in knowing that the murderers of their loved ones will face justice.*"

"*We are going to take a quick break, but we'll be back with updates.*"

Elena lowered the volume and the murmuring amongst the room increased. Everyone knew what those American kids were—the early days of the haeman takeover were exactly the same: increased violence, unexplainable terror amongst average people, a slow acceptance that all of it was normal. In time, those types of news stories stopped being reported in Russia because they were so common. Watching haemanism start over again in another country was terrifying.

"When do you think they'll discover it's all due to a Russian-born drug brought over by Mikhail?" Elena asked Alexsei.

"Soon, I imagine, though I fear it's too late. We'll get more details later, but it sounds like these three are only a few of many. They were weeding out the weak links. Reminds me of when Ruslan and

I escaped to the woods because similar assassinations were happening here. In a city, the societal cause and effect unfolds much slower. In a high school overtaken by haemanism, the effects unravel faster. Schools are mini cities, mini societies, and things that happen in the adult world happen much faster and with more intensity in such a small and juvenile social structure. This event lets us know that haemanism is festering amongst the adults too, they just haven't self-imploded yet."

"Once the truth is revealed I hope it's enough to get foreign leaders to take action against Mikhail."

"Let's just hope the kids blab. If they've been trained by haeman moles, I'm sure they've been told to stay quiet."

"They carried out a school shooting. Seems to me any restrictions given by their suppliers are out the window and the drug rules them now."

"Time will tell."

The people in the room dispersed to carry on with their day. Though they were gone now, the atmosphere remained on edge. Everyone knew this was the start of something big and they couldn't hide their fear. There was no telling how it would unfold, or who would emerge on the other side as the victor.

A few hours passed before the news program came back on. Elena sat in the same spot next to Alexsei and others trickled in slowly to watch. The Americans were running recurring segments covering the tragedy. Mindy Chen and Parker Brown were still on the job, reporting updates and keeping their audience informed.

"This just in: video from the arrest has been released to the news stations. Take a look."

The video left out the capture of the first two teenagers and began with the third. From the cop's point of view the boy was seen charging full force at him. He was even blurrier in this version of the footage. As the cop stood to take aim, the boy's face shifted with rage. Instead of fear of being caught, like most humans would naturally feel, he only doubled in fury. The sight of the cop and gun did not register as a threat; it did not stop his momentum, it fueled him. The teenager rushed at his attacker with ferocity when the gun fired and hit him in the leg. A shaky video of the boy falling was captured as the cop ran to handcuff him while he was down and unable to get away.

"*Get off me, you weak pig,*" the boy spat. "*I'll destroy you the moment I get my strength back.*"

"*That's enough out of you,*" the cop said, ignoring the threat and forcing the boy to stand up. He slammed the boy against the hood of the car and his head hit the metal with a loud thud. The force sounded like it would knock most people out, but the boy kept shouting nonsense and fighting the cop's hold.

"*This isn't over. We aren't alone. We'll come to the light in droves.*"

"*Shut your mouth you little punk. You're done. You'll be in jail till the day you die.*"

The boy laughed.

The video shifted to the car camera, which sat perched upon the front grill. The other cops now headed toward the cars with the two unconscious killers in tow.

"*We've got a live one,*" the policeman warned his fellow officers as they approached. Two cops hurried forward to help him with the resistant teenager. The blood gushed from his leg as they dragged him backward toward an alternate car.

"*Blessed be our veins by which we rid this world of misuse,*" the boy shouted before being shoved into the backseat. The door slammed and he began pounding on the window with his fist. His strength caused the glass to splinter, then break. It sliced the side of his hand and he licked the blood off his wound.

"Blessed be our veins by which we rid this world of misuse!"

Chapter 26

"A what?" Mikhail shouted.

"A school shooting," Kirill answered. "In San Francisco. The teenagers were haeman. They revealed everything when authorities interrogated them."

"How much?"

"That they shot up the school to rid it of the condemned, which they explained meant non-haemans. They told them all about silve, the blood," Kirill paused, "and you."

"Me?"

"That you are their idol. That they are part of your remote empire."

"I warned Timofey and Yana to be careful with the adolescents. How could they let this happen?"

"According to reports, they had one of the fastest growing areas. That high school was almost 75% haeman. All the teenagers were in on it and a few took it too far. Maybe they thought it was safe because they were in the majority, not realizing the world extended beyond their school."

"Idiots. Am I going to have to address the situation?"

"Your call. The foreign press is slamming our phone lines, asking for a comment. International leaders have sent official requests for an explanation. Your name was linked to the drug and lifestyle, they want to know if you are involved."

"How far along are we in our progress?"

Kirill pulled up the map. "We can begin our attack within the month."

"Then, on my behalf, tell whoever is asking that I know nothing about it. I will not go on camera to say this; I cannot let my foreign followers think I am forsaking them."

"I think that's wise."

"Timofey and Yana are cut off. No salary for a month. They need to be punished for this. Every new haeman was supposed to stay quiet. I understand they've done a great job in San Francisco, so the punishment will be slight, but this happened on their watch. They need to know I'm not happy with them. They need to fear my wrath."

"Absolutely. I'll give them a call, let them know. I'm sure they'll be expecting worse and will appreciate your mercy."

Mikhail nodded. "Has Arinadya been given her dose of scopolamine yet?"

"I upped the dosage yesterday to see if we could make it last longer."

"Fine, just don't mess it up."

"She'll be good until tomorrow. I'll make sure to get to her room extra early to prepare for the drug's decline in her system."

"Is it going to screw up my child?"

"There are no tests on it, but the dose is so low I imagine the baby will be fine. Kids are resilient."

"You better be right." Mikhail stood and brushed his fingers through his wild, brown curls. "I'm going to go see her now. Take care of the San Francisco dilemma."

Mikhail departed and headed towards Arinadya's room. When he got there, she was sitting in a rocking chair staring at the wall.

"Hello, beautiful." She shifted her gaze and smiled at her oppressive husband. "What are you thinking about?" he asked.

Her eyes squinted as she tried to recall her thoughts. "Nothing. I think I was admiring the color of the wall."

"And what's your consensus on it?"

Arinadya looked at the golden paint again. She studied it before answering.

"I like it."

"Wonderful. How's the baby doing?"

Arinadya was aloof; everything he said hit her like it was the first time she was hearing it. She knew what he was referring to, but the questions took time to process. Eventually she placed a hand over her belly.

"It is happy."

"I'm glad to hear that. It's a lucky child. Not only will he be born into wealth and fame, but with us as his parents, he is guaranteed to be stunning."

"Is it a boy?" she asked.

"We will find out next week, but I think so. I hope so."

Arinadya nodded without expression. Nothing mattered much to her. If Mikhail was in good spirits, so was she.

"I'll leave you alone," Mikhail said. He left without showing any affection or tenderness toward her, and she returned to her blank state of awareness.

Time passed, but she did not move from her chair. No one came, no one asked anything of her, so she sat alone, unmoving, and oblivious to the world around her for hours. It wasn't until a nurse entered the room to get her ready for bed that she snapped back into reality.

"Did you have a nice day?" the nurse asked.

"Oh, yes, I think it was a good one," Arinadya answered as the nurse undressed her and helped her into her nightgown.

"Good to hear. Take these vitamins, they're for the baby." In this case, the nurse was not lying. She gave Arinadya a handful of neonatal vitamins. Without question, she swallowed each. "Now get to bed. Tomorrow is only a few hours away."

The nurse flipped the light switch, shut the door, and left. At the nurse's command, Arinadya fell asleep. It was easier to pass out when her mind was inclined to obey every order she was given.

Arinadya's eyes shot open at 3 a.m. Unsure where she was, how she got there, or what day it was, she was afraid to move.. She held her breath and scanned the room for a sign.

The Winter Palace.

Yes, she remembered being kidnapped in the woods and returned to Mikhail's prison. Her eyes darted around the room. When she felt sure that no one was there with her, she turned her head to look at the calendar.

The month was April.

But it was December when they captured her. She remembered being sedated, but was it possible they kept her knocked out for four months? Her heart quickened as she wondered if they put her back on silve. She sat up to see if she felt its effects, but she didn't. All she felt was the uncomfortable bump of her belly. Horrified, she lifted her dress to reveal a small pregnant belly. She grasped her stomach, not believing it was real. Hands on skin, she felt a kick. *No.* She waited and it kicked again. *A baby?* Quiet tears streamed down her face at this doomed revelation. She could not have Mikhail's baby; she'd rather die than live out that fate.

What happened in the past four months? Did he rape her while she was under sedation? The room held no sign of struggle. It was tidy, her bed no longer had restraints, and no one was there to babysit her. There was nothing to clue her into the truth and she could not wait to ask someone, they'd only knock her back out once they realized she was awake.

There's a computer in the neighboring bedroom, she recalled from her days living here in the past. Before leaving she noticed a syringe on the bedside table. The word *Scopolamine* was written onto the side label. It was full and ready to be dispensed. She had to hurry. She put on the slippers sitting next to her bed and snuck out of her room. The hallway was empty, so she crept to the computer without any trouble.

The Internet was connected and the moment she logged on she was greeted by her smiling face. The webpage was for Russian news and the picture showed her with her new, short haircut standing next to Mikhail. She wore a fancy dress and was waving to a crowd of adoring haemans. The article was posted in March. She had no memory of this, but in the picture, she appeared to be participating happily. Fear set in as she realized her memories were stolen from her, or perhaps they were giving her something that caused her to blackout. The baby in her stomach kicked again.

"Stop," she hissed down at her belly. It replied by kicking her again. She already hated the creature growing inside her. Not only was Mikhail controlling her outside world, but now he lived inside her too.

Unaware of what she was doing, she found herself scratching at her belly, trying to claw it open and remove the cancer. Tears fell onto her skin and rolled down the small hill the bump created.

"I'm sorry," she whispered. "It's not your fault."

She wiped her cheeks dry and refocused. Back on track, she searched for scopolamine in the browser and was greeted by an onslaught of terrifying articles:

Drug Turns Victims into Zombies
Most Dangerous Drug in the World Blocks Free Will
12 Evil Mind Control Drugs
Scopolamine: The Devil's Breath

She read one, a documentary piece done in Colombia where they called the drug Devil's Breath. It explained how criminals used the narcotic to force others to commit crimes for them. They blew the powder into the face of an unsuspecting bystander and the victim was rendered into a mindless puppet. All free-will was eliminated. And though the victim was blacked out, they remained awake and articulate. They collected no memory of their actions while under the influence of scopolamine.

Rina exited out of the article and did not have the stomach to open another. She looked at the clock to find an hour had passed. Afraid of being caught, she snuck back into her bedroom and crawled into bed. Though she wished to run, there were too many guards scattered throughout the palace. She'd never make it out unseen. The dose of scopolamine sat on her nightstand, ready to be injected into her blood stream. She crawled back out of bed and took the needle into her connected bathroom. Without thinking of the consequences, she smashed the glass barrel against the porcelain sink and the liquid drug dripped down the drain. Panicked that she made a mistake, she wrapped the broken glass in tissue and threw it in the trash. She got back into bed and waited for the inevitable consequences.

Kirill entered the room at 6 a.m. She stayed quiet and waited for him to realize what she'd done. He sat in a chair facing her bed and watched her, waiting for her to show him the drug had worn off. A half hour passed before he noticed the syringe was missing from her bedside table. He stood and stormed toward the barren countertop. He looked in the crevices between the bed and the nightstand to see if it fell, but found nothing. He stood above her, close and unmoving. She could feel him staring down at her.

His breathing was heavy as he read her demeanor: tense facial expression, sweat along her hairline, rigid muscles.

"You can stop pretending to be asleep."

Rina took a deep breath and opened her eyes. Staring up at Kirill's angry face, she wished she could fall unconscious again.

"What have you done?" he went on.

"I shattered the syringe," she said quietly, waiting for the brunt of his punishment to cross her face. But he did not strike her.

"Why didn't you run?"

This was her chance to lie. It was her opportunity to craft some story that would prevent him from ever giving her that terrifying drug again.

"The baby." She forced a smile, faking a look of motherly love. "I need to take care of my child. Leaving the palace would kill us both."

Kirill was taken aback by this confession. He scrutinized her face, looking for any indication of deception, but she kept her façade strong.

"You were a disobedient terror before we started giving you scopolamine. I have trouble believing after four months blacked out from the drug, you gained consciousness and no longer desire to run away."

"The power of motherhood is strong. My bond with this child is more important than anything else. I have to keep my child safe. I must protect my baby."

"Interesting," Kirill mused. "If this is true you've made my life a whole lot easier. You'll be under strict watch; your haeman babysitters will be informed to act however they please if you try anything sneaky. They won't kill you, but they will be ruthless. So if you're lying to me now, you're only hurting yourself."

"I'm not lying."

"We'll see."

He exited the room and summoned the nurses, who were tasked to watch her carefully. Roksana and Isidor joined later in the day and were also instructed to babysit Arinadya.

Time was on her side. If she stopped fighting, they'd stop giving her the drug. No silve while she was pregnant, so for now she was safe from that too. She wasn't sure what her next move would be but remaining conscious was key. Without her own thoughts at the forefront, she was her own worst enemy.

It was time to save herself from this nightmare.

Chapter 27

Reports about the new and mysterious Russian drug were surfacing nation by nation. Each various location was witnessing the same type of effects: increased violence, addicts gathering in hoards, threats to non-users. Those who used the foreign drug were exponentially stronger and faster. Their personalities shifted, making them heartless and morally numb. Sevrick and his friends knew the culprit was Mikhail. During his international tour he spread silve across the globe, and it wasn't long before Norwegian Prime Minister Greta Calland finally agreed to take their story with her to the next U.N. meeting.

The addiction spread like a virus through multiple countries, but the masses still did not understand what it was. Surprisingly, despite their inability to hide their transformation, the new haemans were able to keep the secret behind haemanism under wraps. All anyone knew was the phenomenon was caused by a new narcotic from Russia and that it made its victims volatile and unpredictable.

Greta Calland had a list of facts written out for her by the Clandes and Primos:

- The addiction is called *haemanism*. The users refer to themselves as *haemans*.
- The drug is called *silve*. It is a mixture of cocaine and an unknown chemical created by Mikhail's right-hand man, Kirill Mikvonski.
- Silve is silver and is usually taken in powder form. It can be liquefied or smoked, but those methods are less common and it was doubtful any Russian haeman was doing the work to provide the drug in those forms.
- The Russian government has silve filtering through the public water supply, in all toothpaste sold, and in the

"vitamins" given to Russian citizens. Any ingestible products imported from Russia should be checked for silve.

- The drug alone does not cause haemanism. It only works when the user takes the silve, then drinks their own blood, recirculating their chemically enhanced blood back into their system. This process boosts their senses and abilities.

- Side effects are increased speed, strength, and pain tolerance. Previous beliefs and morals are muted, causing the addict to become violent and apathetic, as they no longer care about consequences or the effect they are having on the people around them.

- Worst of all is the undying loyalty toward Prince Mikhail. The cravings for the drug are intense; once addicted, they rule the user's world. Mikhail is the originator, the idol, the provider; therefore, haemans worship him.

- If Mikhail has spread this disease, it's likely he plans to seize control of lands beyond Russia. With an army scattered through other nations, it would be wise to prepare for battle. One haeman soldier is equivalent to five of the strongest human soldiers.

She held their detailed points of discussion in hand as she left for New York City to meet with the U.N.

President Dobrynin was not included on this particular invite. They reached out numerous times to the Russian government to try and squash this issue at the source, but all they ever received were well-rehearsed responses from the Russian public relations team.

After seeing Rina back on TV with Mikhail, all Sevrick wanted to do was go home and find her. He had to know what happened and why, but his friends stopped him. Once the word of the spread was out, the stories came through faster and they realized there was no way they could return to Russia just yet. They needed to keep an eye on the situation and attempting a three-week trip back through the forest would toss them straight into the dark. By staying put, they also had direct access to the leaders of Norway, Denmark, Sweden, and Finland. Losing those connections now was foolish. They were on the front lines and would be receiving top secret information; things that would never be reported on the news. They needed to stay until things really unraveled. Then, if they wanted, they could go back to the white elm and rescue their fellow survivors. Many of the Primos wanted to stay and fight against the haemans when they breached the borders of Finland and Norway. The Clandes felt more inclined to retrieve their friends from the white elm before engaging in battle.

When they went back for the rest of the Clandes, Sevrick planned to go back for Rina. Surely his friends would have some information to tell him regarding her departure from the white elm and once he knew the facts, he'd move forward accordingly. His gut told him she needed his help, and if that proved true, he'd stop at nothing to save her.

Chapter 28

"Nazar Yedemsky, our haeman spy in Washington, D.C., has informed us that President Ward was summoned to New York for a meeting at the U.N.," Air Force Supreme Officer Dominika Mikvonskaia told Mikhail. "Abram Gusev and Sabine Drugova of New York confirmed it."

"Were we told about this meeting?" Mikhail asked, his temper rising.

"No," President Dobrynin answered. "I never got a call."

"Find out why."

"I know why. Norwegian Prime Minister Greta Calland asked for the meeting to be private. A secret from us. It's about the spread of silve. They are going to discuss how to handle it," he paused, "and us."

"How do you know this?"

"Our spies in Finland made their way into the government over there. Finnish Prime Minister Fredriik Kurtti is against us with Greta."

"Along with Swedish Prime Minister Emelie Braff and Danish President Absalon Hummel," Army Supreme Officer Aliona Rusanova added. "Appears our northwest borders were compromised."

"Are we ready to attack?" Mikhail asked.

"Almost. I'd advise waiting one more week," Dominika answered.

"We don't have another week. Send my haeman army, by foot and tank, into our southwest neighbors. I want control of Kazakhstan, Ukraine, Belarus, Latvia, and Estonia by the end of the week."

"Understood," Aliona said as she wrote in her notebook. "Those will be easy defeats; the majority of their populations have already converted to haemanism." She pointed at the map. Most of Europe was colored in red, indicating the expansive spread of haemanism. "I don't expect much resistance. It's more likely we'll arrive and they'll be ready for your orders."

"Good. If that happens, have them join your ranks as you continue west. According to your map, Poland and France aren't completely devoted to me. We will need the extra soldiers when infiltrating those nations." Mikhail examined the interactive map. "Germany looks ready, as does Spain and Ireland. Dominika, have your airmen fly west to Spain and Ireland. We can have two haeman forces pushing toward the center of Europe simultaneously." Mikhail stood up and uncapped a black marker. He circled Austria. "The city of Graz is our center, our meeting point."

"What about the Americans?" Kirill asked. "They will catch word and try to stop us."

"If these countries are as contaminated by my influence as this map implies, I don't foresee much of a fight. To be safe we will cut the power in each city we seize. I'll have divers from our navy attack the submarine cables connecting the countries in Europe with each other and the rest of the world. Though I suspect the uproar against us will be quiet, I know it won't go unnoticed, but it also won't be desperate cries for foreign assistance. By the time we meet up in Graz, we will outnumber the U.S. army by thousands. Not only in our literal size, but also in strength. One haeman for every five of theirs. The battle will already be won."

"You may be right, but we cannot move forward without preparing for retaliation from others," Aliona warned.

"The moment we start collecting others from neighboring nations as we move west, I'll send the order for the American haemans to start wreaking havoc. They'll be too busy sorting out their own troubles to send valuable militiamen overseas to deal with us."

"What about all the countries in Africa and eastern Asia?" Kirill asked. "They are connected to us by land, so we can't rule them out."

"Yes we can. They are weak, with minimal militia, and most do not have strong bonds with the countries we are attacking first."

"But they are under the U.N.'s protection. Many of those nations are obligated to protect those they are in alliance with."

"Have you listened to a word I've said? I'm cutting all Internet and telephone cables. By the time they catch word of what we've done, there won't be any more alliances. I will be in control and they will not come after me. Once I spread into their countries, perhaps they'll fight back, but not until then. Why would they enter into a guaranteed slaughter?" The room answered him with silence. "We will keep an eye on our other neighbors, but I suspect they won't be a factor. Call in your lead army lieutenants," Mikhail ordered. Kirill and Aliona obliged, hailing their subordinates into the meeting via their two-way radios.

Filipp, Edik, Roman, and a healed-but-scarred Sergei entered.

"It's time to strike. You'll each be leading troops across our European borders." The young haemans smiled with malevolent anticipation. "As you move west, you'll collect foreign haemans and add them to your ranks. They will assist in your fight. Kill anyone who challenges you, along with anyone who refuses to join the haeman lifestyle. I don't have time to set up prison camps, so give them the choice and if they refuse, execute. This will be a sweep of the continent that cleanses the land of those who resist me."

"Got it," Filipp answered for all four lieutenants.

"Get to work. I want the march to begin by tomorrow's sunrise." The men understood and exited the meeting room to prepare. "Dominika, you'll assign specific airmen to the task of beginning in Ireland and Spain. Have them ready to depart before dawn."

"Yes, sir," she responded and left the room to inform her lieutenants of their mission.

The start to Mikhail's takeover was now in the hands of his military leaders. There was nothing left for him to do but give orders from afar and receive updates on his success.

He walked to Arinadya's bedroom where she was being watched by Roksana and Isidor. Kirill told him about her change of heart after accidentally waking up from a dose of scopolamine and realizing she was pregnant. He was happy she no longer wished to fight him and valued the importance of their unborn child, but he wasn't sure if he believed the genuineness of her claims to behave. With all that was unfolding he hadn't found the time to visit her after they stopped giving her the mind-control drug. This was the first time he'd see her and he planned to interrogate her thoroughly to determine the truth behind her intentions.

"Hello, my love," he cooed as he walked in. Roksana scoffed at his endearing greeting for the woman who took her place as his wife.

Rina forced a smile. "It's been a long time."

"Not really, just on your end. I've seen plenty of you recently." He pointed at her belly with a mischievous grin.

"Well, I'm happy to have my mind back."

"Ladies, please leave us." Isidor left without complaint and Roksana followed wearing a potent scowl. The trail she left was bitter. Rina was grateful to have a break from her quiet and brooding presence.

"So, what have I missed?" She cradled her belly like she held great concern over its living contents. Every time it kicked she had to hide her urge to cringe.

"The only thing you missed that is of any concern to you is the creation of our child. He is of great importance to me and I am pleased to find we agree on the matter."

"It's a boy?"

"Yes." His smile was wicked. "A new prince will be delivered to Russia. Someone to carry out my reign once I am gone."

"That's wonderful." She couldn't mask her dread, but Mikhail didn't notice. He was too wrapped up in thoughts of his lineage continuing beyond him.

"His name will be Maxim and he will be great."

"That's a lovely name."

"So tell me, you are truly changed by the idea of motherhood?"

"Yes. I have found new purpose in life." She looked down at her belly faking a look of true love. "This gives me a reason to live. He, Maxim, is my heart. I will love him wholly."

"Good. That makes my life a lot easier. Fighting you while preparing to fight the world was a stress I did not need. I am glad we are on the same team again."

"Fight the *world*?"

"Ah, yes. I forgot you have no memory of your recent time by my side. I've planted the seed of haemanism across the globe. Been patiently waiting as it spread. Without going into details, let's just say you'll be grateful you conceded to stand by my side once you see the fate of the world revealed in the next few months."

She nodded without asking for more details. He believed her lie; that's all that mattered. Now, she needed to find a way out of his clutches and out of Russia. The further along her pregnancy progressed, the harder it would be to escape. If she didn't act soon

187

she'd need to wait until after the baby was born, which she did not wish to do.

Mikhail's expression shifted as his mind wandered to another topic. "When you were under the drug, I asked you some questions I needed answers to. You answered many but not the ones most important to me."

"I don't recall any of that."

"Of course you don't. The drug is designed to make its user completely compliant, unable to lie, and though I believe it did I need to ask again. Now that I have your cooperation, I need you to dive into your memory for any pieces of information you can give me."

"What is the question?"

"How did they heal you? Everyone here dies from the withdrawals. Yet you, and Leonid, and probably countless others, were saved in the woods. I need to know how."

"They never told me how. The process was painful and very difficult to get through. I wasn't there long enough to learn their methods."

Mikhail huffed. "You said the same thing under the drug."

"It's the truth."

He sat and stewed inside his thoughts, trying to think of a way to remedy this problem. "Can you lead me to their hiding location?"

"I don't know where it is. When they captured me, I was by the lagoon. I was knocked out and carried to their hideout. I have no memory of how I got there."

"But if you saw it, you'd remember."

She took a deep breath. "I suppose."

"Once the baby is delivered, we will get you back on silve and have you journey with my best scouts to find the location."

"Why do you need to know how to heal a person from haemanism?"

"If I had the cure, Milena would still be alive." His voice wavered as he recalled his sister. "Also, I am confident you being clean for a short stretch of time is the only reason you were able to get pregnant. We cannot let this be the first and last generation of haemans. I need the cure so I can set up a clinic that helps haeman women get pregnant."

"Do you really think the regular lot of haemans should be allowed to raise children? Just because they give birth doesn't mean they are capable of taking care of their baby. I'd bet most children would die before they reached adolescence. Haemans are too violent."

"We'd deal with that as it came. Perhaps I'll set up a strict screening process, or only give the most esteemed members of the council a chance at procreating. The entire process would be under my strict control. I could even have the children raised in a secluded and structured setting until they hit puberty. I'll find a way to make it work."

"I have no doubt you will."

"Problem is, I can't rehabilitate a haeman without killing them. I need you to help me find those survivors so I can start the next phase of our evolution."

"I understand. I cannot promise anything, but I'll do my best when the time comes."

"Let's hope your best is good enough." His eyes narrowed in on her as he spoke. The only thing keeping him from hitting her into compliance was the little prince living inside her belly. The child was her shield; it was her protection. The feelings she had toward the infant were mixed and confusing: she hated it, but needed it. Motherhood was tearing her apart.

He turned the conversation toward a more dangerous confession she made during her drug-induced blackout.

"A few weeks ago, when I sat you down for the interrogation, I asked who rehabilitated you. Along with Leonid, you mentioned a man named Sevrick." Rina's eyes grew wide; she couldn't deny his existence now. He continued, "Do you recall the night we fought over the imaginary ghost haunting your dreams? If my memory serves, that supposed phantom was also named Sevrick. Not a common name, you know."

"What's your point?" Her attitude returned. She didn't like being toyed with, especially when he dangled the man she loved in front of her.

"Do you remember what you told me about him when I dug deeper?"

"You know I don't."

"Supposedly he is your one true love. The only man you ever cared for, yet you chose haemanism over him and subsequently destroyed him in the process. You sobbed as you revealed all the nitty gritty details of your betrayal. It was comical, but also infuriating. And when I learned that the man made me look like a fool on a few occasions, I decided he was my next conquest."

"He's a powerless man. He has no strength, no speed, no influence. Why can't you just leave him alone?"

"Because you love him." His expression twisted. "You've been a bad girl and the best way to punish you is through him."

"You realize there was an alternate storyline where I died. You almost lost me and my influence over your people forever. If Sevrick hadn't saved me, I'd be dead and your people would have accused you of pushing me to my death."

"Yeah, yeah, you told me all about it. You tried to jump. How could that be misconstrued as my fault?"

"Because, mentally, you tossed me over the edge. Everyone knows you're an egomaniac. I'd be seen as the victim and you the murderer. You ought to be thanking Sevrick for altering the course of your fate. I bet your haeman army would have dwindled knowing their beloved princess would have rather died than stand by your side."

His glare was lethal and his words threatening. "Good thing we no longer have such tension between us."

"Keep your malicious intentions away from Sevrick and it will remain cordial."

Mikhail laughed. "Your disillusion that you hold any control over me is adorable. I'll have the entire world on my side in a few months. I can make you disappear in a way where no one would suspect foul play. It's not hard, dear." He leaned in and whispered into her ear, "Your life is mine." He kissed her neck. "I suggest you focus on those motherly vibes keeping you in line. Seems all other topics still bring out the worst in you."

She said nothing as he exited the room. Playing nice was going to be a true test of her will power. But she had to, for her safety and for Sevrick's.

Chapter 29

At 6 a.m., Roman and Sergei had their troops and tanks lined up along the Estonian, Latvian, and Belarusian borders. As the sun rose, they began their march. Haemans living abroad were informed this invasion was coming. They were told to prepare to join the Russian flanks as they arrived. These small countries neighboring Russia were already primarily haeman. Their conversion was fast and the takeover would be easy.

It wasn't an hour before troops in all three countries reached civilization. Sergei reached the town of Tartu in Estonia first and had an enormous hoard of Estonian haemans waiting for him in the town square.

As he approached, he addressed them. "Hello, friends. My name is Sergei Greshnev and I am an Army Lieutenant in the Russian Armed Forces. Are you ready to fight for our common cause?" The crowd murmured excitedly in unison. The tension was high; the new haemans had been anticipating this moment. "Tell me how the transition went here. Where are those who refused to join?"

An old woman in front answered. "We've been waiting a long time for Prince Mikhail to give us a sign that we were part of his regime. We weren't able to contain ourselves. Most of those who refused haemanism are already dead." Her voice held uncertainty; she wasn't sure if her confession would be looked upon as a good or bad thing.

"Don't look so nervous, that saves us a lot of time. Less people to eliminate before joining the troops in Latvia and crossing into Lithuania. I am going to move south while two of my troops filter through the rest of Estonia, collecting other haemans and eliminating outliers. How many are gathered here?"

"Three thousand," a young man answered.

"Fantastic. I'd like the lot of you to follow me into Latvia. There, we will meet up with Lieutenant Roman Vershinin, join forces, and enter Poland. Along the way we will teach you what you need to know and answer any questions you may have. We understand that other than your local haeman correspondent, you've been in the dark. That will no longer be the case. You're with us now."

The crowd cheered and his captains walked through the masses delivering small baggies of silve to their new recruits. The Estonians fueled up, snorting the drug and ripping at their skin to draw blood. It was an empowering mess. Their high was fierce and red streaks smeared their vision as they followed Sergei. The trek was long but no one noticed. They moved at unnatural speeds and were distracted by their raging highs. They only encountered fellow haemans on their drug-laced trip to the border. When they reached it, they were greeted by their first opposing force.

Latvia's State Border Guard was protecting their territory. The general stood at the main gate's watchtower, observing the threat now approaching. They were warned; perhaps by surveillance but more likely by Southern Latvians already facing the wrath of Roman and his haeman troops. The border patrol was ready to fight, but so was Sergei and his army.

The border, once friendly and devoid of walls or barriers, now had a crudely installed electric fence. It appeared to have been put up with speed and careless haste. Breaking it down would be easy for the haemans.

"Stay back," the Latvian general commanded over a speaker. Sergei did not pause. "If you don't, we will open fire."

The haemans laughed as they continued their approach without worry. As they neared the fence, Sergei could see Roman and his haeman soldiers approaching the border patrol from the inside.

"Looks like you've got backup," Sergei shouted sarcastically. The general whipped his head around and saw the fleet of murderous haemans skulking toward him from inside the fence.

Roman broke into a sprint and Sergei took this as his cue to do the same. The Latvian Border Control was stampeded from both sides. Shots were fired but it was too late. The haemans were upon the guards in a matter of seconds. Those clipped by the bullets licked their wounds and applied the extra boost toward the slaughter.

Sergei climbed the side of the watchtower with inhuman grace. He smashed the glass window with his fist and climbed inside. The general had his rifle aimed at Sergei but did not shoot in time. Sergei was already behind him with an arm wrapped around his neck by the time the general fired.

"You should've joined us," he whispered before snapping the man's neck. He looked out the broken window and saw the massacre of Latvian guards strewn across the ground. The body count was high; Sergei estimated they killed at least one hundred guardsmen.

"We needed only a fraction of our men for that victory," he shouted down to Roman while pointing at the field still full of Estonian haemans. He looked past Roman and saw a large group of Latvian haemans weren't needed to fight either. He climbed down the side of the tower.

"We outmatched them quite severely," Roman said. "Our journey through Latvia was a stroll in the park."

"Same in Estonia. Poland might be harder since their population is bigger and their percentage of haeman conversions is smaller."

"But they don't know we are coming and by the time we get there we will have the majority of Estonia, Latvia, Lithuania, and Belarus behind us."

After assigning a group of haemans to stay behind and guard the newly seized border, the men traveled south with their enormous following. They crossed through Lithuania without any trouble, then entered Belarus. Their border patrol was just as easy to defeat as Latvia's.

Upon entering, they radioed their troops assigned to this country and made plans to meet in the city of Minsk. After a few hours of traveling, they reconnected and their army was larger than anticipated.

"We don't need this many men," Roman whispered to Sergei. "It's almost *too* many. The large numbers are a hindrance; it's too many to control."

Sergei nodded in agreement and spoke to the crowd.

"We are very pleased to have so many new haemans in our extended family. We gathered you all in Minsk and request anyone not of fighting age to stay here. We need haemans to remain scattered throughout Europe in case opposing foreign forces attempt to thwart us. If you wish to return to your homelands and act as guards there, that is fine too. Now that we have control, we will have our Russian correspondents delivering silve directly to you. The following cities will be your depository locations: Tartu, Estonia; Riga, Latvia; Vilnius, Lithuania; and Minsk, Belarus. In time, we will work the silve into the water systems."

The crowd did not object and were content with the assignment to guard their homelands. Roman and Sergei carried on with the remaining haemans. They approached the Polish border near the city of Bialystok. Roman stopped the group before the Polish guardsmen saw them.

"Everyone, spread out but stay hidden within the forest. When I give the command, charge. Their defenses are better than any we've faced yet, so it will be better to surprise them with an attack as a large mass."

The command was passed through the crowd and the haemans scattered quietly among the trees. They crept forward, staying as hidden as possible and the Polish guards were none the wiser. They were not on high alert; no one warned them of what happened in their neighboring countries over the last three days. Cutting the power cables was working. Men were talking casually behind the fence, sitting in chairs and eating pastries. They had no clue what slunk toward them from across the border.

As the haemans grew closer, their anticipation for a good fight grew larger. They thirsted for violence, for strange blood on their hands. Roman turned to the crowd crouched behind him.

"On my count," he whispered. With his fingers, he counted down from three. As his last finger dropped, the haemans left their hiding spots and stampeded toward the fence. The roar of vicious shouts and aggressive war cries filled the air, alerting the Polish guard to the invasion. The men, startled, raced to their stations and readied their weapons.

There was no opportunity to talk reason with their assailants so they opened fire. Bullets rained over the haemans like a storm, hitting many but failing to stop the majority. They reached the fence and while some climbed, others reached through the chain links and strangled the guards who stood too close. Like a swarm, the haemans crossed the fenced border and swallowed the Polish guardsmen. They were so outnumbered they seemingly disappeared as the haemans surrounded them. When the fight was over and the haemans scattered to refuel on silve, the guards' mangled bodies reappeared at their feet. Leaving their victims dead on the ground, the haemans continued their march southwest toward Warsaw.

The walk only took one day. With the bottomless supply of silve, they were unstoppable. As they reached the city, it was eerily quiet. Sergei extended an arm to stop the progression forward.

"Guns out," he commanded before waving the group forward. "Spread out."

Large groups filtered down different streets, all of which housed crowded buildings in cramped spaces. A few blocks in, gunshots erupted. They were followed by a downpour of bullets on the street. Sergei found cover, but many of his men were not as lucky.

"They are shooting from the top windows," Roman shouted from the next street over.

Sergei looked up and saw the barrels of rifles angled out of the highest windows. He broke into the nearest door and ascended the stairs. On the top floor he found two men with sniper rifles. With impeccable stealth, he snuck up behind them, grabbed the nearest man's neck and snapped it, which alerted the second to his arrival. The gun shifted aim to Sergei, but he ducked before the man pulled the trigger. Driven by rage, Sergei dragged out this murder. He pummeled the man repeatedly, knocking out teeth and denting his skull. Once his victim stopped fighting back he stood and stomped on his neck, breaking it. The kill felt good.

He grabbed his radio and addressed Roman.

"Send our haemans to the rooftops. The buildings are close enough, we can travel through town from above, dipping into the buildings as we go."

"Good idea," Roman answered over the speaker.

Their first real fight. This would be perfect training for the new recruits. Sergei raced to the rooftop, adrenaline still pumping from his brutal kill. He was ready for more, ready to wear the blood of his victims proudly.

197

Chapter 30

While Roman and Sergei worked through their assigned borders, Edik and Filipp tackled Ukraine. A few skilled troops were assigned to Kazakhstan, which was reported to be an easy capture, so they crossed into the Ukrainian city of Kharkiv together. The journey to the western border of Ukraine was unpredictable and their success through the eastern side was no indicator for what lay ahead. The Ukrainians were passionate and strong willed. If they were properly warned of the incoming intruders, they'd surely set up some form of defense. It wouldn't change the outcome, the haemans would win, but Edik and Filipp hoped the Ukrainians were not given time to prepare. They'd rather not lose any Russian haemans this early into their quest.

The collection of Ukrainian haemans was steady as they spread out to cover the width of the country. They encountered many resistant people along the way, but none gathered in large enough numbers to take them on. Every defiant person was silenced by death.

When they reached Poltava, they found word had spread of their invasion. Small pacts of non-haemans gathered in various locations, hoping to ambush the haemans, but they never won. Their numbers were too small, their weaponry minimal, and their physical strength outmatched. Each time Edik, Filipp, and their soldiers came across a pocket of rebellion, it ended up being only a momentary pause in their trek. Within minutes, the fight was over and they moved on.

While Edik and half their crew went south to seize the small country of Moldova, Filipp took the rest of their soldiers to sweep the western side of Ukraine. They planned to meet up again in Botosani, Romania. It would be a few days apart but when they rejoined forces, their numbers would be even greater.

They moved swiftly across the landscape, fueled by silve and blood. They barely stopped, moving at speeds that would tire the most athletic humans. A trip that would take weeks for a non-haeman only took them days, sometimes hours. Tanks followed their pursuit west but the large armory was yet to be needed. The fight was a farce. The ease with which they conquered their neighboring countries was comical.

The further west they got, the more resistance they faced. And though the battles increased, the outcome never changed. The haemans always won without suffering many casualties. It was a swift massacre across Europe.

Mikhail was pleased. Kirill updated him often on the progress. Edik and Filipp led their haeman army through Romania, Bulgaria, Macedonia, Albania, Kosovo, Serbia, Bosnia-Herzegovina, Croatia, and Slovenia. All small countries, but huge gains in numbers. Their haeman army was enormous. By the time they reached Budapest, the mission was beginning to feel monotonous. Once they cleared the city of policemen and government officials who resisted haemanism, they set up for the night in the Parliament building. It was massive, so as the enormous haeman army found spots to sleep among the 691 rooms, Edik and Filipp sat in the vacant assembly room and talked.

"I thought it would be more fun," Edik complained in private.

"I'm kind of surprised we got this far without much backlash," Filipp commented.

"Do you think the rest of the world knows what we are doing?"

"It's hard to imagine they don't."

"Well we better enjoy these easy victories while they last. Wouldn't be surprised if the bigger nations are keeping their knowledge secret until they're ready to strike."

"Has any word come through about the airmen in Ireland and Spain? Are they having as easy a time as we are?"

"No clue. Kirill hasn't mentioned it," Edik shook his head. "I guess we just continue this way. We will reach the meeting point by tomorrow evening. Graz is less than a day away."

"Are Sergei and Roman close too?"

"Last I heard, they made it through Poland and Czech Republic. I can't imagine Slovakia put up much of a fight. We might beat them there, but they'll be close behind."

"They had no causalities either?"

"Barely, though Poland was a feat. Thousands of Polish people were gathered at Warsaw upon their arrival. They managed to kill a hundred haemans by hiding out and shooting down from apartment windows. They mostly got the new haemans, foreigners from the recently seized countries."

"How do you think Germany will be?"

"Half and half. According to reports, the majority are transitioned to haemanism. The culture latched onto the power and strength of the lifestyle, embracing it fully. But those who did not give in will be angry and eager to fight us. Germany is one of the few countries that openly battled the new addiction taking over their people. So those who are not part of it will be ready to face us."

"Think they know we've conquered so much land?"

"Hard to tell. We killed every traitor in our path, and we did it so fast they had minimal time to send out warnings before we found and cut the cable lines. But I suppose it's logical to assume some outliers remain hidden in our new territory that could sneak around by foot to spread the word. But a grand game of telephone doesn't pose much of a threat."

"Maybe. I still think we need to keep moving fast. We've covered this much land in less than two weeks; that's not possible for normal humans. The element of surprise has played a huge part in our success. If we keep conquering at this speed, they'll never have time to warn others, prepare themselves, or fight us off."

"Exactly. Which is why we move toward Graz tomorrow, meet up with Roman, Sergei, and all their new soldiers, and move immediately into Germany."

"I agree. I don't think it's smart to wait for the airmen moving east from Ireland and Spain. I'll check with Kirill first, but I think it's best we keep moving. We need to sweep Europe before the U.S. catches wind of what we're doing. They could wipe us out easily if they intervene too soon."

"Are they onto us?" Edik asked.

"Last I heard, our American haemans were instructed to create havoc throughout the States. They should be causing a big enough distraction that the U.S. military won't be able to worry about Europe until their homeland problems are fixed." Filipp smiled. "I wish I could see the mayhem they've stirred up. I bet it's a never-ending train wreck over there."

Edik pondered, "We might not need to travel to the States at all if the haemans there take care of it for us."

"That would be ideal." Filipp yawned. "Let's get some rest. Good chance the next few days will be sleepless."

The men found comfortable places to lay down. Their journey was still long and they had many battles left to fight.

Chapter 31

"Prime Minister Emelie Braff of Sweden called this morning with reports of Polish refugees landing on her shores," Prime Minister Calland announced to the table of men. All leaders returned to their native lands after the U.N. meeting. Their concerns and warnings were heard, but put on the backburner until signs of war began to surface. Those signs were now piling up with great speed. The United States was dealing with large cases of civil unrest. The population outnumbered the policemen and military, making the uproar uncontrollable. Their internal revolution, raised by those afflicted by haemanism, was enough to keep them preoccupied domestically and disconnected from the war unfolding in Europe.

The Nordic countries heard no word of movement from the Russians until the Swedish military received a distress call from the Romanian army. The message was sent out as a blast to anyone with a radio receiving their signal, but the call for help was short and the message unclear. After announcing who they were and that they needed aide, the frequency became filled with screams, both Russian and Romanian. It was enough to determine the Russians were there, but not enough to let them in on what was happening. All other attempts at communication were unsuccessful. No one in Romania answered their calls or reached back out for help. It was as if the entire country went dark: no telephones, no Internet, no connection to the outside world. The Nordic Union formed quickly after this alarming warning and began preparing for the worst.

Denmark beefed up their border patrol. Their borders connected the Scandinavian region to the northern bulk of Europe. It was the land the haemans would try to travel north through.

Norway began prepping their hospitals and schools for more refugees. Their land was furthest from the devastation and it also housed the coast with the easiest path for escape. Prime Minister Emelie Braff was ready and eager to save all survivors who made it to them.

All leaders of the Nordic Union did their best to reach out to the eastern European countries but like Romania, they were unreachable. Every city east of Czech Republic was cut off from the rest of the world and every city west had no clue what they were talking about when asked about the haemans. They knew of the new Russian drug affecting their citizens, and had plans to absolve its existence from their countries, but they had no reason to believe they were on the brink of an uprising, like the U.S., or that the Armed Forces of the Russian Federation were approaching their borders.

Since they could do no more than warn their southern neighbors, they prepared to defend themselves. All Nordic military gathered in Sweden. Finnish, Danish, and Norwegian soldiers met the Swedes there and prepped to protect their small pocket of land with all they had. Haemans and refugees could easily cross either the North Sea or the Baltic Sea to reach them. They were ready to receive the welcomed travelers and expel the unwanted haemans. Until they could get assistance from larger militaries from around the globe, it was essential they kept their land safe and haeman-free.

Finnish locals began a civilian coalition and called themselves the Exonerators. They went from village to town to city, doing their best to apprehend anyone who had fallen victim to haemanism. To their luck, it hadn't spread like a virus in the Nordic region as it had in other countries. The Scandinavians weren't nearly as infiltrated as their European neighbors, but the disease still trickled through their land. A decent amount of people fell into the addiction and they needed to rid haemanism from existence in the Nordic Union. It wasn't easy, but the Clandes and Primos helped. They were used

203

to hunting haemans and their experience proved crucial. They stalked and captured their prey with tranquilizer guns and once caught, they placed the haemans into a high security prison. There, Leonid turned each prison cell into a medical room where the haeman prisoners were forcefully rehabilitated.

As the Exonerators collected more haemans, Leonid made beds for them in the prison. The job was enormous, and he could only heal so many at a time, but he did the best he could. Many Scandinavian nurses came from all over to learn the process and assist him, but it wouldn't be enough to heal them all simultaneously. They'd need to take it one day at a time with raging haemans on one side of the building and healing haemans on the other.

Sevrick did not feel connected to any of it. All he could think about was getting back to St. Petersburg and saving Rina. His gut told him this was not what she wanted, that all of what he'd seen on TV was forced upon her. He helped the Exonerators capture haemans, but he felt hollow inside. He was making a difference, helping the greater good, but his heart pulled him back to Russia and he wouldn't feel right until he was tackling the mission he prioritized. He bided his time, knowing the battle he currently fought was important to the masses, but when the opportunity to return to Russia came, he'd jump on it.

The phone rang on speaker as they waited for the leaders of the Nordic Union to get on the line. Greta Calland led the meeting and she let the allied Russian men sit in to hear the updates. The phone beeped.

"Hello all, Absalon here." President Hummel of Denmark joined the conference call first. "Who else is on the line?"

It beeped again. "Emelie," Prime Minister Braff of Sweden said as she joined.

"Greta," Prime Minister Calland said, "and I also have our Russian friends with me. Wanted them filled in on all updates."

"Of course," Absalon said. The line beeped.

"Fredriik here. Sorry I'm late," Prime Minister Kurtti of Finland said.

"No worries," Greta responded. "Emelie, can you start off by telling them what you told me this morning?"

"Sure. Polish refugees floated onto our shores early this morning. The sun wasn't even up. They came in rafts and small boats, towing extra people and their personal belongings behind them on flotation apparatuses. The first round landed on our beaches in Karlskrona all the way from Leba. They were on the ocean for days before reaching us. A few hours later, another round of Polish refugees washed ashore in Ystad. They came from Kolobrzeg. All stories were the same: the Russian military invaded, stronger than any normal human army, and took over without any trouble at all. They fought back, but it didn't matter. The Russian's were on the silve, they were haemans, and they had an unfair advantage. No fight put forth was enough, not even by their most skilled military men. They said they were lucky, that most who would not succumb to the haeman lifestyle were executed on the spot, but they escaped. They got to their coast and set sail, praying that Sweden was still a safe spot."

"Did they know what other countries were taken?" Absalon asked.

"No, just their own. But we know Romania is conquered and I think we can assume all countries in between and to the east have been lost to Russia as well."

"The leader of Ukraine was *at* our U.N. meeting only two weeks ago," Fredriik said in astonishment. "Could they really cover and conquer so much land in such a short time frame?"

205

All the Russians nodded their heads. Greta observed and reported their response with dread. "Yes. We are fighting a super race; a breed of human we've never known before."

"We must protect our corner of the world. We can house as many displaced neighbors as possible, but we *have* to protect our own in the meantime," Absalon advised. "For all we know, our land will be one of the few remaining places free of haemanism in the near future."

"That's why we must continue warning people. We cannot let that happen," Greta implored. "After this meeting, I am going to begin a round of phone calls to all leaders I can reach. Tell them what's coming."

"We've been doing that and no one has understood the gravity of our warnings," Fredriik sighed.

"I'll make them hear me, I'll demand they take my words seriously."

"No one will take action until they see the horror for themselves on the news," Absalon jumped in. "And unfortunately, the haemans are moving so fast and cutting each country's power that no one has gotten a chance to document the battles because they are conquered before they get the chance."

"I'm going to keep trying anyway," Greta concluded. "It can't hurt."

"Of course not," Emelie agreed. "Best we can do is try."

"What we really need is the United States on our side. They need to realize *their* internal battles are directly correlated with *our* internal battles and that we need to work together to end this madness."

"They are on my list of contacts to call."

The Nordic Union leaders wrapped up their call and Greta hung up.

"What really needs to happen is an execution," Sevrick said, driven by his desire to return to Russia and his hatred for the prince. "Mikhail needs to be killed. It's the only way to stop this."

"He's right," Ruslan agreed. "Without a leader the remaining haemans would have no focus. They'd still be vicious and dangerous, but their organized plans of attack would crumble and we'd have a better chance at defeating them."

"Remove the head, kill the body," Vladimir added.

Greta bit her lip in worry. "Is that something you and your men would be comfortable doing? Attempting an assassination is risky, especially since most of the information we have is based off assumptions and guesses. There still isn't proof he's behind this. We are just placing the pieces of this puzzle where they seem to fit. I can't risk my nation's safety by sending my soldiers on a task like this, just in case we end up being wrong about everything. It has to be an inside job."

"We can do it alone. We have plenty of other survivors hiding out in Russia who will help us, but we need more weapons. We need to be able to put up a good fight, otherwise it's all for nothing. We'd lose if we stormed the palace armed with what we have now," Ruslan answered.

"I'll get you all the arsenal you need, but you need to discard it the moment you succeed. I don't want a target on our back once they find out you used Norwegian weapons to kill the prince."

"Not a problem."

"You'll be given radios that will allow you to contact the leaders of the Nordic Union directly."

"Your help is greatly appreciated."

Greta instructed her guard to contact the leader of their military and have him put together a suitable cache of guns, bombs, and ammunition. She exited the room, doling out instructions as she and her people left.

"Looks like we're headed back to the motherland." Konstantin smirked as he spoke. His mind was on thoughts of Mikhail's death; taking part in the murder brought joy to his face. It was a sentiment every man in the room could relate to.

"Looks like it," Vladimir said. "Feels right that we're in charge of this mission. It's only appropriate that we deliver justice."

All the men mumbled in agreement. Sevrick could not wait to get his hands on Mikhail; he hoped he was the one to steal his final breath. He had a personal vendetta to resolve and this mission was the key to his retribution.

Chapter 32

The journey back into Russia was long and arduous, just as it had been on the journey out. The only difference was the ease with which they crossed the border. The patrol over the Russian border was significantly decreased and they snuck back in without any trouble at all.

"They must be busy taking over benign and unprepared countries," Jurg scoffed.

"Maybe," Artem countered, "but if they are preoccupied hundreds of kilometers away, that means there will be less haeman fighters trying to stop us from completing our mission."

"I doubt the palace was left unguarded," Benedikt retorted. "Mikhail isn't stupid. He'd never let his best warriors leave his side."

"We won't know till we scope it out," Zakhar interjected. "Speculation is fine but we can't treat it like it's fact. We just take it as it comes."

"We don't even have a tactical plan yet," Nikolai said with a mouthful of Tupla. He chewed the Finnish chocolate as he spoke. "Scratch that, we haven't even gotten back to the white elm yet. It'll be a few weeks before we get to another TV. Who knows what will change by then." He handed a piece of chocolate to Isaak, who was never far from his side.

"Lots might change, but the fact that Mikhail needs to die will always remain," Sevrick reminded him. Everyone silently agreed.

The remainder of the trip was quiet. Nikolai continued mentoring Isaak. Zakhar was constantly trying to remind Leonid that the Scandinavians would be fine without him, that they had mastered the rehabilitation process and would function fine on their own. Leonid worried he was needed there more than in Russia, but he also knew Nina would be devastated to see all the men return without him. Eventually they'd need his expertise in Russia more than anyplace else. Once Mikhail was defeated and they were able to round up the Russian haemans, he was going to be swarmed with patients to heal and not just regular patients, but addicts deeper into haemanism than any other place on the planet. His presence in Russia would be crucial then.

Artem stayed by Sevrick's side, chatting with him about all the thoughts he didn't dare tell his Clandes friends. This journey had turned them into very close friends. Artem was the only person he felt safe confiding in about Rina; he was the only one who did not judge him for it. Everyone else rolled their eyes or advised him not to feel how he felt, even when they knew he could not control it. He loved her, he always would, and this fundamental fact annoyed the friends who spent years dealing with it. They were over it. Leonid and Ruslan tried to be patient but Sevrick could sense their annoyance. Zakhar and Nikolai didn't bother pretending anymore. The few times they overheard his chats with Artem, they intervened with their blunt and harsh opinions on the matter. Sevrick learned to keep his fears, worries, and feelings to himself, but Artem made sure to check in on him from time to time.

"Where's your head at?" he asked Sevrick.

"With her."

"Least we're headed back to Russia now. You'll be able to tackle that issue soon."

"When looking at the bigger picture, I know killing Mikhail is more important than saving Rina. I get it. I just can't make the majority's priority match my own."

"We still don't know the conditions by which she left the underground fortress. I know you don't want to hear this, but if she

210

left willingly with intentions to take back her life as a haeman princess, I think your internal battle will cease."

"If she chose to go back to that life, then I'm done with her. I won't try to save her and I will let go. But I don't think that's what happened. I can't believe it. My gut instincts are telling me it didn't happen that way."

"Then let it go until we get to the white elm and talk to the people who were supposed to be watching her. Stressing out the next two weeks while we walk won't do you any good. There's nothing you can do until we get you the truth."

Sevrick nodded. Of course it would stay on his mind, but he had to stop overanalyzing it until he had solid facts to contribute to his mind's wanderings.

A week into their journey they began running into haeman scouts. Though they were no longer near the border, there were still many lurking about the closer they got to St. Petersburg. They still had a two-week walk ahead of them before reaching the white elm, but the further they went, the more they had to be careful.

Time passed slower now that they occasionally needed to hide out for periods of time until it was safe to travel. They observed the haemans as they hid. They were always loud, arrogant, and destructive, but now they walked around with an air of entitlement. Even the lowliest of haemans, those marking their poor social standings with bloodstained clothes and unruly outbursts, acted as if the world belonged to them. Seeing this behavior further confirmed the Clandes and Primos belief that Mikhail was carrying out a plan for world domination. His haemans were aware they'd be top of the food chain once all the foreign, infant haemans were onboard. They wore their new power with pride. They reveled in a victory yet to be received. There was no doubt in their minds their leader would succeed and they celebrated amongst themselves far too early.

The sight of this fueled their mission to assassinate Mikhail.

"It's getting dark. Let's camp here," Ruslan suggested as he threw his pack beneath a large and thick Scots pine tree. The men followed suit and bunkered down for the night. A great grey owl cooed above them as they settled in. Sevrick wondered if it was the same bird that attacked them on their trip into Norway. It was docile now, and he hoped it stayed that way.

"Goodnight," Nikolai called out from the opposite side of the tree trunk.

"Night," Ivan responded.

"Sleep well," Marat added.

"Stop touching me," Konstantin griped while shoving Benedikt.

"But I'm cold," he laughed, trying to cuddle up next to his resistant friend. "You can be the big spoon if it makes you feel better."

"I'll turn your face into a spoon if you don't stop," Konstantin threatened.

"Shut it," Vladimir roared but the situation had escalated and everyone was laughing now.

They had evolved into a family. The connection came suddenly, but their epic journey sealed their bond to one another. All tensions and barriers between them had dissolved over the countless days spent together and though they still fought and bickered, they had a connection that was non-replicable. No one would ever understand what they went through together and this journey made them a stronger unit. They were a true team and there was an unspoken oath of loyalty between them that could never be broken.

"Enough," Ruslan said amused. "We still have a long way to go and I'm not entertaining any cranky attitudes tomorrow because you spent the night awake, giggling like teenage girls."

"You heard the man," Konstantin gave Benedikt a final shove and ended the tomfoolery. Everyone went quiet like they were trying to fall asleep.

"Goodnight, my lovers," Nikolai chimed in, breaking the silence and causing the men to lose their cool and roar in laughter again. Isaak's pre-pubescent laughs were louder than the rest. Sevrick looked to the teenage boy lying next to him and saw tears of merriment rolling down his cheeks. Seeing him act his age brought warmth to Sevrick's soul. It was a rough world to grow up in and Isaak was born and raised in it. The only home he knew was the white elm and he never got to experience life as a carefree adolescent. Sevrick was tired, but seeing him laugh was worth staying up for. It reminded him of a time when there was more to life than just surviving.

"You're all freaking delirious," Ruslan sighed. After a few minutes the laughter trickled off and they began falling asleep one by one. Sevrick wasn't sure but he had a feeling he was the last to surrender to slumber. The disharmonious snoring all around him gave his position in sleeping order away. He tried to ignore the noise but found it impossible. His thoughts, combined with the symphony of snoring, kept him wide-awake.

Dawn was approaching, Sevrick could sense the warmth of a new day. It was still dark and he only slipped in and out of sleep a few times that night, but he would champion through until the next time they got to rest. He waited for the sun's arrival. The sky lightened up gradually. The wait was tiring but he couldn't fall asleep now. It would only make him more tired when they started the next leg of their journey.

The longer it took for the sun to rise, the harder it was to fight off the sleep that finally greeted him. He shut his eyes for a moment, caving into the weight now pressing upon his eyelids. A moment after closing them, he heard a scream. He opened his eyes and saw Isaak being pulled out from under the tree by his ankle. Startled, he reached for his young friend. Isaak's arms reached back but they could not connect. He grabbed Sevrick's ankle instead, latching on and stalling the horror momentarily. As Sevrick tried to grab hold of him, his boot slipped off and Isaak disappeared with it. There was a cackling of laughter from beyond Sevrick's sight.

The haemans had found them.

He shook Artem and kicked Nikolai before exiting the shelter of the tree branches. His friends heard the scream and were slowly rustling awake but none of them understood the gravity of the situation yet. Isaak was already gagged with a rag and couldn't make any more noise.

Alone, Sevrick faced three haemans in their young twenties; two men and a female. They were low-class. The fresh blood dripping from their mouths and forearms onto their clothes indicated that.

"We can give you what you need, just give back the boy," Sevrick pleaded calmly.

"His neck is so fragile in my grip," the haeman holding Isaak sneered.

"Unharmed," Sevrick added.

The female haeman took a step closer to Sevrick. He prayed his friends were assessing the situation from beneath the tree and coming up with a plan to attack.

"We aren't in the business of making deals with traitors," she purred as she reached him where he stood. She breathed on his neck flirtatiously and ran her hand down the front of his thigh, fingers slowly creeping inward. He took a step back.

"What do you want? There must be a reason you're in the middle of the woods instead of the city. Tell me why. Maybe I can help."

The male haeman not holding Isaak stepped forward and pulled a piece of paper from his pocket. He unfolded it and held it in front of Sevrick's face. It was a picture of Leonid.

"Who is that?"

"Knew you couldn't help." The haeman refolded the paper and stepped back. He wore a semi-automatic rifle over his back.

"His name is Leonid Federoff," the female haeman answered. "The prince requires his retrieval."

"What for?"

"That's none of your concern," she said as she stepped closer to him again.

"Let the boy go and I'll help you find him."

"You don't even know who he is." The haeman holding Isaak spat and tightened his grip.

"How'd you find us?"

"This little idiot fell asleep with his feet exposed beyond the branches." He laughed and traced his sharp fingernail down the side of Isaak's cheek. It drew blood.

"How many more of you are there?" the female asked, bending to peer beneath the thick set of branches. She took her time, taunting Sevrick and touching him inappropriately as she crouched closer to the forest floor. Once at eye level with the tree trunk, she shifted her gaze to what hid beneath.

"Boo," Nikolai said, then pulled the trigger. The bullet tore apart her pretty face. She fell dead immediately and his friends emerged from beneath the tree with guns blazing. They quickly assessed the situation, aware to take careful aim since Isaak was caught in the middle. While the men fought and dodged the haeman with the

215

gun, Konstantin, unarmed, dove toward the haeman holding their young friend. He made contact, knocking Isaak free and pinning the haeman to the ground. The only advantage he had was his size. He outweighed the haeman by a hundred pounds, but his strength was still no match. He held the haeman down, doing his best to keep him constrained.

"A little help, please."

Nikolai ran to them with his rifle and shot the haeman in the head. It convulsed beneath Konstantin, fighting off death before finally succumbing. The haeman with the rifle was still on the loose. He fired haphazardly, making the situation even more dangerous. Bullets flew in every direction, which made it hard to take him down. The men hid behind trees and rocks, taking shots whenever they got the chance. Konstantin and Nikolai ran toward Isaak, who stood in the middle of it all, frozen with fear.

Nikolai grabbed his arm and pulled him toward safety, but before they made it to the nearest safe spot, Isaak was yanked from his grip and tugged backward.

Nikolai whipped around to see his young comrade back in the arms of the enraged haeman. The bloody haeman, covered with self-inflicted cuts and newly acquired bullet wounds, cackled into the sky before forcing Isaak onto his knees.

"Stay put," he ordered while showering bullets in the direction of his hidden opponents. "Stop shooting!" The men obeyed, hoping their compliance would save Isaak's life.

The haeman rounded the spot where Isaak kneeled and stood behind him.

"All this trouble for him?" He pulled a pistol from his belt and placed its barrel to the back of Isaak's head.

The hammer clicked back. Isaak stood and sprinted toward the spot where Ruslan hid. The haeman fired at him, missed. Cocked the hammer, fired again. Hit him in the shoulder.

Isaak kept running. Nikolai raced toward the haeman, who fired his pistol at Isaak while simultaneously shooting the semi-automatic haphazardly to keep his opponents at bay. The third shot hit Isaak in the calf, causing him to fall. He stood back up and hobbled with determination to safety.

Nikolai reached the haeman as it aimed to take another shot at the boy. The gun fired as he tackled the haeman to the ground. Keeping the haeman pinned and trapped beneath the barrel of his gun, Nikolai turned to see what happened.

Isaak was on the ground.

Fueled by rage, Nikolai turned back on the haeman, dropped the gun, and lashed out with brute force on the monster's face. Fist to face, fist to face, driven by the strength of utter despair. Nikolai beat the haeman until he was so bruised, cut-up, and raw, bone showed beneath the gashes. The haeman was no longer moving, no longer breathing. Nikolai stood up, took a step back, and aimed his gun at the haeman's mangled face. He fired, guaranteeing the monster died. Then he turned back toward the scene unfolding around Isaak.

"Tell me he's still alive," he demanded as he stormed toward the crowd around Isaak. "Tell me he's still alive!"

Sevrick tried to intercept his bereaved friend, but Nikolai pushed past and crouched next to Ruslan.

"The bullet hit his heart," Ruslan said with tears in his eyes. He picked up his nephew's hand and held it. The skin was cold against his.

Nikolai could not process the news, he could not accept this outcome. He shut his eyes as the grief overwhelmed him and all he could see in the darkness was the bravery with which Isaak ran from the haeman in his final moments. He held onto that image as the tears fell.

Chapter 33

Mikhail was cozy in his success: most of Eastern Europe was now his, along with Ireland and Spain. Aliona's soldiers were slowly occupying the United Kingdom and France, both of which were showing great resistance. Dominika's airmen reached the meeting point in Graz two days ago and were instructed to land and turn back west. Eventually they'd move through Italy, Switzerland, Germany, Netherlands, and Belgium, and reach the bulk of the resistance in France. With all of Russia and the majority of Europe pushing in on them, they were bound to secede.

The U.S. was entangled in civil uprisings and rebel mutinies. The rebels were, of course, his haemans. They were causing mayhem and destruction all across America: initiating riots, taking over towns, forming violent insurgencies. The increase in murders was so overwhelming that the U.S. lost control of the situation within the first week. Now his haemans ran rampant, ruling their local territories, turning more people into haemans, and killing anyone who got in their way.

Mikhail assumed the U.S. got word from the French and British leaders that Europe was under siege, but the Americans could not come to their aid for their troubles at home were just as bad. The rest of Europe went dark; all forms of international telecommunication were eliminated, leaving helpless any non-haeman survivors in those countries. They could not call for assistance because telephone lines were disconnected and cell towers were destroyed. They could not post pictures, videos, or articles to the Internet, because after taking control of each country, the haemans sought out and seized all ISPs. In an act of Cyber Warfare, his Russian technicians sent crippling viruses into international Internet service providers, shutting them down permanently. His Russian navy used the official TeleGeography Submarine Cable Map to scuba dive, locate, and shred all international Internet cables off the coasts of the U.K., Spain, and France. They then bombed the cables lying in the Black, Mediterranean, and Tyrrhenian Sea. Taking out the connections in those seas also put most of Africa and the Middle East into virtual darkness, keeping them out of the loop for now. There was currently no documentation of Russia's actions outside the phone calls still possible from the countries he hadn't conquered yet. Everything was unfolding brilliantly and he couldn't have imagined it working out any better.

While he waited for the inevitable downfall of France and the U.K., he spent his time organizing the transformation of local schools, vacant of children, into mothering farms. Arinadya, with her ever-growing belly, was his spokesperson for this endeavor. He spent his days training and prepping her for the project's big reveal.

"You realize, even if the haeman women in Russia agree to this, we don't know how to heal them yet. No one has found Leonid; he is the one with the answers."

"I have no doubt we will find him, but in the meantime I need to get my people ready. It will take time to rehabilitate them and time to get the next generation of eventual haemans into this world."

"It will take time to *convince* them," Arinadya pointed out.

"Not with you as the face of the campaign. You're already doing it. You're a success case. They adore you and want to be like you. If they found out there was a way for them to follow in your footsteps they'd jump at the chance."

"I think you're underestimating their dependence on the silve. Not only would they need to go nine months without it, but also all the prep time: a few months for the rehab plus an undeterminable amount of time to get impregnated. It could be years."

"Like I've told you before, we present this as an honorable sacrifice; a temporary change in their lifestyle. They'd be serving the greater good."

"And what about *after* the babies are born? Assuming you can even get to that point. What then? These haeman mothers aren't going to want to raise an infant. They'd kill it the first time they couldn't get it to stop crying."

"Haeman nurses, trained in self-discipline and patience, will take care of the babies until they are teenagers. This new generation will be raised together, in home and schooling, with the nurses acting as their care providers and educators until they turn sixteen. They will be conditioned to embrace the haeman lifestyle so that when they come of age, they are excited to join their elders."

"You're treating this like it's a farm. The people of Russia are your cattle and their babies are yours to make fat and ready for slaughter."

"I'm not going to kill them."

"You plan to get them hooked on a debilitating narcotic that *will* eventually be their demise. It's prolonged, but not much different than a slaughterhouse. Just because it isn't immediate doesn't mean you aren't responsible. Same with all the others who are dying in droves because the addiction caused them to starve or destroyed their organs or put them in the line of another addict's rage. You may not see the blood, but it's on your hands."

"You're annoying. Why can't you just be happy for me, for us, for all Russians? Why can't you just embrace your role with positivity? This will keep us alive, keep us thriving. You play a pivotal role and will go down in history as the woman who saved the Russian race."

"I don't want to be remembered alongside any of this."

Mikhail slapped her across the face. It was the first time he hit her since she woke up from the scopolamine. She looked at him, shocked, holding her belly with insincere protectiveness to remind him of the precious cargo she carried. To remind him how important she really was to him, now more than ever.

"Oh stop it, it was just your face."

"And when is the Motherhood Summit again?" she asked accusingly, rubbing the feeling back into her cheek. "Feels like a bruiser."

"The summit is next week and I doubt your face will stay red for more than ten minutes. Enough with the dramatics. You know your role and that I will accept no less than your best performance." She looked back at him defiantly and he continued. "This is your test. It's a big one. If you don't deliver a flawless presentation at the summit, you go back on the scopolamine. Understood?"

She hesitated, hating the way he treated her like his slave. But she had no choice. She could not return to the state of unaware obedience; she needed her wits to protect herself. She needed to stay mentally aware for Sevrick's sake too. Eventually Mikhail would reset his sights on punishing her through Sevrick. When that time came, she had to be ready to stop him by any means necessary.

"I understand."

"Good girl. Let me love you before I go back to the war room for updates."

"I don't feel well. The baby has been kicking a lot today."

"I've got a little fighter in there, huh?" He bent down to kiss her belly. "Regardless, I need to release this desire I have for you before I go on with my day. It's amazing how attracted I am to you, even when you're swollen and hostile."

"You like what you can't have."

"Incorrect. I can have you whenever I please."

"Then you like the challenge," Arinadya sighed. "My mistake all along. If I was easy, you would have ditched me after one date and I'd have been free of you ages ago."

"But you didn't and here we are." He kissed the side of her neck and pushed her onto the bed. Her fire red hair contrasted drastically against the white sheets. He crawled on top of her, removing his clothes as he did. She didn't protest his advances anymore, she just accepted them as a means to an end. It was the price to keep her mind, the cost of her mental freedom. She kept her resistance to a minimum and he let her keep her thoughts. It was an unspoken game of strategy and she had to play smart. Her mind was the only thing left in her control.

It was quick; it always was. He left the room after he finished without a word. She was very aware that he got his real pleasure when screwing Roksana. Though it didn't bother Arinadya to share, it infuriated Roksana. Every moment he spent with his wife was an insulting reminder that she didn't come first. She was supposed to be one of Arinadya's new companions, along with Isidor, but the tension between them was high, toxic, and competitive.

It was a one-sided hatred. Arinadya couldn't be bothered with the poisonous melancholy she brought to the room every time she was tasked to tend to her. She had more important things to worry about, her survival being one of them. All that consumed her idle mind were plans of escape and reuniting with Sevrick. Though she needed the time away from the underground fortress to gather her thoughts, she realized now that she was wrong to leave the white elm. It was the overbearing weight of each day that drove her to that unwise decision. She didn't need to run, she just needed fresh air, a temporary change of scenery. With a proper explanation, any of the survivors, except Lizaveta, would have happily taken her into the woods for some time away from the depression of underground life. Looking back on it now, she felt like an idiot. None of this needed to happen but here she was, enslaved by Mikhail again and carrying his baby. Tears of anger formed in her eyes as she accepted the fault was all her own. She made the choice to leave the safety of the white elm in a moment of desperation. All of it was avoidable if she had just calmed down and thought about it rationally, but it was too late now.

The only positive thing to come of this disaster was the answer to her original woes: she still loved Sevrick, unwaveringly. He was the light in her dark; he was the whole of her heart. The time away was crucial, it didn't need to happen this way but it needed to happen. This alternate, unanticipated twist in her original plan sped up the realization of her unending love for Sevrick. Now she lived to return to him. To escape the fate of being tied to Mikhail's evilness as it will be remembered in human history and back to the man with whom she should have been with all along. The man who loved her unconditionally, and who she loved back. It was a rocky journey, and though her haemanism-fueled demons spent a long time trying to convince her she no longer deserved him, she was confident she never stopped loving him. The drugs just got in the way.

The baby kicked with force, catching her off guard. It hurt and she felt like she might throw up. She hurried to her personal bathroom, locked the door, and kneeled before the toilet. Nothing came. She sat back on her heels and tried to swallow the feeling of nausea. She wondered if it wasn't the kick that caused it, but the reminder that a piece of Mikhail was growing inside her.

That was the trigger. Her body lurched over the bowl and she began hurling uncontrollably. The vomit burned her throat as her stomach emptied and it turned into bile. The thick, yellow saliva hung from her lips after her final heaves. She stayed there, staring at the defiled toilet water, waiting to make sure it was really over. A minute passed and she let the side of her face rest against the cold porcelain. She flushed the toilet and the swirl of cool air brushed her face as the water disappeared and returned clean. The worst of it was over.

The week passed in a blur. Mikhail and his team were in and out making sure Arinadya knew exactly what to say and how to say it. They needed women to embrace this new chapter in their culture's history, they needed to be eager to take part in it.

Arinadya couldn't wait for it to be over. She would play along and deliver a compelling speech. It wouldn't take much to convince the masses to follow her lead; they adored her now more than ever. She was the glue holding them to this lifestyle, she was the reason they overlooked Mikhail's callous and demeaning treatment of them. He cared about the millions of nameless faces comprising the population of his empire as a whole, but in his mind they were irrelevant. They really were no better than farm animals to him: they lived on his land, made up his livestock, and were easily replaced. They were part of his collection, a small piece in his enormous empire. In reality, they were the most important piece, the foundation to his empire, but they did not realize it. Instead of recognizing the crucial part they played in all of Mikhail's success, they followed blindly and without purpose, as ignorant to their shepherd's intentions as a herd of cattle.

She woke up with another onslaught of vomiting. After an hour hugging the toilet, she reemerged from her bathroom and saw Isidor and Roksana sitting on her bed, waiting.

"Were you sick?" Isidor asked with minimal concern.

"I'm fine."

"Good, we have to help prep you for the summit. The stylist team will be here in fifteen minutes."

Arinadya took a deep breath and prepared for the fashion assault she was about to endure. She hadn't missed her stylist team; they were overbearing, harsh, uncaring. All that mattered to them was making her appear as pretty as a photoshopped picture. She recalled the days surrounding her wedding and the hair tugging, face painting, and corset-choking calamity of it all. The end product was flawless, but the hours spent with stranger's hands all over her wasn't worth it. Then, she was on silve. Then, she wanted to look like the perfect haeman so the torture provided her with a final image she desired. Now she was checked out, mentally removed from this world and its shallow afflictions.

While she was shocked she maintained her patience as a haeman with her stylists, she supposed she took some small delight in the process. She wasn't nearly as strong physically now, but she imagined her patience would not hold during the oncoming storm of rough pampering.

They arrived on time and entered the foyer with boisterous chatter. Arinadya could hear them from the opposite side of the palace. Their echoes resonated down every hall. She smiled thinking of Mikhail's aggravation at this unwelcome noise.

Gavriil entered her bedroom first, pushing a cart full of hair styling tools. He still wore the contacts that turned his eyes demon-black and sported the same bleach blond buzz cut. He smiled at her, his surgically pointed teeth sharper than she remembered. It was spring and the t-shirt he wore revealed bite-marks along his forearms. The razor teeth indents scarred like shark bites and he had large collections of them anywhere his mouth could reach.

Izolda came in next. She pulled a rack draped with outfit options behind her. Stoic and serious as ever, she made eye contact with no

226

one as she entered. She had a new scar stemming from the corner of her left eye. It was jagged and ugly and Arinadya assumed it wasn't an intentional scar. Her curiosity was piqued. She wanted to know the story behind it, but her better judgment told her not to ask. She wasn't stronger than them anymore; if she angered them and they lashed out, she couldn't defend herself.

Olesya sauntered in last, closing the door behind her. Her wild blonde curls were longer now and she wore bright purple lipstick.

"Can't believe you're no longer haeman," she said, walking right up to Arinadya.

"Yeah, well, you can't have a healthy baby when you're on drugs." No one knew about her escape into the woods or the rehabilitation she went through. No one knew that she was back in the palace against her will. She could not reveal this fact to anyone. Not only would Mikhail find new and more horrific ways to torture her if she did, but the public's adoration for her was the only thing keeping her safe. If she lost it, not only would Mikhail have no reason to keep her alive but there was no telling what the masses would do. While it's possible some might follow her, she had a feeling most would grow to despise her for abandoning them. Their worship would turn into something nasty, a love gone sour, and that kind of hatred was much worse than any they might hold toward Mikhail. She could not turn into the new villain, the new target for their rage, at least not while she was trapped in Russia.

"So how did they cure you? Everyone else who tried has died. How'd you survive the withdrawals?"

She didn't know how to respond, so she lied. "I really wanted to be a mother, so I fought through them."

Gavriil eyed her suspiciously, but Izolda voiced her disbelief.

"I have trouble believing that. If all it took was the will to live, many others would survive the process too. I have friends who

227

have died from the addiction, good people who wanted to live, wanted to decrease their intake in order to get healthy again. It didn't matter how much they decreased their dosage of silve in an attempt to minimize their haemanism, the damage was already done. The withdrawals killed them."

"I don't know what to tell you. I'm not a doctor."

"It's because you were healed by money," Gavriil sneered. "The council is keeping the cure from the public. They are letting us die while the lot of you are able to skip happily in and out of the addiction's grip. You can control the way in which it controls you because you know how to clean out your system every so often. It's why none of *you* are dying but the masses are."

"Then explain Milena," Isidor snapped back. Milena was a close friend of hers and she still struggled with her death daily.

The room went quiet.

Roksana stepped into the conversation. "The difference between those of us in the council and the low-life's dying on the streets is our self-control. Milena was an exception; she had great self-control but was too sick to be saved by the time they tried. As for the rest of us, we know when enough is enough. We can stop ourselves from drowning in narcotics. Our discipline is what separates us from the majority."

"That's a rather broad judgment." Gavriil stepped up to Roksana, getting in her face. "I don't abuse the drugs, I don't drain my blood till I'm on the brink of death. I am a classy and clean haeman. Yet, because I'm only a lowly hairdresser, my application to join the council is continually dismissed. I've sent it five times in the past year and I haven't even received a phone call."

"Perhaps it is because you are an overbearing lunatic who is harassing the council board members instead of waiting patiently for a reply."

Gavriil lost his cool and lunged at Roksana. He was taller than her but just as skinny and his strength was no match for hers. She was in the council and she was among the most powerful haemans. Without much effort, she removed his hands from her neck and turned him so he was in a chokehold.

"You're lucky I need you right now, otherwise I'd have already snapped your neck." She turned him with speed and punched him in the eye. He fell to the floor unconscious.

"You hit him too hard," Isidor huffed. "You better hope he wakes up soon, Arinadya needs to be ready within the hour."

"Dress her first," Roksana instructed Izolda, who immediately got to work. She pulled her two favorite dresses off the rack and held them up for Arinadya's viewing. One was a skin-tight, black turtleneck dress with long sleeves and a short hem. The other was a bright red baby doll frock. In both dresses her long legs would be the main attraction.

"Personally, I say you go with the black dress. Though the red dress has more opportunity to showcase your ever-growing bust, it isn't formfitting and the baby bump will get lost beneath the shape of the dress. The black dress will show off your belly and your skinny legs, which thankfully have not been altered by your pregnancy weight gain."

"That's fine." Arinadya did not care either way. She took off her clothes and held her arm out. "Hand it here."

She slipped the dress on easily and Izolda played with the cloth of the turtleneck.

In a moment of bravery, Arinadya asked about the disfigured scar on Izolda's face.

"What happened to your eye?"

Izolda stopped fussing with the dress and glared at her menacingly.

"Is that any of your concern?"

"No, but I was curious." She tried to sound confident even though she felt Izolda wishing to give her a matching scar. "Didn't mean to upset you."

Izolda went back to fixing the dress so it laid properly.

"My brother did it."

"It looks painful," she replied, unable to disguise her repulsion as she examined the hideous mutilation. "I'm sorry."

"Don't be. I quite like it. It's all I have to remember him by."

"What do you mean?"

"I killed him shortly after he gave it to me."

This confession was enough to kill the conversation as well. Arinadya was now sorry she asked.

Izolda finished the final touches and directed Arinadya to a body length mirror. The black fabric covered her neck, making it disappear and subsequently causing her large, defined skull to stand out. Not only did it enhance the baby bump and her sexy legs, but also her undeniably beautiful face. Despite being free of make-up, it radiated. Her skin was healthy and tight over her jawline, and her cheekbones were high and meaty. Even though she was no longer haeman, she hadn't lost the supermodel beauty she achieved as one. Ever since her recovery she avoided looking at herself in the mirror, so seeing herself dressed up now was overwhelming. She really did look beautiful. As this image of herself cast a permanent mark on her vision, she did her best not to enjoy it. She could not let herself enjoy any part of this life. It was too dangerous. She was still a recovering addict, she could easily slip back down the slippery slope of haemanism if she wasn't careful. She *had* to control her thoughts and keep them far from any happy reminiscing.

"This works," she said, breaking eye contact with herself in the mirror. "What's next?"

"Hair," Izolda answered, giving Gavriil a light push with her foot. He was still unconscious, so Olesya went over to him and tried shaking him awake.

"You're messing up our routine," she complained to Gavriil, who couldn't hear her. "I can't do her makeup until her hair is done. It will melt off beneath the heat of your hairdryer."

"You're going to have to make due," Roksana said and pointed at the clock. "We can't waste any time."

"Fine," she replied. She yanked Arinadya's arm and sat her on the stool she brought. Olesya smacked the gum between her lips as she painted her face. Layer after layer, turning her natural beauty into something fake and unattainable by society. Her skin was smooth, flawless, and glowing. Black eyeliner and mascara framed her blue eyes, making them appear otherworldly. Red lipstick coated her lips and acted as a reminder of who she was: haeman royalty.

"All done," Olesya announced, collapsing into a chair and disappearing behind a tabloid magazine. Roksana successfully coaxed Gavriil awake with a bucket of ice water to the face. Drenched and freezing, he was not happy when he came to. He dried off the best he could before he started to style Arinadya's hair.

Without its previous length, there wasn't much he could do with it. He evened out the ends and gave her blunt bangs to add drama. The red hair framed her face perfectly, enhancing her attractive features even more. Her blue eyes shone at him as he finished.

"Who knew bangs would have that effect on your eyes?" He shivered. "It's almost creepy how they glow."

Arinadya kept her opinion to herself and thought that nothing could possibly be creepier than the blacked out contact lenses he currently wore.

"Am I done?" she asked without looking in the mirror.

"Don't you want to see how you look?" Roksana asked, looking her up and down. She could not mask the jealousy in her voice.

Arinadya shook her head. She did not want to get any more enjoyment out of her haemanized appearance.

"I'm sure I look fine, let's get to the summit. I don't want to forget my speech or lose my nerve."

Roksana shrugged and Izolda took out a pair of stilettos.

"Wear what you like on the drive there, but you'll need to muster the strength to wear these during your speech."

Arinadya took the heels and carried them to the limo with her. She'd dreaded the moment she'd need to put them on. Carrying the baby weight was hard enough in slippers, carrying it while on stilts was miserable to imagine. She wasn't looking forward to it.

Mikhail was waiting for her in the limo. When she slid into the car, he grazed her over with greedy desire.

"This look suits you," he said, keeping his dirty thoughts to himself, though she could feel his perversions fill the entire limo. Roksana entered and could sense her lover's desire on his wife instead of her. Her bitterness only added to the uncomfortable vibes filtering through the car.

"Let's get on with it," Arinadya requested after Isidor, Kirill, and her stylist team took their seats.

"Driver," Mikhail called out, "take us to Marsovo Polye Square."

The car sped out of the Winter Palace driveway and toward their destination. Mikhail slid his hand up the bottom of Arinadya's short skirt. She glanced at him with annoyance but he did not stop.

"You're so sexy," he purred into her ear.

"Quit it," she whispered, slapping his hand away from her. "I'm trying to focus."

His eyes flashed black at her public rejection. Everyone in the car pretended not to notice but they all saw her resist him. He leaned in closer and spoke so low that she could barely hear him.

"Remedy your defiance."

She took a deep breath and grabbed his hand. She then leaned in and kissed his cheek.

"Later, baby," she said seductively for all to hear. He smirked at her, happy with the recovery.

She sat back against her seat and closed her eyes for a moment. She felt overwhelmed and stressed; faking this life was a lot of pressure and she was scared. Any small misstep or mistake could cost her life, or worse, Sevrick's. With a deep breath she re-opened her eyes and put on the fake smile she perfected in the mirror ages ago.

Survival was a game that she planned to win.

Chapter 34

Marsovo Polye Square was crowded with rowdy haemans. As usual, a stage was set up with a chain-link barrier separating it from the masses. The limo inched through the mob and a guard unlocked the fence so the car could drive through. Once inside, the gate was relocked to ensure the royals and their crew were safe from the mob. The cameramen were sending a live feed to the enormous screens set up around the square. Every move made after leaving the limo would be broadcast for everyone in the crowd to see. The recording would be aired to the rest of Russia that evening after a proper edit.

The stylist crew left the limo first, followed by Isidor, Roksana, and Kirill. Mikhail exited next and the crowd erupted in cheers. Arinadya took a deep breath and followed him out. At the sight of her, the adoring crowd burst into a frenzy. They shook the fence and hollered in frantic tones for her attention. She held her composure but could not silence the fear this type of desperate love gave her. It was unstable, unpredictable, and dangerous. Their love was suffocating and she feared it might kill her one day, like a child who hugs a puppy too tight and accidentally kills it in their grip.

She couldn't think about it. She ignored the noise her followers made and climbed the steps to the stage with Mikhail. President Dobrynin was already there and as soon as they took their throne-like seats, he spoke.

"My people," he said into the microphone, "thank you for coming this afternoon. As you all know, an issue we face as haemans is the lack of reproduction. Without younger generations being born into our world we will die out within the next few decades. We are well on our way to controlling all regions of the planet and cannot let all our hard work go to waste. We cannot become extinct; we will not let that happen. We are a new race of human and we must endure until the end of time." The crowd cheered, feeding into the president's speech. "Today, our beloved haeman leaders have come to deliver great news. If we listen and engage in their plans to save our race, we can thrive long after Russia conquers the world."

The crowd cheered as Mikhail stood, took Arinadya's hand, and escorted her to the microphone. He kissed her on the cheek before taking a step back and leaving her front and center. The crowd became hushed. All eyes were on her and everyone patiently waited for her to speak. She was nervous but she couldn't show it. Haemans don't get nervous, certainly not the powerful haeman princess. She was sexy, confident, and commanding. She needed to fake her old persona if she wanted to make it through this day without tarnishing the only safety net keeping her protected: her image.

"Hello, my dear haemans," she began. "It is lovely to see all of your faces once more. I have been gone too long, though you surely understand my reasons." She placed a hand over her small baby bump and the crowd murmured in fascination. "Now that it has been a few months adjusting to my pregnancy, I feel secure in leaving the palace to address all of you. You may be wondering how this was possible, how did I manage to be with child as a haeman? The drugs are surely a hindrance to the process, hence why no one has gotten pregnant in ages, and exposure to them is, of course, unhealthy for a developing fetus. The answer is simple. I am currently free of silve."

The crowd's whispering grew louder and she could tell they were unsure how to feel about their haeman role model abandoning the lifestyle, even if only for a short amount of time for a noble purpose. She scanned the faces nearest to her and saw a range of emotions displayed. Some were visibly angry and wore scowls of betrayal. Others wore expressions of admiration that their devoted haeman leader was willing to give up something precious for the greater good of their community. But what peaked her interest were those whose faces shifted to deep contemplation. Their curiosity was apparent, and while some were simply unsure how she survived the rehabilitation process, she saw a handful of people whose questions went further. Could they be rehabilitated too? Could their own haemanism be stripped, returning them to their old selves? Though there were few, she caught the small vibe amongst the larger one: there were haemans amongst them that wished to abandon this life. Hearing her speak was an unexpected realization that there was a way out. They had no clue of her attempt to escape and figured she was only doing this in order to have a baby, but hearing her say she was clean but still alive gave them quiet hope.

"The process of rehabilitation is complicated, but not impossible. I'm sure this angers some of you but please do not jump to conclusions. We are not hiding a cure from anyone, we only just perfected it recently. Though it worked on me about four months ago, we wanted to make sure the procedure was flawless before revealing it to all of you. Now that it is ready, we must begin the process of repopulating our culture. As you may have heard, this gathering is being referred to as the Motherhood Summit. That's because our intention this afternoon is to recruit strong and willing females for this journey. We need mothers; we need women who see the bigger picture and want to play a pivotal role in our history. I understand the thought of cleaning your system of silve is frightening; many of us can no longer remember our lives without the strength of haemanism, but we must do this if we want our legacy to go beyond current times. We need women who understand the importance of the sacrifice they'd be making and who aren't afraid to make it. I did it, and so can you."

The crowd's suspicious and angry emotions seemed to level off after hearing her explanation, request, and encouragement. Now that the wide range of anger was temporarily muted, she could feel the curiosity and implications of this revelation much more. It wasn't something she expected to encounter today, or ever. She always thought she was alone in her constant internal battle while she was still haeman, that no one else felt the conflicting struggle between accepting life as a haeman and craving something different, something more; whether it be their old life or a new one. But she wasn't alone. She could feel the secretive hope radiate out of the crowd. The feeling was in the minority but she felt it and recognized it as the feeling she felt before almost jumping to her death. She wasn't sure how to reach these people, but it gave her hope that there were others hidden within the evil that wanted out.

Mikhail stepped to the microphone. "There are sign-up stations located around the perimeter of Marsovo Poyle Square. It won't start right away, but we want to get the process started. We need to get organized so we can begin as soon as our facilities are ready. If you have any questions, submit them at the registration hubs and we will address them publically at our next summit. Sign-up is open indefinitely and we hope to find many willing participants." His last line was a threat, indicating if there weren't enough willing participants they'd enlist women against their will. Arinadya scanned the crowd to see if they caught his warning but no one appeared outraged. If they were, they hid it.

"Thank you again for coming," President Dobrynin said after taking the microphone back from Mikhail. "We will keep you updated on the status of the motherhood initiative."

They exited the stage and joined their crew on the ground floor. The crowd grew loud again and those closest to the fence became unruly as they watched their idolized leaders enter the limo and leave their sight.

"You did well," Mikhail said to Arinadya once everyone was in their seats and the door was shut. "I suspect there will be droves of women hoping to follow in your footsteps."

Arinadya did not respond; she hoped he was wrong. All she wanted was the spark of doubt she felt emanating from the crowd to be real. If it was and if those people stepped forward, maybe she could help them. The men would be tricky, but the women could be freed if they volunteered to be a mother. After they were healed she could carefully determine who was looking for an escape. All she had to do was tell them how and where to go, then the rest was on them. It was the least she could do after enabling this lifestyle for so long. She wasn't to blame—that would be an unfair burden to carry. They were all adults capable of making their own choices, but she could take responsibility for promoting the haeman way with enthusiasm to people who looked up to her. They followed her guidance and she should have been stronger in the early days. Instead of inviting death, she should have taken a stand and rallied any who felt similarly to follow her out. To lead them to a new and better life without the drugs. She supposed it never crossed her mind because she did not realize others felt the same as her. She always assumed she was an anomaly hidden within the masses, that her desire to end the mental torture that came with the haemanism was a strange side effect that only affected her. But she was wrong, she knew that now, and if she could find a way to go about it carefully, maybe she could begin that revolution this time around. It would be hard because no one, except those on her side, could be privy to what she was doing. She wasn't sure how to find the few amongst thousands who wanted to be saved, but if Mikhail found a way to make the rehabilitation process work, with or without Leonid, then the best place to start was with the mothers.

Chapter 35

The remaining trek back to the white elm was miserable. Anytime someone tried to talk, Nikolai found a way to snap at them. Though everyone was grieving Isaak's death, he was handling it the worst and everyone suffered because of it. Ruslan stayed toward the back of the crowd with Zakhar contemplating and overthinking how to break the news to his brother. Alexsei was going to be devastated. The stress kept Ruslan on the brink of tears. His strong, unbreakable demeanor was now weak and shattered. Their leader was incapacitated with grief; Isaak was like a son to him.

They had to keep Nikolai and Ruslan separated. Although they were both hit hardest by the death, their coping methods were so opposite they almost got into a brawl the one time they tried to talk about it. The situation was tense and the remaining men dealt with the tragedy the best they could. Getting home without any more casualties, from haemans or each other, was the immediate priority.

Nikolai insisted on being the one to transport Isaak's body back. Both Konstantin and Benedikt offered, but he refused their help. For two weeks, he dragged the lifeless adolescent body on a makeshift sled. It did not slide easily in the snow because it had no blades and the wood needed constant replacing, but Nikolai would not let anyone help.

"Everyone, wait," Benedikt called out to the rest of the group. He stayed close to Nikolai during their journey back to the white elm. He did not bother him with conversation, but offered him silent support. He felt like an older brother to Isaak too, treating him as he had treated Filipp back when things were good. Being nearby, ready to help, eased his own grief.

The men who walked ahead of them turned and saw Isaak's body lying face first in the snow. Nikolai's face contorted with enraged agony. He went to the body and turned it upright, then went to find wood to replace the broken piece. All the men walked closer to wait as he stubbornly fixed the sled by himself. If they tried to help he'd scream at them, and when they didn't help he screamed at himself. It was hard to watch. Every time it happened, Nikolai had a breakdown.

"Should I offer a hand?" Marat asked the men around him.

"I wouldn't bother. He never lets anyone help," Leonid answered.

Nikolai came back with a thick branch that would fit in the spot of the broken one. It still had pine needles attached that would drag in the back with the rest of the branches. Somehow, despite his grief, Nikolai made the sled double as a tool to cover their tracks.

He began to mend the sled and Marat stepped forward, unable to resist the urge to help.

"Go away," Nikolai yelled as Marat perched next to him and tried to help him with all the pieces.

"Let me help. I won't say a word."

Nikolai glared up at him with unwarranted fury. His face was covered in angry tears. "I said go away." Then he shoved Marat so hard he fell backward. After absorbing the shock, he stood up and cursed beneath his breath. He left Nikolai alone and joined the other men where they watched. After ten minutes, Nikolai fixed the sled for his fallen friend and started walking forward without a word.

The trip was tough, but they made it. As they crossed beneath the abandoned homes of the Scots, they saw the white elm in the distance. After determining the coast was clear, the men could not contain their relief. They jogged with smiles toward their home and made their way beneath the root-laced entrance of the white elm to the friends they hadn't seen for so long.

There was a large crowd welcoming them home. It was hard to filter through but Sevrick made it to the other side and found Elena.

"Isaak?" Elena had tears in her eyes.

"Yeah. It was horrible."

"What happened?" she asked with sincere despair. He buried his face into his hands. He did not want to relive the last two weeks. Part of him felt he could've prevented it if he hadn't dozed off. It was a terrible thought and it ate him up.

"It has been the worst two weeks of my life. Out of all the men there, the youngest one died. It wasn't fair, it wasn't right. I keep playing the incident over and over in my mind, futilely trying to change the outcome in my memory, driving myself to insanity in the process. I haven't even come to terms with it in my own head yet." His voice was growing in volume as he spoke, "If I rehash it out loud right now I will freak out."

"Okay, calm down, I get it," Elena said. "Answer one question and we can talk about it another time. Was it the haemans?"

"Yes."

She nodded, accepting his answer with grave understanding. During their remaining trek they were so busy trying to handle the meltdowns of Nikolai and Ruslan that the rest of the men didn't really get the chance to grieve. They had to contain their sorrow in order to keep their dangerous journey through the forest on track. If anyone else had a breakdown, the whole situation would have become impossible to contain. Now that he was safe at the white elm he was allowed a moment of weakness. The despair hit him all at once and he retreated to his room.

He knew he shouldn't feel guilty; even if he had stayed awake there was no telling whether he could have prevented the haemans from yanking Isaak out from under the tree. But the memory looped vividly and the more he thought about it, the more he fabricated the truth and twisted it into something he could have controlled. He wasn't sure why he was torturing himself, but the torment felt deserved. If Isaak had to die, he and the other men better suffer too.

By nightfall, the memory was so warped he couldn't distinguish reality from his mind's tricks. It was exhausting trying to differentiate the two. Eventually, the effort knocked him out.

He woke up fifteen hours later. He changed out of his filthy clothes and headed to the washroom. A family was already using the well, but they knew who he was and what he went through, so they finished washing their youngest son and let him cut in front of them.

The lukewarm water trickled over his body, creating trails through the dirt collected on his skin. After a brief moment reveling in the shower's warmth, he scrubbed himself and cleaned his hair. His dark hair had gotten long and he had to keep the strands away from his face as the shampoo rinsed out. He wrapped himself in a towel and left the stall.

"Thanks for letting me cut. Hope I didn't take too long," he said to the family still waiting.

"You barely took five minutes. It was no problem at all," the father said. "We appreciate what you and the others did. The least you deserve is a warm shower."

Sevrick smiled and nodded at the man with gratitude. It was a new day and his distress over Isaak's death would stay quiet. It wasn't about him, it was about Isaak and his grieving family. His sorrow did not compare to theirs and it was more important for him to act as their rock than to burden them with his own tormented feelings surrounding the boy's death. His focus was to be a stable friend during this tragic time.

A memorial service was organized for the weekend, so today he had time to refocus on Rina. He needed to find Elena and ask her what happened.

He found her with Nina and Sofiya. They were watching Agnessa, Kira, and Maks huddled around a complicated puzzle. The image of a horse was almost complete but they were struggling with the face. Sevrick knelt down and found two pieces for one of the nostrils.

Maks snapped his head toward him and lost all focus on the puzzle.

"Did you find a DVD player during your travels?"

He had completely forgotten about that.

"No, we didn't. I'm so sorry. We will be heading toward St. Petersburg soon. I will try again when I'm there."

He was disappointed but did not express it verbally. He was young but understood a device to play movies was the least of anyone's concerns. He focused on the puzzle and fit a piece near the horse's eye.

Sevrick stood up and went to Elena.

"We need to talk."

"I know."

"What happened with Rina?"

"She left of her own free will."

Kira's attention was perked. She turned her head and addressed the adults.

"I'm sorry, Sevrick," she said, her voice heavy with a burden that was not hers to carry. "I thought she was getting wood for Alexsei. She tricked me."

Nina sighed. "We already told you, you did nothing wrong."

"I still feel bad."

"It's not your fault," Elena reminded the girl. "You didn't know who she was, what she had been through, or what she intended to do. You were just trying to help."

"I'm sorry you got dragged into this," Sevrick added, then knelt next to Kira and gave her a hug. He knew Kira held his opinion in high-esteem. "It's not your fault, okay?"

He let go and Kira looked up at him with relief.

"Okay," she agreed, focusing back on the puzzle. Sevrick realized he needed to take the conversation elsewhere. He took Elena's hand and escorted her into the hall.

"I don't understand how this happened, or why."

"Me either. There was no warning sign, no reason to believe she had any intention of leaving. She and Liza weren't getting along but the rest of us were helping her out and trying to bond with her."

"Is Lizaveta the reason she left?"

"It's hard to say." Elena was torn between protecting Lizaveta's feelings and holding her accountable. She did not want to hurt her any further after their fight, so she was honest but neutral. "I'm sure their heated conversation helped shape Rina's thought process, but the decision to leave was all her own. Liza was tough on her, but the rest of us were on her side."

"Did she say anything before she left? Any clue why she was leaving or what her intentions were?"

"No," Elena said, "but she left a note for you."

"Where is it?"

"Leonid's desk in the laboratory. Top drawer."

Sevrick left without saying another word. He darted through the long maze of hallways toward the medical laboratory. In the main common room, he bumped into Lizaveta mid-dash.

"What's wrong?" she asked, startled by his frantic demeanor. The sight of her angered him. He placed a hand between them to prevent her from getting any closer.

"Not now." Then he continued on his way, leaving a confused and offended Lizaveta behind.

He made it to Leonid's desk and retrieved the letter from the drawer.

Sevrick,

I'm sorry I left without saying goodbye. I love you too much to stay. I will head away from the city and cross the border. I will heal and learn to love myself again outside of Russia and away from the haemanism. I will do it on my own, as I told you I believe I need to. You will never be happy with me around in this condition. Being here is holding us both back, so I must go. I hope you can understand my choice. I will be okay, and so will you. I am grateful for all you have done for me but it's time I go. It's what's best for us both, so please don't fight it.

I'll love you always, in this life and the next.

Rina

His heart raced. She had no intention of finding Mikhail and reclaiming her old life. Everything he saw on the news was forced upon her. *Was she kidnapped in her attempt to leave Russia? How were they making her behave so compliantly in front of the cameras?* His thoughts ran wild and his fear for her grew as the answers he came up with were terrifying. He had to save her. She was a prisoner in Mikhail's clutches and no one knew it but him. The rest of the haemans thought she was her regular haeman self and the Clandes did not know her well enough to trust she hadn't changed back. She was alone, trapped, and the only person who could help her now was him.

He'd be heading into the city soon to attempt an assassination on Mikhail, but his plans needed to involve Rina's rescue as well. His friends would not want any part of this additional mission; they spent enough time trying to help him save her prior to this new development. They were over it. Once their assassination plan was set, he'd find a way to work Rina into it too. Maybe Artem would help.

She still loved him, she said so in the letter. That was all he needed to know. Confidence restored, his quest to save his love was revived.

Chapter 36

Melanie Cane was one of the haeman leaders of the New York City rebellion. WMBN was entirely converted and the station was in a slow transition toward haemanized news stories. At first they kept the content similar to their old stuff but as the revolution grew larger and the haemans garnered victories throughout the city, their stories shifted and their tone became more sympathetic to the cause. Having the news play a part in the conversion was huge. The American citizens listened to what they said, they believed what they were selling, and they trusted them. Today was their first story on the "science" behind haemanism. It was a last ditch effort to convert those who still resisted.

Melanie helped prepare the script Parker Brown and Mindy Chen would recite during *News Day New York*. The belief that the lifestyle was a biological phenomenon and intended for humans by nature was the pitch they planned to use on those who were still against it. The lie that it was natural wouldn't work like it had in the early days in Russia; they didn't have the means to place silve into their water system. The government wasn't on their side, therefore they could not slip the drug to the population to convince them it was a natural blessing. They'd know their blood was only powerful due to the silve, so they needed to present it in a light that appeared less harmful.

In the greenroom, Melanie laid out three lines of silve for her and the news anchors to snort. They each took a hit then drew blood. Melanie slit the side of her wrist and sucked on the wet cut, Mindy pricked her pointer finger on a needle, making a minimal mark, and Parker chewed on the inside of his cheek until it bled. After the high was ripe, the anchors took their seats in front of the cameras and prepared to go live. The anchors wore make-up to hide the marks but they couldn't disguise the overall transformation: their faces were gaunt, their eyes sunken, and their demeanors intensified.

Melanie stood in the dark next to the main camera and counted down from five. Her fingers were visible to the show's hosts and they saw their cue to begin.

"Rise and shine. It's time for *News Day New York*. I'm Mindy Chen."

"And I'm Parker Brown. Today we have a riveting story to share with you regarding the science behind haemanism and why so many passionate citizens are rioting to be heard."

"Scientists have studied the silve and its effect on our blood to see what is *really* going on. The story is eye-opening."

"But before we get to that, we have a clip sent in from Russia of the beloved royals at the park. Take a look."

The show cut to a video of Mikhail and Arinadya strolling through Catherine Garden. The princess was visibly pregnant and showing off her baby bump beneath a tight red shirt. The prince was holding her hand and waving to the cameras.

"We are very excited for the arrival of our son," Mikhail said to the nearest reporter. "We cannot wait to share our joy with the world."

The feed cut back to Mindy and Parker.

"Beautiful couple. Such an inspiration to us all."

"It's a shame our government is accusing them of instigating the current violence in America," Parker expressed. "The country is dramatically divided on this issue, but once you see what our scientists discovered, I think you'll understand the uproar. If they were behind the spread of silve, then they gave us a gift, not a curse."

"It's only turned sour because leading officials have ignored the desperate pleas of our citizens. They refuse to listen, driving innocent people to extremes in order to be heard."

"It's not much different than other pivotal turning points in American history. The leadership is stubborn, set in their old ways. The people are evolving while the government remains stagnant. And of course, those prone to listen to what politicians say without questioning their motives or authenticity have been a plague to our culture for centuries. If we don't challenge old mindsets and remain open to new ones, we will never evolve as a race. We've seen it time and time again with the acceptance of different genders, races, religions, sexual orientations, and cultures. Now it's an internal lifestyle change, adopted by humans across the board. The government is fighting against the change we all want. Science backs it up as the next step in our evolutionary development. If we resist it and choose not to take part in this revolution, we will be left behind."

Parker stepped back in. "We, as Americans, will disappear as the rest of the world overpowers us. We will become primitive versions of humans, being cast aside as insignificant because we denied this gift from nature. Yes, there is a chemical component involved, but that small aide is minor in the greater picture. It is a means to an end, it is the key to the enhancement of our species."

"Take a look at this video created by the National Academy of Science. It explains everything."

The clip opened up with a scientist in a white lab jacket. He stood in front of a table with microscopes and a large chemistry set. His eyes were dark and his face emaciated. The scars on the backs of his hands indicated he was haeman, though an oblivious viewer would never notice.

"My name is Elias Steinhardt, PhD in Science from Princeton University, and I am here to breakdown the new phenomenon sweeping America. Many of you have heard the terms silve and haeman thrown around the past few months. The words have created a scary connotation as many correlate them with violence, immorality, and death. While those assumptions are valid concerns, they are subjective effects of the new lifestyle taking over our culture. Let me break the words down." Elias walked to a chalkboard and began scribbling as he talked.

"Silve is a form of benzoyl-methyl-ecgonine with an unknown chemical component that turns the substance silver. Hence the name. The base of the matter is more commonly known as cocaine, which understandably scares most people. What changes this narcotic from harmful to productive is the unknown component. Though we do not have a name for it, we were able to isolate and dissect the chemical to determine its base. It shows traces of botanical and herbal roots, as well as a combination of terpenoids and pheromones. What that tells us is that the unknown chemical is made up of natural elements; all components that can be found in nature. Cocaine is also found in nature. This gives us reason to believe that silve is not in fact meant to be harmful to humans if used correctly. Like anything created and grown from the earth, it has a valid and useful purpose. It was placed on earth for us to discover. With moderation and care, silve will rocket humans into our next phase of evolution." He erased his frenzied notes from the board and began again.

"The term haeman comes from the word hematophagy, also spelt haematophagy, which is the practice of feeding on blood. This new breed of human, while complicated to understand, is a non-threat to others as the subject only consumes its *own* blood. Recirculating the silve-laced blood through one's system increases

251

all human functions. Haemans are more lucid, their physical strength is amplified, their motor skills are augmented, and the chemicals in their brains are rewired to work cohesively. Thoughts become fluid and neurons operate more logically instead of firing against each other, creating the messy dilemma of human emotions. A haeman's mental functions are crisp, deliberate, and comprehensive. They can organize their intentions around a solid goal without worry of the various implications that often thwart us from achieving what we set out to do. The lifestyle that has been brought into our country is not a bad thing. If we embrace it as a gift from nature, we can thrive as an evolved version of our former selves. Granted, nothing was wrong with us before, but imagine the accomplishments we could make as a race if we adopted this new way of life. We made great strides as humans in the past hundred years, but as haemans, we could double the progress. What we accomplished in a century could be completed in five decades. The growth would be exponential and would benefit the entire planet. I know everyone has heard the pleas of their local haemans begging them to join in this new life. I implore everyone who doubts their sincerity to absorb what I've said today and reconsider their stand on the issue. The NAS website has added an inquiry board for those of you with additional questions. Please reach out to us if you are confused or unsure and we will do our best to help you make the decision that's best for your future."

The screen flashed with the National Academy of Sciences website as well as a number to call with questions. The feed cut back to Mindy and Parker.

"Powerful information, Mindy. So nice to see the scientific breakdown of the lifestyle brought to us through haemanism. If you think about it, it really is natural. Why would something so advantageous be put on this earth if it wasn't intended for us to discover and utilize for the greater good?" Parker said.

"Agreed. Just like all things in life, it is only harmful if it is abused."

"Everything in moderation," Parker agreed.

"Haemans are being detained and imprisoned, in some cases killed, all over the country. What have these people done to deserve such treatment?"

"Accepting a gift from nature into their lives is no grounds for prejudice," Parker added. "As a race, we should have learned by now. Hatred solves nothing."

They were aware this was not a case of injustice similar to situations Americans had faced in the past, but they hoped to make it seem as such. They wanted to exploit the masses. Utilizing their media leverage, they manipulated their viewers and strategically used their sympathies against them.

"So true. Fantastic segment. If you have any thoughts or insight, please share it with us on our social media page. Let's get the conversation for acceptance started!"

"Until next time," Parker said, signing off.

The station cut to commercials and the hosts relaxed. Melanie approached their anchor desk with a vile of silve. She arranged three lines and they enjoyed a hit together.

"Brilliant," she told them. "This should spark the other haeman-operated stations to follow suit."

"That's all the stations in New York, except WCTX." Mindy rubbed her nose as she complained about the only outlier. "It's likely they'll never convert."

"Too conventional. They belong to the government. The right-wing owns them."

"Oh well," Melanie said. "No one ever took them seriously anyway. They are a joke in their own right. We sell lies, but so do they. It's arguable whose agenda is more detrimental."

"Not ours," Mindy retorted. "I understand it's a bit medieval to force a lifestyle upon a country, but it really is for the greater good. We all know it, we all believe in what haemanism has to offer us as a species. At least we have confidence in the propaganda we spout."

"Agreed." Parker stood, chewing his cheek as he did so.

The three left their stations and prepared for the night's riot. Times Square was a scene of rebellion every evening from dusk till dawn. It had gotten to a point where it was no longer safe for non-haemans. It began as a rally to recruit; now it was a party for the recruited. The sins committed beneath the bright lights each night were immeasurable. The daily disorderly gathering that once called for unification had turned into a depraved rager. The cops didn't bother regulating it anymore; too many had died trying.

They changed from their business clothes into their new haeman fashion. Melanie wore a tight black dress and smeared a thick layer of black eyeliner around her hazel eyes. She and Mindy both wore dagger rings meant for slashing wounds wherever they pleased when they needed a hit. Parker wore a necklace with a sword pendant. All three were in the phase of haemanism where collecting scars was a priority. They wanted to prove their loyalty to the cause and showcase their commitment. Their addictions were deep and they reveled in the upcoming war. They heard rumors that the Russian military was slowly moving through Europe. There was no proof or documentation of it, but word was being passed along through the state-based haeman contacts. Soon the United States would succumb to Mikhail's reign. The majority of the population was already converted. The U.S. government, military, and conservative population would be in the sparse minority by the time the fight was brought to them, and it would be an easy feat to eliminate them with Russia's military on their side.

It was a shame their leaders did not see haemanism in the same light as their people. Melanie couldn't help but feel a bit disappointed that her country was refusing to partner with Russia in the next phase of human history. It wasn't worth dwelling on though. Alliances were made and lines were drawn; now, they waited for their side to conquer all.

Chapter 37

The Irish haemans had struggled for weeks to sway the street rats of Britain to join their side. While Spain and Portugal tackled France, their job was converting the United Kingdom. It was a daunting task. Ireland was significantly smaller, less influential, and already dismissed as irrelevant by most Brits. They did their best to sneak through the alleyways and infect those already corrupt, but it wasn't enough. Their neighboring countrymen were stubborn and they couldn't get the silve to spread beyond the British underworld. They got half of Scotland on their side but many were resistant. Those who adopted haemanism moved to Ireland, which eliminated any foothold they had in Scotland. The Russian haemans placed in Ireland, Scotland, and the U.K. were of no help; they weren't well-versed in the landscape and had no useful insight or strategy to put on the table. Nothing was working in their favor.

Cassidy Flanagan was mid-meeting with her team when her radio came to life.

"Any progress?" Carlos Amador's smooth, Spanish accent projected for all to hear. He was the leader of the haeman street team in Spain. His question was an annoying reminder that there was no progress. She took a deep breath, contained her anger, and replied.

"None yet," she replied in a thick Irish brogue. A strand of her long ringlet curls came free, falling in front of her face and blocking her view of the map. She tucked it behind her ear before continuing. "We've hit a wall."

"Place that mission on hold and meet us in France. Though we are making progress, it is slow and we could use some backup. The Russians should be through Germany by tomorrow night. If all goes well, we will conquer France as they seize the Netherlands and

Belgium, then together we can overpower the U.K. and the rest of Scotland."

"Where should we meet you?"

"We've taken over most of the French coast. Easiest spot for you to reach would be somewhere along the coast of Brittany."

"I know the ports of Roscoff pretty well. Are your haemans stationed there?"

"Yes. Leave immediately. I'll meet you there."

"What's your status in France so far?"

"Our soldiers have formed a solid wall along the western coast but we are having trouble moving inland. If we don't make a dent soon, the French will overpower us. The whole country is aware of what's happening and they've formed an even greater wall of bodies stopping us from moving east. If we push through them, which we could, we'd lose all our soldiers in the process."

"We'll leave within the hour."

The radio call disconnected and Cassidy had her men prepare their ships in Kinsale. The port was in plain view of Wales. The British who paid attention would see their boats leave in flocks, but it was unlikely they'd try to stop them. Though they would not succumb to Ireland's attempts at conversion, they were very aware of their little neighbor's new strength. During the early stages, the Isle of Man was their original mid-way point to meet and trade silve. Once the British police became aware of the drug trade happening there, they infiltrated in an attempt to thwart the illegal commerce. None of the British police officers made it off the isle alive.

Since then, the British kept their distance from the Irish and increased their border patrol so the Irish couldn't enter their land. They found ways around it, but it was difficult.

Happy to have a new mission, Cassidy watched as her haemans loaded the patrol boats, then got on the lead ship. They sailed across the Celtic Sea toward Roscoff. The trip would take an entire day.

The boats were cramped with agitated haemans. The lack of progress was affecting everyone and tensions were high. Cassidy did her best to control the infighting but the aggression was inevitable. They were too amped up not to get in each other's way.

Halfway through their trip a fight broke out on the lower deck. The sounds of men shouting and guns firing echoed through the night air. Cassidy ran down the steps from the captain's cabin toward the source of the noise. When she arrived, the scuffle had escalated from a one-on-one to a full brawl. Everyone was involved and many fought just to fight. They slugged whoever was closest to them with no valid reason behind it. The adrenaline was flowing and all the haemans were caught up in the moment. Cassidy had to break it up before they all killed each other or she would arrive in France with a boatload of dead haemans.

As a new leader, her daily allowance of silve was greater than her subordinates. She was stronger and faster than the lot. As she pushed through the fight, she recruited those who would listen to help her end the brawl; and anyone who ignored her received a hard blow to the head, knocking them out cold. Slowly, the fight disintegrated. After an hour of diligent, physical mediating, she managed to stop the fight. With the help of those who aided in breaking the volatile haemans apart, they dragged the unconscious bodies into the bunks and handcuffed them to their beds in case they were still enraged when they woke up.

"We need to get to France," she growled as they restrained their last unconscious haeman. "If we don't get there soon, I will end up murdering my own people."

"We will be there in five hours," one of her high-ranking subordinates said. Cassidy groaned and stormed back to the captain's cabin, punching and denting a metal wall on the way.

A few hours after sunrise, they arrived at their destination. All rowdy haemans from the night before had regained their composure and were released from their bindings. The boats docked and the Irish and Scottish haemans filtered onto French soil. Their arrival was large and foreboding. They were rough, brash, and disheveled, ready to fight. Carlos greeted Cassidy with a suave kiss on the hand.

"Welcome, my beautiful Irish blossom. It's a pleasure to meet you in person." He scanned her silhouette, seeing through the dirt and grime to the delicate and curvy female shape beneath. His lust covered her as he spoke and she yanked her hand from his grasp.

"Let's get one thing straight," she spat at him, "I am a warrior. I am your equal. I am not a goddamned flower. Nor am I a plaything with boobs that has arrived for your pleasure. So wipe that look of sex off your face because I will rip your dick off before it ever gets close to me."

"Oh, I like you." His expression of desire intensified.

"I mean it." She shot him a nasty glare and stormed away.

By noon, the haeman defensive lines were ready to switch to offense. They began their march forward, toward the line of French resistance waiting a few kilometers away. Armed with guns, tanks, and—most importantly—a haeman high, they approached their opponents and unleashed hell upon them. Though their numbers were matched, their strength was not. It wasn't a fight; it was a massacre. By dusk, the battle was over and the haemans were victorious. They shared a hit of silve together in celebration, then marched onward toward Paris. They moved with swift velocity, covering more land in a few hours than most would believe possible. Most of the French outliers had congregated during the first fight, hoping to stop the haemans before they had a chance to move east, but some still remained scattered through France. Paris housed many, so after eliminating them the haemans spent the rest of the night partying. They stole booze and cigarettes from the local shops and dipped into their travel satchels for more silve. They celebrated beneath the light of the Eiffel Tower and over the dead bodies scattered in the streets.

In the morning, the Russian troops, along with an international assortment of newly recruited haemans, entered Paris. The previous night's partiers spent the early hours sobering up from the alcohol and slapping their senses awake with silve. The Russians filled them in on their plan to invade Britain. Without much discussion, their march headed north. It wouldn't be long before all of Europe was under Russia's control.

Chapter 38

"We've conquered France," Kirill said, barging in on Mikhail and Roksana. She quickly pulled the sheets to cover her naked body. "Sorry," Kirill stammered. He turned to face the wall but Mikhail jumped out of bed.

"Don't apologize." He pulled up his boxer briefs. "This is great news."

"The Irish joined the Spanish and together they took Paris, along with the rest of the country. Our Russian soldiers conquered Germany, Netherlands, and Belgium during the takeover of France. Now that all forces are united, they are going to take down the United Kingdom."

Mikhail could not hide his giddiness. He was as chipper as a schoolgirl. He looked back at Roksana who lay naked and rejected beneath the sheets. "Sorry, love. This is more important." He turned his attention back to Kirill and they left the room deep in strategic conversation.

Roksana fumed, alone and disgraced. She hated how easily the prince dismissed her and loathed the attention he gave to Arinadya. Kirill would have never interrupted an intimate moment with Arinadya for a war meeting and she suspected Mikhail would have told him to wait a moment if he accidentally did. Roksana meant nothing to him and she didn't understand why. Being across the globe with space and time to ponder his feelings toward her was bearable. She could imagine she meant more to him than she did. But now she was at the palace every day, drowning in his presence and indifference toward her. It was too much. It was too real and there was no way to make excuses for his behavior anymore. She couldn't pretend he secretly longed for her when she was at his beck and call and he barely ever called. The complexity of her conflicting emotions made her feel murderous. She could not define his apathy or understand why she could not control how it was affecting her. Flipping between opposing feelings so frequently was confusing and the only emotion that remained constant was desperation. Desperate to keep his love, desperate to make him pay for his callousness, desperate to eliminate the barrier between them—none of which she could achieve. Every time she was forced to be near Arinadya it pushed her closer to the edge. The sight of the princess made her insides roar with envy and she had to restrain herself from jumping over the edge and down Arinadya's throat. Slicing it open and watching her bleed would soothe her fury, but it would only cause a larger battle beyond the confines of her mind. It would infuriate Mikhail, leading to his final dismissal of her: rejection by death. It wasn't an option.

Isidor barged into the room.

"We need to prep Arinadya for a follow up announcement to the Motherhood Summit."

Roksana pulled the sheets over her head. "Why can't she prep herself?"

"You do realize she is the only reason we are here, right? If Milena was alive and Mikhail didn't need a female team around the princess, we'd still be in the States. It was terrible there."

Roksana reemerged from beneath the sheets and began putting her undergarments on.

"That's because you were in Philadelphia. Filthy little hell hole."

"You liked Las Vegas?"

"It was fun. I was treated like a queen." Her nostrils flared in resentment. "Unlike here."

"You shouldn't expect special treatment just because you're Mikhail's mistress." She shook her head. "You act like you're

262

entitled to something more. You must realize you're not the only one he sleeps with on the side."

Roksana shot out of bed and slammed Isidor against the bedroom wall with force.

"Who else? Surely not you." She scanned Isidor's flat silhouette with disgust as she held her up by the neck.

"Let me go," Isidor demanded with her last bit of breath.

"Tell me who. I can't get rid of Arinadya, but there's nothing stopping me from killing the others."

With the same speed Roksana displayed, Isidor threw a punch into the side of her aggressor's ribcage. Roksana let go and stumbled backward, clutching the spot where she was hit.

"What the hell?"

"I told you to let me go." Isidor massaged her neck. "Next time I'll knock you out."

"I'd kill you before you got the chance." Roksana's temper escalated the unnecessary tension between them.

"You're fucking crazy," Isidor proclaimed. "I don't know who you think you are but your role here is minimal: screw the prince at his leisure and take care of his wife. Stop acting like you are so significant. You are replaceable."

"And so are you. Just because we've tolerated each other so far doesn't mean I won't kill you if you push me."

"I'm stronger than you," Isidor threatened. "Mentally and physically. Good luck." She sauntered out of the room.

Roksana finished getting dressed and followed her. She was in a foul mood and seeing the princess was last on the list of things to improve her state of mind. When she got to the room, she leaned against the doorway but did not enter. She watched as Isidor, Gavriil, Olesya, and Izolda dressed her for the cameras. The amount of pampering Arinadya received was sickening.

263

"Are you going to help?" Gavriil asked with a mouth full of bobby pins and a fist full of red hair. "Or are you just going to stand there and pout?"

"Seems like you have it under control."

"Where is her speech?" Izolda asked as she yanked the zipper up the back of her dress.

"I left it in the foyer," Olesya said between snaps of her gum. Her eyes never strayed from the lines she was drawing around Arinadya's eyes. "On that little table by the lion statue."

"Go get it," Isidor demanded of Roksana. With a huff, she left their chaotic scene of hurried fashion and went to retrieve the script. She was happy to get away from them but hated being bossed around. The camera crew was setting up. They were grouchy and pushy as they arranged the lighting and tested the sound in the great hall. She did her best to stay out of their way – for their safety, not her own. Any reason to snap and she would.

By the time she located the script amidst the mess created in the foyer, Arinadya and her stylist team were already finished. They walked down the grand staircase to where she stood with the paper.

"She was supposed to practice while we got her ready." Gavriil snatched the paper out of Roksana's hand. "Now she's going in cold."

"Don't bitch at me about it. Your makeup artist is the one who left it down here."

"What took you so long to bring it back to the room?" Gavriil got in her face. "Did you make a quick pit stop to screw the prince on the way?"

"You better watch your tone with me. I may not outrank many, but I certainly outrank you."

"Maybe, but unlike you, my role holds value in the greater picture. I have styled the princess's perfect look since day one.

There are tons of hair stylists out there, but none who can be trusted. I have earned my spot through talent and discretion. The prince needs me." Gavriil's breath was hot as he spoke inches from her face. "You, well, you're only good for the cave between your legs, and trust me when I say there are thousands like you. If I were you, I'd develop some kind of skill. Fast."

Before Roksana could digest her fury and retort, Gavriil had already walked away. She stormed out of the palace to find someone she could kill without consequence.

"I really don't feel well," Arinadya told Isidor for the twentieth time.

"You need to pretend like you feel great."

Arinadya said nothing more. No one cared, so she stopped warning them that she felt too queasy and lightheaded to put on a good performance. They were determined to make this little video happen now, so they'd get the best she could give them.

They escorted her to a spot in front of the camera. The lights were set up and shining down on her with blinding radiance. Though she felt horrible, she probably looked like a flawless doll on screen; the flood of light would wash out any imperfections not covered by makeup.

A teleprompter was set up with the introduction and wording she was supposed to use when answering each pre-approved question from the public.

"We go live in five, four, three," the cameraman counted the rest down with his fingers.

"Hello. We have organized this live Q&A session due to the large volume of questions brought forth by the public. There were so many valid questions and concerns that we decided it best to address them as quickly as possible." Arinadya smiled, but sounded like a robot. "We have recorded some of the common questions that were raised by multiple parties and plan to answer them here today."

A spell of nausea hit her like a wave, but she regained her composure as the recording played.

"If I volunteer to be a mother, do I also need to raise the child?"

"A popular question asked by many females interested in participating. The next generation needs to be raised properly. They need to be healthy, educated, and taken care of. We assume many mothers will want to return to their haeman lifestyles after giving birth, which is understandable, so we plan to train our nurses how to raise the next generation of future haemans. They are already patient, their self-control is better than we could possibly expect an untrained civilian's to be, and they have the medical background to nurture and care for each child as they grow." Another wave of nausea rose but she swallowed it. "While most mothers will find relief knowing the burden is off their back once the baby is delivered, some may feel obligated to participate in the child's life. All children will go to the group homes run by nurses, but each mother will have a choice after labor. They can permanently sign away their rights then, or they may sign a waiver that allows them visitation rights to the children as they grow. You must return to haemanism, so you cannot raise the child, but if your heart feels torn about an irreversible separation, there will be ways to watch your child grow from afar. The child won't know you, but you can know them."

Her head grew hot and her mind went fuzzy as the next question was read. She couldn't hear the words being said in the recording. She tried to focus but it hurt to do so. Her face scrunched as she battled another wave of nausea. A warm liquid dripped over her lips and down her chin. It flowed with speed and she looked down to see her white pumps splattered with blood.

266

With wide eyes, she looked back up at the camera in fear. They were still recording despite the blood dripping down her face. The voice recording stopped and the teleprompter waited for her to read. With the back of her wrist she wiped the blood from the bottom half of her face, smearing it everywhere and making it look worse. The blood kept flowing from her nose and new trails formed beneath her nostrils.

A hand emerged from the darkness to hand her a clump of tissues. She took the offer in disbelief, amazed that they wanted her to carry on this way. She wiped her face, drenching the white tissues in red. As she went to read the prompter, the nausea returned. The first word was "Generally," but as she tried to say it, the word turned into a heave and she barfed blood all over her hands.

"Cut," someone finally barked, "stop filming, cut the live feed."

The red light on the camera turned off and the chandelier in the foyer turned back on.

"Well, that's going to hurt the cause," Isidor said bluntly.

"I told you I didn't feel well," Arinadya shouted in anger at her team. Then she barfed again. By the time they got her a towel and a bucket, she was drenched in regurgitated blood.

"Everyone is going to think this is due to the pregnancy," Gavriil said. "That this is what happens when you reject haemanism, even if it's only for temporary sobriety."

"No one is going to sign up after seeing that," Olesya said. "Totally gross."

"Yeah, and painful," Arinadya said, interrupting their callous conversation. "It would be nice if instead of worrying how my bloody collapse mid-video will affect volunteers, you focused on getting me to the nurses. I'd like to know why I'm bleeding out of half the orifices in my head."

267

"Right, right." Izolda took Arinadya's arm and begrudgingly wrapped it around her shoulder. Now they both had her blood on them. "Let's get you checked out."

An hour with the nurses determined the baby was fine and her episode was caused by regular symptoms of pregnancy. She just happened to get a bloody nose at the same time the nausea hit, which caused her vomit to be filled with blood.

They escorted her back to her room and left her alone to clean up. They departed so fast it made her feel like a leper. She was surprised that she felt a bit offended considering she craved such moments of total solitude.

The shower water heated up fast. She stripped down and got in. As the water hit her body, the spots covered in blood slowly returned to normal. She watched as the water caused the blood, both dried and wet, to lift and swirl off her skin. The blood collected on her chest ran like red rivers over her breasts and pooled at the top of her growing belly. Once enough watery blood collected there, it ran down her baby bump and onto the floor of the porcelain tub. Seeing the blood on her stomach brought her conflicted feelings for the child back to the forefront of her mind. It was a product of blood, this demon child growing inside her. It was half Mikhail, who was fueled by drug-laced blood, and half her, who fell into Mikhail's world due to her own blood addiction. This would be a child of death; one formed by two evils. It was doomed. There was nothing good that could come from its delivery into the world. Its birth would only bring more heartache. She could feel its suffering growing inside her. Its negative aura was already blossoming.

Then again, the child was hers. What if she ran away with him? What if she escaped and hid with the baby until he was grown, raised him into a man she could be proud of, a man she could love, a man without any trace of Mikhail in him? But it was impossible to assume she could strip the child of its father's DNA. He had the traits in him inherently; there was no way to eradicate them.

The blood continued to drip off her and onto the tub's floor. It painted a pretty picture as it swirled throughout the water on its way to the drain.

Not too long ago she would have licked all this blood off herself. Remembering its taste, remembering the act of cutting and consuming her wounds' secretions was enough to bring her nausea back. The memory hurt. It made her feel weak all over again. She belonged to the addiction and it tore her apart. It still called to her from the depths of her mind, shouting out from the prison she locked it in. It begged to be released, it fought to win back her love. Recalling the hold it had over her was suffocating; it transported her back to a time when she was a slave to her demons.

Tears fell as she relived her old torment. She wiped them away angrily. She wasn't weak anymore; she was saved, she was strong. The addiction was behind her. She shook her head. She may be cured, but her demons were always there, waiting in the shadows. Waiting for any glimpse of weakness they could capitalize on. She'd never be able to remove their stain from her soul.

The blood was off her and gone from beneath her feet, but she didn't want to leave the shower. It was private and peaceful. She was free to feel however she wanted and wasn't forced to smile despite it. Time went on and she stood beneath the showerhead, letting the water hit her face. Her mascara ran down her cheeks, leaving black teardrop stains. It was quiet and she pretended there wasn't a palace full of haemans outside her bathroom door. Time passed and she lost track of it until someone slammed their fist against the door.

"What are you doing in there?" Kirill demanded. She had gone unaccounted for far too long.

"Sorry, just enjoying a nice shower."

"Hurry up."

She didn't know why she needed to hurry, but she did anyway. As she bent to turn the water off, a sharp pain seared through her abdomen. It hurt so intensely it took her breath away. She squeezed her eyes shut and waited for the pain to pass. It did, so she tried again. Before she could reach the faucet, the pain returned. This time it brought her to her knees. Hands on the floor of the tub in front of her, she leaned forward and breathed slowly as the pain persisted. She tried to breathe through it but it sliced at her insides relentlessly, like the little demon child had a knife and was carving its way out of her body.

"Stop," she whispered, delirious from the pain. "Leave me alone," she begged of the baby, praying it wouldn't kill her before she got the chance to eject it.

The sharp abdomen pain continued and she swore she was being murdered from the inside out. She opened her eyes and saw a stream of red water going down the drain. Petrified, she sat up to determine where it came from. The throbbing ache endured, but the blood wasn't coming from her belly. There was no blood left on her body from the bloody nose or vomiting. She looked down and saw that the bright red blood flowed heavily from between her legs. She was having a miscarriage.

Kirill banged on the door again.

"Why is the water still running?"

"Give me a second." Arinadya was panicked. No one could know. "I still have conditioner in my hair."

Tears fell from her eyes as she stood through the pain. She did her best to clean the blood off her legs, but it kept flowing. Enormous blood clots and large chunks of placenta fell from her body. She braced herself against the wall, biting the side of her forearm as she waited for the pain and blood to cease.

She was crying, but she wasn't sad. The tears were forged from joy and fear. She no longer had a piece of Mikhail living inside her. She was free of him once more. But now she had no leverage against him while she remained prisoner in his kingdom. The baby was her only source of control; the promise of an heir kept Mikhail in line and Arinadya safe from his physical abuse. Without his baby inside her, she was vulnerable. He'd rape her again in order to put another little life into her. This could not happen. This miscarriage was a gift from the universe, quite possibly a one-time deal, and she would not fall victim to the fate he designed for her again. She could not let this secret get out. She had to hold onto control for as long as possible until she figured out her next move.

The pain dwindled and the blood stopped. She cleaned herself off and squeezed some of her soap onto the floor and washed away the evidence of her miscarriage with her foot.

She closed her eyes, put the larger pieces into the toilet, and flushed. It was traumatizing. She did not want the baby, but she didn't want to murder it either. Discarding the pieces of the child she'd never know was hitting her harder than she ever dreamed it would. Maybe the baby would have been a blessing. Maybe, despite all odds, the child would have turned out decent. She couldn't dwell on it. In this moment, the miscarriage was a new chance to escape a life forever tied to Mikhail.

The belly was still there, it hadn't gotten any smaller yet. She wondered how long that would last. Luckily, she knew where the fake pregnancy bellies they used during her early days back at the palace were kept.

The baby was gone. Part of her felt guilty that this loss brought her joy, but she couldn't deny the freedom it gave her. She was raped by a monster, by an evil man that she loathed. She never asked for the child, and while she was ready to have it and do her best to eradicate the traits it received from its father, she never wanted that life. She never asked for it; she was never a willing participant in that decision. This miscarriage was another blessing she didn't deserve, it was another chance to set her life right.

Chapter 39

Artem agreed to accompany Sevrick back to St. Petersburg on a scouting mission. They'd scope out Rina's situation as well as monitor Mikhail's regular activities. After a week watching both parties, they could determine a way to rescue Rina and report their findings on the Prince back to the rest of the assassination crew. From there, tactical plans could be made to achieve their goals.

Sevrick visited Pasha as many times as he could before they left for the city. There were a few days between the memorial service for Isaak and their departure date where he got to spend a lot of time with his old friend.

He sat by his bed now, using his last hours before leaving to garner as much wisdom as possible.

"I brought the letter."

"Finally." Pasha extended a hand. "Let me read it."

Sevrick handed it to him. Pasha read it silently, scanning over it a few times before handing it back.

"I wonder what happened between here and the border that landed her back in Mikhail's clutches."

"They must have spotted her. There were haeman scouts everywhere looking for her and Leonid."

Pasha nodded, deep in thought. "So, what's your next move?"

"Go back for her."

"You realize it's more dangerous now than ever. Mikhail lost her once, I imagine he's done everything in his power to prevent that from happening again."

"Yeah, that's why we are scouting and assessing the situation for a week before taking any action."

"Good. You need to determine if she is back on the silve or still sober. You need to figure out if she really is pregnant with Mikhail's kid. You need to see if she readjusted back into that life and is happy there. Once you get those answers, I hope you are able to see clearly enough to determine if saving her is still worth the risk." He paused. "It really might kill you this time."

"I know. If she's back on silve and happily embracing the return of her haemanism, I'd turn around and never look back. That would be enough to make me let go for good."

"All right, what about the baby?"

"I hope it's fake. I'm praying it's a publicity stunt."

"She's at least four months in. They would've found a way to publicly terminate the pregnancy by now if it wasn't real. A miscarriage or something. I doubt they'd go to the trouble to find a baby to play the part. Then they'd need to raise it. Plus, there are no babies in Russia anymore. I think you need to prepare to face the hard truth that Rina is pregnant with Mikhail's child."

"It makes me sick."

"But it's more than likely your new reality. What happens if that's part of the deal?"

"I save her and we raise the baby like it was our own. Away from Mikhail's evil influence. Hopefully, the child will turn out decent." Sevrick's head dipped for a moment. "Do you think I am making a mistake?"

"No. You'd be making a mistake if you gave up now. She said she loved you in that letter. I imagine it was tough for her to admit that to you. I really believe she doesn't want to hurt you anymore than she already has. She wouldn't have written it if she didn't mean it. I've got a feeling she might need you now more than anyone realizes."

"I think so too. No one knows she needs saving except a few of us here. She's all alone."

"That being said, you need to be smart. You need to check your heart at the forest's edge before entering the city. Your decisions must be driven by logic, not emotion."

"You're right. I have Artem accompanying me so if I get irrational he'll knock sense back into me."

"Good. Listen to him. He'll have your best interests in mind."

Sevrick stood and leaned over the bed to give Pasha a hug. "I have to get going, but I'll see you again soon."

Pasha coughed as he spoke. "Yes, you will. Take care of yourself."

"Right back at you. I'll have lots to fill you in on when I return."

"I look forward to it."

Sevrick left the bedroom and headed to meet Artem.

"You ready?" Artem asked, pack secured to his back and a rifle slung over his shoulder.

"Yup. Let's go."

Sevrick threw his own pack and rifle over his shoulder. He also kept his Tokarev pistol and a small tranquilizer gun on his belt holster. Artem had a Makarov pistol and a Spetsnaz machete hanging from his belt. They headed out. It was early and no one was awake to say goodbye. Many were still drained from the emotional days spent grieving Isaak. The days surrounding the burial were filled with funeral rituals and traditions. The whole week had been emotionally exhausting. Sevrick was grateful to have a reason to leave the gloomy underground fortress behind. It was dark enough inside his head whenever he thought about Isaak, and being surrounded by everyone else's negative energy only made it harder to cope with his own. A week away and focused on something new would be good for his psyche. At least he hoped so. There was no telling the curveballs they'd encounter once they reached the city.

They spoke about Artem's late wife, who died a few years into the addiction. Like Sevrick, Artem went back and forth between the Primos hiding place and the city to visit her. It was a harder trip because the Primos were originally stationed much farther north of St. Petersburg, but he did it anyway. He tried to save her, did everything he could to make her see reason, but she couldn't escape the grip of haemanism.

"I hope you have a better outcome than I did," Artem said.

"I thought this ordeal was over when I finally got her back to the white elm and rehabilitated. I never dreamt I'd be making this trek again." A tidal wave of memories flooded his mind as he made the same journey he used to make during the days Rina was still haeman. "This time, it doesn't feel as hopeless. It was tough watching her heal, but I know she was happier without the addiction and I can say with certainty that she still loves me." He tapped the pocket where he kept the letter. "I used to make this trip with nothing but speculations and desperate hope driving me. Now I know recovering our love is attainable."

"Absolutely. I'd say this is harder than what I went through. I would have died to save Lidiya but death got to her first. Just like you, I would've gone to the ends of the earth in order to save her. It was driving me mad. I miss her every day but the more time that goes by, the more I realize I was never going to succeed in saving her. She wouldn't let me and I wouldn't give up. The cycle was disastrous. In a way, her death put us both out of our misery." The words hurt as he said them; Sevrick could hear the strain in his friend's voice. "I know it may seem like a terrible thing to say, maybe it's a strange way to look at it, but it's the truth. It brought her peace and restored my sanity. Her monsters beat me. They took her from me. The only way I can cope is to keep her alive in my heart. The Lidiya I knew, prior to haemanism, is safe inside me; I guard her memory with stubborn determination. I am eternally devoted to her."

"I don't know," Sevrick expressed, "that sounds way more devastating than what I'm dealing with. At least Arinadya is alive and there is hope. I wish I could've been there to help you with Lidiya."

"No, it happened how it had to. From what you've told me, our loves treated us very differently as haemans. Rina was patient, she physically restrained herself from hurting you. Lidiya didn't even try. She left me broken and battered more times than I can count."

"But she didn't kill you."

"She tried. She was half my size, so I was able to wrestle her and get away before any death blows. But there were numerous times she would've killed me if I was any weaker. I promise you, our situations are not similar. I never would have had an outcome like yours."

"How did she die? You never actually told me."

"She killed herself." Artem's jaw tightened. "With my gun."

Sevrick stopped in his tracks. "What? How?"

"I went to see her. We fought, as usual. It got more physical than normal and I had to pull my gun on her. I never planned to fire it, it was just meant to act as a barrier between us, something that would hold her back. I was backing toward the door when she lunged at me and knocked the gun out of my hand. She snatched it up and pointed it at me. I was sure she'd pull the trigger. She was crazed, you know? Doped and volatile. She glared at me like she didn't even know who I was, like I was a stranger. Then her expression twisted and her breathing got heavy. She never said anything, never explained what was going on in her head. She turned the gun on herself and placed it under her chin. I raced to her, hoping to stop her or knock the gun away, but she pulled the trigger without hesitating. It happened so fast." Artem was holding back tears. "A moment before she did it I would've sworn that bullet was meant for me."

"I'm so sorry."

"I wish she said something before she did it."

"She loved you, in spite of the addiction and the terrible things it made her do, and she didn't want to hurt you anymore. Seems like seeing herself aim a gun at you woke her up to the reality of what she'd become; a threat to everything she ever loved."

"Yeah, I've thought a lot about it and that theory crossed my mind. Despite the drug wiping away all emotional stability and long-held morals, it doesn't make a person forget people. In a moment of intense clarity, I think she realized what she almost did and couldn't bear it. So she ended it by ending her life. If she was dead, she'd never harm me again."

"I think that's why Rina almost jumped off that cliff. I can't pretend to know what would've happened if I didn't show up, but I'm grateful I did. My gut tells me she would've gone through with it."

"Probably. Still, they were very different creatures as haemans. Arinadya listened to you, Lidiya didn't hear a word I said."

"Really, I'm sorry it happened that way for you. And I'm sorry if me venting about my situation, or dragging you along now, makes it harder to deal with the loss."

"It's the opposite. It helps me. I like to think I may be able to help you have a better outcome. I'd like to see someone get a happy ending."

"If it's ever too much, just tell me."

"Will do."

Night was bearing down on them, so they found shelter and took cover. They only had another day's walk before they reached St.

Petersburg. Sevrick's anticipation for what they'd discover upon finding Rina was at an all-time high.

Chapter 40

"Your little stunt really screwed things up," Mikhail roared at Arinadya.

"I didn't do it on purpose. I warned them I felt sick."

"No one has signed up in days and new questions are pouring in. Everyone is concerned; they think the pregnancy is killing you."

"Nausea is common with pregnancy and I only puked blood because of the bloody nose. Have a nurse go on camera so they can hear it from the mouth of a medical professional."

Mikhail groaned, "This is so aggravating."

"I don't know what to tell you. I already said I was sorry."

"Find a way to fix it," he demanded, as if she had any control over who volunteered and who didn't. He stormed out of the room.

Arinadya collapsed back onto the bed and stared at the ceiling. Soon her belly would become too small to continue faking a pregnancy. The baby bump suits would conceal her secret until Mikhail decided he wanted to screw her.

She still bled occasionally. She didn't know when it would stop but the moment it did she figured the belly would disappear too. The only way to deal with it was day by day. In the middle of the night she cut up and burned her bloody undergarments in the tin trashcan in her bathroom. Destroying the evidence was the only sure way to keep her secret safe.

She was grateful they checked on the baby right after the bloody mess she made on live TV. It was still alive then. She had three weeks until her next checkup, three weeks to find a way out.

To her delight, her accidental sickness on TV stopped many women from volunteering. Though she had plans to help any who showed relief when they were free of the addiction, stopping them from volunteering was good too. Once she was out of Russia, she would find a way to send a message to the lost souls buried beneath the sea of haemanism. An international TV spot or a well-placed Internet article with an offer to help them would suffice. If they wanted out from the haeman lifestyle, they'd leave to find their recovered princess and follow her lead toward rehabilitation. If she could get away from Mikhail and find a safe place outside of Russia, she could accomplish this. She suspected there weren't many locations left on the planet free from Mikhail's grip, but she had to find out. She needed to know what he'd done and what he planned to do next.

It was late and most of the palace was asleep. She didn't know where the war room was, but she needed to find it. At 3 a.m. when the palace was at its most serene, she snuck out of her room and explored. Careful not to be seen, she tiptoed down the long corridors, pressed her ear against each door, and peeked into every quiet room. The palace was enormous, so it took a long time before she found her destination.

The war room was vacant; all leaders of Mikhail's war were fast asleep. The room was dark but she could see a small projector facing a white wall. She turned it on and the room came alive with red light. A map of the world appeared on the wall. Crimson lines illuminated each country's border and every country west of Russia was smeared with red light. She didn't know what it meant, but she figured anything colored in red now belonged to Mikhail. She couldn't go west toward Ukraine, Belarus, Latvia, or Estonia. She couldn't head south east toward Georgia, Azerbaijan, or Kazakhstan. Mongolia and China weren't under Russian rule, but they were too far east and she'd never make it there alive. Finland, Norway, Sweden, and Denmark were still untouched, but she hesitated to latch onto that route; trying to sneak into Finland is what landed her back in the palace.

North America and South America weren't marked as haeman yet, but the United States had tons of red spots littered across its territories. Mikhail infected them and it was still spreading.

The United Kingdom, Iceland, and Greenland still looked safe, but she had no way to get to any of them. She wished more than anything to return to the white elm but she did not know where it was and she could not risk leading any haemans to it if she happened to find it. She had too many eyes on her and she'd never jeopardize the lives of the innocent people at the white elm because she failed to consider their safety in her attempt to break free. It wasn't an option.

It appeared that Finland was her only choice. She sat back in a chair and sighed. It saddened her to see Mikhail winning. He was taking over the world and no one was stopping him.

She could stop him.

She let that digest. All she had to do was kill him. His death would bring forth her own but she'd save millions. It was worth it. It would set all her wrongs right. Any influence she had in propelling this horrid lifestyle into mass existence would be counter-balanced. She could end what she helped grow. She'd need a weapon, something that would require minimal contact with her opponent. A gun. She wasn't sure how she'd manage to get her hands on one or keep it hidden; her babysitters still watched her like a hawk. No one trusted her, and they were waiting for any reason to stick her back on the scopolamine.

She'd mull it over and come up with something. If she couldn't kill Mikhail, she needed to find a way to get to Finland. Either way, it needed to happen before her next checkup.

She crept back to her bedroom and got under the covers.

The week flew by and Arinadya made no progress on her plan to escape. She did find a small armory closet during a late night escapade, which she planned to raid the moment she found a suitable hiding spot for the gun.

Roksana startled her awake Friday morning.

"Up, up, up. There's work to do."

"Work?" Arinadya was never required to do anything more than provide comfy housing for the future prince.

"Yes. Since you clearly weren't brainstorming a way to fix your epic failure last week, the rest of us were. There is a fair being held in your honor," she said, the last word tasted sour. "You need to go out and socialize with your admirers. Assure them that you are fine, the baby is fine, and getting pregnant as a temporarily recovered haeman won't kill them."

"Okay, fine. Give me a moment of privacy to get ready."

"No time for that," Roksana said harshly, grabbing the blanket that covered Arinadya. She tossed it off her to find the princess sitting in a small puddle of blood. "What on earth?" Roksana muttered as she examined the scene.

Arinadya sat up, exposed and frightened. Her secret was out. The next few moments shared between her and Roksana were critical to her survival.

"Why are you in a pool of blood?"

"I cut my upper thigh while shaving; it's hard to get to all areas with this belly in the way. The cut must have opened while I slept."

"Liar." With haeman strength she flipped Arinadya over and yanked her shorts up to look for the cut. "There's no wound." She ruthlessly scoured her body, pushing and pulling at her skin while she did so.

"Stop, you're hurting me."

She flipped Arinadya back over and grabbed her face. "Tell me the truth." Arinadya refused to speak. "Is it a miscarriage? Did you lose the baby?"

A tear of fear fell down Arinadya's cheek. Roksana took her defeated silence as confirmation. She let go of her face and excitedly paced around the room, deciding how best to use this information.

"Please don't tell him."

"Why shouldn't I?"

Arinadya couldn't reveal her fear of going back on silve, she couldn't express her desire to run away, and most importantly, she couldn't disclose her fear that Mikhail would try again. He'd rape her relentlessly, not stopping until he successfully planted another child in her. The thought of going through that without the scopolamine to black her out was petrifying.

"I don't want to disappoint him."

Roksana laughed. "The problem is I *do* want you to disappoint him. I want to see his rage turned on you. I want to watch you fall from grace."

"I'm begging you, don't tell him. *I'll* do it. I need to be the one to tell him what happened."

Roksana looked down at Arinadya and reveled in the new power she had over her.

"You are at my mercy."

"I know."

"What can you offer me in return for my discretion?"

"The prince."

"You can't promise him to me."

"No, but I promise to leave. The moment he has won and doesn't need me anymore, I'll vanish and he will be all yours. You can take my place. We can start now. Today, at this event, you'll be by my side. The people will see you as my friend, they'll learn to love you too. Then when I 'die' and you step in, they'll be happy Mikhail has a good woman by his side as he grieves his late wife and moves on with life."

"That's awfully thought out."

"It makes sense."

"There's no guaranteeing how the people would respond to me. There's also no saying Mikhail would choose me in your absence."

"He would. You're his number one mistress." Roksana cringed at the dishonorable title but Arinadya covered her tracks. "I don't mean that with disrespect but I'm positive he'd rocket you into the limelight if I was out of the picture. You're beautiful, strong, and have the capacity to be influential. I bet he would've chosen you if he never met me."

"So would I," Roksana fumed as the life she almost had replayed in her mind. Hearing the girl who stole it away confess that she also believed that alternate fate was a possibility eased her hostility. She was just as good a fit to be Mikhail's wife as Arinadya; the girl who got in her way just confirmed it. The validation was intoxicating.

"Deal?" Arinadya asked. She prayed Roksana played nice.

"Never," Roksana seethed. "I want to watch you burn." After a moment of pure loathing, she straightened her stature and regained her composure. She flashed a devious smile at Arinadya and turned to leave.

Watching her exit the room with her secret in hand kicked Arinadya's perseverance into full gear. Her brain panicked, firing neurons at full speed in all directions. The moment Roksana left, her life was over. She had to stop the spread of truths before they were shared.

She quietly opened the drawer of her bedside table and removed the vile of scopolamine they had ready for her in case she ever misbehaved. With stealth, she jumped onto Roksana's back and plunged the syringe into her neck. She got half the contents into her system before Roksana fought her off. She threw Arinadya across the room and stared at her with fury.

"Are you fucking kidding me?" Roksana spat as she rubbed the spot on her neck where the drug entered. Her eyes narrowed on Arinadya. She lunged for her, but before she made contact the drug kicked in and induced her with a feverish spell of dizziness. Arinadya saw the drug weaken her opponent and took the opportunity to knock her onto the bed. Without hesitation, she grabbed a pillow and held it over Roksana's face. Roksana bucked like a horse, trying to free herself from her attacker, but the scopolamine weakened her. Arinadya kept her pinned beneath the pillow.

Punch after punch to the abdomen, Roksana did all she could to break free. Arinadya took the blows in stride, holding her breath as the pain resonated. It would all be over soon.

It took a minute and a half to deplete Roksana's oxygen and kill her. Once the fight was won, Arinadya collapsed next to her on the bed and heaved with exhaustion. If the baby wasn't dead previous to this, it certainly was now. Her ribs were bright red and already forming deep bruises. Another kill; she felt like she was back in her haeman days. She reached a hand around her back and touched the golden tattoo on her spine. Number 25. She wasn't a haeman but the kill still counted. She fought back tears and looked at the murder scene around her.

Frantic, she scoured the room for a way to cover her tracks. The windows were set low. She could push the body out.

Roksana was thin, but her dead weight was heavy. Arinadya pulled her body off the bed and dragged it to the window. She opened it and looked down. The three story drop onto frozen ground would easily kill a person. There was so much going on that maybe the coroner wouldn't care to look too closely at her death. She checked to make sure the coast was clear then got to work.

As she bent down to lift up the body, something hit the top part of the window. Startled, she dropped Roksana's shoulders and looked to see what made the noise. The lawn was empty. There was a thick patch of evergreens but she saw no movement. Wondering if the noise was a product of her paranoia, she went back to her mission. She didn't have much time. If anyone saw what she had done, a whole new world of problems would open up.

She tugged Roksana by the shoulders and propped the top half of her body over the windowsill. After a brief moment to catch her breath, she picked up her legs and pushed her over the ledge. Roksana's dead body plummeted to the ground, hitting head first and leaving her sprawled in a very broken position.

Tears streamed down Arinadya's face as she stared at the body below. She wasn't sad that Roksana was dead, she was terrified that she was able to commit such an act without the assistance of her haemanism. Was she really still a monster after all? Or was this an act of self-preservation? Roksana initiated the attack with words; she threatened her safety. She knew her secret and could not be trusted. Killing her was the only way to ensure her own survival.

She hoped.

Seeing the body made her long for her old addiction. Silve could numb the guilt she felt and being haeman would justify this deed. But it was a cop out, she understood that now. The drug was a convenient excuse, a way to defend indefensible behavior. It was an empty way to live and she never wanted to return to such a shallow existence. The problem was, if she was forced to live among them, she was going to have to act like them in order to stay alive. She needed to get out soon or else she would *need* the drug to justify all the terrible things she'd end up doing for the sake of survival. She couldn't go on this way. Roksana was her first kill as a recovered haeman and if she stayed here much longer, she had a feeling it wouldn't be her last.

She buried her face into the palms of her hands. Something hit the window again. When she searched for the source this time, she found it.

Sevrick stood near the tree line with a tall blonde man a few meters behind him. They both stared up at her in horror. She looked down at Roksana's body again, then back at Sevrick.

After all this time, he was finally seeing the dark side she warned him about. He saw the monster that still lived inside her. He saw her for who she had become.

He was scared of her, he didn't really know her anymore, and all those years he spent fighting for their love was a waste. He didn't need to say it, the look in his eyes told her so.

Chapter 41

"Prime Minister," his secretary poked her head into his office, "the President of the United States is on the telephone. Do you have a minute to speak with him?"

"Of course I do. They are one of our few allies left standing. Transfer his call to my line."

The phone rang.

"Prime Minister Archibald Dabney on the line."

"Archie, it's Nate. We need to talk."

"I know. I'm surprised it's taken this long for us to get on the same page. We've been battling the Irish off our streets for months now. Didn't you get any of our distress calls?"

"Yes, but we've been dealing with our own crisis. You're battling foreigners, we are fighting off our own. Half my population, if not more, has turned into those Russian-born monsters. It's chaos here. All that's left standing is a frail shadow of our government and the military. People who refuse to convert to haemanism are struggling to survive. There are caravans traveling in large numbers to Canada, hoping to find refuge there, but the Canadians aren't interested. They've turned everyone away, leaving thousands at our northern borders as easy pickings for the rebel haemans," President Ward sighed, "karma for how we handled immigration with Mexico, I guess."

"Greta Calland of Norway gave me a call yesterday to fill me in on what's happening there. Norway, Finland, Denmark, and Sweden formed a pact called the Nordic Union. They've banded together and are working hard to keep their lands safe from the haeman invasion. Refugees from all over Europe are flooding their borders, begging for asylum from the ongoing massacres in their own countries."

"Have they been letting them in?"

"Yes. They are housing as many as they can. She asked me if I had talked to you and if the U.S. could take some of the overflow, but I told her the rumors I heard of your own struggle against the haemans."

"They do not want to come here, trust me. My *own* people are clamoring to get out. They are desperate for a safe haven too. Canada might take the Europeans in. I think they are being assholes to us to teach us a lesson, though it's a foul time to do so. My people are dying in masses."

"I suggested Iceland or Greenland. They haven't been seized yet and according to their leaders, there have been no signs of haemans on their land at all. It's likely Mikhail and Dobrynin skipped over those countries, assuming they weren't big enough players to waste men there."

"I can have all boats along the east coast head north toward Maine if we get word they'd take my survivors in. I need to get my people to safety."

"I'll talk to Canadian Prime Minister Bruce Dumont to see why they are giving you a hard time. They know what's going on and how dire the situation has become. Perhaps you're just overwhelming them. The sight of people showing up at their borders in droves is likely discouraging. What will they do with all those people flooding their streets without a home? From what I've been told, Norway currently looks like a Woodstock or Glastonbury festival, minus the drugs. People are living in tents and scavenging for food to survive. No one speaks the same language and regulating the sudden overflow of people has been a feat. They are scared, therefore unruly. Their behavior is unpredictable; they have digressed to their primitive instincts in an attempt to survive. Bruce has surely talked to Greta. If she told him this, it's likely he's reluctant to follow her lead. And I hope you don't take offense when I say this, but your people have a reputation of taking over when they arrive places. If they were put into a situation similar to our neighbors in Europe, I doubt they'd handle it as well as those camping out in Norway are."

"I know we are an entitled lot, but I think my people would adapt fine. We have a worse reputation than we deserve. In all instances of natural disasters or terrorist attacks, moments when we needed to band together and be strong, my people have excelled. I have complete faith they'd act similarly during these grim times."

"I'm sure you're right. Canada is in the wrong, they shouldn't be locking their borders against you. I just need to talk to Bruce."

"Please do. Our media has adopted a pro-haemanism slant and they are spouting lies and detrimental propaganda. They are converting stragglers and scaring anyone who remains. Within the last week, they've started airing the riots and the violence and the murders, siding with the perpetrators. The casual way in which they report the brutality is disturbing. I'm losing a civil war I never got a chance to fight."

"So are we. Once we caught onto the Irish, we closed our borders and isolated the existing British haemans. They are in confinement. I regrettably must report that most of them are also dying there. The withdrawals are too intense to live through. I have my best doctors on the case, but regular rehabilitation doesn't work and they haven't been able to figure out an alternative. Our streets are safe again, but we are losing good people in the meantime."

"Do you think the Russians know how to heal a haeman? Or have they placed this virus-like addiction upon us with no cure?"

"Greta mentioned something about it but never went into detail. Our conversation was brief. Let's just hope the Russians weren't reckless enough to send the entire planet down stream without a paddle."

"What do we do now? I can't fight the battle on my own land any harder. I've already lost. Best thing I can do is partake in the global initiative so I can help the American citizens still fighting to survive and save the countries not yet affected by the disease. My military is fully intact. I want to use them for the greater good before I lose them too."

"Let's convene with the Nordic Union and derive a plan together. We have zero access to the rest of Europe; it's gone dark. Maybe China, Japan, and India can help. We can also reach out to leaders in Africa, Australia, and South America. Their armies aren't large but every additional ally helps. The Middle East has lots of passionate fighters too."

"No. We aren't involving them." President Ward refused the suggestion. "Their armies are littered with and corrupted by terrorism. They've harmed all of us at one point or another. I don't trust them. I don't want the terrorists on our side. They'll turn on us the moment this ends."

"I understand." Archibald knew too well the grief left covering a country after the terrorists struck.

"We can win without them."

"Greta mentioned a small task force sent into Russia on a mission to assassinate Mikhail."

"Norwegian soldiers?"

"No, Russians apparently. Remember when she warned us this would happen at that U.N. meeting a while back? Well, the Russians on this mission are the same ones who snuck across the border to warn her about Mikhail. They are the only reason she had the information to alert the rest of the world."

"I believed her. I knew Mikhail was up to something. I saw him last December during his international tour. I never would have guessed it was this, but the moment she made that announcement my gut told me she was right. I just wish I took more preventative action locally. I never thought it would grow from the inside. I always suspected an external attack."

"That's how it happened everywhere, internal sabotage. It was well thought out by the Russian haemans. Have to give them that much."

"Infuriating. So, all the Russians aren't on board, just like many of our citizens have resisted the tempting lifestyle change. Good to know. I hope they succeed."

"If they do, they might end this for all of us. But until then, we need to protect ourselves and come up with a plan to defeat them in case they fail."

"Absolutely. Let's get Greta on the line. We need to eradicate the damage caused by this so-called evolutionary gift. It's a sham, nature never intended for us to find and combine this strange mixture of human and earthly chemicals. It's time to save the human race from itself."

Chapter 42

After making sure the coast was clear, Sevrick and Artem approached the body Rina dropped from the window. The body was bent in unnatural directions and the female's head twisted and cracked from the impact. Her neck broke post-mortem, unless Rina snapped it before she disposed of it. The woman was long and lanky, her jet-black hair was wet with sweat, and her forest green eyes were wide open. Sevrick wasn't sure who this was or what happened, but if Rina killed her there must have been a good reason.

"I had to do it," she called down to Sevrick in her quietest voice. "She threatened me. There's so much to it, you'd have to know all the details to understand. *I* would have died if she didn't. You have to believe me."

"Are you on silve?" Artem asked. Rina shot the stranger an annoyed glare before looking back at Sevrick.

"This is Artem. He's a very good friend of mine," Sevrick explained. "Are you haeman again?"

"No. When Mikhail's men kidnapped me, they brought me back here and I was kept sedated for days. Mikhail wanted to get me pregnant so instead of putting me back on silve, they kept me knocked out until they figured out a way to control me."

"So you didn't come back here by your own choice," Sevrick said to himself with relief.

"Of course not. Didn't you get my note?"

"Yes, but it's hard to take anything at face value anymore. I needed to hear it from you."

"I meant everything in it."

"How far along are you in your pregnancy?" Artem asked, speeding the information process along. They were out in the open and couldn't chat long.

"I'm not pregnant anymore, but no one knows that except me. And Roksana, but I took care of that. She hated me and planned to tell Mikhail I was no longer carrying his child. I couldn't let them find out. Mikhail would rape me until I was pregnant again. If I fought it, they'd put me back on scopolamine."

"Devil's Breath?" Artem asked. His voice was alarmed.

"Yeah, that's another name for it. They kept me on it the first few months I was here. I woke up one day after they miscalculated the dosage and found I was pregnant with Mikhail's child. I have no memory of anything that happened during that time."

"Nasty drug. How'd you convince them to stop using it on you?" Artem asked.

"When I came to, it was early morning and everyone was asleep. I had a few hours to figure out what had happened and when Kirill came in the next day to give me another dose I begged him not to. Told him I was happy to have a baby growing inside me, told him it gave me a new purpose in life and a reason to live. I promised I would behave and put on the perfect show for Mikhail. They bought it. A few days ago I had a miscarriage." She wore a look of fear and desperation. "I need to get away from here."

"We can help you," Sevrick said. "We will help you escape."

"I have so many eyes on me at all times. Only reason no one is here now is because they think I'm with Roksana. If I go back to the white elm with you there's a good chance we will lead the haemans right to it. They'd stalk us all the way there."

"We will think of something," Artem said. "For now, you need to keep fighting. Where is Mikhail?"

"No clue."

295

"Are you in your bedroom now?

"Yes, but we don't share a room. His sleeping chambers are located on the complete opposite side of the palace. His room is the only one with purple and gold curtains." She examined both their determined faces. "Why?"

"We are going to kill him," Sevrick answered with conviction.

"No. Not you," Rina said to him, remembering Mikhail's secondary mission to find and kill her old lover. "He knows about you. He knows I still love you. To punish me for all the trouble I've caused him he plans to kill you. You can't make it easy for him. You shouldn't even be here now." Suddenly, his presence was no longer welcome. This reminder triggered her paranoia and she needed him to leave. "You must go. I can't be the reason you die."

"We will be covert and have additional men backing us up. You don't need to worry."

"Sevrick, you need to go back to the white elm and stay there. The other men can help me and they can kill Mikhail. It can't be you. The moment he figures out who you are his motivation will amplify and he won't let anyone defeat him until he's defeated you."

"I'm not going to walk up and introduce myself. Do you think I'm crazy? He'd never know."

Footsteps appeared beyond her bedroom door. She stopped talking and waited for them to pass.

"You need to leave. They are coming." She looked at Sevrick imploringly. "Please don't come back."

"Can you meet me at the lagoon?"

"Do you promise not to come back here?"

"I'm not promising that."

She hesitated. "Fine. Tomorrow. They let me sleep alone now. I'll have a few hours during early morning when it should be safe."

"I'll be there."

"Now go," she begged. The men checked their surroundings, then ran back toward the patch of evergreens. They disappeared from sight in less than a minute. Arinadya quickly ripped the sheets from her bed and hid them so she could burn them later. She made the bed before returning to the window.

A blood-curdling scream left her lips. In less than twenty seconds, Kirill came barging through her bedroom door.

"She's dead." She managed a few fake tears. "She jumped."

"Who?" Kirill stormed toward the window.

"Roksana."

He peered over the ledge and saw the lifeless body dead on the ground.

"You've got to be kidding me. She was supposed to be up here getting you ready. We are already running late." He stormed back toward the bedroom door, completely unconcerned about the dead woman or why she jumped to her death. "I'll send Isidor. Move fast when she gets here."

Isidor arrived a minute later. She examined the scene and eyed Arinadya suspiciously.

"She jumped?"

"I guess so. I woke up and my window was open, letting in a cold breeze. When I went to shut it, I saw her body lying there. Why would she do something like that?"

"Looks like her insecurities finally got the best of her. Count your lucky stars that she took it out on herself and not you. I was waiting for the day I woke up to find she killed you in your sleep." Isidor stopped questioning the truth of the situation and attributed it to her late friend's unstable emotions. She handed Arinadya an outfit and played with her hair as she put it on. "Better this way," she continued, "she was a liability. If it had to happen, at least she didn't tear down the rest of us in the process. Killing you would have messed up everything."

Arinadya was taken aback by the callous resolution Isidor came to, but she didn't question it. She was just happy Isidor didn't scrutinize her story. She didn't want to have to kill her too.

"I need fresh air. Am I almost ready?"

"Yes, they are keeping your look casual today. Only thing the stylists are doing is your makeup. They want you to look relatable. The haeman women you meet with today need to connect with you, they need to trust you. We need them to volunteer."

"I understand."

"Let's go," Isidor said, pulling Arinadya by the arm out the bedroom, down the hall, and into the foyer. Mikhail, Kirill, and the rest of their team were waiting there for her.

"Beautiful. Time to roll," Mikhail said, wrapping an arm in Arinadya's and escorting her to their limo. "I heard there was an incident this morning."

"With Roksana, yeah. I woke up and found she had jumped from my window. It was a terrible way to start my day."

Mikhail's eyes narrowed. "I knew Roksana well, she wasn't the suicidal type. Sure, she was a little unstable, but she was a fighter. I have a hard time believing she'd ever sacrifice herself in a moment of desperation."

"Well, she did. The proof is splattered all over the palace lawn."

"Are you sure you're telling me the whole story?" He was onto her, his gaze pierced through her and she had to look away to prevent him from reading through her lies.

"I'm not sure what you're implying. Do you really think I could have taken her on in my current state?" She placed a hand on her belly. "When I was in my haeman prime, sure. I could've taken her down without much effort at all. But right now I am weak. I am sober and carrying a child. I have no energy to fight someone to the death, and definitely not a freakishly strong super human."

"True," he leaned in closer and spoke in her ear, "but still. The thought of you overpowering her gives me great delight. Don't get me wrong, I enjoyed her company and did not wish her dead, but you're my wife. You're the one standing by my side in a position of authority. Knowing you still have your ruthless haeman roots is an incredible turn on."

Everyone else was now in the car.

"Then I wish I could take credit for her death, but I can't. I'm sorry to disappoint you."

He leaned back and tilted his head in examination of her. After taking in her words, demeanor, and expression, he let it go.

They arrived at Marsovo Polye Square and drove through the crowd to the safe spot designated for their drop off. A circle of haeman guards surrounded them as they exited the limo, keeping the frenzied idolizers at bay. The point of today was to socialize with the local haemans, but they'd need to calm down before the guards let them get too close.

A few park benches were set up for them, so Arinadya and Mikhail took their seats while the haeman guards screened the crowd for haemans suitable to approach the royals. After a few minutes, five women were let into the circle. They approached Arinadya, who smiled at them with believable sincerity.

"Are you women interested in becoming mothers?" she asked them.

"Maybe," the tallest said. "I was sure about it a week ago, but then I saw what happened to you during your live broadcast and it scared me. Now I'm not so sure."

"I can promise you it had nothing to do with my former haemanism or the health of my child. I was feeling nauseous that

299

day, like any normal pregnant woman, and I just so happened to get a bloody nose at the same time. I got them as a haeman and they've carried over to my rehabilitated life as well. It is a residual effect; it isn't a sign of any deeper issue. The combination caused my vomit to be filled with blood. All those channels in our skulls are connected, it would happen to anyone whether they are haeman, non-haeman, pregnant, or without child. I am sorry it frightened you and so many others. It was a very misfortunate situation."

"Are you excited to be a mother?" the shortest lady asked.

"Absolutely. It's a very empowering feeling to bring life into the world. I can't properly describe the way it has improved my view on life or the exciting new purpose it has given me, but I can say I am so glad to be blessed with by motherhood. Nothing compares."

"How did it feel to lose your haemanism?" a lady with blonde hair asked. She did not ask it with malice; her voice was filled with cautious curiosity. This was one of the individual's whose energy Arinadya felt at the Motherhood Summit. She wanted out of her haeman life.

"I was scared, there were moments I thought I wouldn't survive the withdrawals, but I fought through the pain and came out a new woman." She had to be careful with her word choice. Mikhail was listening closely. She wanted to give this woman hope that there was life beyond haemanism, but she couldn't risk Mikhail suspecting that she was encouraging others to follow their desires to run away like she had. "While I, like everyone else, feared losing my haeman strength, I must say that it isn't as detrimental to my mind, body, or soul as I thought it might be. I feel refreshed. I feel recharged." Mikhail's nostrils flared; she was going overboard. "And I look forward to returning to my haeman lifestyle the moment my little prince is born."

"Thank you for your time," Mikhail cut in. He handed them business cards. "Now that you've met with Arinadya personally, you're allowed access to a private email exchange where she will answer your questions directly. All your concerns, fears, doubts, and queries will go right to your princess and she will converse with you. Please do not share the email address with anyone else; you've been chosen specifically to receive this olive branch because we enjoyed your company. It is a way for us to stay connected. We want you to feel safe. We care about you."

Mikhail laid it on thick and they ate it up. The eyes of all five women lit up with excitement. They received direct contact to their idol and they could not hide their joy. They left the inner circle and the guards looked for the next batch to send in.

"An email exchange with me?"

"Of course not. I have someone assigned to answer anyone who writes to the address. They'll just think they are talking to you."

"I see."

"Careful how you describe your brief leave from haemanism. You sounded a bit too excited about your sobriety for a moment."

"Did I? I apologize. That wasn't my intention. I'll choose my words more carefully."

"Good."

The next batch of women came in and they went through a similar spiel with them. Even though she changed her wording each time, Mikhail was never happy with how she described the rehabilitation process or how the sobriety felt. Each group had at least one individual who seemed eager to be healed and she couldn't let them leave without giving them a smidgen of hope. She played dumb every time he called her out on it, pretending she was trying her best to sound exactly how he wished. Eventually, she claimed he was being paranoid, and after a dozen rounds of her adjusting her approach to the questions, he conceded that maybe he was overreacting.

Another victory for Arinadya.

The day went off without a hitch and they returned to the Winter Palace for dinner. A romantic supper was set up for them by the fireplace in the White Hall. All Arinadya could think about was her late-night meeting with Sevrick by the lagoon. She tried not to anticipate it too much; she couldn't let it distract her from giving Mikhail her full attention right now. He needed no additional reasons to be suspicious of her.

"We are alone now. You can tell me the truth about Roksana," he said after slurping a spoonful of his okroshka.

"I told you the truth earlier. I didn't do that to her."

Mikhail sighed, "I wish you did."

His desire to know she was a cold-blooded murderer without the help of her haemanism made her stomach turn. He liked her for who she was when her demons took the reins. They were a part of her and always would be, and Mikhail *liked* that side of her. He loved her dark and Sevrick loved her light. Unfortunately, she'd always be a combination of both. There was no way to eradicate the dark that lived inside her. She could keep it in check, but she couldn't erase it and she hoped Sevrick could learn to love her despite it. His face after seeing her push Roksana's body out the window would be stained in her mind forever. He was appalled, disgusted, frightened; he looked up at her like she was a stranger. It was brief, but clear. Seeing him look at her like that was her greatest fear. Though she always planned to come clean about her past behavior as a haeman to him, she never imagined he'd see her demons in action. But if they wanted true and honest love, he'd need to know her, inside and out.

Maybe it was good he saw the truth now. If he could love her after seeing her push a dead body out of a window, maybe he'd absorb her past terrible deeds in stride. But killing Roksana was necessary to survive; it was self-defense. Sevrick would see it in that light. Everything she did as a haeman was ruthless and unwarranted: she killed for pleasure, killed for personal gain, killed out of anger, killed by mistake. The kill count tattooed on her back was a grave reminder that none of those deaths were warranted; none of them had any justifiable cause behind them. She still feared he'd fall out of love with her once he heard the unbridled details of her time as a haeman.

Murdering Roksana proved that wisps of her haemanism still ran free inside her. Though she killed her out of self-preservation, it verified that her demons were alive and well. She never would have resorted to such violence in her life prior to the haemanism. Killing a person to survive never would have been an option; she'd have found another way. Now, she was sober post-haemanism and she had no qualms murdering anyone who got in her way. She had no doubt she'd do it again if need be and it frightened her.

"How is my son doing?" Mikhail asked, snapping her out of her thoughts.

"He's good. Lively little boy growing in there, kicks me all the time. He makes sure he isn't forgotten." She did not miss the constant reminder the child gave her of its presence.

"He is his father's son, demanding and driven. He will be a fine addition to our legacy."

"I have no doubt."

Mikhail whipped out a vile of silve and poured two lines for himself. He snorted them through a golden cylinder and sat back to let the high hit him. To Arinadya's dismay, she caught herself watching his actions with nostalgia. Her subconscious took over.

The sight, the smell, the memories; her demons were awakened. She glazed over with longing and a deep-rooted craving she never really abolished.

"Don't worry, my love. You'll be able to join me again soon."

His words snapped her out of her coveted daze. Ashamed, she punished herself internally, chastising her momentary lapse of strength and pushing her demons back into their dark cellar.

She nodded at Mikhail, but silently swore she'd never let it come to that. Returning to her addiction was choosing death over life, and Arinadya intended to survive. No more giving up, no more giving in; she'd never let it take her again.

Chapter 43

Halfway through the walk back, the men parted ways. Artem headed to the white elm to report their findings and gather more men for the trip back, while Sevrick headed to the lagoon in order to intercept Rina.

Midnight came and went fast. The hours following passed slower as he waited eagerly for his love to arrive. At 3 a.m., she emerged from the shadows.

The sight of him standing there, waiting for her with an open heart, brought tears to her eyes. All the trauma, mental torture, and self-harm she suffered since she left him years ago surfaced at once. She ran into his arms and let her bodyweight collapse into him. He held her up, carrying the heaviness she finally buckled beneath.

"I love you," she sobbed into his chest. "I'm so sorry it took so much for me to realize it again, but I do. I always have. I never stopped, even when I forced myself to believe that I had."

"I love you too." He kissed the top of her head.

"The fact that you are still here, willingly embracing me after all I've put you through, is overwhelming. I don't deserve it, but I am so grateful for it."

"I told you I wouldn't give up on you."

The tears fell faster. She breathed him in, trying to absorb all of his love in a single breath. It was too much; his love for her was enough to drown in. She let herself get lost in his embrace, swimming through the endless comfort he provided her. She never wanted to let him go.

"Let's sit by the lagoon," he suggested, kissing her head again and guiding her toward a dry spot. They took off their spring jackets and sat down. He held her hand as they got comfortable, keeping a tight hold as she started the conversation.

"Are you afraid of me now?"

"Afraid?"

"After seeing my demons take over. After seeing me throw a dead body out of a window. That had to shake you up a bit."

"It did, but you did it in self-defense. I don't question your judgment. I'd never fault you for doing what needed to be done in order to survive."

"A lot of the dreadful things I did as a haeman were not grounded by noble intentions. I did those things out of malice, anger, fear, and selfishness. I killed a lot of people and my reasoning was never to protect myself. I just did it because I felt like it." She stared at the ground and the tears fell onto the mossy rock covering.

"You were an addict. Yeah, those decisions were yours, but they were made by your drug-fueled mind, not your sober one. You should take responsibility and feel remorse, but you cannot believe that who you were then is who you are now."

"It still lives in me."

"Maybe, but you have control over it. You'll be okay."

Rina nodded and rested her head on his shoulder.

"So you lost the baby?"

"Yeah. No one knows yet. I'm trying to keep it a secret as long as possible, but I have a checkup in two weeks and they'll find out then. I can play dumb, like I didn't realize I miscarried, but the secret will be out and Mikhail will put me through hell to remedy it. I'm trying to find a way out before that happens."

"Leave with me tonight."

"I can't." She needed to kill Mikhail before Sevrick came back to try and do it with his team of assassins. She would do anything to keep him out of harm's way, but she couldn't tell him that. He'd only object. "This isn't the right time. I need to stay on the inside for now; I get valuable information by being there. I'll start taking notes. When I get out for good, I can report his war plans back to you."

"Your safety is more important."

"I've helped cause this disastrous turn of events for humankind. I need to help make it right. I can't go down in history as Prince Mikhail's royal bitch. I need to help stop him."

"I'll be back at the palace soon to kill Mikhail. I'll get you out then."

"I really don't want you coming back. Let your friends do that mission without you. Mikhail has no vendetta against them, they are safer in my presence than you are. They'll help me escape."

"None of them feel as passionately about saving you as I do either. I know they'd mean well, but if push came to shove, they'd leave you behind if it meant their survival. I can't risk that."

"You need to. While I was under the scopolamine I told Mikhail *everything*. Our love before I was a haeman, your visits during my haemanism, that night where you shot him with a tranquilizer gun. The fact that I loved you through all of it. He was enraged. When I came to, he let me know what I divulged and filled me in on his quest to destroy you. Not only to punish you for whatever delusional reasons he has, but also to punish me for all the trouble I've caused him."

"I can handle him. I'll have back up."

"So will he."

"He won't know who I am."

"Someone might call you by name in front of him, or in a fit of anger you might say it, I don't know. It's not worth the risk."

Sevrick sighed, "I don't want to argue about this right now. I just want to enjoy having you back."

Rina stopped her rant and relaxed. He was right; this was a moment to enjoy. And maybe she could prevent him from ever having to face Mikhail if she found a way to assassinate him herself. She let the topic drop and snuggled into him. He laid them back onto the moss.

She kissed his cheek twice, and he turned his head to kiss her lips. Their soft, tender kiss evolved into a passionate one. Lost in each other's love, they rolled to face each other, body against body. The chemistry between them was alive and their body heat radiated in the places where they touched. Rina pushed his shoulder and straddled him. She unbuckled his belt while continuing to kiss him and he lifted her nightgown over her head and placed his hands on her hips. He pressed her against him, increasing the fire between them.

The moment escalated quickly. With one arm he held her close and flipped their bodies over. She smiled at him, blue eyes glowing, and he kissed her again with fervor. It felt like it did years ago, before the heartache, before the trauma. She pulled him in closer and they reignited their love. Having him inside her again was pure bliss; he was her only love and she was his. The tragic time apart seemed to melt away as they intertwined as one.

When it ended, they exhaled with exhausted ecstasy. They remained in a quiet and loving embrace as their hearts returned to a normal pace. The time slipped away and when the birds began to chirp, Rina realized she had to get back.

"The sun is about to rise. I need to return to the palace."

"Please run away with me now. No one followed you here, we would've known by now."

She thought of her own mission to end Mikhail's reign; it was a crusade she felt obligated to carry out. To gain retribution for all the torment he put her through over the years, and to protect Sevrick from having to do it.

"Please don't make this harder than it already is."

Sevrick hated the idea of letting her go back, but knew he'd never change her mind.

"Fine, but you're getting out before your next doctor's appointment."

"Yes. I'll spend the week spying."

"Can I still see you?"

She grinned at him. "The wee hours of morning are yours."

"I'll be here every day, waiting for you."

She kissed him again and they lingered, lips connected for a minute before she grabbed her coat.

"I love you," he said as she put her jacket on.

"I love you too." She gave him a relieved and genuine smile before darting away.

For the first time in years, Sevrick breathed easy. Finally, everything felt like it would be okay.

Chapter 44

The week passed in slow motion. Rina snuck out and met with Sevrick every night. They spent the wee hours of morning together, talking, reconnecting, and making love. It was a small slice of heaven amidst the terror that surrounded them. Mikhail had all of Europe under his control, minus the United Kingdom and Nordic countries. His haeman soldiers continued their efforts, but Mikhail began making plans to move onward. The United States was next on his list. His air force was ready and waiting for his signal to strike, as were the multiple militaries he acquired upon the acquisition of other countries. His fleet was enormous and he had no doubt his air strike would end in success. President Ward would surrender and Mikhail would gain the greatest powerhouse on the planet.

Rina relayed all of this information to Sevrick when they met. She updated him daily so he could tell his friends at the white elm, who relayed the message to the Nordic Union via radio. After Isaak's funeral, Pasha and a few other technically savvy individuals were assigned to get in radio contact with the leaders of the Nordic Union. A few days into Sevrick and Artem's scouting trip they succeeded and now the white elm had free-flowing communication with their allies. Everything Rina reported to Sevrick was relayed to them and they made their plans around the inside information.

Her doctor's appointment was rapidly approaching. She wasn't sure how to post-pone it. Mikhail was still alive and the men from the white elm were on their way in an attempt to assassinate him. Sevrick refused to stay behind, so she suspected he'd be with them. It scared her to know he'd be in such close proximity to the monster who wished him dead. She needed to get to Mikhail before they did.

It was Friday and everything was scheduled to happen on Sunday: her checkup, her rescue, the assassination. She had minimal time to alleviate the situation before it became out of her control.

She spent the day roaming the palace, looking for any unattended armory closets that she could steal a pistol from. She knew where they were located, but she couldn't get to any of them without being seen. Isidor strolled with her up and down the corridors for the first half of the day, refusing to converse but insisting on staying by her side. Isidor was always cold and calculated, but ever since Roksana's death her suspicion and dislike for Rina had tripled.

"I am going to take a nap," she told her haeman watchdog.

"Finally," Isidor said. "I've been dying to have a moment to myself."

She escorted her back to her room and after a half hour alone, Rina snuck out again. She barely made it down the hall when Kirill turned a corner and bumped into her.

"What are you doing out here alone?"

"I was taking a nap, but got restless and needed to walk it off."

He rolled his eyes. "Fine, walk with me."

She wasn't going to get anything productive done until they were all asleep. Sevrick already knew not to expect her at the lagoon that night; he had to help gather his troop and Rina needed to take care of her own, secretive obligations. Mikhail was so busy prepping to attack the Americans that he left her alone all week. She was incredibly grateful that he hadn't touched her since she and Sevrick reignited their love, but she knew it wouldn't last. Especially if Sunday came and went and he discovered she no longer carried his child.

That night, while the rest of the palace slept, she crept through the hallways to search for a gun to steal. The first armory closet she came across was locked. She continued to the next one to find it bolted shut as well. Cursing beneath her breath, she moved on to the storage room at the end of her hall. It was unlocked. She pushed her way through the door and found shelves upon shelves of weapons. The walls were lined with crossbows, spears, and machetes. Racks were set up with endless rows of rifles slung by their straps. She headed to the back wall where the shelf of pistols was located. She grabbed a TT-30 and a box of Tokarev cartridges and snuck out of the room. She considered grabbing more to aid Sevrick's men when they arrived, but she didn't think she could hide anything bigger than a small pistol. She'd sneak back here to acquire more if it proved necessary, but if all went according to plan Mikhail would be dead before Sunday.

Once back in her bedroom, she made sure the gun was loaded and wedged it between her bed's large headboard and the wall. There was just enough space for it to fit. No one would find it there. She dumped the bullets into a tissue box, burying them beneath the remaining tissues. The box stayed next to her on the nightstand.

Now she just needed to get Mikhail alone. She had no clue how to pull this off without him suspecting her. Or how she would get away with it without being killed herself, but she had to try.

The morning arrived draped in rain. Everything outside was drenched and she wondered how Sevrick and his men were doing in the forest. They were likely on their way, probably camped out last night in order to make the last leg of the trip today. The weather concerned her.

"Get dressed," Isidor commanded as she barged in. "Doctor appointment got moved to today. You've got ten minutes."

312

"Why?" she asked, panic in her voice.

"What does it matter?" Isidor said with great distrust.

"It doesn't." Arinadya changed the tone of her voice and came up with an excuse. "I just haven't showered. I don't know if I'll be ready in time."

"Skip the shower. The doctor needs to be in Moscow by nightfall."

"I smell."

"Who cares?"

There was no way out. The gun was lodged behind her headboard, out of reach, and Isidor blocked the doorway. She was going to have to obey and suffer the consequences.

On their walk to the newly designated medical wing of the palace, Arinadya prepped herself mentally for what was to come. She needed to act surprised when they told her she lost the baby; she needed to seem distraught and remorseful. They couldn't know she'd been living with this truth for a few weeks.

She got on the examining table and the haeman doctor placed a stethoscope to her stomach. He didn't ask her how she was feeling or try to make her feel comfortable, he just began the physical exam. After listening to her belly, his facial expression shifted from apathy to alarm. He spread her legs and began a pelvic exam. His hands were cold and his touch was rough. It hurt, but she bit her lip to offset the pain.

After a minute of looking around, he peered up at her through her legs. He stood, not breaking eye contact with her, and placed a stethoscope to her belly again. He listened, glaring at her with mistrust as he did so.

"Have you experienced any abnormal bleeding?"

"Like what happened during my live segment a few weeks ago?"

"Yes, but from your vagina," he answered condescendingly.

"There's been some spotting but I've heard that's normal."

"Any sharp abdominal pain?"

"No," she lied.

"Your baby is dead."

Arinadya faked a look of pure dread. "No. That's not possible."

"You had a miscarriage, and based on how the ruptured membranes are healing, it didn't happen recently. My guess is it happened a week or two ago."

"How did this happen? Why didn't I know?"

"Are you sure you didn't know?" His eyes narrowed down on her.

"Of course I didn't know. What are you trying to imply? I could have you tried for treason for making such hurtful and treacherous accusations against me. I am the princess. I am above you," she seethed, "never forget that."

"My apologies," he said in a bored, apathetic tone. "It's just hard to believe you did not have substantial bleeding this late into your pregnancy. A miscarriage four months in rarely comes and goes without making a scene."

"Well, I guess I'm a rare case. Now tell me why this happened? I've been very careful."

"The reasons are numerous, so there's no way to tell why you miscarried without additional testing."

Arinadya focused on the memory of her mother-in-law Dafna passing away, and tears began to stream from her eyes.

"Let me get Mikhail," the doctor said uncomfortably at the sight of her crying. "Acting as your therapist is beyond my pay grade."

He left the room and she kept the tears going. She needed to put on a good performance if she wanted Mikhail to go easy on her.

A few moments later, Mikhail stormed into the room, Kirill following close behind.

314

"We lost the baby," she sobbed.

"*You* lost the baby." He slapped her hard across the face. His ring sliced her cheek and the blood mixed with her tears.

"I didn't mean to! I was taking good care of our child. It's not my fault this happened."

Mikhail roared with aggravation. She foiled his plans once again. As he raised his hand to strike her a second time, a deafening explosion erupted and shook the entire palace. Mikhail's eyes grew wide with crazed disbelief. He looked to Kirill.

"What the hell was that?"

Kirill ran out of the room to investigate the situation. Mikhail returned his attention to Arinadya.

"This isn't over." He grabbed her face and squeezed, pulling her in close while he did so. "You *will* have my child. You *will* deliver me a healthy heir."

He stormed out of the room as Isidor entered with fury in her eyes. She grabbed her arm and dragged her through the palace and back to her bedroom.

"You're a devilish little bitch," she hissed as she threw Arinadya onto the bed. "You've been hiding this secret all along, haven't you?"

"No."

"That's why Roksana is dead, huh? She found out so you killed her?"

"No!"

Isidor picked her up by the throat and pinned her against the wall.

"I can't kill you, but Mikhail gave me permission to punish you however I saw fit." She squeezed her neck tighter, cutting off her flow of oxygen.

Arinadya's hands scoured the wall desperately, hoping she was within reach of the gun. With a little struggle, she was able to get her hand low enough to reach it. Her fingers wiggled it loose and she snagged it by the trigger guard. Isidor was too engrossed in her moment of power to notice what was happening beneath eye level.

As another bomb went off, shaking the foundation of the palace, Arinadya fired a bullet into Isidor's abdomen. The palace echoing from the explosion's aftershock muted the gunshot.

Her eyes grew wide as the bullet went straight through her, piercing a few vital organs on the way out. She fell to the floor, dropping Arinadya in the process.

Isidor crawled away, holding her wound. She licked the blood from her fingers, but it wasn't enough to increase her high and help her muscle through the injury. She hadn't taken silve recently. She stopped moving once she reached the opposite wall. Her head rested against the windowsill. Arinadya approached, gun in hand.

"Are you going to toss *me* out the window too?"

"No. I don't have time for that." She changed into a pair of jeans and tucked the pistol into the back of them. "You'll bleed out soon enough."

She threw on a t-shirt, a long sleeved shirt, a sweater, and her red fur-lined pea coat. It wasn't cold enough to warrant so many layers, but she wasn't planning on coming back and she needed all the clothes she could bring. There was no telling the next time she'd have solid shelter. She grabbed her biggest designer handbag and began stuffing it with items that would help her survive: the bullets, extra socks, a bottle of water off her bed stand, a first-aid kit that was beneath her bathroom sink, and the syringe she hid behind the toilet that still had a few drops of scopolamine left in it. She zippered the bag and threw it over her shoulder. With her rubber-soled boots on, she climbed out the window and perched onto the window's exterior molding. With careful steps and strategic foot placement, she was able to climb down. Another bomb exploded in the distance. She looked over her shoulder and saw Marsovo Polye Square covered in flames and smoke. The impact shook the ground beneath the palace but she had a firm grip and held on through the worst of it. No one was outside—they all were in the palace strategizing—so she made it to the ground without being seen.

For fear she might be seen, she headed north toward the lagoon instead of west into the forest where she thought the white elm might be. The unexpected onslaught of bombings was likely keeping Sevrick and his friends at bay for now. They were smart enough to stay far from a city under attack by foreign aerial forces. She just hoped Sevrick was smart enough to stay behind too. The sight of bombs dropping over where she resided might cause him to act irrationally, but she prayed he had people talking sense into him. He couldn't race into the line of fire for her. He had to trust she could take care of herself. The bombs would take care of Mikhail.

She was excited to reunite with Sevrick without the usual, ever-present danger looming over them. They could finally be together again.

The city was on fire. Everyone was distracted by the war raining down on them and no one noticed their princess slip away through the chaos and into the forest.

Chapter 45

They hid in the forest, a few hours outside of the suburbs of St. Petersburg. Sevrick and Artem brought six men back with them: Zakhar, Konstantin, Benedikt, Marat, Ivan, and Jurg. They only brought those who were physically fit and mentally stable; many of their friends still weren't handling Isaak's death well.

"Do we wait?" Jurg asked.

"I say we go now," Artem answered. "The bombs are falling, the haemans are distracted. This may be our best shot to get Mikhail alone."

"There's no guarantee the missiles will strike his location and kill him," Konstantin agreed. "We are here to make sure he dies."

The men conceded and walked toward the burning city. The air strikes were continual. Radio reports from the Nordic Union confirmed that they had aligned with the United Kingdom and the United States, they just never told them their plan after that. Bombing Russia into ruins was their apparent strategy, and though it hurt the men to see their once beloved city go up in flames, they understood that there weren't many other options. Mikhail, President Dobrynin, and their entire population were monsters, jacked up super-freaks with incomparable strength and speed. They wouldn't stop until they got what they wanted. If extreme measures were the only way to stop them, then they needed to be taken.

They snuck through the suburbs, which were untouched. At least their faraway allies were attempting to leave the haeman civilians out of this. When they reached the palace, they searched for the window with purple curtains. Many haemans ran past them, but they were so distracted by the war tearing apart their homeland that they didn't even notice the men strapped in weapons charging toward the palace.

They rounded the enormous building to the opposite side from where they saw Rina. It wasn't hard to find the windows draped in purple; they were the largest ones there. Around each palace window was an elaborate frame with molding that provided firm handholds. The men scaled the wall using these aesthetic pieces as grips. Sevrick led the way, leading them to the window next to Mikhail's bedroom. The spare room was empty so Sevrick smashed the glass, cleared out the debris, and they climbed through.

Another bomb landed a few kilometers west of their location. It shook the building and the men clung to their baroque pediments as the frame of the palace trembled dangerously beneath them. Once it stopped, they followed Sevrick through the window.

Ivan cracked open the door to the hallway and a flood of chaotic yelling filtered into the room. The haemans were disorganized, they weren't sure how to fight something they could not physically access. So long as the bombs continued to fall, they couldn't return a counter-strike.

"We need to get to Mikhail before they run out of bombs to launch," Ivan said. "We can't let him give the order to strike back."

Everyone agreed. They waited until the coast was clear and snuck out of the spare room. They peeked into Mikhail's bedroom, but no one was there.

"We need to find their war room or wherever they do their planning," Benedikt announced.

They scurried through the corridor, trying to be as small and unnoticeable as possible, which was impractical. Haemans saw them, but the men did their best to act concerned about the bombings and their enemies didn't have time to register that these men weren't on their side. Time after time they let the threat pass and the men were able to keep looking for their target.

Peering into every door, they searched for any sign of Mikhail. When they reached the middle point of the palace, Kirill whipped around a corner and they had just enough time to dip into an empty room before he saw them.

"Dominika," he shouted down the hall. A female haeman dressed in the official military uniform paused in her stride to face him. "She's gone."

"Excuse me?"

"Arinadya. She's gone."

"Again? How?"

"I went to grab her from her bedroom so she could hide in the safe room with us, but when I got there I found Isidor dead near the window. She bled out. On the wall, in her blood, she left us a cryptic note."

"Does Mikhail know?"

"No, and you cannot tell him. She's not our concern anymore. We have bigger issues to deal with and if he learns she's outwitted him again, he will freak out. She is the smaller picture, we need him to focus on the bigger one."

"Agreed."

"Let's follow them," Marat whispered to his friends. "They will lead us right to him."

"She left," Sevrick said to himself.

"That should make you happy," Artem reminded him. "She's safe. No bombs to worry about, no evil prince trying to keep her prisoner. Take that as good news."

Artem was right. Now Sevrick could focus on this mission without Rina's safety lingering at the back of his mind. They left the room and followed Kirill and Dominika at a safe distance. It wasn't long before they turned a corner and stopped at a heavily guarded door. The men hid around the bend, watching.

Kirill paused deliberately. His head snapped toward where the men hid and they dipped back behind the wall.

"Did he see us?" Marat whispered, but before they could speculate, Kirill had Marat gripped by the neck and airborne. He tossed him across the hall, catapulting him into a marble pillar. Marat was out cold.

Two against seven; their odds were okay so long as no other haemans came to help. The men readjusted their guns and began firing. The echoes caused by the gunfire was too loud; there was no chance they'd keep their ratio for long.

The men fired, backing up as they did so. Kirill and Dominika dodged the bullets, zigzagging as they rushed the men. They moved so fast it looked like they were flying. Both haemans used the pillars and walls as launching points, making them even harder to hit. Without breaking stride, they used these unnatural spots to place a foot or hand and propel themselves forward. They charged like animals from another planet. There was nothing human about the way they moved.

The men kept the ammunition firing. Sevrick had his automatic rifle in one hand and his pistol in the other. Though the quantity of gunfire was immense, it wasn't enough. The haemans moved too fast and were quickly backing them into a corner.

Zakhar shouted for everyone to split up and the group dispersed in opposite directions. Kirill and Dominika were forced to separate as well.

Dominika chased Ivan, Jurg, and Benedikt back toward Mikhail's bedroom, while Kirill raced after Zakhar, Artem, Sevrick, and Konstantin. Marat was still knocked out.

Zakhar led the way while the others ran backwards, shooting at Kirill. They were almost at the end of the hallway when a blast erupted, throwing them all to the ground. A piercing ring shot

321

through Sevrick's brain. It pulsed in his ears as the dust around him settled.

The rest of the corridor in the direction they were running was gone. He looked out and saw the city of St. Petersburg before him. The historical buildings were engulfed in fire and smoke. One second later and he and his friends would have died in the blast.

Everyone was okay, just struggling. Even Kirill was tossed back and having a hard time adjusting in the aftermath of the explosion. He placed his hands over his ears and coughed out dust and smoke.

This was their chance.

Sevrick pushed through the pain and charged at Kirill. Artem, Zakhar, and Konstantin saw his move and followed suit. No one was operating at full capacity, but their unbeatable haeman foe was temporarily debilitated. If they wanted a chance to take him out, the opportunity was now.

Sevrick opened fire, hitting Kirill down the length of his left arm. The pain reawakened him to the fact that he was on a murder hunt. His haeman eyes came alive and he crouched, ready to pounce. Sevrick let out an animal cry, aiming for Kirill's head but missing because his opponent was too quick. He dodged, blurring out of sight and reappearing on the opposite side of the men.

Another female haeman had arrived at the scene. Kirill stood on one side of the blast and she on the other. The men were boxed in.

"Aliona," Kirill shouted to the Army Supreme Officer. "Take them out."

The men stood back to back in a small circle, firing at the haemans as they charged from both sides. Like before, they used the walls to bounce back and forth, distorting their image and making themselves a difficult target to hit.

Konstantin shut one eye and focused on the female. All he needed was one good shot to slow her down.

"Why aren't you shooting?" Zakhar screamed, appalled.

Konstantin ignored him and waited for the right moment. Aliona hesitated after flipping off a marble pillar and landing on the opposite side of the hall. She paused a second too long and Konstantin's bullet went straight through her neck. Blood spurted from the wound, splattering all over the white walls. She stumbled and her body slammed against the nearest pillar. Like an injured animal, she staggered, still approaching her prey but failing to move fluidly. She was blinded by pain. Her adrenaline and determination were the only things keeping her standing. Konstantin took the kill shot, hitting her in the forehead. She crumbled to the floor in a pool of her own blood.

The sight of his fallen comrade only fueled Kirill's rage. With two extra guns on him, he needed to move faster than before. The men made a wall of gunfire; there was no way Kirill could pass without getting hit.

To their dismay, once he was a few meters from them, he slid and glided along the marble floor between where they stood. He grabbed hold of Zakhar and Artem's ankles as he did so, taking them down with him. The force knocked their rifles out of their hands and Kirill was fast to get up and drag them away from their weapons. They had nothing to fight him with now. He grabbed both men by their collars and quickly tightened his hold around each of their necks. They were now his shield and Sevrick and Konstantin had to cease fire. The only part of Kirill that was visible were his arms and head.

Kirill laughed, waiting to see what his opponents did next.

"Take the shot," Artem mouthed to Konstantin.

He raised his gun and shut an eye to aim. Simultaneously, Kirill jerked to the left, switching the target from himself to Artem. He cackled callously as Konstantin jerked from the shock of seeing his friend's face at the end of his barrel.

"You'll never hit me, but go ahead and try. Highlight of my day will be watching you kill your friends."

In a moment of desperation, Sevrick stepped forward and revealed the one thing that might save his friends.

"I am Sevrick," he shouted as Kirill tightened his grip around their necks. "Let them go and you can have me."

"You're *who*?"

"Sevrick Bykovsky."

"Is that supposed to mean something to me?"

"I am the guy Mikhail wants to kill after this is all over. Rina was my fiancée."

Kirill let out a wild laugh, recalling the story now. "Why on earth would you ever step foot into this palace?"

He moved forward with Zakhar and Artem still acting as his shield. Konstantin kept his gun raised, ready for a chance to strike. Sevrick hoped he fired before Kirill took him to his slaughter.

"I take it you came here to save her?"

"Yes," Sevrick answered, leaving out their primary mission.

"Sorry to tell you, but your quest is a waste. She's gone. Looks like the whore really doesn't care about a damn soul but her own." Kirill smirked. "You should've left her behind years ago. Her love has killed you."

"We'll see."

"Drop your weapon and step in front of me," Kirill directed and Sevrick obeyed. He put his rifle down but left his pistol tucked into the front of his pants. Once he was blocking Konstantin's rifle, Kirill let Artem and Zakhar go, replacing them with Sevrick. "The rest of you can go. I won't kill you. Just leave before I change my mind."

All rifles were raised.

"We won't leave without Sevrick," Zakhar spat back.

"I plan to send a pack of haemans after you. You should leave now before they catch your scent and follow your trail."

They refused to back down.

"Have it your way," Kirill continued, backing away with Sevrick in front of him. The hallway was still filled with smoke from the earlier explosion, and though the men followed Kirill, he managed to make an unexpected dash and disappear with Sevrick.

They raced after them but by the time they made it through the thick and cloudy air, they were gone.

"Split up," Artem commanded. "He sacrificed himself for us. We aren't leaving without him."

Chapter 46

The words were clear. Isidor lay lifeless in a puddle of her own blood, fingers stained red. Mikhail let out a roar.

A bomb hit but the blast did not drown out his furious howl. The palace shook. He didn't feel it. All he felt was rage. She bested him again, she tricked him into trusting her again; he felt like a fool and all he could envision were his hands squeezing the life out of her. She'd never deceive him again.

He took out his vile of silve, snorted six silver lines, and then waited a few minutes before slicing his forearm open and guzzling his intoxicated blood. It was more than he'd normally take, but he needed the extra sensory enhancements. He had to track her down. Her parting gift to him was treachery; his gift to her would be death.

He let the high take over his body. Once his senses were fully heightened, he grabbed her nightgown and inhaled its scent. It was pure; there was still an innocence to her natural fragrance and it hit Mikhail like a train. She was evil, just like him. She'd done terrible, unforgivable things, just like him. Yet he sensed her pure nature all over her clothes. How was that possible? He meant to destroy her, corrupt her, and turn her into a monster just like him. There should be no lingering traces of the girl she was before the haemanism; not in her scent, not in her mind, not in her personality. Sensing it there angered him further. Not only did he fail in making her his obedient wife, but he also failed on a much more fundamental level. Haemanism was meant to break a person down. Once you're guilty of the terrors it encourages you to commit, your soul is shattered forever. She shouldn't have survived the rehabilitation; she shouldn't be thriving as a recovered haeman. The forced wake-up should have sent Arinadya's conscious into a tizzy, eating her alive from the inside out. Instead, she was running free, unbroken by the girl she used to be.

He needed to destroy her, or else her lack of submission might destroy him. He could feel his heart pounding with frustration. It was confusing, it did not make sense; why didn't this life cause her insides to rot, just like it had done to his? Since she would not obey, would not submit, would not let her demons beat her, he'd have to finish the job himself. If he couldn't have her, no one could. She wasn't allowed to be free of him.

He ripped a piece of the nightgown off and placed it in his pocket. Ripe with a fresh and powerful high, he climbed out the window and scaled down the wall with three brief catch and releases. The window frames cracked beneath his strong grip as he used them to propel himself to the ground. Once on land, he took another sniff of her dress and found her scent through the exploded concrete, chemicals, and death that filled the air. He followed it into the woods.

She thought she outsmarted him, but the joke was on her. Her demise was on its way.

Chapter 47

Kirill dragged Sevrick to the war room. Dominika stood in front of the map with Filipp and Edik, who returned from Paris yesterday afternoon. Roman and Sergei were holding down the fort in France with Spanish haeman Carlos Amador and Irish haeman Cassidy Flanagan. All of Europe was under their command and they needed their Russian soldiers back on the home front. They already determined the source of their current attack and they needed to begin planning a counter-strike.

Before Kirill could ask why Mikhail was absent, a desperate call came in over their radio.

"Cassidy Flanagan calling in. Can anyone hear me?" The sound of low-flying planes accompanied her voice.

"We hear you loud and clear. What's wrong?"

"They've sent fighter planes in. We've been in touch with our German counterparts and they told us they are dropping bombs filled with some kind of fog. It works like sleeping gas. It lingers at face level and spreads. If the explosion doesn't kill you, the chemical reaches you and knocks you out. We lost touch with the Germans hours ago. The Italians called a few minutes ago reporting something similar."

"Are you still in Paris?" Dominika asked.

"Yes, we've seen the jets but they haven't hit us yet. There's nothing we can do from the ground. We need the Russian air force to come and take these planes down."

"We are currently being bombed as well, but with explosive bombs. They are leveling our city. I need you to contact the leaders of each country in Europe with an air force. It's time they donate their resources to this battle."

"I'll try. Many have gone silent like Germany. We are beginning to feel cut off."

"Call us back in an hour with an update on your status." Dominika hung up. They didn't have time for this, they needed to counter-strike on a larger scale in order to stop the attack. "Where is Mikhail?" she asked Kirill.

"I thought he'd be here."

"He left a half hour before you got here, Dominika," Filipp explained.

"Where did he go? We need to bomb the U.S. and the U.K., then the Nordic region of Europe. We can't execute this order without his approval. He has the codes."

"I don't know where he went. When Aliona radioed up from the safe room explaining Arinadya still wasn't there yet, he freaked and stormed out of the room."

Sevrick listened closely, trying to piece this puzzle together and determine what it meant for him, Rina, and his friends who still roamed the palace looking for Mikhail.

"We need to find him," Kirill groaned. "Edik, stay behind and watch over our captive." He shoved Sevrick into Edik's grip. Once he was firmly transferred to a new guard, Kirill, Dominika, and Filipp left to look for Mikhail.

"Is there any chance I can convince you to let me go?" Sevrick asked, unable to think of any good trade or bargain.

"No," Edik replied.

"Didn't think so."

Sevrick yanked his pistol out from the front of his pants, aimed down, and shot Edik in the foot. Edik threw a punch, knocking Sevrick hard in the side of the head before stumbling backward. Sevrick fired two more times, hitting the haeman in the shoulder and thigh.

He didn't have much ammo left, so he saved the remaining shots and left Edik writhing on the floor in pain. When he left the room, he rounded a corner and was yanked into a large closet unexpectedly. Ready to fight, he cocked the trigger of his pistol.

"Stop. Hold your fire, it's me."

Sevrick took a better look and saw it was Konstantin. Benedikt stood next to him, towering in the cramped corner of the closet.

"Where are Artem and Zakhar?"

"They are looking for you on the opposite side of the palace. We spilt up. Marat was still unconscious, so Jurg and Ivan carried him back to the white elm. Benedikt joined me to make the groups even."

"How'd you find each other again?"

"Luck. How'd *you* get away?"

"They've lost track of Mikhail's whereabouts, so Kirill and his cohorts left me with some kid while they went to look for him. I still had my pistol on me so I crippled him and ran."

"We saw them leave. My younger brother was with them," Benedikt said. He tried to mask the pain it caused him but failed. Seeing Filipp help lead this invasion tore him apart.

"Are you okay?"

"Yeah. Nothing I can do to change it. Just a shame, that's all." Benedikt wore a brave face but it killed him inside. He wanted nothing more than to rescue his brother from this mess.

"Learn anything helpful while you were with the haemans?" Konstantin asked, changing the subject.

"The Nordic Union, United States, and United Kingdom are behind the bombings here, which we figured. They are also attacking the rest of Europe with chemical bombs that hover and spread at face level. It's knocking out the haemans across Europe."

"Good stuff," Konstantin commented.

"Have either of you seen Mikhail?" Sevrick asked.

"No," they answered in unison.

Sevrick sighed, "I have a feeling our target has left the building."

"Where would he have gone?"

"To chase down my love." Sevrick's heart raced as his suspicion began to feel justified.

"There's no way he left mid-war to track her down."

"I hope I'm wrong, but I need to go. Find the others and leave here."

"You can't go alone. What if you run into him in the woods? He will kill you."

"I'll move slow and stay concealed. Tell Zakhar I'm headed to the lagoon. He knows where it is. You can meet me there."

Sevrick bolted without another word.

Chapter 48

Mikhail watched Arinadya wade in the shallow lagoon water. His high still roared in his ears and he felt like a lion stalking its prey. She had no clue he was there, yet he had a clear view and easy access whenever the moment to pounce felt right.

For now, he observed. Her scent was strong and he found her with no trouble. The ease with which he trailed her to this location amazed him and her oblivious nature brought him great delight. Hunting her was fun.

He waited for hours, reveling in her unsuspecting behavior. When his high began to falter, he poured himself another line and snorted it off the side of his pointer finger. He lost count of how many hits he'd taken but he was sure he'd never been this high on silve before. He reopened his forearm wound, cleaning off the dried blood so fresh blood could reemerge, and then he ravenously devoured it. He could hear the bombs that continued to drop on his beloved city. Once he took care of his perfidious princess he would return to his palace and unleash hell over those who dared attack his home.

The sun was setting, so he found an early evening shadow to hide in. As he watched his lover and licked the flowing blood off his arm, the sound of cracking twigs came from behind where he crouched. A tall man with dark hair and a slender, muscular build tip-toed toward the lagoon. Mikhail looked closer. The definition in the man's face indicated he was in his late-twenties but his youthfulness was unnatural. He had healthy skin, vibrant blue eyes, and an air of confidence about him. The man was handsome. Mikhail's interest and jealousy peaked.

Arinadya spun around at the sound of the man crossing the tree line. A beaming smile took over her expression and she ran to him.

"Sevrick," she sighed as she buried herself in his embrace.

The name rang inside Mikhail's mind like a clock striking midnight. His body went numb as the deafening repetition of the name brought forth his irrepressible quest for revenge. He was submerged in hatred. There was no light, there was no air, there was only Sevrick standing a few meters from him.

He pounced.

Instead of victimizing Arinadya, his violence shifted onto Sevrick. The man who prevented her from completely caving into his will, into his life, into his grip. The man who made a fool of him from afar. The man who got in his way time and time again.

Mikhail body slammed him to the ground. He pounded Sevrick's face and Arinadya tried to pull him off.

"Back off or I'll kill you too," Mikhail screamed, backhanding her so hard she fell and blacked out for a moment. She shouted and cried through the fog, begging Mikhail to stop, but he didn't listen. He continued mashing Sevrick's face into bloody putty.

Sevrick reached for his gun, trying to grab it and shoot the prince, but Mikhail's knees locked the pistol tight to Sevrick's hip. As darkness settled in over his vision, gunshots fired. Zakhar ran through the tree line, leading Artem, Konstantin, and Benedikt into the lagoon. Mikhail immediately maneuvered to prevent the new arrivals from getting an easy shot.

Rina's eyesight returned and she crawled to Sevrick's side as his friends opened fire at Mikhail. Their blaze of ammunition was futile; Mikhail moved faster than any haeman they had ever seen. Not only did he blur, he disappeared. They kept the bullets flying; they'd die if they didn't. It was the only thing keeping Mikhail at bay.

Sevrick sat up, taking deep breaths and regaining his wits. His head throbbed and his face was already bruised, but he fought off the pain. He needed to protect Rina and help his friends.

He struggled to stand, so Rina helped him. Another moment to recover and he'd be good to go.

"You need to hide," he said.

"No, I can help."

"I will not watch you die today. Find a safe place to disappear until this settles." He grabbed her face and kissed her. "I love you."

"I love you too."

He ran to his pack of friends and Rina looked around for a way to help. She ran to her bag and took her own pistol out. Ready to join the fire fight, an enormous forearm clubbed the side of her skull.

Kirill.

She was knocked down as he, Dominika, and Filipp walked over her to take on the men firing at Mikhail.

"Watch out," she hollered, catching Artem's attention, who then shifted his gunfire toward their newly approaching opponents.

Rina scrambled to get out of the line of fire, cradling her head as she did so. It throbbed. Kirill's blow was significant. She did her best to silence the ringing.

"Filipp?" Artem said beneath his breath as he scanned their new haeman opponents. Benedikt heard him and whipped around to see. The sight of his younger brother charging toward them with murder in his eyes froze him in place. His rifle dropped to his side and he lost all will to fight. Filipp showed no signs of slowing down at the appearance of his long lost brother; it appeared he did not care at all.

"Keep fighting." Artem elbowed Benedikt in the ribcage, waking him up from his heartbreaking nostalgia.

Less gunfire was being directed at Mikhail and he had time to swoop in and snatch Sevrick by his jacket collar. He dragged him away from the fray all while receiving death punches to the gut from Sevrick. The hits were hard and Mikhail would feel it later, but right now he was too jacked up on silve, blood, and pure adrenaline to feel any pain.

It had turned into a one-on-one fight. Artem took on Kirill, Zakhar brawled with Dominika, and Benedikt half-heartedly fought his brother.

Filipp separated his older brother from the pack.

"I can't believe you work for him," Benedikt said while dodging a full-force swing at his jaw. He was taller and sturdier than Filipp; if drugs weren't involved, Filipp wouldn't stand a chance against him.

"Don't be jealous, brother," Filipp snapped. "I'm finally out of your shadow, doing big things on my own. I don't need your approval anymore, I have Mikhail's."

"You're breaking my heart. Let me help you."

"I don't need your help." He lunged at Benedikt and threw a solid punch into his eye socket. His older brother stumbled, but did not fall.

"It's crumbling down around you. Mikhail will never get away with what he has done and anyone still standing by his side when the smoke has cleared will go down with him."

"We have all of Europe and the United States. Just because they are bombing us and trying to fight back doesn't mean they will succeed in stopping what we've started. It's too late, brother." Filipp rubbed his nose; his rampant high caused it to itch. "We've already won. The only one going down is you."

He charged at his enormous older brother, slamming into his chest with both hands and pinning him up against a tree. Benedikt tried to push back but his scrawny little brother was too strong as a haeman. He couldn't match his strength.

"Mamochka would be so sad to see you like this." Benedikt stopped fighting back and tears formed in his eyes. He wasn't old but his face looked weathered with despair.

"Don't speak of mama." Filipp grabbed his neck and slammed his head against the tree trunk. "Don't pretend to know her. She's dead. Died when we were boys. You don't know a damn thing about who she is or what side she would have chosen when Mikhail took over."

"I knew her better than you. I was seven when she passed. She would have never let you turn into this." Benedikt's face quivered. "I'm sorry I failed you."

"You aren't my keeper!" Filipp slammed his brother's head against the trunk again. "You've hovered over me all my life." Another head slam. "Kept me hidden in your shadow, buried beneath its frigid darkness. The lack of light left me weak. The only oxygen I got was the stagnant air left in your wake. It turned me rotten."

"I was trying to keep you safe."

"You smothered me," Filipp roared. "Haemanism saved me. It turned me into the man you prevented me from being. It made me strong and gave me purpose."

"I'll help you heal."

"No. I choose this over you every time." Filipp's vision was streaked in red and the anger boiling within him scorched his insides. He took his pain out on his brother.

The back of Benedikt's head was gushing blood.

"You know I love you," he said through the agony. "You are my family."

"Stop," another head bash, "talking." One final hit against the tree and Benedikt was dead. Filipp didn't notice until his body went limp in his grip as he completed four more slams. He examined Benedikt's blank stare and held his lifeless body in his grasp. He barely tried to stop him. He accepted Filipp's unprovoked wrath without trying to return the hurt.

His high began to waver and the gravity of what he'd done finally sunk in. He killed hundreds before this and never thought twice about it, but now he knew the face of his victim; he knew the depth of the man whose life he stole. It was his brother, the person who took care of him his entire life. He ruthlessly murdered the only person who cared about the boy beneath the monster. He never doubted his choice to be a haeman until this moment, until his brother's blood was all over his hands. What mind games did the haemanism play on him? How did it twist all his good memories into toxic ones? His anger turned to fear, which quickly shifted into panic. He stepped away from the dead body, unable to break eye contact with Benedikt's lifeless gaze.

Everything went black. Filipp raised his pistol to his temple and fired. Maybe he'd be able to atone for this sin in death.

No one else saw this exchange, they were too busy fighting for their own lives. Artem and Zakhar were doing a good job holding Kirill and Dominika back, but they were so consumed with making the kill shot while simultaneously trying to survive that they didn't notice Sevrick being dragged away from the heat of the quarrel.

Rina noticed.

She chased after them, screaming at Mikhail to let Sevrick go. But her cries were ignored. He dragged her love around the lagoon and up the sloping incline of the cliff. He moved with haeman speed, so Rina could not keep up. While he easily ran over the jagged rocks, she found herself tripping and furthering her injuries.

They were at the top of the cliff while she still battled the bottom terrain. She could see their silhouettes fighting against the orange sky.

The fight was one sided; Mikhail threw punches and Sevrick received them. Though Sevrick was strong and able, he was no match for a monster fueled by superhuman narcotics. Tears fell down Rina's face as she got closer and saw the damage being caused to Sevrick's body.

She screeched, stumbling as she ran. "Let him go!"

"So nice of you to join us, love," Mikhail crooned at his wife. He then yanked Sevrick by the neck to his feet. He held him up with his left hand while casually speaking. He sneered. "You'll enjoy this."

Without any warning, he propelled his right hand into Sevrick's chest. The strength fueling the punch broke skin and bone, letting his fingers curl around Sevrick's heart. He yanked the organ from his body and held it into the sky like a trophy.

Sevrick fell to the ground and Rina let out a blood-curdling shriek. She raced over the remaining distance to be by Sevrick's side, but there was nothing she could do to help him now. He was gone.

She glared up at Mikhail, who stood over them with Sevrick's life dripping from his hand.

"I thought I'd keep his heart as a souvenir, mount it over my fireplace as a token of my victory, but then I realized you might want it. It did belong to you, after all."

Rina stood, trembling with rage. She grabbed the pistol from the waist of her pants and aimed it at Mikhail. It shook in her grip.

"Oh," Mikhail mocked, "You're going to kill me? You can't blame anyone but yourself for his death. You know that as well as I do."

"Shut up." She cocked the hammer. "Your reign of terror over me is through."

"Do it," he seethed, "I dare you."

She pulled the trigger and sent a bullet into Mikhail's shoulder. He stumbled backwards, more in shock than in pain. His high pushed him through the injury.

He placed a hand over the gushing wound and licked the blood off his fingers. "Do you really think I won't kill you?" he laughed. "You think you're safe? That I will keep protecting you? My use for you is through. I don't need you anymore. I planned to punish you by killing him, but I'll gladly rip your heart out too."

"You already did."

As she cocked the hammer, he dove. She fired the gun as he tackled her to the ground. The bullet passed through his chest, but he didn't stop. He bled out on her while pinning her to the ground by her neck. It was a race to the death. His blood drained just as fast as her oxygen. Part of her didn't care if she lived or died; she had no interest in a world where Sevrick did not exist. But the other half needed to stay alive to make sure the deed was done. Mikhail needed to die. There was no giving up until she knew he was gone for good.

She fought for her last breath, remaining calm beneath his grip and clinging on to whatever remnants of air she had left. She could feel his warm blood drenching her torso.

The sun was setting so she couldn't tell if the lack of light was the sky's transition into night or her body shutting down, but the end was coming for her too. She held on, clutching tightly to the only shred of light she could still see. Then suddenly, a weight landed on top of her and blackness covered her sight. Death.

She sobbed.

Tears fell.

She could breath again.

Surprised she was still alive, she pushed the weight off her and scrambled away, swallowing as much fresh air as her body would allow. It was the weight of Mikhail's dead body that landed on her. She outlasted him.

Tears of relief rushed down her face; Mikhail would never hurt anyone again. It was too late for her and Sevrick, but the rest of the world was safe. Her grief would be immense, but at least she gave the rest of humanity a chance to save itself.

She crawled back to Sevrick's body. She cradled his head in her lap and kissed his forehead over and over, weeping as she did so.

"I love you. I'm so sorry." No words eased the misery she was feeling. How could she go on? How could she live without him? How could she live with herself knowing his death was a result of her choices? The answer was, she couldn't.

Through the tears she glared at the cliff's edge, her old friend. She stood and walked to it. Peering over and absorbing its massive height, she felt a momentary reprieve from her suffering. The freefall would free her; it would right the wrongs that led her to this fate. It would send her to a place where she could be with Sevrick again. Or so she hoped.

She took a step closer.

Sevrick would not want her to do this. He'd tell her to go on, to keep fighting. But how could she when the crux of her being caused the demise of her only love? He never deserved to die, she did. She was guilty, not him. It was unfair.

She looked back at his body and grew weak. The tears returned with force, causing her entire body to crumble beneath its own weight. She landed next to Sevrick's dead body and curled up next to it, crying onto his shoulder. Maybe her broken heart would kill her instead.

"What happened?" a voice called out in question from the middle of the cliff's rock bed. Rina looked up and saw Artem and Zakhar, Sevrick's two best friends, approach carefully. They were covered in blood. She wished now more than ever that her heart would stop and deliver her the justice she deserved. Instead she was forced to face them. She stayed silent. Speaking felt wrong.

When they got close enough to see the murder scene they picked up their pace. They also struggled over the rough terrain, but moved as fast as they could.

"No," Zakhar said in a pant. "There's a hole in his chest."

They both looked to Mikhail's body and saw the bloody organ laying a few meters from his dead body.

"He ripped his heart out?" Artem asked, appalled.

Rina sat up, her face clenched in agony. She nodded.

"Who killed Mikhail?" Artem asked. "You?"

She nodded.

No one knew what to say. Their mission to kill the haeman prince was complete, but their best friend lay dead right beside him. The price to succeed should not have cost Sevrick his life.

Artem crouched down next to Rina. "Are you okay?"

She shook her head. "I want to die."

"Sevrick fought his whole damn life to save you. Quitting now would be just as bad as you killing him yourself. He wanted you to live, to be healthy, to be happy. You better snap out of this and honor his memory by surviving."

"How do I cope? I didn't kill him but he's dead because of me. It's my fault."

"You couldn't have stopped him from coming back for you no matter how hard you tried. People sacrifice everything for those they love. He'd die for you a million times if it meant you got to live."

"But we could have killed Mikhail without him here. He didn't need to die for this."

"You can't dwell on speculations. What you need to do is pick your head up and carry on. If you give up now, it was all for nothing. Do not waste his love."

He was right.

"Let's go," Zakhar said, choking back tears. He grabbed Sevrick by the armpits and Artem carried his legs. Rina retrieved his heart. Though it hurt to hold it in her hands, leaving it disgraced on the dirty ground was worse. He deserved respect, honor, and decency in death. He needed to be buried with his heart in place. It was the best part about him.

Chapter 49

The white elm was alive with emotion: grief, relief, uncertainty. After Zakhar, Artem, and Rina returned, Jurg and Nikolai went back to help Konstantin carry Benedikt's body home. A beautiful memorial service was held for both valiant men who died in battle. Now everyone was trying to get back to normal.

Things would never be normal again for Rina, but she tried her best to keep a brave face.

Two months had already passed beneath the white elm. Leonid examined them all after they returned from St. Petersburg, but after learning Rina was under scopolamine for an extended period of time, he requested she come back for weekly checkups. She told him about the miscarriage and all the trauma she'd been through. He listened to her when she expressed her fears and concerns about the future, he sympathized when she told him about the crippling guilt she felt for Sevrick's death. He was haeman once too, he understood the deep internal dilemmas she'd face for the rest of her life. Not only was he her doctor, but he'd become her greatest confidant as well.

Artem tried, but he was also grieving Sevrick. None of his other friends bothered with her. He was dead, and deep down they blamed her, just like she did. They were cordial in passing but nothing more. An honest conversation could not be held because they saw her as the reason their best friend died. The shame was debilitating. Polina helped counter-balance the hateful vibes, but Leonid helped her the most. He loved Sevrick too, yet he was able to see past his own grief to know Rina never intended for this to happen and that she was hurting worse than anyone else.

Though the world above their underground fortress was slowly being remedied, it still wasn't safe to leave. The Nordic Union checked in with them regularly to give them updates and fill them in on their progress. The United States and the United Kingdom provided the heavy artillery, and with the help of armed forces from China, Japan, India, Israel, Egypt, Canada, and Australia, they managed to take back control of Europe. They turned all hospitals and schools into centers for rehabilitation, but since it took so long to heal such large quantities of people, these establishments would look more like haeman prisons for a while. Leonid and the Scandinavian nurses taught the rehabilitation process to medical practitioners from all over the world. Doctors and nurses from all over the globe traveled to Europe and were assigned to different rehabilitation centers. Many haemans were dying in the process, but many also survived. After they were rehabilitated, they were sent to local prisons where they were treated with care, psychologically analyzed, and given the final treatments in their recovery. It seemed that many were grateful to be ripped from their addiction, though plenty woke up angry and confused. It would take time to determine a humane way to handle those who fought the recovery process. With so many hands helping, they had high hopes that the fate of humanity could be salvaged.

Rina headed to Leonid's medical laboratory for her weekly checkup. He was beginning to see there were no long-term effects from the scopolamine and he'd probably need to see her less often. She hoped he'd still let her visit regularly though, since he was the only person she could talk with freely.

She sat on the table and he began the medical exam. He checked her pulse and blood pressure before grabbing the otoscope to check her eyes and ears.

"How have you been feeling in general?"

"Mentally? Awful. But physically I am okay. Still haven't gotten my period but everything else seems normal."

"Still?" he asked as he flashed the small light across her eyes. "How long has it been?"

"Two to three months," Rina estimated.

"That's not normal. It isn't unusual for the menstrual cycle to be late or irregular after a miscarriage, but yours should be back on track by now." He took a step away from her, breathing heavily in contemplation. He walked to a cabinet full of medical supplies, pulled out a small package, and handed it to her.

"A pregnancy test?"

"Humor me."

"Is that even possible so soon after I miscarried?"

"Absolutely."

Rina raced through her memories to recall the short time frame between the miscarriage and Mikhail's death. He never touched her.

Her heart fluttered with dangerous hope.

"If it's positive," she said softly, "the baby will be Sevrick's."

"When on earth did you two find time for that?"

"Yeah, I left out that detail when I told you everything. But we had one really beautiful and loving week together before it all fell apart. I snuck out every night to meet him at the lagoon. Mikhail was too busy with his war to notice. He didn't even kiss me during that time frame."

"Well," Leonid couldn't hide his excited anticipation now either. "Go take the damned test!"

She left the room and headed to the watering well. On the bathroom side, she found an empty curtained-off bucket and dipped inside. She pressed the test against her heart, holding it there with hope for a moment before unwrapping the plastic and squatting over the stick.

When she was done, she put the cap back on the test so the results could formulate while she emptied the bucket down the communal, underground drain.

She ran back to Leonid and they waited together for the result. He held her hand and she tapped her foot impatiently. The screen began to shift as the colors moved to reveal her answer. Lines formed, slowly spelling out a word.

A minute later, her hopes were validated.

Rina smiled.

Their love was not wasted.

Thank you for reading *Haemanism: The Spread* – I hope you enjoyed it! If you have a moment, please consider rating and reviewing it on Amazon and sharing your thoughts with me via social media. All feedback is greatly appreciated!

Amazon Author Account:

www.amazon.com/author/nicolineevans

Instagram:

www.instagram.com/nicolinenovels

Facebook:

www.facebook.com/nicolinenovels

Twitter:

www.twitter.com/nicolinenovels

To learn more, please visit my official author website:

www.nicolineevans.com

Made in the USA
Monee, IL
28 October 2021

80607995R00193